I0831920

Voltaire

The History of Peter the Great

Outlook

Voltaire

The History of Peter the Great

1. Auflage | ISBN: 978-3-73262-482-9

Erscheinungsort: Frankfurt am Main, Deutschland

Erscheinungsjahr: 2018

Outlook Verlag GmbH, Frankfurt.

Voltaire

The History of Peter the Great

Outlook

The History of Peter the Great

H. Corbould. W. Chevalier.

He ran every where in person to put a stop to the pillage and slaughter.

Chap. 13.

THE
HISTORY
OF
PETER THE GREAT.

Council him for his own safety, not to pardon me.

Chap. 36.

London:

ENGRAVED FOR THE ENGLISHCLASSICS.

PUBLISHED BY SAMUEL JOHNSON & SON. MANCHESTER.

THE HISTORY OF PETER THE GREAT,

EMPEROR OF RUSSIA.

FROM THE FRENCH OF VOLTAIRE,
BY SMOLLETT.

MANCHESTER:
S. JOHNSON & SON, No. 3, OLDHAM-STREET;
AND 48, CHURCH-ST., LIVERPOOL.

MDCCCXLV.

CONTENTS

CHAPTER

Ordinance of the Emperor Peter I. for the crowning of the Empress Catherine.

PETER THE GREAT.

CHAP. I.

DESCRIPTION OF RUSSIA.

The empire of Russia is the largest in the whole globe, extending from west to east upwards of two thousand common leagues of France,[1] and about eight hundred in its greatest breadth from north to south. It borders upon Poland and the Frozen Sea, and joins to Sweden and China. Its length from the island of Dago, in the westernmost part of Livonia, to its most eastern limits, takes in near one hundred and seventy degrees, so that when it is noon in the western parts of the empire, it is nearly midnight in the eastern. Its breadth from north to south is three thousand six hundred wersts, which make eight hundred and fifty of our common French leagues.

The limits of this country were so little known in the last century, that, in 1689, when it was reported, that the Chinese and the Russians were at war, and that in order to terminate their differences, the emperor *Camhi* on the one hand, and the czars Ivan or John, and Peter, on the other, had sent their ministers to meet an embassy within three hundred leagues of Pekin, on the frontiers of the two empires, the account was at first treated as a fiction.

The country now comprehended under the name of Russia, or the Russias, is of a greater extent than all the rest of Europe, or than ever the Roman empire was, or that of Darius subdued by Alexander; for it contains upwards of one million one hundred thousand square leagues. Neither the Roman empire, nor that of Alexander, contained more than five hundred and fifty thousand each; and there is not a kingdom in Europe the twelfth part so extensive as the Roman empire; but to make Russia as populous, as plentiful, and as well stored with towns as our southern countries, would require whole ages, and a race of monarchs such as Peter the Great.

The English ambassador, who resided at Petersburg in 1733, and who had been at Madrid, says, in his manuscript relation, that in Spain, which is the least populous state in Europe, there may be reckoned forty persons to every square mile, and in Russia not above five. We shall see in the second chapter, whether this minister was mistaken. Marshal Vauban, the greatest of engineers, and the best of citizens, computes, that, in France, every square mile contains two hundred inhabitants. These calculations are never very exact, but they serve to shew the amazing disproportion in the population of two different countries.

I shall observe here, that from Petersburg to Pekin, there is hardly one mountain to be met with in the route which the caravans might take through independent Tartary, and that from Petersburg to the north of France, by the road of Dantzic, Hamburg, and Amsterdam, there is not even a hill of any eminence to be seen. This observation leaves room to doubt of the truth of that theory, which makes the mountains to have been formed by the rolling of the waves of the sea, and supposes all that is at present dry land, to have been for a long time covered with water: but how comes it to pass, that the waves, which, according to the supposition, formed the Alps, the Pyrenees, and Mount Taurus, did not likewise form some eminence or hill from Normandy to China, which is a winding space of above three thousand leagues? Geography, thus considered, may furnish lights to natural philosophy, or at least give room for rational doubts.

Formerly we called Russia by the name of Muscovy, from the city of Moscow, the capital of that empire, and the residence of the grand dukes: but at present the ancient name of Russia prevails.

It is not my business in this place to inquire, why the countries from Smolensko, to the other side of Moscow, were called White Russia, or why Hubner gives it the name of Black, nor for what reason the government of Kiow should be named Red Russia.

It is very likely that Madies the Scythian, who made an irruption into Asia, near seven hundred years before our vulgar æra, might have carried his arms into these regions, as Gengis-Khan and Tamerlane did afterwards, and as probably others had done long before Madies. Every part of antiquity is not deserving of our inquiries; that of the Chinese, the Indians, the Persians, and the Egyptians, is ascertained from illustrious and interesting monuments; but these monuments suppose others of a far more ancient date, since it required many ages to teach men the art of transmitting their thoughts by permanent signs, and no less time was required to form a regular language; and yet we have no such monuments even in this polite part of Europe. The art of writing was a long time unknown to all the North: the patriarch Constantine, who wrote the history of Kiow in the Russian language, acknowledges, that the use of writing was not known in these countries in the fifth century.

Let others examine whether the Huns, the Slavi, and the Tartars, formerly led their wandering and famished tribes towards the source of the Boristhenes;[2] my design is to shew what czar Peter created, and not to engage in a useless attempt, to clear up the chaos of antiquity. We should always keep in mind, that no family upon earth knows its first founder, and consequently, that no nation knows its first origin.

I use the name of Russians to designate the inhabitants of this great empire.

That of Roxolanians, which was formerly given them, would indeed be more sonorous, but we shall conform to the custom of the language in which we write. News-papers and other memoirs have for some time used the word Russians; but as this name comes too near to that of Prussians, I shall abide by that of Russ, which almost all our writers have given them. Besides, it appeared to me, that the most extensive people on the earth ought to be known by some appellation that may distinguish them absolutely from all other nations.[3]

This empire is at present divided into sixteen large governments, that will one day be subdivided, when the northern and eastern countries come to be more inhabited.

These sixteen governments, which contain several immense provinces are the following:—

LIVONIA.

The nearest province to our part of the world is that of Livonia, one of the most fruitful in the whole North. In the twelfth century the inhabitants were pagans; at this time certain merchants of Bremen and Lubeck traded to this country, and a body of religious crusaders, called *port-glaives*, or sword- bearers, who were afterwards incorporated in the Teutonic order, made themselves masters of this province in the thirteenth century, at the time when the fury of the crusades armed the Christians against every one who was not of their religion. Albert, margrave of Brandenburg, grand-master of these religious conquerors, made himself sovereign of Livonia and of Brandenburg- Prussia, about the year 1514. From that time, the Russians and Poles began to dispute for the possession of this province. Soon afterwards it was invaded by the Swedes, and for a long while continued to be ravaged by these several powers. Gustavus Adolphus having conquered it, it was then ceded to the Swedes in 1660, by the famous treaty of Oliva; and, at length, czar Peter wrested it from these latter, as will be seen in the course of this history.

Courland, which joins to Livonia, is still in vassalage to Poland, though it depends greatly upon Russia. These are the western limits of this empire in Christendom.

Of the Governments of REVEL, PETERSBURG, *and* WYBURG.

More northward is the government of Revel and Esthonia. Revel was built by the Danes in the thirteenth century. The Swedes were in possession of this province, from the time that country put itself under the protection of that crown in 1561. This is another of the conquests of Peter the Great.

On the borders of Esthonia lies the gulf of Finland. To the eastward of this sea, and at the junction of the Neva with the lake Ladoga,[4] is situated Petersburg, the most modern and best built city in the whole empire, founded by czar Peter, in spite of all the united obstacles which opposed its foundation.

This city is situated on the bay of Kronstat, in the midst of nine rivers, by which its different quarters are divided. In the centre of this city is almost an impregnable fortress, built on an island, formed by the main-stream of the river Neva: seven canals are cut from the rivers, and wash the walls of one of the royal palaces of the admiralty, of the dock-yard for the galleys, and of several buildings of manufactories. Thirty-five large churches contribute to adorn the city; among which five are allotted for foreigners of the Roman Catholic, Calvinist, and Lutheran religions: these are as so many temples raised to toleration, and examples to other nations. There are five palaces; the old one, called the summer palace, situated on the river Neva, has a very large and beautiful stone balustrade, which runs all along the river side. The new summer palace near the triumphal gate, is one of the finest pieces of architecture in Europe. The admiralty buildings, the school for cadets, the imperial college, the academy of sciences, the exchange, and the merchants' warehouses, are all magnificent structures, and monuments of taste and public utility. The town-house, the public dispensary, where all the vessels are of porcelain, the court magazines, the foundery, the arsenal, the bridges, the markets, the squares, the barracks for the horse and foot guards, contribute at once to the embellishment and safety of the city, which is said to contain at present four hundred thousand souls. In the environs of the city are several villas or country-seats, which surprise all travellers by their magnificence. There is one in particular which has water-works superior to those of Versailles. There was nothing of all this in 1702, the whole being then an impassable morass. Petersburg is considered as the capital of Ingria, a small province subdued by Peter I. Wyburg, another of his conquests, and that part of Finland which was lost, and ceded by the Swedes in 1742, make another government.

ARCHANGEL.

Higher up, proceeding towards the north, is the province of Archangel, a country entirely new to the southern nations of Europe. It took its name from St. Michael, the Archangel, under whose patronage it was put long after the Russians had embraced Christianity, which did not happen till the beginning of the eleventh century; and they were not known to the other nations of Europe till the middle of the sixteenth. The English, in 1533, endeavouring to find out a north-east passage to the East Indies, Chancellor, captain of one of the ships fitted out for this expedition, discovered the port of Archangel in the White Sea; at that time it was a desert place, having only one convent, and a little church, dedicated to St. Michael, the Archangel.

The English sailing up the river Dwina,[5] arrived at the midland part of the country, and at length at Moscow. Here they easily made themselves masters of the trade of Russia, which was removed from the city of Novogorod, where it was carried on by land to this sea-port, which is inaccessible indeed during seven months in the year; but, nevertheless, this trade proved more beneficial to the empire than the fairs of Novogorod, that had fallen to decay in consequence of the wars with Sweden. The English obtained the privilege of trading thither without paying any duties; a manner of trading which is apparently the most beneficial to all nations. The Dutch soon came in for a share of the trade of Archangel, then unknown to other nations.

Long before this time, the Genoese and Venetians had established a trade with the Russians by the mouth of the Tanais or Don,[6] where they had built a town called Tana. This branch of the Italian commerce was destroyed by the ravages of Tamerlane, in that part of the world; but that of Archangel continued, with great advantages both to the English and Dutch, till the time that Peter the Great opened a passage into his dominions by the Baltic Sea.

RUSSIAN LAPLAND.

Of the Government of Archangel.

To the west of Archangel, and within its government, lies Russian Lapland, the third part of this country, the other two belonging to Sweden and Denmark. This is a very large tract, occupying about eight degrees of longitude, and extending in latitude from one polar circle to the North Cape[7]. The natives of this country were confusedly known to the ancients, under the name of troglodytes and northern pigmies; appellations suitable enough to men, who, for the most part, are not above four feet and a half high, and dwell in caverns; they are just the same people they were at that time. They are of a tawny complexion, though the other people of the north are white, and for the most part very low in stature; though their neighbours, and the people of Iceland, under the polar circle, are tall: they seem made for their mountainous country, being nimble, squat, and robust; their skins are hard, the better to resist the cold, their thighs and legs are slender, their feet small, to enable them to run more nimbly amongst the rocks, with which their province is covered. They are passionately fond of their own country, which none but themselves can be pleased with, and are able to live no where else. Some have affirmed, upon the credit of Olaus, that these people were originally natives of Finland, and that they removed into Lapland, where they diminished in stature: but why might they not as well have made choice of lands less northerly, where the conveniences of life were to be had in greater plenty? How comes it that they differ so totally from their pretended ancestors in features, figure, and complexion? Methinks we might, with as great reason, suppose that the grass which grows in Lapland is produced from that of Denmark, and that the fishes, peculiar to their lakes, came from those of Sweden. It is most likely that the Laplanders are, like their animals, the produce of their own country, and that nature has made the one for the other.

Those who inhabit the frontiers of Finland, have adopted some of the expressions of their neighbours, as happens to every people: but when two nations give to things of common use, to objects which are continually before their eyes, names absolutely different, it affords a strong presumption, that one of them is not a colony from the other. The Finlanders call a bear Karu, the Laplanders Muriet: the sun in the Finnish language is called Auringa, in the Lapland tongue Beve. Here is not the least analogy. The inhabitants of Finland, and Swedish Lapland, formerly worshipped an idol whom they called Iumalac, and since the reign of Gustavus Adolphus, to whom they are indebted for the appellation of Lutherans, they call Jesus Christ the son of Iumalac. The Muscovite or Russian Laplanders, are at present thought to be of the Greek church; but those who wander about the mountains of the North Cape, are satisfied with adoring one God under certain rude forms, as has been the ancient custom of all the nations called Nomades, or wandering nations.

This race of people, who are inconsiderable in numbers, have but very few ideas, and are happy in not having more, which would only occasion them to have new wants which they could not satisfy: at present they live contented, and free from diseases, notwithstanding the excessive coldness of their climate; they drink nothing but water, and attain to a great age. The custom imputed to them of entreating strangers to lie with their wives and daughters, which they esteem as an honour done to them, probably arose from a notion of the superiority of strangers, and a desire of amending, by their means, the defects of their own race. This was a custom established amongst the virtuous Lacedemonians. A husband would entreat a favour of a comely young man, to give him handsome children, whom he might adopt. Jealousy, and the laws, prevent the rest of mankind from giving their wives up to the embraces of another; but the Laplanders have few or no laws, and are in all probability, strangers to jealousy.

MOSCOW.

Ascending the river Dwina from north to south, we travel up the country till we come to Moscow, the capital of the empire. This city was long the centre of the Russian dominions, before they were extended on the side of China and Persia.

Moscow, lying in 55 degrees and a half, north latitude, in a warmer climate, and more fruitful soil than that of Petersburg, is situated in the midst of a large and delightful plain on the river Moskwa, and two lesser rivers, which with the former lose themselves in the Occa, and afterwards help to swell the stream of the Wolga. This city, in the 13th century, was only a collection of huts inhabited by a set of miserable wretches, oppressed by the descendants of Gengis Khan.

The Kremlin, or ancient palace of the great dukes, was not built till the 14th century; of such modern date are cities in this part of the world. This palace was built by Italian architects, as were several churches in the Gothic taste which then prevailed throughout all Europe. There are two built by the famous Aristotle, of Bologna, who flourished in the 15th century; but the private houses were no better than wooden huts.

The first writer who brought us acquainted with Moscow, was Olearius; who, in 1633, went thither as the companion of an embassy from the duke of Holstein. A native of Holstein must naturally be struck with wonder at the immense extent of the city of Moscow, with its five quarters, especially the magnificent one belonging to the czars, and with the Asiatic splendour which then reigned at that court. There was nothing equal to it in Germany at that time, nor any city by far so extensive or well peopled.

On the contrary, the earl of Carlisle, who was ambassador from Charles II. to the czar Alexis, in 1633, complains in his relation that he could not meet with any one convenience of life in Moscow; no inns on the road, nor refreshments of any kind. One judged as a German, the other as an Englishman, and both by comparison. The Englishman was shocked to see most of the Boyards or Muscovite noblemen, sleep upon boards or benches, with only the skins of animals under them; but this was the ancient practice of all nations. The houses, which were almost all built of wood, had scarcely any furniture, few or none of their tables were covered with cloth; there was no pavement in the streets; nothing agreeable; nothing convenient; very few artificers, and those few extremely awkward, and employed only in works of absolute necessity. These people might have passed for Spartans, had they been sober.

But, on public days, the court displays all the splendour of a Persian monarch.

The earl says, he could see nothing but gold and precious stones on the robes of the czar and his courtiers. These dresses were not manufactured in the country; and yet, it is evident, that the people might be rendered industrious long before that time. In the reign of the czar Boris Godonow, the largest bell was cast at Moscow, in Europe; and in the patriarchal church there were several ornaments in silver, worked in a very curious manner. These pieces of workmanship, which were made under the direction of Germans and Italians, were only transient efforts. It is daily industry, and the continual exercise of a great number of arts, that makes a nation flourishing. Poland, and the neighbouring nations, were at that time very little superior to the Russians. The handicraft trades were not in greater perfection in the north of Germany, nor were the polite arts much better known, than in the middle of the seventeenth century.

Though the city of Moscow, at that time, had neither the magnificence nor arts of our great cities in Europe, yet its circumference of twenty miles; the part called the Chinese town, where all the rarities of China are exhibited; the spacious quarter of the Kremlin, where stood the palace of the czars; the gilded domes, the lofty and conspicuous turrets; and, lastly, the prodigious number of its inhabitants, amounting to near 500,000. All this together, rendered Moscow one of the most considerable cities in the world.

Theodore, or Fœdor, eldest brother to Peter the Great, began to improve Moscow. He ordered several large houses to be built of stone, though without any regular architecture. He encouraged the principal persons of his court to build, advancing them sums of money, and furnishing them with materials. He was the first who collected studs of fine horses, and made several useful embellishments. Peter, who was attentive to every thing, did not neglect Moscow at the time he was building Petersburg; for he caused it to be paved, adorned it with noble edifices, and enriched it with manufactures; and, within these few years, M. de Showalow, high chamberlain to the empress Elizabeth, daughter to Peter the Great, has founded an university in this city. This is the same person who furnished me with the memorials, from which I have compiled the present history, and who was himself much more capable to have done it, even in the French language, had not his great modesty determined him to resign the task to me, as will evidently appear from his own letters on this subject, which I have deposited in the public library of Geneva.

SMOLENSKO.

Westward of the duchy of Moscow, is that of Smolensko, a part of the ancient Sarmatia Europea. The duchies of Moscow and Smolensko composed what is properly called White Russia. Smolensko, which at first belonged to the great dukes of Russia, was conquered by the great duke of Lithuania, in the beginning of the fifteenth century, and was retaken one hundred years afterwards by its old masters. Sigismund III. king of Poland, got possession of it in 1611. The czar Alexis, father of Peter I. recovered it again in 1654, since which time it has always constituted part of the Russian empire. The panegyric of Peter the Great, pronounced in the academy of sciences at Paris, takes notice, that before his time the Russians had made no conquests either to the west or south; but this is evidently a mistake.

Of the Governments of **NOVOGOROD** *and* **KIOW**, *or the* **UKRAINE.**

Between Petersburg and Smolensko, lies the province of Novogorod;[8] and is said to be the country in which the ancient *Slavi*, or Sclavonians, made their first settlements. But from whence came these *Slavi*, whose language has spread over all the north-east part of Europe? *Sla* signifies a chief, and *slave* one belonging to a chief. All that we know concerning these ancient *Slaves* is, that they were a race of conquerors; that they built the city of Novogorod the Great, at the head of a navigable river; and that this city was for a long time in possession of a flourishing trade, and was a potent ally to the Hanse Towns. Czar Iwan Wassiliawitsch (or John Basilowitz) made a conquest of it in 1467, and carried away all its riches, which contributed to the magnificence of the court of Moscow, till then almost unknown.

To the south of the province of Smolensko, we meet with the province of Kiow, otherwise called the Lesser Russia, Red Russia, or the Ukraine, through which runs the Dnieper, called by the Greeks the Boristhenes. The difference of these two names, the one so harsh to pronounce, and the other so melodious, served to shew us, together with a hundred other like instances, the rudeness of all the ancient people of the North, in comparison with the graces of the Greek language. Kiow, the capital city, formerly Kisow, was built by the emperors of Constantinople, who made it a colony: here are still to be seen several Greek inscriptions upwards of twelve hundred years old. This is the only city of any antiquity in these countries, where men lived so long together without building walls. Here it was that the great dukes of Russia held their residence in the eleventh century, before the Tartars brought it under their subjection.

The inhabitants of the Ukraine, called Cossacks, are a mixture of the ancient Roxolanians, Sarmatians, and Tartars, blended together. Rome and Constantinople, though so long the mistress of other nations, are not to compare in fertility of country with the Ukraine. Nature has there exerted her utmost efforts for the service of mankind; but they have not seconded those efforts by industry, living only upon the spontaneous productions of an uncultivated, but fruitful soil, and the exercise of rapine. Though fond, to a degree of enthusiasm, of that most valuable of all blessings, liberty; yet they were always in subjection, either to the Poles or to the Turks, till the year 1654, when they threw themselves into the arms of Russia, but with some limitations. At length they were entirely subdued by Peter the Great.

Other nations are divided into cities and towns; this into ten regiments. At the head of which is a chief, who used to be elected by a majority of votes, and is called by the name of Hetman, or Itman. This captain of the nation was not invested with supreme power. At present the itman is a person nominated by the czar, from among the great lords of the court; and is, in fact, no more that the governor of the province, like governors of the *pays d'etats* in France, that have retained some privileges.

At first the inhabitants of this country were all either Pagans or Mahometans; but, when they entered into the service of Poland, they were baptized Christians of the Roman communion; and now, that they are in the service of Russia, they belong to the Greek church.

Amongst these are comprehended the Zaporavian Cossacks, who are much the same as our Bucaniers, or freebooters, living upon rapine. They are distinguished from all other people, by never admitting women to live among them; as the Amazons are said never to have admitted any man. The women, whom they make use of for propagation, live upon other islands on the river; they have no marriages amongst them, nor any domestic economy; they inroll the male children in their militia, and leave the girls to the care of their mothers. A brother has frequently children by his sister, and a father by his daughter. They know no other laws than customs, introduced by necessity: however, they make use of some prayers from the Greek ritual. Fort St. Elizabeth has been lately built on the Boristhenes, to keep them in awe. They serve as irregulars in the Russian armies, and hapless is the fate of those who fall into their hands.

Of the Governments of **BELGOROD, WORONITZ,** *and* **NISCHGOROD.**

To the north-east of the province of Kiow, between the Boristhenes and the Tanais, or Don, is the government of Belgorod, which is as large as that of Kiow. This is one of the most fruitful provinces of Russia, and furnishes Poland with a prodigious number of that large cattle known by the name of

Ukraine oxen. These two provinces are secured from the incursions of the petty Tartar tribes, by lines extending from the Boristhenes to the Tanais, and well furnished with forts and redoubts.

Farther northward we cross the Tanais, and come into the government of Worownitz, or Veronise, which extends as far as the banks of the Palus Mæotis. In the neighbourhood of the capital of this province, which is called, by the Russians, Woronestch, at the mouth of the river of the same name, which falls into the Don, Peter the Great built his first fleet; an undertaking which was at that time entirely new to the inhabitants of these vast dominions. From thence we come to the government of Nischgorod, abounding with grain, and is watered by the river Wolga.

ASTRACAN.

From the latter province we proceed southward to the kingdom of Astracan. This country reaches from forty-three and a half degrees north latitude (in a most delightful climate) to near fifty, including about as many degrees of longitude as of latitude. It is bounded on one side by the Caspian Sea, and on the other by the mountains of Circassia, projecting beyond the Caspian, along mount Caucasus. It is watered by the great river Wolga, the Jaick, and several other lesser streams, between which, according to Mr. Perry, the English engineer, canals might be cut, that would serve as reservoirs to receive the overflowing of the waters; and by that means answer the same purposes as the canals of the Nile, and make the soil more fruitful: but to the right and left of the Wolga and Jaick, this fine country was inhabited, or rather infested, by Tartars, who never apply themselves to agriculture, but have always lived as strangers and sojourners upon the face of the earth.

The above named engineer, Perry, who was employed by Peter the Great in these parts, found a vast track of land covered with pasture, leguminous plants, cherry and almond trees, and large flocks of wild sheep, who fed in these solitary places, and whose flesh was excellent. The inhabitants of these countries must be conquered and civilized, in order to second the efforts of nature, who has been forced in the climate of Petersburg.

The kingdom of Astracan is a part of the ancient Capshak, conquered by Gengis-Khan, and afterwards by Tamerlane, whose dominion extended as far as Moscow. The czar, John Basilides, grandson of John Basilowitz, and the greatest conqueror of all the Russian princes, delivered his country from the Tartarian yoke, in the sixteenth century, and added the kingdom of Astracan to his other conquests, in 1554.

Astracan is the boundary of Asia and Europe, and is so situated as to be able to carry on a trade with both; as merchandizes may be conveyed from the Caspian Sea, up to this town, by means of the Wolga. This was one of the grand schemes of Peter the Great, and has been partly carried into execution. An entire suburb of Astracan is inhabited by Indians.

OREMBURG.

To the south-east of the kingdom of Astracan, is a small country, newly planted, called Oremburg. The town of this name was built in the year 1734, on the banks of the river Jaick. This province is thick covered with hills, that are parts of Mount Caucasus. The passes in these mountains, and of the rivers that run down from them, are defended by forts raised at equal distances. In this region, formerly uninhabited, the Persians come at present, to hide from the rapacity of robbers, such of their effects as have escaped the fury of the civil wars. The city of Oremburg is become the asylum of the Persians and their riches, and is grown considerable by their calamities. The natives of Great Bukari come hither to trade, so that it is become the mart of Asia.

Of the Government of CASAN, *and of* GREAT PERMIA.

Beyond the Wolga and Jaick, towards the north, lies the kingdom of Casan, which, like that of Astracan, fell by partition to one of the sons of Gengis Khan, and afterwards to a son of Tamerlane, and was at length conquered by John Basilides. It is still inhabited by a number of Mahometan Tartars. This vast country stretches as far as Siberia; it is allowed to have been formerly very flourishing and rich, and still retains some part of its pristine opulence. A province of this kingdom, called Great Permia, and since Solikam, was the staple for the merchandizes of Persia, and the furs of Tartary. There has been found in Permia a great quantity of the coin of the first Caliphs, and some Tartarian idols, made of gold;[9] but these monuments of ancient opulence were found in the midst of barren deserts and extreme poverty, where there were not the least traces of commerce: revolutions of this nature may easily happen to a barren country, seeing they are so soon brought about in the most fruitful provinces.

The famous Swedish prisoner, Strahlemberg, who made such advantageous use of his misfortunes, and who examined those extensive countries with so much attention, was the first who gave an air of probability to a fact, which before had been always thought incredible; namely, concerning the ancient commerce of these provinces. Pliny and Pomponius Mela relate, that, in the reign of Augustus, a king of the Suevi made a present to Metellus Celer of some Indians who had been cast by a storm upon the coasts bordering on the

Elbe. But how could inhabitants of India navigate the Germanic seas? This adventure was deemed fabulous by all our moderns, especially after the change made in the commerce of our hemisphere by the discovery of the Cape of Good Hope. But formerly it was no more extraordinary to see an Indian trading to the parts to the north west of his country, than to see a Roman go from India by the way of Arabia. The Indians went to Persia, and thence embarked on the Hyrcanian Sea, and ascending the Rha, now the Wolga, got to Great Permia through the river Kama; from whence they might take shipping again on the Black Sea, or the Baltic. They have, in all times, been enterprising men. The Tyrians undertook most surprising voyages.

If after surveying all these vast provinces, we direct our view towards the east, we shall find the limits of Europe and Asia again confounded. A new name is wanting for a considerable part of the globe. The ancients divided their known world into Europe, Asia, and Africa: but they had not seen the tenth part of it: hence it happens, that when we pass the Palus Mæotis we are at a loss to know where Europe ends, or Asia begins; all that tract of country lying beyond mount Taurus was distinguished by the general appellation of Scythia, and afterwards by that of Tartary. It might not be improper, perhaps, to give the name of Terræ Arcticæ, or Northern Lands, to the country extending from the Baltic Sea to the confines of China; as that of Terræ Australes, or Southern Lands, are to that equally extensive part of the world, situated under the Antarctic Pole, and which serves to counterpoise the globe.

Of the Governments of SIBERIA, *of the* SAMOJEDES, *the* OSTIAKS KAMTSHATKA, *&c.*

Siberia, with the territories beyond it, extends from the frontiers of the provinces of Archangel, Casan, and Astracan, eastward as far as the sea of Japan: it joined the southern parts of Russia by Mount Caucasus; from thence, to the country of Kamtshatka, is about one thousand two hundred computed French leagues; and from southern Tartary, which serves as its boundary, to the Frozen Sea, about four hundred, which is the least breadth of the Russian empire. This country produces the richest furs; and this occasioned the discovery of it in the year 1563.

In the sixteenth century, in the reign of the czar, John Basilides, and not in that of Fœdor Johannowitz, a private person in the neighbourhood of Archangel, named Anika, one tolerably rich for his condition of life and country, took notice that certain men of an extraordinary figure, and dressed in a manner unknown to that country, and who spoke a language understood by none but themselves, came every year down a river which falls into the

Dwina,[10] and brought martens and black foxes, which they trucked for nails and pieces of glass; just as the first savages of America used to exchange their gold with the Spaniards: he caused them to be followed by his sons and servants, as far as their own country. These were the Samojedes, a people who seem to resemble the Laplanders, but are of a different race. They are, like that people, unacquainted with the use of bread; and like them, they yoke rein-deer to draw their sledges. They live in caverns and huts, amidst the snow;[11] but in other respects, nature has made a visible difference between this species of men and the Laplanders. Their upper jaw projects forward, so as to be on a level with their nose, and their ears are placed higher. Both the men and women have no hair in any other part of their bodies, but their heads; and their nipple is of a deep black, like ebony. The Lapland men and women are distinguished by no such marks. By memoirs sent from these countries so little known, I have been informed, that the author of the curious natural history of the king's garden, is mistaken, where, in speaking of the many curiosities of human nature, he confounds the Lapland race with that of the Samojedes. There are many more different species of men than is commonly thought. The Samojedes, and the Hottentots, seem to be the two extremes of our continent; and if we observe the black nipples of the Samojedian women, and the apron with which nature has furnished the Hottentot females, and which hangs half way down their thighs, we may have some idea of the great variety of our animal species, a variety unknown to those inhabiting great cities, who are generally strangers to almost every thing that is not immediately within their view.

The Samojedes are as singular in their moral as in their physical distinctions; they pay no worship to the Supreme Being; they border upon Manicheism, or rather upon the religion of the ancient Magi in this one point, that they acknowledge a good and an evil principle. The horrible climate they inhabit may in some measure excuse this belief, which is of such ancient date, and so natural to those who are ignorant and unhappy.

Theft, or murder, is never heard of amongst them; being in a manner devoid of passions, they are strangers to injustice; they have no terms in their language to denote vice and virtue, their extreme simplicity has not yet permitted them to form abstract ideas, they are wholly guided by pensation, and this is perhaps an incontestable proof that men naturally love justice, when not blinded by inordinate passions.

Some of these savages were prevailed on to suffer themselves to be carried to Moscow, where many things they saw struck them with admiration. They gazed upon the emperor as their god, and voluntarily engaged for themselves and countrymen a present of two martens, or sables, every year for each inhabitant. Colonies were soon settled beyond the Oby,[12] and the Irtis,[13] and some forts built. In the year 1595, a Cossack officer was sent into this country, who conquered it for the czar with only a few soldiers and some artillery, as Cortez did Mexico; but he only made a conquest of barren deserts.

In sailing up the Oby to the junction of the river Irtis with the Tobol, they found a petty settlement, which they converted into the town of Tobol,[14] now the capital of Siberia, and a considerable place. Who could imagine that this country was for a long time the residence of those very Huns, who under Attila carried their depredations as far as the gates of Rome, and that these Huns came from the north of China? The Usbeck Tartars succeeded the Huns, and the Russians the Usbecks. The possession of these savage countries has been disputed with as much murderous fury, as that of the most fruitful provinces. Siberia was formerly better peopled than it is at present, especially towards the southern parts; if we may judge from the rivers and sepulchral monuments.

All this part of the world, from the sixtieth degree of latitude, or thereabouts, as far as those mountains of perpetual ice which border the north seas, is totally different from the regions of the temperate zone, the earth produces neither the same plants, nor the same animals, nor are there the same sort of fishes in their lakes and rivers.

Below the country of the Samojedes lies that of the Ostiaks, along the river Oby. These people have no resemblance in any respect with the Samojedes, save that like them and all the first race of men, they are hunters, fishermen, and shepherds; some of them have no religion, not being formed into any society, and the others who live together in herds or clans, have a kind of worship, and pray to the principal object of their wants; they adore the skin of a sheep, because this creature is of all others the most serviceable to them; just as the Egyptian husbandmen made choice of an ox, as an emblem of the Deity who created that creature for the use of man.

The Ostiaks have likewise other idols, whose origin and worship are as little deserving our notice as their worshippers. There were some converts to Christianity made amongst them in the year 1712; but these, like the lowest of our peasants, are Christians without knowing what they profess. Several writers pretend that these people were natives of Great Permia, but as Great Permia is in a manner a desert, how comes it that its inhabitants should settle themselves at such a distance, and so inconveniently? This is a difficulty not worth clearing up. Every nation which has not cultivated the polite arts, deserves to remain in obscurity.

In the country of the Ostiaks in particular, and amongst their neighbours the

Burates and Jakutians, they often discover a kind of ivory under ground, the nature of which is as yet unknown. Some take it to be a sort of fossil, and others the tooth of a species of elephants, the breed of which have been destroyed: but where is the country that does not afford some natural productions, which at once astonish and confound philosophy.

Several mountains in this country abound with the amianthes or asbestos, a kind of incombustible flax, of which a sort of cloth and paper is sometimes made.

To the south of the Ostiaks are the Burates, another people, who have not yet been made Christians. Eastward there are several hordes, whom the Russians have not as yet entirely subdued.

None of these people have the least knowledge of the calendar: they reckon their time by snows, and not by the apparent motion of the sun: as it snows regularly, and for a long time every winter, they say, 'I am so many snows old,' just as we say, I am so many years.

And here I must relate the accounts given by the Swedish officer Strahlemberg, who was taken prisoner in the battle of Pultowa, and lived fifteen years in Siberia, and made the entire tour of that country. He says, that there are still some remains of an ancient people, whose skin is spotted or variegated with different colours, and that he himself had seen some of them, and the fact has been confirmed to me by Russians born at Tobolsky. The variety of the human species seems to be greatly diminished, as we find very few of these extraordinary people, and they have probably been exterminated by some other race: for instance there are very few Albinos, or White Moors; one of them was presented to the academy of sciences at Paris, which I saw. It is the same with respect to several other species of animals which are rare.

As to the Borandians, of whom mention is made so frequently in the learned history of the king's garden, my memoirs say, that this race of people is entirely unknown to the Russians.

All the southern part of these countries is peopled by numerous hordes of Tartars. The ancient Turks came from this part of Tartary to conquer these extensive countries, of which they are at present in possession. The Calmucs and Monguls are the very Scythians who, under Madies, made themselves masters of Upper Asia, and conquered Cyaxares, king of the Medes. They are the men, whom Gengis Khan and his sons led afterwards as far as Germany, and was termed the Mogul empire under Tamerlane. These people afford a lively instance of the vicissitudes which have happened to all nations; some of their hordes, so far from being formidable now, are become vassals to Russia.

Among these is a nation of Calmucs, dwelling between Siberia and the

Caspian Sea, where, in the year 1720, there was discovered a subterraneous house of stone, with urns, lamps, earrings, an equestrian statue of an oriental prince, with a diadem on his head, two women seated on thrones, and a roll of manuscripts, which were sent by Peter the Great to the academy of inscriptions at Paris, and proved to be written in the Thibet language: all these are striking proofs, that the liberal arts formerly resided in this now barbarous country, and are lasting evidences of the truth of what Peter the Great was wont several times to say, viz. that the arts had made the tour of the globe.

The last province is Kamtshatka, the most eastern part of the continent. The inhabitants were absolutely void of all religion when they were first discovered. The north part of this country likewise affords fine furs, with which the inhabitants clothed themselves in winter, though they went naked all the summer season. The first discoverers were surprised to find in the southern parts men with long beards, while in the northern parts, from the country of the Samojedes, as far as the mouth of the river Amur, they have no more beards than the Americans. Thus, in the empire of Russia, there is a greater number of different species, more singularities, and a greater diversity of manners and customs, than in any country in the known world.

The first discovery of this country was made by a Cossack officer, who went by land from Siberia to Kamtshatka, in 1701, by order of Peter the Great, who, notwithstanding his misfortune at Narva, still continued to extend his care from one extremity of the continent to the other. Afterwards, in 1725, some time before death surprised him, in the midst of his great exploits, he sent Captain Bering, a Dane, with express orders to find out, if possible, a passage by the sea of Kamtshatka, to the coast of America. Bering did not succeed in his first attempt; but the empress Anne sent him out again in 1733.
M. Spengenberg, captain of a ship, his associate in this voyage, set out the first from Kamtshatka, but could not put to sea till the year 1739, so much time was taken up in getting to the port where they were to embark, in building and fitting out the ships, and providing the necessaries. Spengenberg sailed as far as the north part of Japan, through a streight, formed by a long chain of islands, and returned without having discovered the passage.

In 1741, Bering cruised all over this sea, in company with De Lisle de la Croyere, the astronomer, of the same family of L'Isle, which has produced such excellent geographers: another captain likewise went upon the same discovery. They both made the coast of America, to the northward of California. Thus the north-east passage, so long sought after, was at length discovered, but there were no refreshments to be met with in those barren coasts. Their fresh water failed them, and part of the crew perished with the scurvy. They saw the northern bank of California for above a hundred miles, and saw some leathern canoes, with just such a sort of people in them as the Canadians. All their endeavours however proved fruitless: Bering ended his life in an island, to which he gave his name. The other captain, happening to be closer in with the Californian coast, sent ten of his people on shore, who never returned. The captain, after waiting for them in vain, found himself obliged to return back to Kamtshatka, and De Lisle died as he was going on shore. Such are the disasters that have generally attended every new attempt upon the northern seas. But what advantages may yet arise from these powerful and dangerous discoveries, time alone can prove.

We have now described all the different provinces that compose the Russian dominions, from Finland to the sea of Japan. The largest parts of this empire have been all united at different times, as has been the case in all other kingdoms in the world. The Scythians, Huns, Massagetes, Slavians, Cimbrians, Getes, and Sarmatians, are now subjects of the czar. The Russians, properly so called, are the ancient Roxolani or Slavi.

Upon reflection, we shall find that most states were formed in the same manner. The French are an assemblage of Goths, of Danes called Normands, of northern Germans, called Burgundians; of Franks, Allmans, and some Romans, mixed with the ancient Celtæ. In Rome and Italy there are several families descended from the people of the North, but none that we know of from the ancient Romans. The supreme pontiff is frequently the offspring ofa Lombard, a Goth, a Teuton, or a Cimbrian. The Spaniards are a race of Arabs, Carthaginians, Jews, Tyrians, Visigoths, and Vandals, incorporated with the ancient inhabitants of the country. When nations are thus intermixed, it is a long time before they are civilized, or even before their language is formed. Some, indeed, receive these sooner, others later. Polity and the liberal arts are so difficult to establish, and the new raised structure is so often destroyed by revolutions, that we may wonder all nations are not so barbarous as Tartars.

CHAP. II.

Continuation of the description of Russia, population, finances, armies, customs, religion: state of Russia before Peter the Great.

The more civilized a country is, the better it is peopled. Thus China and India are more populous than any other empires, because, after a multitude of revolutions, which changed the face of sublunary affairs, these two nations made the earliest establishments in civil society: the antiquity of their government, which has subsisted upwards of four thousand years, supposes, as we have already observed, many essays and efforts in preceding ages. The Russians came very late; but the arts having been introduced amongst them in their full perfection, it has happened, that they have made more progress in fifty years, than any other nation had done before them in five hundred. The country is far from being populous, in proportion to its extent; but, such as it is, it has as great a number of inhabitants as any other state in Christendom. From the capitation lists, and the register of merchants, artificers, and male peasants, I might safely assert, that Russia, at present, contains at least twenty-four millions of male inhabitants: of these twenty-four millions, the greatest part are villains or bondmen, as in Poland, several provinces of Germany, and formerly throughout all Europe. The estate of a gentleman in Russia and Poland is computed, not by his increase in money, but by the number of his slaves.

The following is a list, taken in 1747, of all the males who paid the capitation or poll-tax:—

Merchants or tradesmen	198000
Handicrafts	16500
Peasants incorporated with the merchants and handicrafts	1950
Peasants called Odonoskis, who contribute to maintain the militia	430220
Others who do not contribute thereto	26080
Workmen of different trades, whose parents are not known	1000
Others who are not incorporated with the companies of tradesmen	4700

Peasants immediately dependent on the crown, about	555000
Persons employed in the mines belonging to the crown, partly Christians, partly Mahometans and Pagans	64000
Other peasants belonging to the crown, who work in the mines, and in private manufactories	24200
New converts to the Greek church	57000
Tartars and Ostiaks (peasants)	241000
Mourses, Tartars, Mordauts, and others, whether Pagans or Christians, employed by the admiralty	7800
Tartars subject to contribution, called Tepteris, Bobilitz, &c.	28900
Bondmen to several merchants, and other privileged persons, who though not landholders, are allowed to have slaves	9100
Peasants in the lands set apart for the support of the crown	418000
Peasants on the lands belonging to her majesty, independently of the rights of the crown	60500
Peasants on the lands confiscated to the crown	13600
Bondmen belonging to the assembly of the clergy, and who defray other expenses	37500
Bondmen belonging to gentlemen	3550000
Bondmen belonging to bishops	116400
Bondmen belonging to convents, whose numbers were reduced by Peter the Great	721500
Bondmen belonging to cathedral and parish churches	23700
Peasants employed as labourers in the docks of the admiralty, or in other public works, about	4000

Labourers in the mines, and in private manufactures	16000
Peasants on the lands assigned to the principal manufactures	14500
Labourers in the mines belonging to the crown	3000
Bastards brought up by the clergy	40
Sectaries called Raskolniky	2200
Total	6646390

Here we have a round number of six millions six hundred forty-six thousand three hundred and ninety male persons, who pay the poll-tax. In this number are included boys and old men, but girls and women are not reckoned, nor boys born between the making of one register of the lands and another. Now, if we only reckon triple the number of heads subject to be taxed, including women and girls, we shall find near twenty millions of souls.

To this number we may add the military list, which amounts to three hundred and fifty thousand men: besides, neither the nobility nor clergy, who are computed at two hundred thousand, are subject to this capitation.

Foreigners, of whatever country or profession, are likewise exempt: as also the inhabitants of the conquered countries, namely, Livonia, Esthonia, Ingria, Carelia, and a part of Finland, the Ukraine, and the Don Cossacks, the Calmucks, and other Tartars, Samojedes, the Laplanders, the Ostiaks, and all the idolatrous people of Siberia, a country of greater extent than China.

By the same calculation, it is impossible that the total of the inhabitants of Russia should amount to less than twenty-four millions. At this rate, there are eight persons to every square mile. The English ambassador, whom I have mentioned before, allows only five; but he certainly was not furnished with such faithful memoirs as those with which I have been favoured.

Russia therefore is exactly five times less populous than Spain, but contains near four times the number of inhabitants: it is almost as populous as France or Germany; but, if we consider its vast extent, the number of souls is thirty times less.

There is one important remark to be made in regard to this enumeration, namely, that out of six million six hundred and forty thousand people liable to the poll-tax, there are about nine hundred thousand that belong to the Russian clergy, without reckoning either the ecclesiastics of the conquered countries, of the Ukraine, or of Siberia.

Therefore, out of seven persons liable to the poll-tax, the clergy have one; but, nevertheless, they are far from possessing the seventh part of the whole revenues of the state, as is the case in many other kingdoms, where they have at least a seventh of all estates; for their peasants pay a capitation to the sovereign; and the other taxes of the crown of Russia, in which the clergy have no share, are very considerable.

This valuation is very different from that of all other writers, on the affairs of Russia; so that foreign ministers, who have transmitted memoirs of this state to their courts, have been greatly mistaken. The archives of the empire are the only things to be consulted.

It is very probable, that Russia has been better peopled than it is at present; before the small-pox, that came from the extremities of Arabia, and the great-pox that came from America, had spread over these climates, where they have now taken root. The world owes these two dreadful scourges, which have depopulated it more than all its wars, the one to Mahomet, and the other to Christopher Columbus. The plague, which is a native of Africa, seldom approached the countries of the North: besides, the people of those countries, from Sarmatia to the Tartars, who dwell beyond the great wall, having overspread the world by their irruptions, this ancient nursery of the human species must have been surprisingly diminished.

In this vast extent of country, there are said to be about seventy-four thousand monks, and five thousand nuns, notwithstanding the care taken by Peter the Great to reduce their number; a care worthy the legislator of an empire where the human race is so remarkably deficient. These thirteen thousand persons, thus immured and lost to the state, have, as the reader may have observed, seventy-two thousand bondmen to till their lands, which is evidently too great a number: there cannot be a stronger proof how difficult it is to eradicate abuses of a long standing.

I find, by a list of the revenues of the empire in 1735, that reckoning the tribute paid by the Tartars, with all taxes and duties in money, the sum total amounted to thirteen millions of rubles, which makes sixty-five millions of French livres, exclusive of tributes in kind. This moderate sum was at that time sufficient to maintain three hundred and thirty-nine thousand five hundred, as well sea as land forces: but both the revenues and troops are augmented since that time.

The customs, diets, and manners of the Russians, ever bore a greater affinity to those of Asia than to those of Europe: such was the old custom of receiving tributes in kind, of defraying the expenses of ambassadors on their journeys, and during their residence in the country, and of never appearing at church, or in the royal presence with a sword; an oriental custom, directly the reverse of that ridiculous and barbarous one amongst us, of addressing ourselves to God, to our king, to our friends, and to our women, with an offensive weapon, which hangs down to the bottom of the leg. The long robe worn on public days, had a more noble air than the short habits of the western nations of Europe. A vest lined and turned up with fur, with a long scimar, adorned with jewels for festival days; and those high turbans, which add to the stature, were much more striking to the eye than our perukes and close coats, and more suitable to cold climates; but this ancient dress of all nations seems to be not so well contrived for war, nor so convenient for working people. Most of their other customs were rustic; but we must not imagine, that their manners were so barbarous as some writers would have us believe. Albert Krants relates a story of an Italian ambassador, whom the czar ordered to have his hat nailed to his head, for not pulling it off while he was making his speech to him. Others attribute this adventure to a Tartar, and others again to a French ambassador.

Olearius pretends, that the czar Michael Theodorowitz, banished the marquis of Exideüil, ambassador from Henry IV. of France, into Siberia; but it is certain, that this monarch sent no ambassador to Moscow, and that there never was a marquis of Exideüil in France. In the same manner do travellers speak about the country of Borandia, and of the trade they have carried on with the people of Nova Zémbla, which is scarcely inhabited at all, and the long conversations they have had with some of the Samojedes, as if they understood their language. Were the enormous compilations of voyages to be cleared of every thing that is not true nor useful in them, both the works and the public would be gainers by it.

The Russian government resembled that of the Turks, in respect to the standing forces, or guards, called Strelitzes, who, like the janissaries, sometimes disposed of the crown, and frequently disturbed the state as much as they defended it. Their number was about forty thousand. Those who were dispersed in the provinces, subsisted by rapine and plunder; those in Moscow lived like citizens, followed trades, did no duty, and carried their insolence to the greatest excess: in short, there was no other way to preserve peace and good order in the kingdom, but by breaking them; a very necessary, and at the same time a very dangerous step.

The public revenues did not exceed five millions of rubles, or about twenty-five millions of French livres. This was sufficient when czar Peter came to the crown to maintain the ancient mediocrity, but was not a third part of what was necessary to go certain lengths, and to render himself and people considerable in Europe: but at the same time many of their taxes were paid in kind, according to the Turkish custom, which is less burthensome to the people than that of paying their tributes in money.

OF THE TITLE OF CZAR.

As to the title of czar, it may possibly come from the tzars or tchars of the kingdom of Casan. When John, or Ivan Basilides, completed the conquest of this kingdom in the sixteenth century, which had been begun by his grandfather, who afterwards lost it, he assumed this title, which his successors have retained ever since. Before John Basilides, the sovereign of Russia, took the title of Welike Knez, i. e. great prince, great lord, great chief, which the Christian nations afterwards rendered by that of great duke. Czar Michael Theodorowitz, when he received the Holstein embassy, took to himself the following titles: 'Great knez, and great lord, conservator of all the Russias, prince of Wolodomer, Moscow, Novogorod, &c. tzar of Casan, tzar of Astracan, and tzar of Siberia.' Tzar was, therefore, a title belonging to these eastern princes; and, therefore, it is more probable to have been derived from the tshas of Persia, than from the Roman Cæsars, whom the Siberian tzars, on the banks of the Oby, can hardly be supposed to have ever heard.

No title, however pompous, is of any consequence, if those who bear it are not great and powerful themselves. The word emperor, which originally signified no more than general of the army, became the title of the sovereign of the Roman republic: it is now given to the supreme governor of all the Russias, more justly than to any other potentate, if we consider the power and extent of his dominions.

RELIGION.

The established religion of this country has, ever since the eleventh century, been that of the Greek church, so called in opposition to the Latin; though there were always a greater number of Mahometan and Pagan provinces, than of those inhabited by Christians. Siberia, as far as China, was in a state of idolatry; and, in some of the provinces, they were utter strangers to all kind of religion.

Perry, the engineer, and baron Strahlemberg, who both resided so many years in Russia, tell us, that they found more sincerity and probity among the Pagans than the other inhabitants; not that paganism made them more virtuous, but their manner of living, which, was that of the primitive ages, as they are called, freed them from all the tumultuous passions; and, in consequence, they were known for their integrity.

Christianity did not get footing in Russia and the other countries of the North, till very late. It is said, that a princess, named Olha, first introduced it, about the end of the tenth century, as Clotilda, niece to an Arian prince, did among the Franks; the wife of Miceslaus, duke of Poland, among the Poles; and the sister of the emperor Henry II. among the Hungarians. Women are naturally easily persuaded by the ministers of religion, and as easily persuade the other part of mankind.

It is further added, that the princess Olha caused herself to be baptized at Constantinople, by the name of Helena; and that, as soon as she embraced Christianity, the emperor John Zimisces fell in love with her. It is most likely that she was a widow; however, she refused the emperor. The example of the princess Olha, or Olga, as she is called, did not at first make many proselytes. Her son,[15] who reigned a long time, was not of the same way of thinking as his mother, but her grandson, Wolodomer, who was born of a concubine, having murdered his brother and mounted the throne, sued for the alliance of Basiles, emperor of Constantinople, but could obtain it only on condition of receiving baptism: and this event, which happened in the year 987, is the epocha when the Greek church was first established in Russia. Photius, the patriarch, so famous for his immense erudition, his disputes with the church of Rome, and for his misfortunes, sent a person to baptize Wolodomer, in order to add this part of the world to the patriarchal see.[16]

Wolodimer, or Wolodomer, therefore completed the work which his grandmother had begun. A Greek was made the first metropolitan, or patriarch of Russia; and from this time the Russians adopted an alphabet, taken partly from the Greek. This would have been of advantage to them, had they not still retained the principles of their own language, which is the Sclavonian in every thing, but a few terms relating to their liturgy and church government. One of the Greek patriarchs, named Jeremiah, having a suit depending before the divan, came to Moscow to solicit it; where, after some time, he resigned his authority over the Russian churches, and consecrated patriarch, the archbishop of Novogorod, named Job. This was in the year 1588, from which time the Russian church became as independent as its empire. The patriarch of Russia has ever since been consecrated by the Russian bishops, and not by the patriarch of Constantinople. He ranked in the Greek church next to the patriarch of Jerusalem, but he was in fact the only free and powerful patriarch; and, consequently, the only real one. Those of Jerusalem, Constantinople, Antioch, Alexandria, are mercenary chiefs of a church, enslaved by the Turks; and even the patriarchs of Jerusalem and Antioch are no longer considered as such, having no more credit or influence in Turkey, than the rabbins of the Jewish synagogues settled there.

It was from a person who was a patriarch of all the Russias, that Peter the

Great was descended in a right line. These new prelates soon wanted to share the sovereign authority with the czars. They thought it not enough that their prince walked bare-headed, once a year before the patriarch, leading his horse by the bridle. These external marks of respect only served to increase their thirst for rule; a passion which proved the source of great troubles in Russia, as well as in other countries.

Nicon, a person whom the monks look upon as a saint, and who was patriarch in the reign of Alexis, the father of Peter the Great, wanted to raise his dignity above that of the throne; for he not only assumed the privilege of sitting by the side of the czar in the senate, but pretended that neither war nor peace could be made without his consent. His authority was so great, that, being supported by his immense wealth, and by his intrigues with the clergy andthe people, he kept his master in a kind of subjection. He had the boldness to excommunicate some senators who opposed his excessive insolence; till at last, Alexis, finding himself not powerful enough to depose him by his own authority, was obliged to convene a synod of all the bishops. There the patriarch was accused of having received money from the Poles; and being convicted, was deposed, and confined for the remainder of his days in a monastery, after which the prelates chose another patriarch in his stead.

From the first infancy of Christianity in Russia, there have been several sects there, as well as in other countries; for sects are as frequently the fruits of ignorance, as of pretended knowledge: but Russia is the only Christian state of any considerable extent, in which religion has not excited civil wars, though it has felt some occasional tumults.

The Raskolnikys, who consist at present of about two thousand males, and who are mentioned in the foregoing list,[17] are the most ancient sect of any in this country. It was established in the twelfth century, by some enthusiasts, who had a superficial knowledge of the New Testament: they made use then, and still do, of the old pretence of all sectaries, that of following the letter, and accused all other Christians of remissness. They would not permit a priest, who had drank brandy, to confer baptism; they affirmed, in the words of our Saviour, that there is neither a first nor a last, among the faithful; and held, that one of the elect might kill himself for the love of his Saviour. According to them it is a great sin to repeat the hallelujah three times; and, therefore, repeat it only twice. The benediction is to be given only with three fingers. In other respects, no society can be more regular, or strict in its morals. They live like the quakers, and, like them, do not admit any other Christians into their assemblies, which is the reason that these have accused them of all the abominations of which the heathens accused the primitive Galileans: these latter, the gnostics, and with which the Roman catholics have charged the protestants. They have been frequently accused of cutting the throat of an infant, and drinking its blood; and of mixing together in their private ceremonies, without distinction of kindred, age, or even of sex. They have been persecuted at times, and then they shut themselves up in their hamlets, set fire to their houses, and thrown themselves into the flames. Peter took the only method of reclaiming them, which was by letting them live in peace.

But to conclude, in all this vast empire, there are but twenty-eight episcopal sees; and in Peter's time there were but twenty-two. This small number was, perhaps, one of the causes to which the Russian church owes its tranquillity. So very circumscribed was the knowledge of the clergy, that czar Theodore, brother to Peter the Great, was the first who introduced the custom of singing Psalms in churches.

Theodore and Peter, especially the latter, admitted indifferently, into their councils and their armies, those of the Greek, the Latin, the Lutheran, and the Calvinist communion, leaving every one at liberty to serve God after his own conscience, provided he did his duty to the state. At that time there was not one Latin church in this great empire of two thousand leagues, till Peter established some new manufactures at Astracan, when there were about sixty Roman catholic families, under the direction of the capuchins; but the jesuits endeavouring to establish themselves in his dominions, he drove them out by an edict, published in the month of April, 1718. He tolerated the capuchins as an insignificant set of monks, but considered the jesuits as dangerous politicians.

The Greek church has at once the honour and satisfaction to see its communion extended throughout an empire of two thousand leagues in length, while that of Rome is not in possession of half that tract in Europe. Those of the Greek communion have, at all times, been particularly attentive to maintain an equality between theirs and the Latin church; and always upon their guard against the zeal of the see of Rome, which they look upon as ambition; because, in fact, that church, whose power is very much circumscribed in our hemisphere, and yet assumes the title of universal, has always endeavoured to act up to that title.

The Jews never made any settlements in Russia, as they have done in most of the other states of Europe, from Constantinople to Rome. The Russians have carried on their trade by themselves, or by the help of the nations settled amongst them. Theirs is the only country of the Greek communion, where synagogues are not seen by the side of Christian temples.

Conclusion of the State of **RUSSIA** *before* **PETER** *the* **GREAT.**

Russia is indebted solely to czar Peter for its great influence in the affairs of Europe; being of no consideration in any other reign, since it embraced Christianity. Before this period, the Russians made the same figure on the Black Sea, that the Normans did afterwards on the coasts of the ocean. In the reign of the emperor Heraclius, they fitted out an armament of forty thousand small barks; appeared before Constantinople, which they besieged, and imposed a tribute on the Greek emperors; but the grand knez Wolodimar, being wholly taken up with the care of establishing Christianity in his dominions, and wearied out with intestine broils in his own family, weakened his dominions by dividing them between his children. They almost all fell a prey to the Tartars, who held Russia in subjection near two hundred years. At length John Basilides freed it from slavery, and enlarged its boundaries: but, after his time, it was ruined again by civil wars.

Before the time of Peter the Great, Russia was neither so powerful, so well cultivated, so populous, nor so rich as at present. It had no possessions in Finland, nor in Livonia; and this latter alone had long been worth more than all Siberia. The Cossacks were still unsubjected, nor were the people of Astracan reduced to obedience; what little trade was carried on, was rather to their disadvantage. The White Sea, the Baltic, the Pontus Euxinus, the sea of Azoph, and the Caspian Sea, were entirely useless to a nation that had not a single ship, nor even a term in their language to express a fleet. If nothing more had been wanting but to be superior to the Tartars, and the other nations of the north, as far as China, the Russians undoubtedly had that advantage, but they were to be brought upon an equality with civilized nations, and to be in a condition, one day, of even surpassing several of them. Such an undertaking appeared altogether impracticable, inasmuch as they had not a single ship at sea, and were absolutely ignorant of military discipline by land: nay, the most common manufactures were hardly encouraged, and agriculture itself, that *primum mobile* of trade, was neglected. This requires the utmost attention and encouragement on the part of a government; and it is to this that the English are indebted, for finding in their corn a treasure far superior to their woollen manufacture.

This gross neglect of the necessary arts, sufficiently shews that the people of Russia had no idea of the polite arts, which become necessary, in their turn, when we have cultivated the others. They might indeed, have sent some of the natives to gain instruction among foreigners, but the difference of languages, manners, and religion, opposed it. Besides, there was a law of state and religion, equally sacred and pernicious, which prohibited any Russian from going out of his country, and thus seemed to devote this people to eternal ignorance. They were in possession of the most extensive dominions in the universe, and yet every thing was wanted amongst them. At length Peter was born, and Russia became a civilized state.

Happily, of all the great lawgivers who have lived in the world, Peter is the only one whose history is well known. Those of Theseus and Romulus, who did far less than him, and of the founders of all well-governed states, are blended with the most absurd fictions: whereas here, we have the advantage of written truths, which would pass for fictions, were they not so well attested.

CHAP. III.

The ancestors of Peter the Great.

The family of Peter the Great have been in possession of the throne ever since the year 1613. Before that time, Russia had undergone revolutions, which had retarded the reformation of her police, and the introduction of the liberal arts. This has been the fate of all human societies. No kingdom ever experienced more cruel troubles. In the year 1597, the tyrant Boris Godonow assassinated Demetrius (or Demetri, as he was called), the lawful heir, and usurped the empire. A young monk took the name of Demetrius, pretending to be that prince who had escaped from his murderers; and with the assistance of the Poles, and a considerable party (which every tyrant has against him), he drove out the usurper, and seized the crown himself. The imposture was discovered as soon as he came to the sovereignty, because the people were not pleased with him; and he was murdered. Three other false Demetrius's started up, one after another. Such a succession of impostors, supposes a country in the utmost distraction. The less men are civilized, the more easily they are imposed on. It may readily be conceived, how much these frauds augmented the public confusion and misfortunes. The Poles, who had begun the revolutions, by setting up the first false Demetrius, were on the point of being masters of Russia. The Swedes shared in the spoils on the coast of Finland, and laid claim to the crown. The state seemed on the verge of utter destruction.

In the midst of these calamities, an assembly, composed of the principal boyards, chose for their sovereign a young man of fifteen years of age: this happened in 1613, and did not seem a very likely method of putting an end to these troubles. This young man was Michael Romanow,[18] grandfather to czar Peter, and son to the archbishop of Rotow, surnamed Philaretes, and of a nun, and related by the mother's side to the ancient czars.

It must be observed, that this archbishop was a powerful nobleman, whom the tyrant Boris had obliged to become priest. His wife, Scheremetow, was likewise compelled to take the veil; this was the ancient custom of the western tyrants of the Latin church, as that of putting out the eyes was with the Greek Christians. The tyrant Demetrius made Philaretes archbishop of Rostow, and sent him ambassador to Poland, where he was detained prisoner by the Poles, who were then at war with the Russians; so little was the law of nations known to the different people of these times. During his father's confinement, young Romanow was elected czar. The archbishop was exchanged against some Polish prisoners; and, at his return, his son created him patriarch, and the old man was in fact king, under his son's name.

If such a government appears extraordinary to strangers, the marriages of czar Michael Romanow, will seem still more so. The Russian princes had never intermarried with foreign states since the year 1490, or after they became masters of Casan and Astracan; they seem to have followed the Asiatic customs in almost every thing, and especially in that of marrying only among their own subjects.

This conformity to the ancient customs of Asia, was still more conspicuous at the ceremonies observed at the marriage of a czar. A number of the most beautiful women in the provinces were sent for to court, where they were received by the grand gouvernante of the court, who provided apartments for them in her own house, where they all eat together. The czar paid them visits, sometimes incognito, and sometimes in his real character. The wedding-day was fixed, without its being declared on whom the choice had fallen. At the appointed time, the happy she was presented with a rich wedding-suit, and other dresses were given to the rest of the fair candidates, who then returned home. There have been four instances of these marriages.

In this manner was Michael Romanow espoused to Eudocia, the daughter ofa poor gentleman, named Streschneu. He was employed in ploughing his grounds with his servants, when the lords of the bed-chamber came to him with presents from the czar, and to acquaint him that his daughter was placed on the throne. The name of the princess is still held in the highest veneration by the Russians. This custom is greatly different from ours, but not the less respectable on that account.

It is necessary to observe, that before Romanow was elected czar, a strong party had made choice of prince Ladislaus, son to Sigismund III. king of Poland. At the same time, the provinces bordering on Sweden had offered the crown to a brother of Gustavus Adolphus: so that Russia was in the same situation then in which we have so frequently seen Poland, where the right of electing a king has been the source of civil wars. But the Russians did not follow the example of the Poles, who entered into a compact with the prince whom they elected; notwithstanding they had smarted from the oppression of tyrants, yet they voluntarily submitted to a young man, without making any conditions with him.

Russia never was an elective kingdom; but the male issue of the ancient sovereigns failing, and six czars, or pretenders, having perished miserably in the late troubles, there was, as we have observed, a necessity for electing a monarch; and this election occasioned fresh wars with Poland and Sweden, who maintained, with force of arms, their pretended rights to the crown of

Russia. The right of governing a nation against its own will, can never be long supported. The Poles, on their side, after having advanced as far as Moscow, and exercised all the ravages in which the military expeditions of those times chiefly consisted, concluded a truce for fourteen years. By this truce, Poland remained in possession of the duchy of Smolensko, in which the Boristhenes has its source. The Swedes also made peace, in virtue of which theyremained in possession of Ingria, and deprived the Russians of all communication with the Baltic Sea, so that this empire was separated more than ever from the rest of Europe.

Michael Romanow, after this peace, reigned quietly, without making any alteration in the state, either to the improvement or corruption of the administration. After his death, which happened in 1645, his son, Alexis Michaelowitz (or son of Michael), ascended the throne by hereditary right. It may be observed, that the czars were crowned by the patriarch of Russia, according to the ceremonies in use at Constantinople, except that the patriarch of Russia, was seated on the same ascent with the sovereign, and constantly affected an equality highly insulting to the supreme power.

ALEXIS MICHAELOWITZ.

Alexis was married in the same manner as his father, and from among the young women presented, he chose the one who appeared the most amiable in his eyes. He married a daughter of the boyard Meloslauski, in 1647; his second wife, whom he married in 1671, was of the family of Nariskin, and his favourite Morosow was married to another. There cannot be a more suitable title found for this favourite than that of vizier, for he governed the empire in a despotic manner; and, by his great power, excited several commotions among the strelitzes and the populace, as frequently happens at Constantinople.

The reign of Alexis was disturbed by bloody insurrections, and by domestic and foreign wars. A chief of the Don Cossacks, named Stenko-Rasin, endeavoured to make himself king of Astracan, and was for a long time very formidable; but, being at length defeated and taken prisoner, he ended his life by the hands of the executioner; like all those of this stamp, who have nothing to expect but a throne or a scaffold. About twelve thousand of his adherents are said to have been hanged on the high road to Astracan. In this part of the world, men being uninfluenced by morality, were to be governed only by rigour; and from this severity, frequently carried on to a degree of cruelty, arose slavery, and a secret thirst of revenge.

Alexis had a war with the Poles that proved successful, and terminated in a peace, which secured to him the possession of Smolensko, Kiow, and the Ukraine: but he was unfortunate against the Swedes, and the boundaries of the Russian empire were contracted within a very narrow compass on that side of the kingdom.

The Turks were at that time his most formidable enemies: they invaded Poland, and threatened the dominions of the czar that bordered upon Crim Tartary, the ancient Taurica Chersonesus. In 1671, they took the important city of Kaminiek, and all that belonged to Poland in the Ukraine. The Cossacks of that country, ever averse to subjection, knew not whether they belonged to the Turks, Poland, or Russia. Sultan Mahomet IV. who had conquered the Poles, and had just imposed a tribute upon them, demanded, with all the haughtiness of an Ottoman victor, that the czar should evacuate his possessions in the Ukraine, but received as haughty a denial from that prince. Men did not know at that time how to disguise their pride, by an outside of civility. The sultan, in his letter, styled the sovereign of the Russias only Christian Hospodar, and entitled himself 'most gracious majesty, king of the universe.' The czar replied in these terms, 'that he scorned to submit to a Mahometan dog, and that his scimetar was as good as the grand seignior's sabre.'

Alexis at that time formed a design which seemed to presage the influence which the Russian empire would one day obtain in the Christian world. He sent ambassadors to the pope, and to almost all the great sovereigns in Europe, excepting France (which was in alliance with the Turks), in order to establish a league against the Ottoman Porte. His ambassadors at the court of Rome succeeded only in not being obliged to kiss the pope's toe; and in other courts they met with only unprofitable good wishes; the quarrels of the Christian princes between themselves, and the jarring interests arising from those quarrels, having constantly prevented them from uniting against the common enemy of Christianity.

In the mean time, the Turks threatened to chastise the Poles, who refused to pay their tribute: czar Alexis assisted on the side of Crim Tartary, and John Sobieski, general of the crown, wiped off his country's stain in the blood of the Turks, at the famous battle of Choczim,[19] in 1674, which paved his way to the throne. Alexis disputed this very throne with him, and proposed to unite his extensive dominions to Poland, as the Jagellons had done; but in regard to Lithuania, the greatness of his offer was the cause of its being rejected. He is said to have been very deserving of the new kingdom, by the manner in which he governed his own. He was the first who caused a body of laws to be digested in Russia, though imperfect; and introduced both linen and silk manufactures, which indeed were not long kept up; nevertheless, he had the merit of their first establishment. He peopled the deserts about the Wolga and the Kama, with Lithuanian, Polish, and Tartarian families, whom he had taken prisoners in his wars: before his reign, all prisoners of war were the slaves of those to whose lot they fell. Alexis employed them in agriculture: he did his utmost endeavours to introduce discipline among his troops. In a word, he was worthy of being the father of Peter the Great; but he had no time to perfect what he had begun, being snatched away by a sudden death, at the age of forty-six, in the beginning of the year 1677, according to our style, which is eleven days forwarder than that of Russia.

FŒDOR, or THEODORE ALEXIOWITZ.

Upon the death of Alexis, son of Michael, all fell again into confusion. He left, by his first marriage, two princes, and six princesses. Theodore, the eldest, ascended the throne at fifteen years of age. He was a prince of a weak and sickly constitution, but of merit superior to his bodily infirmities. His father Alexis had caused him to be acknowledged his successor, a year before his death: a conduct observed by the kings of France from Hugh Capet down to Lewis the Young, and by many other crowned heads.

The second son of Alexis was Iwan, or John, who was still worse treated by nature than his brother Theodore, being almost blind and dumb, very infirm, and frequently attacked with convulsions. Of six daughters, born of this first marriage, the only one who made any figure in Europe was the princess Sophia, who was remarkable for her great talents; but unhappily still more so for the mischief she intended against Peter the Great.

Alexis, by his second marriage with another of his subjects, daughter of the boyard Nariskin, had Peter and the princess Nathalia. Peter was born the 30th of May (or the 10th of June new stile), in the year 1672, and was but four years old when he lost his father. As the children of a second marriage were not much regarded in Russia, it was little expected that he would one day mount the throne.

It had ever been the character of the family of Romanow to civilize their state. It was also that of Theodore. We have already remarked, in speaking of Moscow, that this prince encouraged the inhabitants of that city to build a great number of stone houses. He likewise enlarged that capital, and made several useful regulations in the general police; but, by attempting to reform the boyards, he made them all his enemies: besides, he was not possessed of sufficient knowledge, vigour, or resolution, to venture upon making a general reformation. The war with the Turks, or rather with the Crim Tartars, in which he was constantly engaged with alternate success, would not permit a prince of his weak state of health to attempt so great a work. Theodore, like the rest of his predecessors, married one of his own subjects, a native of the frontiers of Poland; but having lost her in less than a year after their nuptials, he took for his second wife, in 1682, Martha Matweowna, daughter of the secretary Nariskin.[20] Some months after this marriage, he was seized with the disorder which ended his days, and died without leaving any children. As the czars married without regard to birth, they might likewise (at least at that time) appoint a successor without respect to primogeniture. The dignity of consort and heir to the sovereign seemed to be entirely the reward of merit; and, in that respect, the custom of this empire was much preferable to the customs of more civilized states.

Theodore, before he expired, seeing that his brother Iwan was by his natural infirmities incapable of governing, nominated his younger brother Peter, heir to the empire of Russia. Peter, who was then only in his tenth year, had already given the most promising hopes.

If, on the one hand, the custom of raising a subject to the rank of czarina, was favourable to the females, there was another which was no less hard upon them; namely, that the daughters of the czars were very seldom married, but were most of them obliged to pass their lives in a monastery.

The princess Sophia, third daughter of czar Alexis, by his first marriage, was possessed of abilities, equally great and dangerous. Perceiving that her brother Theodore had not long to live, she did not retire to a convent; but finding herself situated between two brothers, one of whom was incapable of governing, through his natural inability; and the other, on account of his youth, she conceived the design of placing herself at the head of the empire. Hence, in the last hours of czar Theodore, she attempted to act the part that Pulcheria had formerly played with her brother, the emperor Theodosius.

CHAP. IV.

JOHN AND PETER.

Horrible Sedition among the Strelitzes.[21]

1682.

Czar Theodore's eyes were scarcely closed, when the nomination of a prince of only ten years old to the throne, the exclusion of the elder brother, and the intrigues of the princess Sophia, their sister, excited a most bloody revolt among the strelitzes. Never did the janissaries, nor the prætorian guards, exercise more horrible barbarities. The insurrection began two days after the interment of Theodore, when they all ran to arms in the Kremlin, which is the imperial palace at Moscow. There they began with accusing nine of their colonels, for keeping back part of their pay. The ministry was obliged to break the colonels, and to pay the strelitzes the money they demanded: but this did not satisfy them, they insisted upon having these nine officers delivered up to them, and condemned them, by a majority of votes, to suffer the Battogs, or Knout; the manner of which punishment is as follows:—

The delinquent is stripped naked, and laid flat on his belly, while two executioners beat him over the back with switches, or small canes, till the judge, who stands by to see the sentence put in execution, says, 'It is enough.' The colonels, after being thus treated by their men, were obliged to return them thanks, according to the custom of the eastern nations; where criminals, after undergoing their punishment, must kiss the judge's hand. Besides complying with this custom, the officers gave them a sum of money, which was something more than the custom.

While the strelitzes thus began to make themselves formidable, the princess Sophia, who secretly encouraged them, in order to lead them by degrees from crime to crime, held a meeting at her house, consisting of the princesses of the blood, the generals of the army, the boyards, the patriarch, the bishops, and even some of the principal merchants; where she represented to them, that prince John, by right of birth and merit, was entitled to the empire, the reins of which she intended to keep in her own hands. At the breaking up of the assembly, she caused a promise to be made to the strelitzes, of an augmentation of pay, besides considerable presents. Her emissaries were in particular employed to stir up the soldiery against the Nariskin family, especially the two brothers of the young dowager czarina, the mother of Peter the First. These persuaded the strelitzes, that one of the brothers, named John, had put on the imperial robes, had seated himself on the throne, and had attempted to strangle prince John; adding, moreover, that the late czar Theodore had been poisoned by a villain, named Daniel Vongad, a Dutch physician. At last Sophia put into their hands a list of forty noblemen, whom she stiled enemies to their corps, and to the state, and as such worthy of death. These proceedings exactly resembled the proscriptions of Sylla, and the Roman triumvirate, which had been revived by Christian II. in Denmark and Sweden. This may serve to shew, that such cruelties prevail in all countries in times of anarchy and confusion. The mutineers began the tragedy with throwing the two knez, or princes, Dolgorouki and Matheof, out of the palace-windows; whom the strelitzes received upon the points of their spears, then stripped them, and dragged their dead bodies into the great square; after this they rushed into the palace, where meeting with Athanasius Nariskin, a brother of the young czarina, and one of the uncles of czar Peter, they murdered him in like manner; then breaking open the door of a neighbouring church, where three of the proscribed persons had taken refuge, they drag them from the altar, strip them naked, and stab them to death with knives.

They were so blinded with their fury, that seeing a young nobleman of the family of Soltikoff, a great favourite of theirs, and who was not included in the list of the proscribed, and some of them mistaking him for John Nariskin, whom they were in search of, they murdered him upon the spot; and what plainly shews the manners of those times, after having discovered their error, they carried the body of young Soltikoff, to his father to bury it; and the wretched parent, far from daring to complain, gave them a considerable reward for bringing him the mangled body of his son. Being reproached by his wife, his daughters, and the widow of the deceased, for his weakness, 'Let us wait for an opportunity of being revenged,' said the old man. These words being overheard by some of the soldiers, they returned furiously back into the room, dragged the aged parent by the hair, and cut his throat at his own door.

Another party of the strelitzes, who were scouring the city in search of the Dutch physician, Vongad, met with his son, of whom they inquired for his father; the youth trembling, replied, he did not know where he was, upon which they immediately dispatched him. Soon after, a German physician falling in their way, 'You are a doctor,' said they, 'and if you did not poison our master, Theodore, you have poisoned others, and therefore merit death;' and thereupon killed him.

At length they found the Dutchman, of whom they were in quest, disguised in the garb of a beggar; they instantly drag him before the palace. The princesses who loved this worthy man, and placed great confidence in his skill, begged the strelitzes to spare him, assuring them that he was a very good physician, and had taken all possible care of their brother Theodore. The strelitzes made answer, that he not only deserved to die as a physician, but also as a sorcerer; and that they had found in his house, a great dried toad, and the skin of a serpent. They furthermore required to have young Nariskin delivered up to them, whom they had searched for in vain for two days: alleging, that he was certainly in the palace, and that they would set fire to it, unless he was put into their hands. The sister of John Nariskin, and the other princesses, terrified by their menaces, went to acquaint their unhappy brother in the place of his concealment, with what had passed; upon which the patriarch heard his confession, administers the viaticum, and extreme unction to him, and then, taking an image of the blessed Virgin, which was said to perform miracles, he leads the young man forth by the hand, and presents him to the strelitzes, shewing them, at the same time, the image of the Virgin. The princesses, who in tears surrounded Nariskin, falling upon their knees before the soldiers, besought them, in the name of the blessed Virgin, to spare their relation's life; but the inhuman wretches tore him from their arms, and dragged him to the foot of the stairs, together with the physician Vongad, where they held a kind of tribunal among themselves, and condemned them both to be put to the torture. One of the soldiers, who could write, drew up a form of accusation, and sentenced the two unfortunate princes to be cut in pieces; a punishment inflicted in China and Tartary on parricides, and called the punishment of ten thousand slices. After having thus used Nariskin and Vongad, they exposed their heads, feet, and hands, on the iron points of a balustrade.

While this party of the strelitzes were thus glutting their fury in the sight of the princesses, the rest massacred every one who was obnoxious to them, or suspected by the princess Sophia.

This horrid tragedy concluded with proclaiming the two princes, John and Peter, in June, 1682, joint sovereigns, and associating their sister Sophia with them, in the quality of co-regent; who then publicly approved of all their outrages, gave them rewards, confiscated the estates of the proscribed, and bestowed them upon their murderers. She even permitted them to erect a monument, with the names of the persons they had murdered, as being traitors to their country: and to crown all, she published letters-patent, thanking them for their zeal and fidelity.

CHAP. V.

Administration of the princess Sophia. Extraordinary quarrel about religion. A conspiracy.

Such were the steps by which the princess Sophia did in effect ascend the throne of Russia, though without being declared czarina; and such the examples that Peter the First had before his eyes. Sophia enjoyed all the honours of a sovereign; her bust was on the public coin; she signed all dispatches, held the first place in council, and enjoyed a power without control. She was possessed of a great share of understanding, and some wit; made verses in the Russian language, and both spoke and wrote extremely well. These talents were set off by the addition of an agreeable person, and sullied only by her ambition.

She procured a wife for her brother John, in the manner already described in several examples. A young lady named Soltikoff, of the family with the nobleman of that name who had been assassinated by the seditious strelitzes, was sent for from the heart of Siberia, where her father commanded a fortress, to be presented to czar John at Moscow. Her beauty triumphed over all the intrigues of her rivals, and John was married to her in 1684. At every marriage of a czar we seem to read the history of Ahasuerus, or that of Theodosius the Younger.

In the midst of the rejoicings on account of this marriage, the strelitzes raised a new insurrection, and (who would believe it?) on account of religion! of a particular tenet! Had they been mere soldiers, they would never have become controvertists, but they were also citizens of Moscow. Whosoever has, or assumes a right of speaking in an authoritative manner to the populace, may found a sect. This has been seen in all ages, and all parts of the world, especially since the passion of dogmatizing has become the instrument of ambition, and the terror of weak minds.

Russia had experienced some previous disturbances on occasion of a dispute, whether the sign of the cross was to be made with three fingers, or with two! One Abakum, who was also a priest, had set up some new tenets at Moscow, in regard to the Holy Spirit; which according to the Scriptures, enlightened all the faithful; as likewise with respect to the equality of the primitive Christians, and these words of Christ:—'There shall be amongst you neither first nor last.' Several citizens and many of the strelitzes, embraced the opinions of Abakum. One Raspop[22] was the chief of this party, which became considerable. The sectaries, at length, entered (July 16, 1682, new stile) the cathedral, where the patriarch and his clergy were officiating; drove them out of the church with stones, and seated themselves very devoutly in their places, to receive the Holy Spirit. They called the patriarch the 'ravenous wolf in the sheepfold;' a title which all sects have liberally bestowed on each other. The princess Sophia, and the two czars, were immediately made acquainted with these disturbances: and the other strelitzes, who were staunch to the good old cause, were given to understand, that the czars and the church were in danger. Upon this the strelitzes and burghers of the patriarchal party attacked the Abakumists: but a stop was put to the carnage, by publishing a convocation of a council, which was immediately assembled in a hall of the palace. This took up very little time, for they obliged every priest they met to attend. The patriarch, and a bishop, disputed against Raspop; but at the second syllogism, they began to throw stones at one another. The council ended with ordering Raspop, and some of his faithful disciples to have their heads struck off; and the sentence was executed by the sole order of the three sovereigns, Sophia, John, and Peter.

During these troubles, there was a knez, named Chowanskoi, who having been instrumental in raising the princess Sophia to the dignity she then held, wanted, as a reward for his services, to have a share in the administration.

It may be supposed, that he found Sophia not so grateful as he could wish; upon which he espoused the cause of religion, and the persecuted Raspopians, and stirred up a party among the strelitzes and the people, in defence of God's name.

This conspiracy proved a more serious affair than the enthusiastic riot of Raspop. An ambitious hypocrite always carries things farther than a simple fanatic. Chowanskoi aimed at no less than the imperial dignity; and to rid himself of all cause of fear, he resolved to murder the two czars, Sophia, the other princesses, and every one who was attached to the imperial family. The czars and the princesses were obliged to retire to the monastery of the Holy Trinity, within twelve leagues of Petersburg.[23] This was, at the same time, a convent, a palace, and a fortress, like Mount Cassino,[24] Corhy,[25] Fulda,[26] Kempten,[27] and several others belonging to the Latin church. This monastery of the Trinity belongs to the monks of St. Basil. It is surrounded by deep ditches, and ramparts of brick, on which is planted a numerous artillery. The monks are possessed of all the country round for four leagues. The imperial family were in full safety there, but more on account of the strength, than the sanctity of the place. Here Sophia treated with the rebel knez; and having decoyed him half way, caused his head to be struck off, together with those of one of his sons, and thirty-seven strelitzes who accompanied him.

The body of strelitzes upon this news, fly to arms, and march to attack the convent of Trinity, threatening to destroy every thing that came in their way. The imperial family stood upon their defence; the boyards arm their vassals, all the gentlemen flocked in, and a bloody civil war seemed on the point of beginning. The patriarch somewhat pacified the strelitzes, who began to be intimidated with the number of troops that were marching towards them on all sides: in short, their fury was changed into fear, and their fear into the most abject submission; a change common to the multitude. Three thousand seven hundred of this corps, followed by their wives and children, with ropes tied about their necks, went in procession to the convent of the Trinity, which three days before they had threatened to burn to the ground. In this condition, these unhappy wretches present themselves before the gate of the convent, two by two, one carrying a block and another an axe; and prostrating themselves on the ground, waited for their sentence. They were pardoned upon their submission, and returned back to Moscow, blessing their sovereigns; and still disposed, though unknown to themselves, to commit the same crime upon the very first opportunity.

These commotions being subsided, the state resumed an exterior of tranquillity; but Sophia still remained possessed of the chief authority, leaving John to his incapacity, and keeping Peter in the subjection of a ward. In order to strengthen her power, she shared it with Prince Basil Galitzin, whom she created generalissimo, minister of state, and lord keeper. Galitzin was in every respect superior to any person in that distracted court: he was polite, magnificent, full of great designs, more learned than any of his countrymen, as having received a much better education, and was even master of the Latin tongue, which was, at that time, almost entirely unknown in Russia. He was of an active and indefatigable spirit, had a genius superior to the times he lived in, and capable, had he had leisure and power, as he had inclination, to have changed the face of things in Russia. This is the eulogium given of him by La Neuville, at that time the Polish envoy in Russia; and the encomiums of foreigners are seldom to be suspected.

This minister bridled the insolence of the strelitzes, by distributing the most mutinous of that body among the several regiments in the Ukraine, in Casan, and Siberia. It was under his administration that the Poles, long the rivals of Russia, gave up, in 1686, all pretensions to the large provinces of Smolensko and the Ukraine. He was the first who sent an embassy to France, in 1687; a country which had, for upwards of twenty years, been in the zenith of its glory, by the conquests, new establishments, and the magnificence of Lewis XIV. and especially by the improvement of the arts, there can be not only external grandeur, but solid glory. France had not then entered into any correspondence with Russia, or rather was unacquainted with that empire; and the academy of inscriptions ordered a medal to be struck to commemorate this embassy, as if it had come from the most distant part of the Indies; but notwithstanding all this, the ambassador Dolgorouski miscarried in his negotiation, and even suffered some gross affronts on account of the behaviour of his domestics, whose mistakes it would have been better to have overlooked; but the court of Lewis XIV. could not then foresee, that France and Russia would one day reckon among the number of their advantages, that of being cemented by the closest union.

Russia was now quiet at home, but she was still pent up on the side of Sweden, though enlarged towards Poland, her new ally, in continual alarms on the side of Crim Tartary, and at variance with China in regard to the frontiers.

The most intolerable circumstance for their empire, and which plainly shewed, that it had not yet attained to a vigorous and regular administration, was, that the khan of the Crim Tartars exacted an annual tribute of 6000 rubles, in the nature of that which the Turk had imposed on the Poles.

Crim Tartary is the ancient Taurica Chersonesus, formerly so famous by the commerce of the Greeks, and still more by their fables, a fruitful but barbarous country. It took its name of Crimea, or Crim, from the title of its first khans, who took this name before the conquests of the sons of Gengis Khan. To free his country from this yoke, and wipe off the disgrace of such tribute, the prime minister, Galitzin, marched in person (1687, 1688,) into Crim Tartary, at the head of a numerous army. These armies were not to be compared to the present troops; they had no discipline; there was hardly one regiment completely armed; they had no uniform clothing, no regularity: their men indeed were inured to hard labour and a scarcity of provisions, but then they carried with them such a prodigious quantity of baggage, as far exceeded any thing of the kind in our camps, where the greatest luxury prevails. Their vast numbers of waggons for carrying ammunition and provisions, in an uninhabitable and desert country, greatly retarded the expedition against Crim Tartary. The army found itself in the midst of the vast deserts, on the river Samara, unprovided with magazines. Here Galitzin did what in my opinion, was never done any where else: he employed thirty thousand men in building a town on the banks of the Samara, to serve as a place for magazines in the ensuing campaign: it was begun in one year, and finished in the third month of the following; the houses indeed were all wood except two, which were brick; the ramparts were of turf, but well lined with artillery; and the whole place was in a tolerable state of defence.

This was all that was done of any consequence in this ruinous expedition. In the mean while Sophia continued to govern in Moscow, while John had only the name of czar; and Peter, now at the age of seventeen, had already the courage to aim at real sovereignty. La Neuville, the Polish envoy, then resident at Moscow, and who was eye-witness to all that passed, pretends that Sophia and Galitzin had engaged the new chief of the strelitzes, to sacrifice to them their young czar: it appears, at least, that six hundred of these strelitzes were to have made themselves masters of his person. The private memoirs which have been entrusted to my perusal by the court of Russia, affirm, that a scheme had actually been laid to murder Peter the First: the blow was on the point of being struck, and Russia for ever deprived of the new existence she has since received. The czar was once more obliged to take refuge in the convent of the Trinity, the usual asylum of the court when threatened by the soldiers. There he assembled the boyards of his party, raised a body of forces, treats with the captains of the strelitzes, and called in the assistance of certain Germans, who had been long settled in Moscow, and were all attached to his person from his having already shewn himself the encourager of strangers. Sophia and John, who continued at Moscow, used every means to engage the strelitzes to remain firm to their interests; but the cause of young Peter, who loudly complained of an attempt meditated against himself and his mother, prevailed over that of the princess, and of a czar, whose very aspect alienated all hearts. All the acomplices were punished with a severity to which that country was as much accustomed as to the crimes which occasioned it. Some were beheaded after undergoing the punishment of the knout or battocks. The chief of the strelitzes was put to death in the same manner, and several other suspected persons had their tongues cut out. Prince Galitzin escaped with his life, through the intercession of one of his relations, who was a favourite of czar Peter; but he was stripped of all his riches, which were immense, and banished to a place in the neighbourhood of Archangel. La Neuville, who was present at the whole of this catastrophe, relates, that the sentence pronounced upon Galitzin was in these terms: 'Thou art commanded, by the most clement czar, to repair to Karga, a town under the pole, and there to continue the remainder of thy days. His majesty, out of his extreme goodness, allows thee three pence per day for thy subsistence.'

There is no town under the pole. Karga is in the 62nd degree of latitude, and only six degrees and a half further north than Moscow. Whoever pronounced this sentence must have been a very bad geographer. La Neuville was probably imposed upon by a false account.

1689.] At length the princess Sophia was once more sent back to her monastery at Moscow,[28] after having so long held the reins of government; and this revolution proved, to a woman of her disposition, a sufficient punishment.

From this instant Peter began to reign in reality; his brother John having no other share in the government, but that of seeing his name to all public acts. He led a retired life, and died in 1696.

CHAP. VI.

The reign of Peter the First.—Beginning of the grand reformation.

Peter the Great was tall, genteel, well made, with a noble aspect, piercing eyes and a robust constitution, fitted for all kinds of hardship and bodily exercise. He had a sound understanding, which is the basis of all real abilities; and to this was joined an active disposition, which prompted him to undertake and execute the greatest things. His education was far from being worthy of his genius. The princess Sophia was, in a peculiar manner, interested to let him remain in ignorance, and to indulge himself in those excesses which youth, idleness, custom, and the high rank he held, made but too allowable. Nevertheless, he had been lately married, (June 1689) like others of his predecessors, to one of his own subjects, the daughter of colonel Lapuchin; but, as he was young, and for some time enjoyed none of the prerogatives of the crown, but that of indulging his pleasures without restraint, the ties of wedlock were not always sufficient to keep him within just bounds. The pleasures of the table, in which he indulged himself rather too freely, with foreigners, who had been invited to Moscow by prince Galitzin, seemed not to presage that he would one day become the reformer of his country; however, in spite of bad examples, and even the allurements of pleasure, he applied himself to the arts of war and government, and which, even then, shewed that he had the seeds of greatness in him.

It was still less expected, that a prince, who was subject to such a constitutional dread of water, as to subject him to cold sweats, and even convulsions, when he was obliged to cross a small river or brook, should become one of the best seamen in all the north. In order to get the better of nature, he began by jumping into the water, notwithstanding the horror he felt at it, till at length this aversion was changed into a fondness for that element.
[29]

He often blushed at the ignorance in which he had been brought up. He learned, almost of himself, without the help of a master, enough of German and high Dutch, to be able to write and explain himself tolerably well in both those languages. The Germans and Dutch appeared to him as the most civilized nations, because the former had already erected, in Moscow, some of those arts and manufactures which he was desirous of seeing established in his empire, and the latter excelled in the art of navigation, which he already began to look upon as the most necessary of all others.

Such were the dispositions which Peter cherished, notwithstanding the follies of his youth. At the same time, he found himself disturbed by factions at home, had the turbulent spirit of the strelitzes to keep under, and an almost uninterrupted war to manage against the Crim Tartars. For though hostilities had been suspended in 1689, by a truce, it had no long continuance.

During this interval, Peter became confirmed in his design of introducing the arts into his country.

His father Alexis had, in his lifetime, entertained the same views, but he wanted leisure, and a favourable opportunity to carry them into execution; he transmitted his genius to his son, who was more clear-sighted, more vigorous, and more unshaken by difficulties and obstacles.

Alexis had been at a great expense in sending for Bothler,[30] a ship builder and sea captain, from Holland, together with a number of shipwrights and sailors. These built a large frigate and a yacht upon the Wolga, which they navigated down that river to Astracan, where they were to be employed in building more vessels, for carrying on an advantageous trade with Persia, by the Caspian Sea. Just at this time the revolt of Stenko-Rasin broke out, and this rebel destroyed these two vessels, which he ought to have preserved for his own sake, and murdered the captain; the rest of the crew fled into Persia, from whence they got to some settlements belonging to the Dutch East India company. A master-builder, who was a good shipwright, staid behind in Russia, where he lived a long time in obscurity.

One day, Peter taking a walk at Ishmaelof, a summer-palace built by his grandfather, he perceived, among several other rarities, an old English shallop, which had lain entirely neglected: upon which he asked Timmerman, a German, and his mathematical teacher, how came that little boat to be of so different a construction from any he had seen on the Moska? Timmerman replied, that it was made to go with sails and oars. The young prince wanted instantly to make a trial of it; but it was first to be repaired and rigged. Brant, the ship-builder abovementioned, was by accident found out at Moscow, where he lived retired; he soon put the boat in order, and worked her upon the river Yauza, which washes the suburbs of the town.

Peter caused his boat to be removed to a great lake, in the neighbourhood of the convent of the Trinity; he likewise made Brant build two more frigates, and three yachts, and piloted them himself. A considerable time afterwards, viz. in 1694, he made a journey to Archangel, and having ordered a small vessel to be built in that port, by the same Brant, he embarked therein on the Frozen Sea, which no sovereign beside himself had ever beheld. On this occasion, he was escorted by a Dutch man of war, under the command of captain Jolson, and attended by all the merchant-vessels then in the port of

Archangel. He had already learned the manner of working a ship; and, notwithstanding the pains his courtiers took to imitate their master, he was the only one who made a proficiency in it.

He found it no less difficult to raise a well disciplined body of land forces, on whom he could depend, than to establish a navy. His first essay in navigation, on a lake, previous to his journey to Archangel, was looked upon only as the amusements of a young prince of genius; and his first attempt to form a body of disciplined troops, likewise appeared as nothing more than that of diversion. This happened during the regency of the princess Sophia; and, had he been suspected of meaning any thing serious by this amusement, it might have been attended with fatal consequences to him.

He placed his confidence in a foreigner, the celebrated Le Fort, of a noble and ancient family in Piedmont, transplanted near two centuries ago to Geneva, where they have filled the most considerable posts in the state. He was intended to have been brought up to the trade, to which the town is indebted for the figure it now makes; having formerly been known only as the seat of religious controversies.

But his genius, which prompted him to the greatest undertakings, engaged him to quit his father's house at the age of fourteen; and he served four months[31] in quality of a cadet in the citadel of Marseilles; from thence he went to Holland, where he served some time as a volunteer, and was wounded at the siege of Grave, a strong fortified town on the Meuse, which the prince of Orange, afterwards king of England, retook from Lewis XIV. in 1674. After this, led by hopes of preferment, wherever he could find it, he embarked with a German colonel, named Verstin, who had obtained a commission from Peter's father, the czar Alexis, to raise soldiers in the Netherlands, and bring them to Archangel. But, when he arrived at that port, after a most fatiguing and dangerous navigation, the czar Alexis was no more; the government was changed, and Russia in confusion. The governor of Archangel suffered Verstin, Le Fort, and his whole troop, to remain a long time, in the utmost poverty and distress, and even threatened to send them into the extremity of Siberia; upon which every man shifted for himself. Le Fort, in want of every thing, repaired to Moscow, where he waited upon the Danish resident, named De Horn, who made him his secretary: there he learned the Russian language, and some time afterwards found means to be introduced to the czar Peter; the elder brother, Iwan, not being a person for his purpose. Peter was taken with him, and immediately gave him a company of foot. Le Fort had seen very little service, he knew but little of letters, not having studied any particular art or science; but he had seen a great deal, and had a talent of making the most of what he saw. Like the czar, he owed every thing to his own genius; he understood the German and Dutch languages, which Peter was learning, as those of two nations that might be of service in his designs. Every thing conspired to make him agreeable to Peter, to whom he strictly attached himself. From being the companion of his pleasures, he became his favourite, and confirmed himself in that station by his abilities. The czar made him his confidant in the most dangerous design that a prince of that country could possibly form, namely, that of putting himself in a condition to be able one day to break the seditious and barbarous body of forces called the strelitzes. It had cost the great sultan or basha Osman his life, for attempting to disband the janissaries. Peter, young as he was, went to work in a much abler manner than Osman.

He began with forming, at his country-seat at Preobrazinski, a company of fifty of his youngest domestics; and some young gentlemen, the sons of boyards, were chosen for their officers: but, in order to teach these young noblemen a subordination, to which they were wholly unaccustomed, he made them pass through all the different military degrees, and himself set them the example, by serving first as a drum, then as a private soldier, a serjeant, and a lieutenant of the company. Nothing was ever more extraordinary, nor more useful, than this conduct. The Russians had hitherto made war in the same manner as our ancestors at the time of the feudal tenures, when the unexperienced nobles took the field at the head of their vassals, undisciplined, and ill armed: a barbarous method, sufficient indeed to act against the like armies, but of no use against regular troops.

This company, which was formed wholly by Peter himself, soon increased in numbers, and became afterwards the regiment of Preobrazinski guards. Another regiment, formed on the same plan, became in time the regiment of Semeniousky guards.

The czar had already a regiment of five thousand men that could be depended upon, trained by general Gordon, a Scotchman, and composed almost entirely of foreigners. Le Fort, who had borne arms but a short time, but whose capacity was equal to every thing, undertook to raise a regiment of twelve thousand men, which he effected: five colonels were appointed to serve under him, and he saw himself on a sudden general of this little army, which had been raised, as much to oppose the strelitzes, as the enemies of the state.

One thing worthy of being remarked,[32] and which fully confutes the hasty error of those who pretend that France lost very few of its inhabitants by the revocation of the edict of Nantz, is, that one-third of his army, which was only called a regiment, consisted of French refugees. Le Fort disciplined his new troops, as if he had been all his lifetime a soldier.

Peter was desirous of seeing one of those images of war, the mock fights, which had lately been introduced in times of peace: a fort was erected, which was to be attacked by one part of his new troops, and defended by the other. The difference between this fight, and others of the like nature, was, that instead of a sham engagement, there was a real one, in which some of his men were slain, and a great many wounded.[33] Le Fort, who commanded the attack, received a considerable wound. These bloody sports were intended to initiate the young troops into the service of the field; but it required much labour, and even some degree of sufferings to compass this end.

These warlike amusements did not take off the czar's attention to his naval project. As he had made Le Fort a general by land, notwithstanding his having never borne a command; he now made him admiral, though he had never had the direction of a ship, but he knew him deserving both of the one and the other. It is true, that he was an admiral without a fleet, and a general with only his regiment for an army.

By degrees the czar reformed that great abuse in the army, viz. the independence of the boyards, who, in time of war, used to bring into the field a multitude of their vassals and peasants: this was exactly the ancient government of the Franks, Huns, Goths, and Vandals, who indeed subdued the Roman empire in its state of decline, but would have been totally destroyed, had they had the warlike disciplined legions of ancient Rome to encounter, or such armies as are now brought into the field.

Admiral Le Fort was not long, however, before he had something more than an empty title. He employed some Dutchmen and Venetians in building a number of barcolongos, or kind of long barks, and also two ships of about thirty guns each, at the mouth of the Woronitz, which falls into the Tanais, or Don: these vessels were to fall down the river, and keep in awe the Crim Tartars, with whom hostilities had been renewed.

The czar was now to determine (in 1689) against which of the following powers he would declare war, whether against the Turks, the Swedes, or the Chinese. But here it will be proper to premise on what terms he then stood with China, and which was the first treaty of peace concluded by that nation.

CHAP. VII.

Congress and Treaty with the Chinese.[34]

We must set out by forming a proper idea of the limits of the Chinese and Russian empires at this period. When we leave Siberia, properly so called, and also far behind us to the south, a hundred hordes of Tartars, with white and black Calmucks, and Mahometan and Pagan Monguls, we come to the 130th degree of longitude, and the 52d of latitude upon the river Amur.[35] To the northward is a great chain of mountains, that stretches as far as the Frozen Sea, beyond the polar circle. This river, which runs upwards of five hundred leagues,[36] through Siberia and Chinese Tartary, falls, after many windings, into the sea of Kamtshatka. It is affirmed for a truth, that at its mouth, which opens with this sea, there is sometimes caught a monstrous fish, much larger than the hippopotamus of the Nile, and that the tooth thereof is the finest ivory. It is furthermore said, that this ivory was formerly an object of trade; that they used to convey it through Siberia, which is the reason why several pieces of it are still found under the ground in that country. This is the most probable account of the fossil ivory, of which we have elsewhere spoken; for it appears highly chimerical to pretend, that there were formerly elephants in Siberia.

This Amur is likewise called the Black River by the Mantechoux Tartars, and the Dragon's River by the Chinese.

It was in these countries, so long unknown, that the Russians and Chinese contested the limits of their empires.[37] The Russians had some forts on the river Amur, about three hundred leagues from the great wall. Many hostilities had arisen between these two nations on account of these forts: at length both began to understand their interests better; the emperor Camhi preferred peace and commerce to an unprofitable war, and sent several ambassadors to Niptchou, one of those settlements. The ambassadors had ten thousand men in their retinue, including their escort: this was Asiatic pomp; but what is very remarkable, is, that there was not an example in the annals of the empire, of an embassy being sent to another potentate; and what is still more singular, that the Chinese had never concluded a treaty of peace since the foundation of their monarchy. Though twice conquered by the Tartars, who attacked and subjected them, they never made war upon any people, excepting a few hordes that were quickly subdued, or as quickly left to themselves, without any treaty. So that this nation, so renowned for morality, knew nothing of what we call the 'Law of nations;' that is to say, of those vague rules of war and peace, of the privileges of foreign ministers, of the formalities of treaties, nor of the obligations resulting from thence, nor of the disputes concerning precedency and point of honour.

But in what language were the Chinese to negotiate with the Russians, in the midst of deserts? This difficulty was removed by two jesuits, the one a Portuguese, named Pereira, the other a Frenchman, whose name was Gerbillon; they set out from Pekin with the Chinese ambassadors, and were themselves the real negotiators. They conferred in Latin with a German belonging to the Russian embassy, who understood this language. The chief of that embassy was Golowin, governor of Siberia, who displayed a greater magnificence than the Chinese themselves, and thereby gave a high idea of the Russian empire, to a people who thought themselves the only powerful nation under the sun.

The two jesuits settled the limits of both empires at the river Kerbechi, near the spot where the treaty was concluded. All the country, to the southward of this line of partition, was adjudged to the Chinese, and the north to the Russians, who only lost a small fort which was found to have been built beyond the limits: a peace was agreed to, and after some few altercations, both parties swore to observe it, in the name of the same God;[38] and in these terms, 'If any of us shall entertain the least thought of kindling anew the flames of war, we beseech the supreme Lord of all things, and who knows all hearts, to punish the traitor with sudden death.'

From this form of treaty, used alike by Chinese and Christians, we may infer two important truths: the first, that the Chinese government is neither atheistical nor idolatrous, as has been so frequently and falsely charged upon it, by contradictory imputations. Secondly, that all nations, who cultivate the gift of reason and understanding, do, in effect, acknowledge the same God, notwithstanding the particular deviations of that reason, through the want of being properly instructed.

The treaty was drawn up in Latin, and two copies were made of it. The Russian ambassadors set their names the first to the copy that remained in their possession, and the Chinese also signed theirs the first, agreeable to the custom observed by European nations, when two equal powers conclude a treaty with each other. On this occasion was observed another custom belonging to the Asiatic nations, and which was indeed, that of the earliest ages. The treaty was engraven on two large marble pillars, erected on the spot, to determine the boundaries of the two empires.

Three years after this, the czar sent Isbrand Ides, a Dane, his ambassador to China; and the commerce he then established between the two nations, continued with advantage to each, till the rupture between them in the year 1722; but since this short interruption, it has been revived with redoubled vigour.

CHAP. VIII.

Expedition to the Palus Mæotis; conquest of Azoph.—The czar sends young gentlemen into foreign countries for improvement.

It was not so easy to have peace with the Turks, and indeed, the time seemed come for the Russians to rise upon their ruins. The republic of Venice, that had long groaned under their yoke, began now to rouse itself. The Doge Morosini, the same who had surrendered Candy to the Turks, afterwards took from them the Peloponnesus, which conquest got him the title of Peloponnesian, an honour which revived the memory of the Roman republic. Leopold, emperor of Germany, had proved successful against the Ottoman power in Hungary; and the Poles made shift to check the incursions of the Crim Tartars.

Peter took advantage of these circumstances, to discipline his troops, and to procure himself the empire of the Black Sea. General Gordon marched along the Tanais, towards Azoph, with his numerous regiment of five thousand men, followed by general Le Fort, with his regiment of twelve thousand; by a body of Strelitzes, under the command of Sheremeto and Schein, natives of Prussia; by a body of Cossacks, and by a large train of artillery: in a word, every thing was ready for this expedition.

1694.] This grand army began its march under the command of marshal Sheremeto, or Scheremetoff, in the beginning of the summer of 1695, to attack the town of Azoph, at the mouth of the Tanais, and at the extremity of the Palus Mæotis, now called the Zaback Sea. The czar himself was with the army, but only in quality of a volunteer, being determined to learn, some time before he took upon him to command. During their march, they stormed two forts which the Turks had built on the banks of the river.

This expedition was attended with some considerable difficulties. The place was well fortified, and defended by a numerous garrison. A number of barcolongos, resembling the Turkish saicks, and built by Venetians, with two small Dutch ships of war, that were to sail out of the Woronitz, could not be got ready soon enough to enter the sea of Azoph. All beginnings meet with obstacles. The Russians had never yet made a regular siege; and the first attempt did not meet with all the success that could be desired.

One Jacob, a native of Dantzic, had the direction of the artillery, under the command of general Schein; for as yet they had none but foreign officers belonging to the train, and none but foreign engineers and pilots. This Jacob had been condemned to the bastinade, or *knout*, by Schein, the Russian general. At that time rigorous discipline was thought to be the only method of strengthening command; and the Russians quietly submitted to it, notwithstanding their natural bent to sedition; and after the punishment, did their duty as usual. But the Dane thought in a different manner, and resolved to be revenged for the treatment he had received, and thereupon nailed up the cannon, deserted to the Turks, turned Mahometan, and defended Azoph, with great success, against his former masters. This instance shews, that the lenity which is now practised in Russia, is much preferable to the former severities; and is better calculated to retain those in their duty, who by a good education, have a proper sense of honour. It was absolutely necessary at that time, to use the utmost rigour towards the common people; but since their manners have been changed, the empress Elizabeth[39] has completed, by clemency, the work her father begun, by the authority of the laws. This lenity has even been carried, by this princess, to a degree unexampled, in the history of any nation. She has promised, that, during her reign, no person shall be punished with death, and she has kept her word. She is the first sovereign who ever shewed so much regard for the lives of men. By an institution, equally prudent and humane, malefactors are now condemned to serve in the mines, and other public works: by which means their very punishments prove of service to the state. In other countries, they know only how to put a criminal to death, with all the apparatus of execution, without being able to prevent the perpetration of crimes. The apprehension of death makes, perhaps, less impression on those miscreants, who are, for the most part, bred up in idleness, than the fear of punishment and hard labour, renewed every day.

To return to the siege of Azoph, which place was now defended by the same person who had before directed the attacks against it; the Russians, in vain, attempted to take it by storm; and after losing a great number of men, were obliged to raise the siege.

Perseverance in his undertakings, was the distinguishing character of Peter the Great. In the spring of 1696, he brought a still more considerable army before Azoph. About this time died czar John, his brother, who though he had not, while living, been the least curb to Peter's authority, having enjoyed only the bare title of czar, yet he had been some restraint upon him in regard to appearances. The money which had been appropriated to the support of John's dignity and household, were now applied to the maintenance of the army. This proved no small help to a government, whose revenues were not near so great as they are at present. Peter wrote to the emperor Leopold, to the states-general, and to the elector of Brandenburg, to obtain engineers, gunners, and seamen. He likewise took some Calmucks into his pay, whose light horse are very useful against the Crim Tartars.

The most agreeable of the czar's successes, was that of his little fleet, which was at length completed, and well commanded. It defeated the Turkish saicks, sent from Constantinople, and took some of them. The siege was carried on regularly by trenches, but not altogether in our method; the trenches being three times deeper than ours, with parapets as high as ramparts. At length the garrison surrendered, the 28th of July, 1696. N. S. without being allowed the honours of war, or to carry out with them either arms or ammunition: they were likewise obliged to deliver up the renegade, Jacob, to the conquerors.

The czar immediately set about fortifying Azoph, built strong forts to protect it, and made a harbour capable of holding large vessels, with a design to make himself master of the Streights of Caffa, or the Cimmerian Bosphorus, which commands the entrance into the Pontus Euxinus, or Black Sea; places famous in ancient times, by the naval armaments of Mithridates. He left thirty-two armed saicks before Azoph,[40] and made all the necessary preparations for fitting out a fleet against the Turks, to consist of nine ships of sixty guns, and of forty-one, from thirty to fifty. He obliged his principal nobles, and the richer merchants, to contribute towards this armament; and thinking that the estates of the clergy ought to help towards the common cause, he obliged the patriarch, the bishops, and principal clergy, to pay down a sum of ready money to forward this expedition, in honour of their country, and the advantage of the Christian faith. The Cossacks were employed in building a number of those light boats in use amongst them, and which were excellent for the purpose of cruising on the coast of Crim Tartary. The Ottoman empire was alarmed at this powerful armament; the first that had ever been attempted on the Palus Mæotis. The czar's scheme was to drive the Turks and the Tartars for ever out of the Taurica Chersonesus, and afterwards to establish a free and easy commerce with Persia through Georgia. This is the very trade which the Greeks formerly carried on to Colchos, and to this peninsula of Crim Tartary, which Peter now seemed on the point of conquering.

Having subdued the Turks and the Tartars, he was willing to accustom his people to splendid shows as well as to military labour. He made his army to enter into Moscow, under triumphal arches, in the midst of superb fire-works, and every thing that could add to the lustre of the festival. The soldiers who had fought on board the Venetian saicks against the Turks, and who were a distinct corps of themselves, marched first. Marshal Sheremeto, the generals Gordon and Schein, admiral Le Fort, and the other general officers, all took the precedence of their monarch in this procession, who declared he had no rank in the army, being desirous to convince the nobility, by his example, that the only way to acquire military preferment, was to deserve it.[41]

This triumphal entry seemed somewhat a-kin to those of the ancient Romans, in which the conquerors were wont to expose the prisoners they had taken, to public view, and sometimes put them to death: in like manner, the slaves, taken in this expedition, follow the army; and the deserter Jacob, who had betrayed them, was drawn in an open cart, in which was a gibbet, to which his body was fastened after he had been broke upon the wheel.

On this occasion was struck the first medal in Russia, with this remarkable legend, in the language of the country. 'Peter the First, august emperor of Muscovy.' On the reverse was the city of Azoph, with these words; 'Victorious by Fire and Water.'

Peter felt a sensible concern in the midst of all these successes, that his ships and gallies in the sea of Azoph, had been built entirely by the hands of foreigners; and wished as earnestly to have a harbour in the Baltic Sea, as upon the Pontus Euxinus.

Accordingly, in the month of March 1697, he sent threescore young Russians of Le Fort's regiment, into Italy, most of them to Venice, and the rest to Leghorn, to instruct themselves in the naval art, and the manner of constructing gallies. He likewise sent forty others into Holland,[42] to learn the method of building and working large ships: and others likewise into Germany, to serve in the land forces, and instruct themselves in the military discipline of that nation. At length he took a resolution to absent himself for a few years from his own dominions, in order to learn how to govern them the better. He had an irresistible inclination to improve himself by his own observation and practice in the knowledge of naval affairs, and of the several arts which he was so desirous to establish in his own country. He proposed to travel *incognito* through Denmark, Brandenburg, Holland, Vienna, Venice, and Rome. France and Spain were the only countries he did not take into his plan; Spain, because the arts he was in quest of, were too much neglected there; and France, because in that kingdom they reigned with too much ostentation, and that the parade and state of Lewis XIV. which had disgusted so many crowned heads, ill agreed with the private manner in which he proposed to travel. Moreover, he was in alliance with most of the powers, whose dominions he intended to visit, except those of France and Rome. He likewise remembered, with some degree of resentment, the little respect shewn by Lewis XIV. to his embassy in 1687, which had proved more famous than successful; and lastly he already began to espouse the cause of Augustus, elector of Saxony, with whom the prince of Conti had lately entered into a competition for the crown of Poland.

CHAP. IX.

Travels of Peter the Great.

1697.

Having thus determined to visit the several countries and courts above-mentioned in a private character, he put himself into the retinue of three ambassadors, in the same manner as he had before mingled in the train of his generals at his triumphant entry into Moscow.

[43] The three ambassadors were, general Le Fort, the boyard Alexis Gollowin, commissary-general of war, and governor of Siberia, the same who signed the perpetual treaty of peace with the plenipotentiaries of China, on the frontiers of that empire; and Wonitzin, diak, or secretary of state, who had been long employed in foreign courts. Four principal secretaries, twelve gentlemen, two pages for each ambassador, a company of fifty guards, with their officers, all of the regiment of Preobrazinski, composed the chief retinue of this embassy, which consisted in the whole of two hundred persons; and the czar, reserving to himself only one valet de chambre, a servant in livery, and a dwarf, mingled with the crowd. It was a thing unparalleled in history, for a king of five-and-twenty years of age, to quit his dominions, in order to learn the art of governing. His victory over the Turks and Tartars, the splendour of his triumphant entry into Moscow, the number of foreign troops attached to his service, the death of his brother John, his co-partner in the empire, and the confinement of the princess Sophia to a cloister, and above all the universal respect shewn to his person, seemed to assure him the tranquillity of his kingdom during his absence. He intrusted the regency in the hands of the boyard Strechnef, and the knez or prince Romadonowski, who were to deliberate with the rest of the boyards in cases ofimportance.

Two troops raised by general Gordon remained behind in Moscow, to keep every thing quiet in that capital. Those strelitzes, who were thought likely to create a disturbance, were distributed in the frontiers of Crim Tartary, to preserve the conquest of Azoph, and to check the incursions of the Tartars. Having provided against every incident, he gave a free scope to his passion and desire of improvement.

As this journey proved the cause, or at least the pretext, of the bloody war, which so long traversed, but in the end promoted, all the designs of the czar; which drove Augustus, king of Poland, from the throne; placed that crown on the head of Stanislaus, and then stript him of it; which made Charles XII. king of Sweden, the first of conquerors for nine years, and the most unfortunate of kings for nine more; it is necessary, in order to enter into a detail of these events, to take a view of the state of Europe at that time.

Sultan Mustapha II. sat at that time on the Ottoman throne; the weakness of whose administration would not permit him to make any great efforts, either against Leopold, emperor of Germany, whose arms were successful in Hungary, nor against the czar, who had lately taken Azoph from him, and threatened to make himself master of the Pontus Euxinus; nor even against the Venetians, who had made themselves masters of all the Peloponnesus.

John Sobieski, king of Poland, for ever famous by the victory of Chocksim, and the deliverance of Vienna, died the 17th of June, 1696, and the possession of that crown was in dispute between Augustus, elector of Saxony, who obtained it, and Armond, prince of Conti, who had only the honour of being elected.

1697.] Sweden had lately lost, but without regret, Charles XI. her sovereign, who was the first king who had ever been really absolute in that country, and who was the father of a prince still more so, and with whom all despotic power ceased. He left the crown to his son Charles XII. a youth of only fifteen years of age. This was in all appearance a conjuncture the most favourable for the czar's design; he had it in his power to extend his dominions on the Gulf of Finland, and on the side of Livonia. But he did not think it enough to harass the Turks on the Black Sea; the settlements on the Palus Mæotis, and the borders of the Caspian Sea, were not sufficient to answer his schemes of navigation, commerce, and power. Besides, glory, which is the darling object of every reformer, was to be found neither in Persia, nor in Turkey, but in our parts of Europe, where great talents are rendered immortal. In a word, Peter did not aim at introducing either the Persian or Turkish manners among his subjects.

Germany, then at war both with the Turks and with the French, and united with Spain, England, and Holland, against the single power of Lewis XIV. was on the point of concluding peace, and the plenipotentiaries were already met at the castle of Ryswick, in the neighbourhood of the Hague.

It was during this situation of affairs, that Peter and his ambassador began their journey in the month of April, 1697, by the way of Great Novogorod: from thence they travelled through Esthonia and Livonia, provinces formerly disputed by the Russians, Swedes, and Poles, and which the Swedes at last acquired by superiority of arms.

The fertility of Livonia, and the situation of its capital, Riga, were temptations to the czar, to possess himself of that country. He expressed a curiosity to see the fortifications of the citadel. But count D'Alberg, governor of Riga, taking umbrage at this request, refused him the satisfaction he desired, and affected to treat the embassy with contempt. This behaviour did not at all contribute to cool the inclination the czar might have, to make himself one day master of those provinces.

From Livonia they proceeded to Brandenburg-Prussia, part of which had been inhabited by the ancient Vandals; Polish Prussia had been included in European Sarmatia. Brandenburg-Prussia was a poor country and badly peopled; but its elector, who afterwards took the name of king, displayed a magnificence on this occasion, equally new and destructive to his dominions. He piqued himself upon receiving this embassy in his city of Konigsberg, with all the pomp of royalty. The most sumptuous presents were made on both sides. The contrast between the French dress which the court of Berlin affected, and the long Asiatic robes of the Russians, with their caps buttoned up with pearls and diamonds, and their scimitars hanging at their belts, produced a singular effect. The czar was dressed after the German fashion. The prince of Georgia, who accompanied him, was clad in a Persian habit, which displayed a different magnificence. This is the same who was taken prisoner afterwards at the battle of Narva, and died in Sweden.

Peter despised all this ostentation; it was to have been wished that he had shewn an equal contempt for the pleasures of the table, in which the Germans, at that time, placed their chiefest glory. It was at one of those entertainments, [44] then too much in fashion, and which are alike fatal to health and morality, that he drew his sword upon his favourite, Le Fort; but he expressed as much contrition for this sudden sally of passion, as Alexander did for the murder of Clytus; he asked pardon of Le Fort, saying, that he wanted to reform his subjects, and could not yet reform himself. General Le Fort, in his manuscript praises the czar more for this goodness of heart, than he blames him for his excess of passion.

The ambassadors then went through Pomerania and Berlin; and, from thence, one part took its way through Magdeburg, and the other by Hamburg, a city which already began to be considerable by its extensive commerce, but not so rich and populous as it has become since. From thence they directed their route towards Minden, crossed Westphalia, and at length, by the way of Cleves, arrived at Amsterdam.

The czar reached this city fifteen days before the ambassadors. At his first coming, he lodged in a house belonging to the East India company; but soon afterwards he took a small apartment in the dock-yard, belonging to the admiralty. He then put on the habit of a Dutch skipper, and in that dress went to the village of Saardam, a place where a great many more ships were built at that times, than at present. This village is as large, as populous, and as rich, and much neater, than many opulent towns. The czar greatly admired the multitude of people who were constantly employed there, the order and regularity of their times of working, the prodigious dispatch with which they built and fitted out ships, the incredible number of warehouses, and machines, for the greater ease and security of labour. The czar began with purchasing a bark, to which he made a mast with his own hands; after that, he worked upon all the different parts in the construction of a vessel, living in the same manner as the workmen at Saardam, dressing and eating the same as them, and working in the forges, the rope-walks, and in the several mills, which are in prodigious numbers in that village, for sawing timber, extracting oil, making paper, and wire-drawing. He caused himself to be enrolled in the list of carpenters, by the name of Peter Michaelhoff, and was commonly called Peter Bas, or Master Peter: the workmen were at first confounded at having a crowned head for a fellow-labourer, but soon became familiarized to the sight.

While he was thus handling the compass and the axe at Saardam, a confirmation was brought him of the division in Poland, and of the double nomination of the elector Augustus, and the prince of Conti. The carpenter of Saardam immediately promised king Augustus to assist him with thirty thousand men; and, from his work-loft, issued out orders to his army that was assembled in the Ukraine against the Turks.

11th Aug. 1697.] His troops gained a victory over the Tartars near Azoph, and a few months afterwards took from them the city of Or, or Orkapi, which we call Precop.[45] As to himself, he still continued improving in different arts: he went frequently from Saardam to Amsterdam, to hear the lectures of the celebrated anatomist, Ruysch; and made himself master of several operations in surgery, which, in case of necessity, might be of use both to himself and his officers. He went through a course of natural philosophy, in the house of the burgomaster Witzen, a person for ever estimable for his patriotic virtue, and the noble use he made of his immense riches, which he distributed like a citizen of the world, sending men of abilities, at a great expense, to all parts of the globe, in search of whatever was most rare and valuable, and fitting out vessels at his own charge to make new discoveries.

Peter Bas gave a truce to his labours for a short time, but it was only to pay a private visit at Utrecht, and at the Hague, to William, king of England, and stadtholder of the United Provinces. General Le Fort was the only one admitted to the private conference of the two monarchs. Peter assisted afterwards at the public entry of his ambassadors, and at their audience: they presented, in his name, to the deputy of the states, six hundred of the most beautiful sables that could be procured; and the states, over and above the customary presents on these occasions, of a gold chain and a medal, gave them three magnificent coaches. They received the first visits of all the plenipotentiaries who were at the congress of Ryswick, excepting those of France, to whom they had not notified their arrival, not only because the czar espoused the cause of Augustus against the prince of Conti, but also because king William, whose friendship he was desirous of cultivating, was averse to a peace with France.

At his return to Amsterdam he resumed his former occupations, and completed with his own hands, a ship of sixty guns, that he had begun himself, and sent her to Archangel; which was the only port he had at that time on the ocean.

He not only engaged in his service several French refugees, Swiss, and Germans; but he also sent all sorts of artists over to Moscow, and he previously made a trial of their several abilities himself. There were few trades or arts which he did not perfectly well understand, in their minutest branches: he took a particular pleasure in correcting with his own hands, the geographical maps, which at that time laid down at hazard the positions of the towns and rivers in his vast dominions, then very little known. There is still preserved, a map, on which he marked out, with his own hand, his projected communication of the Caspian and Black Seas, the execution of which he had given in charge to Mr. Brekel, a German engineer. The junction of these two seas was indeed a less difficult enterprise than that of the Ocean and Mediterranean, which was effected in France; but the very idea of joining the sea of Azoph with the Caspian, astonished the imagination at that time: but new establishments in that country became the object of his attention, in proportion as his successes begat new hopes.

His troops, commanded by general Schein and prince Dolgorowski, had lately gained a victory over the Tartars near Azoph, and likewise over a body of janissaries sent by sultan Mustapha to their assistance. (July 1696.) This success served to make him more respected, even by those who blamed him, as a sovereign, for having quitted his dominions, to turn workman at Amsterdam. They now saw, that the affairs of the monarch did not suffer by the labours of the philosopher, the traveller, and the artificer.

He remained at Amsterdam, constantly employed in his usual occupations of shipbuilding, engineering, geography, and the practice of natural philosophy, till the middle of January 1698, and then he set out for England, but still as one of the retinue of his ambassadors.

King William sent his own yacht to meet him, and two ships of war as convoy. In England he observed the same manner of living as at Amsterdam and Saardam; he took an apartment near the king's dockyard, at Deptford, where he applied himself wholly to gain instruction. The Dutch builders had only taught him their method, and the practical part of shipbuilding. In England he found the art better explained; for there they work according to mathematical proportion. He soon made himself so perfect in this science, that he was able to give lessons to others. He began to build a ship according to the English method of construction, and it proved a prime sailor. The art of watchmaking, which was already brought to perfection in London, next attracted his attention, and he made himself complete master of the whole theory. Captain Perry, the engineer, who followed him from London to Russia, says, that from the casting of cannon, to the spinning of ropes, there was not any one branch of trade belonging to a ship that he did not minutely observe, and even put his hand to, as often as he came into the places where those trades were carried on.

In order to cultivate his friendship, he was allowed to engage several English artificers into his service, as he had done in Holland; but, over and above artificers, he engaged likewise some mathematicians, which he would not so easily have found in Amsterdam. Ferguson, a Scotchman, an excellent geometrician, entered into his service, and was the first person who brought arithmetic into use in the exchequer in Russia, where before that time, they made use only of the Tartarian method of reckoning, with balls strung upon a wire; a method which supplied the place of writing, but was very perplexing and imperfect, because, after the calculation, there was no method of proving it, in order to discover any error. The Indian ciphers, which are now in use, were not introduced among us till the ninth century, by Arabs; and they did not make their way into the Russian empire till one thousand years afterwards. Such has been the fate of the arts, to make their progress slowly round the globe. He took with him two young students from a mathematical school,[46] and this was the beginning of the marine academy, founded afterwards by Peter the Great. He observed and calculated eclipses with Ferguson. Perry, the engineer, though greatly discontented at not being sufficiently rewarded, acknowledges, that Peter made himself a proficient in astronomy; that he perfectly well understood the motions of the heavenly bodies, as well as the laws of gravitation, by which they are directed. This force, now so evidently demonstrated, and before the time of the great Newton so little known, by which all the planets gravitate towards each other, and which retain them in their orbits, was already become familiar to a sovereign of Russia, while other countries amused themselves withimaginary vertices, and, in Galileo's nation, one set of ignorant persons ordered others, as ignorant, to believe the earth to be immoveable.

Perry set out in order to effect a communication between rivers, to build bridges, and construct sluices. The czar's plan was to open a communication by means of canals between the Ocean, the Caspian, and the Black Seas.

We must not forget to observe, that a set of English merchants, with the marquis of Caermarthen[47] at their head, gave Peter fifteen thousand pounds sterling, for the permission of vending tobacco in Russia. The patriarch, by a mistaken severity, had interdicted this branch of trade; for the Russian church forbid smoking, as an unclean and sinful action. Peter, who knew better things, and who, amongst his many projected changes, meditated a reformation of the church, introduced this commodity of trade into his dominions.

Before Peter left England, he was entertained by king William with a spectacle worthy such a guest: this was a mock sea-fight. Little was it then imagined, that the czar would one day fight a real battle on this element against the Swedes, and gain naval victories in the Baltic. In fine, William made him a present of the vessel in which he used to go over to Holland, called the Royal Transport, a beautiful yacht, and magnificently adorned. In this vessel Peter returned to Holland the latter end of 1698, taking with him three captains of ships of war, five and twenty captains of merchant ships, forty lieutenants, thirty pilots, as many surgeons, two hundred and fifty gunners, and upwards of three hundred artificers. This little colony of persons skilful in all branches, sailed from Holland to Archangel, on board the Royal Transport, and from thence were distributed into all the different places where their services were necessary. Those who had been engaged at Amsterdam went by the way of Narva, which then belonged to the Swedes.

While he was thus transplanting the arts and manufacture of England and Holland into his own country, the officers, whom he had sent to Rome, and other places in Italy, had likewise engaged some artists in his service. General Sheremeto, who was at the head of his embassy to Italy, took the tour of Rome, Naples, Venice, and Malta, while the czar proceeded to Vienna with his other ambassadors. He had now only to view the military discipline of the Germans, after having seen the English fleets, and the dock-yards of Holland. Politics had likewise as great a share in this journey as the desire of instruction. The emperor was his natural ally against the Turks. Peter had a private audience of Leopold, and the two monarchs conferred standing, to avoid the trouble of ceremony.

There happened nothing worthy remark during his stay at Vienna, except the celebration of the ancient feast of the landlord and landlady, which had been disused for a considerable time, and which Leopold thought proper to revive on the czar's account. This feast, which by the Germans is called Wurtchafft, is celebrated in the following manner:—

The emperor is landlord and the empress landlady, the king of the Romans, the archdukes and the archduchesses are generally their assistants: they entertain people of all nations as their guests, who come dressed after the most ancient fashion of their respective countries: those who are invited to the feast, draw lots for tickets, on each of which is written the name of the nation, and the character or person they are to represent. One perhaps draws a ticket for a Chinese mandarin; another for a Tartarian mirza; a third a Persian satrap; and a fourth for a Roman senator; a princess may, by her ticket, be a gardener's wife, or a milk-maid; a prince a peasant, or a common soldier. Dances are composed suitable to all those characters, and the landlord and landlady with their family wait at table. Such was the ancient institution; but on this occasion[48] Joseph, king of the Romans, and the countess of Traun, represented the ancient Egyptians. The archduke Charles, and the countess of Walstein, were dressed like Flemings in the time of Charles the Fifth. The archduchess Mary Elizabeth and count Traun were in the habits of Tartars; the archduchess Josephina and the count of Workslaw were habited like Persians, and the archduchess Mariamne and prince Maximilian of Hanover in the character of North Holland peasants. Peter appeared in the dress of a Friesland boor, and all who spoke to him addressed him in that character, at the same time talking to him of the great czar of Muscovy. These are trifling particulars; but whatever revives the remembrance of ancient manners and customs, is in some degree worthy of being recorded.

Peter was ready to set out from Vienna, in order to proceed to Venice, to complete his tour of instruction, when he received the news of a rebellion, which had lately broke out in his dominions.

CHAP. X.

A conspiracy punished.—The corps of strelitzes abolished, alterations in customs, manners, church, and state.

Czar Peter, when he left his dominions to set out on his travels, had provided against every incident, even that of rebellion. But the great and serviceable things he had done for his country, proved the very cause of this rebellion.

Certain old boyards, to whom the ancient customs were still dear, and some priests, to whom the new ones appeared little better than sacrilege, began these disturbances, and the old faction of the princess Sophia took this opportunity to rouse itself anew. It is said, that one of her sisters, who was confined to the same monastery, contributed not a little to excite these seditions. Care was taken to spread abroad the danger to be feared from the introduction of foreigners to instruct the nation. In short, who would believe, that[49] the permission which the czar had given to import tobacco into his empire, contrary to the inclination of the clergy, was one of the chief motives of the insurrection? Superstition, the scourge of every country, yet the darling of the multitude, spread itself from the common people to the strelitzes, who had been scattered on the frontiers of Lithuania: they assembled in a body, and marched towards Moscow, with the intent to place the princess Sophia on the throne, and for ever to prevent the return of a czar who had violated the established customs,[50] by presuming to travel for instruction among foreigners. The forces commanded by Schein and Gordon, who were much better disciplined than the strelitzes, met them fifteen leagues from Moscow, gave them battle, and entirely defeated them: but this advantage, gained by a foreign general over the ancient militia, among whom were several of the burghers of Moscow, contributed still more to irritate the people.

To quell these tumults, the czar sets out privately from Vienna, passes through Poland, has a private interview with Augustus, concerts measures with that prince for extending the Russian dominions on the side of the Baltic, and at length arrived at Moscow, where he surprised every one with his presence: he then confers rewards on the troops who had defeated the strelitzes, (Sept. 1698,) of whom the prisons were now full. If the crimes of these unhappy wretches were great, their punishment was no less so. Their leaders, with several of their officers and priests, were condemned to death; some were broken upon the wheel,[51] and two women were buried alive; upwards of two thousand of the strelitzes were executed, part of whom were hung round about the walls of the city, and others put to death in different manners, and their dead bodies remained exposed for two days in the high roads,[52] particularly about the monastery where the princesses Sophia and Eudocia resided.[53] Monuments of stone were erected, on which their crimes and punishments were set forth. A great number of them who had wives and children at Moscow, were dispersed with their families into Siberia, the kingdom of Astracan, and the country of Azoph. This punishment was at least of service to the state, as they helped to cultivate and people a large tract of waste land.

Perhaps, if the czar had not found it absolutely necessary to make such terrible examples, he might have employed part of those strelitzes whom he put to death, upon the public works; whereas they were now lost both to him and the state: the lives of men ought to be held in great estimation, especially in a country where the increase of inhabitants ought to have been the principal care of the legislature: but he thought it necessary to terrify and break the spirit of the nation by executions, and the parade attending them. The entire corps of the strelitzes, whose number not one of his predecessors had even dared to think of diminishing, was broke for ever, and their very name abolished. This change was effected without any resistance, because matters had been properly prepared beforehand. The Turkish sultan, Osman, as I have already remarked, was deposed and murdered in the same century, only for giving the janissaries room to suspect that he intended to lessen their number. Peter had better success, because he had taken better measures.

Of this powerful and numerous body of the strelitzes, he left only two feeble regiments, from whom there could no longer be any danger; and yet these still retaining their old spirit of mutiny, revolted again in Astracan, in the year 1705, but were quickly suppressed.

But while we are relating Peter's severity in this affair of state, let us not forget to commemorate the more than equal humanity he shewed some time afterwards, when he lost his favourite Le Fort, who was snatched away by an untimely fate, March 12, N. S. 1699, at the age of 46. He paid him the same funeral honours as are bestowed on the greatest sovereigns, and assisted himself in the procession, carrying a pike in his hand, and marching after the captains, in the rank of a lieutenant, which he held in the deceased general's regiment, hereby setting an example to his nobles, of the respect due to merit and the military rank.

After the death of Le Fort, it appeared plainly, that the changes in the state were not owing to that general, but to the czar himself. Peter had indeed been confirmed in his design by his several conversations with Le Fort; but he had formed and executed them all without his assistance.

As soon as he had suppressed the strelitzes, he established regular regiments on the German model, who were all clothed in a short and commodious uniform, in the room of those long and troublesome coats, which they used to wear before; and, at the same time, their exercise was likewise more regular.

The regiment of Preobrazinski guards was already formed; it had taken its name from the first company of fifty men, whom the czar had trained up in his younger days, in his retreat at Preobrazinski, at the time when his sister Sophia governed the state, and the other regiment of guards was also established.

As he had himself passed through the lowest degrees in the army, he was resolved that the sons of his boyards and great men, should serve as common soldiers before they were made officers. He sent some of the young nobility on board of his fleet at Woronitz and Azoph, where he obliged them to serve their apprenticeship as common seamen. No one dared to dispute the commands of a master who had himself set the example. The English and Dutch he had brought over with him were employed in equipping this fleet for sea, in constructing sluices, and building docks, for careening the ships, and to resume the great work of joining the Tanais, or Don, and the Wolga, which had been dropped by Brekel, the German. And now he began to set about his projected reformations in the council of state, in the revenue, in the church, and even in society itself.

The affairs of the revenue had been hitherto administered much in the same manner as in Turkey. Each boyard paid a stipulated sum for his lands, which he raised upon the peasants, his vassals; the czar appointed certain burghers and burgomasters to be his receivers, who were not powerful enough to claim the right of paying only such sums as they thought proper into the public treasury. This new administration of the finances, was what cost him the most trouble: he was obliged to try several methods before he could fix upon a proper one.

The reformation of the church, which in all other countries is looked upon as so dangerous and difficult an attempt, was not so to him. The patriarchs had at times opposed the authority of the crown, as well as the strelitzes; Nicon with insolence, Joachin, one of his successors, in an artful manner.

The bishops had arrogated the power of life and death, a prerogative directly contrary to the spirit of religion, and the subordination of government. This assumed power, which had been of long standing, was now taken from them. The patriarch Adrian, dying at the close of this century, Peter declared that there should for the future be no other.

This dignity then was entirely suppressed, and the great income belonging thereto was united to the public revenue, which stood in need of this addition.

Although the czar did not set himself up as the head of the Russian church, as the kings of Great Britain have done in regard to the church of England; yet he was, in fact, absolute master over it, because the synods did not dare either to disobey the commands of a despotic sovereign, or to dispute with a prince who had more knowledge than themselves.

We need only to cast an eye on the preamble to the edict, concerning his ecclesiastical regulations, issued in 1721, to be convinced that he acted at once as master and legislator: 'We should deem ourselves guilty of ingratitude to the Most High, if, after having reformed the military and civil orders, we neglect the spiritual, &c. For this cause, following the example of the most ancient kings, who have been famed for piety, we have taken upon us to make certain wholesome regulations, touching the clergy.' It is true, he convened a synod for carrying into execution his ecclesiastical decrees, but the members of this synod, at entering upon their office, were to take an oath, the form of which had been drawn up and signed by himself. This was an oath of submission and obedience, and was conceived in the following terms: 'I swear to be a faithful and obedient servant and subject to my true and natural sovereign, and to the august successors whom it shall please him to nominate, in virtue of the incontestable right of which he is possessed: I acknowledge him to be the supreme judge of this spiritual college: I swear by the all-seeing God, that I understand and mean this oath in the full force and sense, which the words convey to those who read or hear it.' This oath is much stronger than that of the supremacy in England. The Russian monarch was not, indeed, one of the fathers of the synod, but he dictated their laws; and, though he did not touch the holy censer, he directed the hands that held it.

Previous to this great work, he thought, that in a state like his, which stood in need of being peopled, the celibacy of the monks was contrary to nature, and to the public good. It was the ancient custom of the Russian church, for secular priests to marry at least once in their lives: they were even obliged so to do: and formerly they ceased to be priests as soon as they lost their wives. But that a multitude of young people of both sexes should make a vow of living useless in a cloister, and at the expense of others, appeared to him a dangerous institution. He, therefore, ordered that no one should be admitted to a monastic life, till they were fifty years old, a time of life very rarely subject to a temptation of this kind; and he forbid any person to be admitted, at any age soever, who was actually in possession of any public employ.

This regulation has been repealed since his death, because the government has thought proper to shew more complaisance to the monasteries: but the patriarchal dignity has never been revived, and its great revenues are now appropriated to the payment of the troops.

These alterations at first excited some murmurings. A certain priest wrote, to prove that Peter was antichrist, because he would not admit of a patriarch; and the art of printing, which the czar encouraged in his kingdom, was made use of to publish libels against him: but, on the other hand, there was another priest who started up to prove that Peter could not be antichrist, because the number 666 was not to be found in his name, and that he had not the sign of the Beast. All complaints, however, were soon quieted. Peter, in fact, gave much more to the church than he took from it; for he made the clergy, by degrees, more regular and more learned. He founded three colleges at Moscow, where they teach the languages, and where those who are designed for the priesthood are obliged to study.

One of the most necessary reforms was the suppression, or at least the mitigation of the Three Lents, an ancient superstition of the Greek church, and as prejudicial with respect to those who are employed in public works, and especially to soldiers, as was the old Jewish superstition of not fighting on the sabbath-day. Accordingly the czar dispensed with his workmen and soldiers at least, observing these lents, in which, though they were not permitted to eat, they were accustomed to get drunk. He likewise dispensed with their observance of meagre days; the chaplains of the fleet and army were obliged to set the example, which they did without much reluctance.

The calendar, another important object. Formerly, in all the countries of the world, the chiefs of religion had the care of regulating the year, not only on account of the feasts to be observed, but because, in ancient times, the priests were the only persons who understood astronomy.

The year began with the Russians on the 1st of September. Peter ordered, that it should for the future commence the first day of January, as among the other nations of Europe. This alteration was to take place in the year 1700, at the beginning of the century, which he celebrated by a jubilee, and other grand solemnities. It was a matter of surprise, to the common people, how the czar should be able to change the course of the sun. Some obstinate persons, persuaded that God had created the world in September, continued their old style: but the alteration took place in all the public offices, in the whole court of chancery, and in a little time throughout the whole empire. Peter did not adopt the Gregorian calendar, because it had been rejected by the English mathematicians; but which must, nevertheless, be one day received in all countries.

Ever since the 5th century, the time when letters first came into use amongst them, they had been accustomed to write upon long rolls, made either of the bark of trees, or of parchment, and afterwards of paper; and the czar was obliged to publish an edict, ordering every one, for the future, to write after our manner.

The reformation now became general. Their marriages were made formerly after the same manner as in Turkey and Persia, where the bridegroom does not see his bride till the contract is signed, and they can no longer go from their words. This custom may do well enough among those people, where polygamy prevails, and where the women are always shut up; but it is a very bad one in countries where a man is confined to one wife, and where divorces are seldom allowed.

The czar was willing to accustom his people to the manners and customs of the nations which he had visited in his travels, and from whence he had taken the masters who were now instructing them.

It appeared necessary that the Russians should not be dressed in a different manner from those who were teaching them the arts and sciences; because the aversion to strangers, which is but too natural to mankind, is not a little kept up by a difference of dress. The full dress, which at that time partook of the fashions of the Poles, the Tartars, and the ancient Hungarians, was, as we have elsewhere observed, very noble; but the dress of the burghers and common people resembled those jackets plaited round the waist, which are still given to the poor children in some of the French hospitals.[54] In general, the robe was formerly the dress of all nations, as being a garment that required the least trouble and art; and, for the same reason, the beard was suffered to grow. The czar met with but little difficulty in introducing our mode of dress, and the custom of shaving among his courtiers; but the people were more obstinate, he found himself obliged to lay a tax on long coats and beards. Patterns of close-bodied coats were hung up in public places; and whoever refused to pay the tax were obliged to suffer their robes and their beards to be curtailed: all this was done in a jocular manner, and this air of pleasantry prevented seditions.

It has ever been the aim of all legislators to render mankind more sociable; but it is not sufficient to effect this end, that they live together in towns, there must be a mutual intercourse of civility. This intercourse sweetens all the bitterness of life. The czar, therefore, introduced those assemblies which the Italians call *ridotti*. To these assemblies he invited all the ladies of his court, with their daughters; and they were to appear dressed after the fashions of the southern nations of Europe. He was even himself at the pains of drawing up rules for all the little decorums to be observed at these social entertainments. Thus, even to good breeding among his subjects, all was his own work, and that of time.

To make his people relish these innovations the better, he abolished the word *golut*, *slave*, always made use of by the Russians when they addressed their czar, or presented any petition to him; and ordered, that, for the future, they should make use of the word *raab*, which signifies *subject*. This alteration in no wise diminished the obedience due to the sovereign, and yet was the most ready means of conciliating their affections. Every month produced some new change or institution. He carried his attention even to the ordering painted posts to be set up in the road between Moscow and Woronitz, to serve as mile stones at the distance of every verst; that is to say, every seven hundredpaces, and had a kind of caravanseras, or public inns, built at the end of every twentieth verst.

While he was thus extending his cares to the common people, to the merchants, and to the traveller, he thought proper to make an addition to the pomp and splendour of his own court; for though he hated pomp or show in his own person, he thought it necessary in those about him; he therefore instituted the order of St. Andrew,[55] in imitation of the several orders with which all the courts of Europe abound. Golowin, who succeeded Le Fort in the dignity of high admiral, was the first knight of this order. It was esteemed a high reward to have the honour of being admitted a member. It was a kind of badge that entitled the person who bore it to the respect of the people. This mark of honour costs nothing to the sovereign, and flatters the self-love of a subject, without rendering him too powerful.

These many useful innovations were received with applause by the wiser part of the nation; and the murmurings and complaints of those who adhered to the ancient customs were drowned in the acclamations of men of sound judgment.

While Peter was thus beginning a new creation in the interior part of his state, he concluded an advantageous truce with the Turks, which gave him the liberty to extend his territories on another side. Mustapha the Second, who had been defeated by prince Eugene, at the battle of Zeuta, in 1697, stripped of the Morea by the Venetians, and unable to defend Azoph, was obliged to make peace with his victorious enemies, which peace was concluded at Carlowitz, (Jan. 26, 1699,) between Peterwaradin and Salankamon, places made famous by his defeats. Temeswaer was made the boundary of the German possessions, and of the Ottoman dominions. Kaminieck was restored to the Poles; the Morea, and some towns in Dalmatia, which had been taken by the Venetians, remained in their hands for some time; and Peter the First continued in possession of Casaph, and of a few forts built in its neighbourhood.

It was not possible for the czar to extend his dominions on the side of Turkey, without drawing upon him the forces of that empire, before divided, but now united. His naval projects were too vast for the Palus Mæotis, and the settlements on the Caspian Sea would not admit of a fleet of men of war: he therefore turned his views towards the Baltic Sea, but without relinquishing those in regard to the Tanais and Wolga.

CHAP. XI.

War with Sweden.—The battle of Narva.

1700.

A grand scene was now opened on the frontiers of Sweden. One of the principal causes of all the revolutions which happened from Ingria, as far as Dresden, and which laid waste so many countries for the space of eighteen years, was the abuse of the supreme power, by Charles XI. king of Sweden, father of Charles XII. This is a fact which cannot be too often repeated, as it concerns every crowned head, and the subjects of every nation. Almost all Livonia, with the whole of Esthonia, had been ceded by the Poles to Charles XI. king of Sweden, who succeeded Charles X. exactly at the time of the treaty of Oliva. It was ceded in the customary manner, with a reservation of rights and privileges. Charles XI. shewing little regard to these privileges, John Reinhold Patkul, a gentleman of Livonia, came to Stockholm in 1692, at the head of six deputies from the province, and laid their complaints at the foot of the throne, in respectful, but strong terms.[56] Instead of an answer, the deputies were ordered to be imprisoned, and Patkul was condemned to lose his honour and his life. But he lost neither, for he made his escape to the country of Vaud, in Switzerland, where he remained some time; when he afterwards was informed, that Augustus, elector of Saxony, had promised, at his accession to the throne of Poland, to recover the provinces that had been wrested from that kingdom; he hastened to Dresden, to represent to that prince, how easily he might make himself master of Livonia, and revenge upon a king, only seventeen years of age, the losses that Poland had sustained by his ancestors.

At this very time czar Peter entertained thoughts of seizing upon Ingria and Carelia. These provinces had formerly belonged to the Russians, but the Swedes had made themselves masters of them by force of arms, in the time of the false Demetriuses, and had retained the possession of them by treaties: another war and new treaties might restore them again to Russia. Patkul went from Dresden to Moscow, and, by exciting up the two monarchs to avenge his private causes, he cemented a close union between them, and directed their preparations for invading all the places situated to the east and south of Finland.

Just at this period, the new king of Denmark, Frederick IV. entered into an alliance with the czar and the king of Poland, against Charles, the young king of Sweden, who seemed in no condition to withstand their united forces.

Patkul had the satisfaction of besieging the Swedes in Riga, the capital of Livonia, and directing the attack in quality of major-general.

The czar marched near eighty thousand men into Ingria. It is true, that, in this numerous army, he had not more than twelve thousand good soldiers, being those he had disciplined himself; namely, the two regiments of guards, and some few others, the rest being a badly armed militia, with some Cossacks, and Circassian Tartars; but he carried with him a train of a hundred and forty-five pieces of cannon. He laid siege to Narva, a small town in Ingria, that had a very commodious harbour, and it was generally thought the place would prove an easy conquest.

Sept.] It is known to all Europe, how Charles XII. when not quite eighteen years of age, made head against all his enemies, and attacked them one after another; he entered Denmark, put an end to the war in that kingdom in less than six weeks, sent succours to Riga, obliged the enemy to raise the siege, and marched against the Russians encamped before Narva, through the midst of ice and snow, in the month of November.

The czar, who looked upon Narva as already in his possession, was gone to Novogorod, (Nov. 18,) and had taken with him his favourite, Menzikoff, then a lieutenant in the company of bombardiers, of the Preobrazinski regiment, and afterwards raised to the rank of field-marshal and prince; a man whose singular fortunes entitle him to be spoken of more at large in another place.

Peter left the command of the army, with his instructions for the siege, with the prince of Croi; whose family came from Flanders, and who had lately entered into the czar's service.[57] Prince Dolgorouki acted as commissary of the army. The jealousy between these two chiefs, and the absence of the czar, were partly the occasion of the unparalleled defeat at Narva.

Charles XII. having landed at Pernau, in Livonia, with his troops, in the month of October advanced northward to Revel, where he defeated an advanced body of Russians. He continued his march, and meeting with another body, routed that likewise. The runaways returned to the camp before Narva, which they filled with consternation. The month of November was now far advanced; Narva, though unskilfully besieged, was on the point of surrendering. The young king of Sweden had not at that time above nine thousand men with him, and could bring only six pieces of cannon to oppose to a hundred and forty-five, with which the Russian intrenchments were defended. All the relations of that time, and all historians without exception, concur in making the Russian army then before Narva amount to eighty thousand men. The memoirs with which I have been furnished say sixty thousand; be that as it may, it is certain, that Charles had not quite nine thousand; and that this battle was one of those which have proved, that the greatest victories have been frequently gained by inferior numbers, ever since the famed one of Arbela.[58]

Nov. 30.] Charles did not hesitate one moment to attack with his small troop this army, so greatly superior; and, taking advantage of a violent wind, and a great storm of snow, which blew directly in the faces of the Russians, he attacked their intrenchments under cover of some pieces of cannon, which he had posted advantageously for the purpose. The Russians had not time to form themselves in the midst of that cloud of snow, that beat full in their faces, and astonished by the discharge of cannon, that they could not see, and never imagined how small a number they had to oppose.

The duke de Croi attempted to give his orders, but prince Dolgorouki would not receive them. The Russian officers rose upon the German officers; the duke's secretary, with Colonel Lyon, and several others, were murdered. Every one abandoned his post; and tumult, confusion, and a panic of terror, spread through the whole army. The Swedish troops had nothing more to do, but to cut in pieces those who were flying. Some threw themselves into the river Narva, where great numbers were drowned; others threw down their arms, and fell upon their knees before the conquering Swedes.

The duke de Croi, general Alland, and the rest of the general officers, dreading the Russians more than the Swedes, went in a body and surrendered themselves prisoners to count Steinbock. The king of Sweden now made himself master of all the artillery. Thirty thousand of the vanquished enemy laid down their arms at his feet, and filed off bare-headed and disarmed before him. Prince Dolgorouki, and all the Russian generals, came and surrendered themselves, as well as the Germans, but did not know till after they had surrendered, that they had been conquered by eight thousand men. Amongst the prisoners, was the son of a king of Georgia, whom Charles sent to Stockholm: his name was Mittelesky Czarovits, or czar's son, an additional proof that the title of czar, or tzar, had not its original from the Roman Cæsars.

Charles XII. did not lose more than one thousand two hundred men in this battle. The czar's journal, which has been sent me from Petersburg, says, that including those who died at the siege of Narva, and in the battle, and those who were drowned in their flight, the Russians lost no more than six thousand men. Want of discipline, and a panic that seized the army, did all the work of that fatal day. The number of those made prisoners of war, was four times greater than that of the conquerors; and if we may believe Norberg,[59] count Piper, who was afterwards taken prisoner by the Russians, reproached them, that the number of their people made prisoners in the battle, exceeded by eight times the number of the whole Swedish army. If this is truth, the Swedes must have made upwards of seventy-two thousand prisoners. This shews how seldom writers are well informed of particular circumstances. One thing, however, equally incontestable and extraordinary, is, that the king of Sweden permitted one half of the Russian soldiers to retire back, after having disarmed them, and the other half to repass the river, with their arms; by this unaccountable presumption, restoring to the czar troops that, being afterwards well disciplined, became invincible.[60]

Charles had all the advantages that could result from a complete victory. Immense magazines, transports loaded with provisions, posts evacuated or taken, and the whole country at the mercy of the Swedish army, were consequences of the fortune of this day. Narva was now relieved, the shattered remains of the Russian army did not shew themselves; the whole country as far as Pleskow lay open; the czar seemed bereft of all resource for carrying on the war; and the king of Sweden, victor in less than twelve months over the monarchs of Denmark, Poland, and Russia, was looked upon as the first prince in Europe, at an age when other princes hardly presume to aspire at reputation. But the unshaken constancy that made a part of Peter's character, prevented him from being discouraged in any of his projects.

A Russian bishop composed a prayer to St. Nicholas,[61] on account of this defeat, which was publicly read in all the churches throughout Russia. This composition shews the spirit of the times, and the inexpressible ignorance from which Peter delivered his country. Amongst other things, it says, that the furious and terrible Swedes were sorcerers; and complains that St. Nicholas had entirely abandoned his Russians. The prelates of that country would blush to write such stuff at present; and, without any offence to the holy St. Nicholas, the people soon perceived that Peter was the most proper person to be applied to, to retrieve their losses.

CHAP. XII.

Resources after the battle of Narva. That disaster entirely repaired. Peter gains a victory near the same place. The person who was afterwards empress made prisoner at the storming of a town. Peter's successes. His triumph at Moscow.[62]

The years 1701 and 1703.

The czar having, as has been already observed, quitted his army before Narva, in the end of November, 1700, in order to go and concert matters with the king of Poland, received the news of the victory gained by the Swedes, as he was on his way. His constancy in all emergencies was equal to the intrepidity and valour of Charles. He deferred the conference with Augustus, and hastened to repair the disordered state of his affairs. The scattered troops rendezvoused at Great Novogorod, and from thence marched to Pleskow, on the lake Peipus.

It was not a little matter to be able to stand upon the defensive, after so severe a check: 'I know very well,' said Peter, 'that the Swedes will have the advantage of us for some time, but they will teach us at length to conquer them.'

1701.] Having provided for the present emergency, and ordered recruits to be raised on every side, he sent to Moscow to cast new cannon, his own having been all taken before Narva. There being a scarcity of metal, he took all the bells of the churches, and of the religious houses in Moscow. This action did not savour much of superstition, but at the same time it was no mark of impiety. With those bells he made one hundred large cannon, one hundred and forty-three field-pieces, from three to six pounders, besides mortars and howitzers, which were all sent to Pleskow. In other countries the sovereign orders, and others execute; but here the czar was obliged to see every thing done himself. While he was hastening these preparations, he entered into a negotiation with the king of Denmark, who engaged to furnish him with three regiments of foot, and three of cavalry; an engagement which that monarch could not fulfil.

As soon as this treaty was signed, he hurried to the theatre of war. He had an interview with king Augustus, at Birzen, (Feb. 27.) on the frontiers of Courland and Lithuania. His object was, to confirm that prince in his resolution of maintaining the war against Charles XII. and at the same time to engage the Polish Diet to enter into the quarrel. It is well known, that a king of Poland is no more than the head person in a republic. The czar had the advantage of being always obeyed; but the kings of Poland, and England, at present the king of Sweden, are all obliged to treat with their subjects.[63] Patkul and a few Poles in the interest of their monarch, assisted at these conferences. Peter promised to aid them with subsidies, and an army of twenty-five thousand men. Livonia was to be restored to Poland, in case the diet would concur with their king, and assist in recovering this province: the diet hearkened more to their fears, than to the czar's proposals. The Poles were apprehensive of having their liberties restrained by the Saxons and Russians, and were still more afraid of Charles XII. It was therefore agreed by the majority, not to serve their king, and not to fight.

The partisans of Augustus grew enraged against the contrary faction, and a civil war was lighted up in the kingdom; because their monarch had an intention to restore to it a considerable province.

Feb.] Peter then had only an impotent ally in king Augustus, and feeble succours in the Saxon troops; and the terror which Charles XII. inspired on every side, reduced Peter to the necessity of depending entirely upon his own strength.

March 1.] After travelling with the greatest expedition from Moscow to Courland, to confer with Augustus: he posted back from Courland to Moscow, to forward the accomplishment of his promises. He actually dispatched Prince Repnin, with four thousand men, to Riga, on the banks of the Duna, where the Saxon troops were intrenched.

July.] The general consternation was now increased; for Charles, passing the Duna in spite of all the Saxons, who were advantageously posted on the opposite side, gained a complete victory over them; and then, without waiting a moment, he made himself master of Courland, advanced into Lithuania, and by his presence encouraged the Polish faction that opposed Augustus.

Peter, notwithstanding all this, still pursued his designs. General Patkul, who had been the soul of the conference at Birzen, and who had engaged in his service, procured him some German officers, disciplined his troops, and supplied the place of general Le Fort: the czar ordered relays of horses to be provided for all the officers, and even for the German, Livonian, and Polish soldiers, who came to serve in his armies. He likewise inspected in person into every particular relating to their arms, their clothing, and subsistence.

On the confines of Livonia and Esthonia, and to the eastward of the province of Novogorod, lies the great lake Peipus, which receives the waters of the river Velika, from out of the middle of Livonia, and gives rise in its northern part to the river Naiova, that washes the walls of the town of Narva, near which the Swedes gained their famous victory. This lake is upwards of thirty leagues in length, and from twelve to fifteen in breadth. It was necessary to keep a fleet there, to prevent the Swedish ships from insulting the province of Novogorod; to be ready to make a descent upon their coasts, and above all, to be a nursery for seamen. Peter employed the greatest part of the year 1701, in building on this lake an hundred half gallies, to carry about fifty men each; and other armed barks were fitted out on the lake Ladoga. He directed all these operations in person, and set his new sailors to work: those who had been employed in 1697, at the Palus Mæotis were then stationed near the Baltic. He frequently quitted those occupations to go to Moscow, and the rest of the provinces, in order to enforce the observance of the late customs he had introduced, or to establish new ones.

Those princes who have employed the leisure moments of peace in raising public works, have acquired to themselves a name: but that Peter, just after his misfortune at Narva, should apply himself to the junction of the Baltic, Caspian, and the Black seas, by canals, has crowned him with more real glory than the most signal victory. It was in the year 1702, that he began to dig that deep canal, intended to join the Tanais and the Wolga. Other communications were likewise to be made, by means of lakes between the Tanais and the Duna; whose waters empty themselves into the Baltic, in the neighbourhood of Riga. But this latter project seemed to be still at a great distance, as Peter was far from having Riga in his possession.

While Charles was laying all Poland waste, Peter caused to be brought from that kingdom, and from Saxony, a number of shepherds, with their flocks, in order to have wool fit for making good cloth; he likewise erected manufactories of linen and paper: gave orders for collecting a number of artificers; such as smiths, braziers, armourers, and founders, and the mines of Siberia were ransacked for ore. Thus was he continually labouring for the embellishment and defence of his dominions.

Charles pursued the course of his victories, and left a sufficient body of troops, as he imagined, on the frontiers of the czar's dominions, to secure all the possessions of Sweden. He had already formed a design to dethrone Augustus, and afterwards to pursue the czar with his victorious army to the very gates of Moscow.

There happened several slight engagements in the course of this year, between the Russians and Swedes, in which the latter did not always prove superior; and even in those where they had the advantage, the Russians improved in the art of war. In short, in little more than twelve months after the battle of Narva, the czar's troops were so well disciplined, that they defeated one of the best generals belonging to the king of Sweden.

Peter was then at Pleskow, from whence he detached numerous bodies of troops, on all sides, to attack the Swedes; who were now defeated by a native of Russia, and not a foreigner. His general, Sheremeto, by a skilful manœuvre, beat up the quarters of the Swedish general, Slipenbak, in several places, near Derpt, on the frontiers of Livonia; and at last obtained a victory over that officer himself. (Jan. 11, 1702.) And now, for the first time, the Russians took from the Swedes four of their colours; which was thought a considerable number.

May.] The lakes Peipus and Ladoga were for some time afterwards the theatres of sea-fights between the Russians and Swedes; in which the latter had the same advantages as by land: namely, that of discipline and long practice; but the Russians had some few successes with their half gallies, at the lake Peipus, and the field-marshal Sheremeto took a Swedish frigate.

By means of this lake, the czar kept Livonia and Esthonia in continual alarms; his gallies frequently landed several regiments in those provinces; who reimbarked whenever they failed of success, or else pursued their advantage: the Swedes were twice beaten in the neighbourhood of Derpt, (June, July,) while they were victorious every where else.

In all these actions the Russians were always superior in number; for this reason, Charles XII. who was so successful in every other place, gave himself little concern about these trifling advantages gained by the czar: but he should have considered, that these numerous forces of his rival were every day growing more accustomed to the business of fighting, and might soon become formidable to himself.

While both parties were thus engaged, by sea and land, in Livonia, Ingria, and Esthonia, the czar is informed that a Swedish fleet had set sail, in order to destroy Archangel; upon which he immediately marched thither, and every one was astonished to hear of him on the coasts of the Frozen Sea, when he was thought to be at Moscow. He put the town into a posture of defence, prevented the intended descent, drew the plan of a citadel, called the New Dwina, laid the first stone, and then returned to Moscow, and from thence to the seat of war.

Charles made some alliances in Poland; but the Russians, on their side, made a progress in Ingria and Livonia. Marshal Sheremeto marched to meet the Swedish army, under the command of Slipenbak, gave that general battle near the little river Embac, and defeated him, taking sixteen colours, and twenty pieces of cannon. Norberg places this action on the first of December, 1701; but the journal of Peter the Great, fixes it on the nineteenth of July, 1702.

6th Aug.] After this advantage, the Russian general marched onwards, laid the whole country under contributions, and takes the little town of Marienburg, on the confines of Ingria and Livonia. There are several towns of this name in the north of Europe; but this, though it no longer exists, is more celebrated in history than all the others, by the adventure of the empress Catherine.

This little town, having surrendered at discretion, the Swedes, who defended it, either through mistake or design, set fire to the magazine. The Russians, incensed at this, destroyed the town, and carried away all the inhabitants. Among the prisoners was a young woman, a native of Livonia, who had been brought up in the house of a Lutheran minister of that place, named Gluck, and who afterwards became the sovereign of those who had taken her captive, and who governed Russia by the name of the empress Catherine.

There had been many instances before this, of private women being raised to the throne; nothing was more common in Russia, and in all Asiatic kingdoms, than for crowned heads to marry their own subjects; but that a poor stranger, who had been taken prisoner in the storming of a town, should become the absolute sovereign of that very empire, whither she was led captive, is an instance which fortune never produced before nor since in the annals of the world.

The Russian arms proved equally successful in Ingria: for their half gallies on the lake Ladoga compelled the Swedish fleet to retire to Wibourg,[64] a town at the other extremity of this great lake, from whence they could see the siege of the fortress of Notebourg, which was then carrying on by general Sheremeto. This was an undertaking of much greater importance than was imagined at that time, as it might open a communication with the Baltic Sea, the constant aim of Peter the Great.

Notebourg was a strong fortified town, built on an island in the lake Ladoga, which it entirely commands, and by that means, whoever is in possession of it, must be masters of that part of the river Neva, which falls into the sea not far from thence. The Russians bombarded the town night and day, from the 18th of September to the 12th October; and at length gave a general assault by three breaches. The Swedish garrison was reduced to a hundred men only capable of defending the place; and, what is very astonishing, they did defend it, and obtain, even in the breach, an honourable capitulation: moreover, colonel Slipenbak, who commanded there, would not surrender the town, but on condition of being permitted to send for two Swedish officers from the nearest post, to examine the breaches (Oct. 16.), in order to be witnesses for him to the king his master, that eighty-three men, who were all then left of the garrison capable of bearing arms, besides one hundred and fifty sick and wounded, did not surrender to a whole army, till it was impossible for them to fight longer, or to preserve the place. This circumstance alone shews what sort of an enemy the czar had to contend with, and the necessity there was of all his great efforts and military discipline. He distributed gold medals among his officers on this occasion, and gave rewards to all the private men; except a few, whom he punished for running away during the assault. Their comrades spit in their faces, and afterwards shot them to death; thus adding ignominy to punishment.

Notebourg was repaired, and its name changed to that of Shlusselburg, or the City of the Key; that place being the key of Ingria and Finland. The first governor was that Menzikoff, whom we have already mentioned, and who was become an excellent officer, and had merited this honour by his gallant behaviour during the siege. His example served as an encouragement to all who have merit without being distinguished by birth.

After this campaign of 1702, the czar resolved that Sheremeto, and the officers who had signalized themselves, should make a triumphal entry into Moscow. (Dec. 17.) All the prisoners taken in this campaign marched in the train of the victors, who had the Swedish colours and standards carried before them, together with the flag of the Swedish frigate taken on the lake Peipus. Peter assisted in the preparations for this triumphal pomp, as he had shared in the great actions it celebrated.

These shows naturally inspired emulation, otherwise they would have been no more than idle ostentation. Charles despised every thing of this kind, and, after the battle of Narva, held his enemies, their efforts, and their triumphs, in equal contempt.

CHAP. XIII.

Reformation at Moscow.—Further successes.—Founding of Petersburg. —The czar takes Narva, &c.

The short stay which the czar made at Moscow, in the beginning of the winter 1703, was employed in seeing all his new regulations put into execution, and in improving the civil as well as the military government. Even his very amusements were calculated to inspire his subjects with a taste for the new manner of living he had introduced amongst them. In this view, he invited all the boyards, and principal ladies of Moscow, to the marriage of one of his sisters, at which every one was required to appear dressed after the ancient fashion. A dinner was served up just in the same manner as those in the sixteenth century.[65] By an old superstitious custom, no one was to light a fire on the wedding-day, even in the coldest season. This custom was rigorously observed upon this occasion. The Russians formerly never drank wine, but only mead and brandy; no other liquors were permitted on this day, and, when the guests made complaints, he replied, in a joking manner, 'This was a custom with your ancestors, and old customs are always the best.' This raillery contributed greatly to the reformation of those who preferred past times to the present, at least it put a stop to their murmurings; and there are several nations that stand in need of the like example.

A still more useful establishment than any of the rest, was that of a printing-press, for Russian and Latin types; the implements of which were all brought from Holland. They began by printing translations in the Russian language of several books of morality and polite literature. Ferguson founded schools for geometry, astronomy, and navigation.

Another foundation, no less necessary, was that of a large hospital; not one of those houses which encourage idleness, and perpetuate the misery of the people, but such as the czar had seen at Amsterdam, where old persons and children are employed at work, and where every one within the walls is made useful in some way or other.

He established several manufactories; and, as soon he had put in motion all those arts to which he gave birth in Moscow, he hastened to Woronitz, to give directions for building two ships, of eighty guns each, with long cradles, or caserns, fitted to the ribs of the vessel, to buoy her up, and carry her safely over the shoals and banks of sand that lay about Azoph; an ingenious contrivance, similar to that used by the Dutch in Holland, to get their large ships over the Pampus.

Having made all the necessary preparations against the Turks, he turned his attention, in the next place, against the Swedes. He went to visit the ships that were building at Olonitz (March 30, 1703.), a town between the lakes Ladago and Onega, where he had established a foundry for making all kinds of arms; and, when every thing bore a military aspect, at Moscow flourished all the arts of peace. A spring of mineral waters, which has been lately discovered near Olonitz, has added to the reputation of that place. From thence he proceeded to Shlusselburg, which he fortified.

We have already observed, that Peter was determined to pass regularly through all the military degrees: he had served as lieutenant of bombardiers, under prince Menzikoff, before that favourite was made governor of Shlusselburg, and he now took the rank of captain, and served under marshal Sheremeto.

There was an important fortress near the lake Ladoga, and not far from the river Neva, named Nyantz, or Nya.[66] It was necessary to make himself master of this place, in order to secure his conquest, and favour his other designs. He therefore undertook to transport a number of small barks, filled with soldiers, and to drive off the Swedish vessels that were bringing supplies, while Sheremeto had the care of the trenches. (May 22.) The citadel surrendered, and two Swedish vessels arrived, too late to assist the besieged, being both attacked and taken by the czar. His journal says, that, as a reward for his service, 'The captain of bombardiers was created knight of the order of St. Andrew by admiral Golowin, the first knight of that order.'

After the taking of the fort of Nya, he resolved upon building the city of Petersburg, at the mouth of the Neva, upon the gulf of Finland.

The affairs of king Augustus were in a desperate way; the excessive victories of the Swedes in Poland had emboldened his enemies in the opposition; and even his friends had obliged him to dismiss a body of twenty thousand Russians, that the czar had sent him to reinforce his army. They thought, by this sacrifice, to deprive the malcontents of all pretext for joining the king of Sweden: but enemies are disarmed by force, a show of weakness serving only to make them more insolent. These twenty thousand men, that had been disciplined by Patkul, proved of infinite service in Livonia and Ingria, while Augustus was losing his dominions. This reinforcement, and, above all, the possession of Nya, enabled the czar to found his new capital.

It was in this barren and marshy spot of ground, which has communication with the main land only by one way, that Peter laid the foundation of Petersburg, in the sixtieth degree of latitude, and the forty-fourth and a half of longitude. The ruins of some of the bastions of Nya was made use of for the first stones of the foundation.[67] They began by building a small fort upon one of the islands, which is now in the centre of the city. The Swedes beheld, without apprehension, a settlement in the midst of a morass, and inaccessible to vessels of burden; but, in a very short time, they saw the fortifications advanced, a town raised, and the little island of Cronstadt, situated over against it, changed, in 1704, into an impregnable fortress, under the cannon of which even the largest fleets may ride in safety.

These works, which seemed to require a time of profound peace, were carried on in the very bosom of war; workmen of every sort were called together, from Moscow, Astracan, Casan, and the Ukraine, to assist in building the new city. Neither the difficulties of the ground, that was to be rendered firm, and raised, the distance of the necessary materials, the unforeseen obstacles, which are for ever starting up in all great undertakings; nor, lastly, the epidemical disorder, which carried off a prodigious number of the workmen, could discourage the royal founder; and, in the space of five months, a new city rose from the ground. It is true, indeed, it was little better than a cluster of huts, with only two brick houses, surrounded by ramparts; but this was all that was then necessary. Time and perseverance accomplished the rest. In less than five months, after the founding of Petersburg, a Dutch ship came to trade there, (Nov.) the captain of which was handsomely rewarded, and the Dutch soon found the way to Petersburg.

While Peter was directing the establishment of this colony, he took care to provide every day for its safety, by making himself master of the neighbouring posts. A Swedish colonel, named Croniort, had taken post on the river Sestra, and thence threatened the rising city. Peter, without delay, marched against him with his two regiments of guards, defeated him, (July 8.) and obliged him to repass the river. Having thus put his town in safety, he repaired to Olonitz,(Sep.) to give directions for building a number of small vessels, and afterwards returned to Petersburg, on board a frigate that had been built by his direction, taking with him six transport vessels, for present use, till the others could be got ready. Even at this juncture he did not forget his ally, the king of Poland, but sent him (Nov.) a reinforcement of twelve thousand foot, and a subsidy in money of three hundred thousand rubles, which make about one million five hundred thousand French livres.[68] It has been remarked, that his annual revenue did not exceed then five million rubles; a sum, which the expense of his fleets, of his armies, and of his new establishments, seemed more than sufficient to exhaust. He had, at almost one and the same time, fortified Novogorod, Pleskow, Kiow, Smolensko, Azoph, Archangel, and founded a capital. Notwithstanding all which, he had still a sufficiency left to assist his ally with men and money. Cornelius le Bruine, a Dutchman, who was on his travels, and at that time in Russia, and with whom he frequently conversed very freely, as indeed he did with all strangers, says, that the czar himself assured him, that he had still three hundred thousand rubles remaining in his coffers, after all the expenses of the war were defrayed.

In order to put his infant city of Petersburg out of danger of insult, he went in person to sound the depth of water thereabouts, fixed upon a place for building the fort of Cronstadt; and, after making the model of it in wood with his own hands, he employed prince Menzikoff to put it in execution. From thence he went to pass the winter at Moscow, (Nov. 5.) in order to establish, by degrees, the several alterations he had made in the laws, manners, and customs of Russia. He regulated the finances, and put them upon a new footing. He expedited the works that were carrying on in the Woronitz, at Azoph, and in a harbour which he had caused to be made on the Palus Mæotis, under the fort of Taganrock.

Jan. 1704.] The Ottoman Porte, alarmed at these preparations, sent an embassy to the czar, complaining thereof: to which he returned for answer that he was master in his own dominions, as well as the grand seignior was in Turkey, and that it was no infringement of the peace to render the Russian power respectable on the Euxine Sea.

March 30.] Upon his return to Petersburg, finding his new citadel of Cronstadt, which had been founded in the bosom of the sea, completely finished, he furnished it with the necessary artillery. But, in order to settle himself firmly in Ingria, and entirely to repair the disgrace he had suffered before Narva, he esteemed it necessary to take that city. While he was making preparations for the siege, a small fleet appeared on the lake of Peipus, to oppose his designs. The Russian half galleys went out to meet them, gave them battle, and took the whole squadron, which had on board ninety-eight pieces of cannon. After this victory, the czar lays siege to Narva both by sea and land, (April.) and, which was most extraordinary, he lays siege to the city of Derpt in Esthonia at the same time.

Who would have imagined, that there was a university in Derpt? Gustavus Adolphus had founded one there, but it did not render that city more famous, Derpt being only known by these two sieges. Peter was incessantly going from the one to the other, forwarding the attacks, and directing all the operations. The Swedish general Slipenbak was in the neighbourhood of Derpt, with a body of two thousand five hundred men.

The besiegers expected every instant when he would throw succours into the place; but Peter, on this occasion, had recourse to a stratagem worthy of more frequent imitation: he ordered two regiments of foot, and one of horse, to be clothed in the same uniform, and to carry the same standards and colours as the Swedes: these sham Swedes attack the trenches, (June 27.) and the Russians pretend to be put to flight; the garrison, deceived by appearances, make a sally; upon which the mock combatants join their forces and fall upon the Swedes, one half of whom were left dead upon the place, and the rest made shift to get back to the town. Slipenbak arrives soon after with succours to relieve it, but is totally defeated. At length Derpt was obliged to capitulate, (July 23.) just as the czar was preparing every thing for a general assault.

At the same time Peter met with a considerable check, on the side of his new city of Petersburg; but this did not prevent him either from going on with the works of that place, or from vigorously prosecuting the siege of Narva. It has already been observed, that he sent a reinforcement of troops and money to king Augustus, when his enemies were driving him from his throne; but both these aids proved useless. The Russians having joined the Lithuanians in the interest of Augustus, were totally defeated in Courland by the Swedish general Levenhaupt: (July 31.) and had the victors directed their efforts towards Livonia, Esthonia, and Ingria, they might have destroyed the czar's new works, and baffled all the fruits of his great undertakings. Peter was every day sapping the breast-work of Sweden, while Charles seemed to neglect all resistance, for the pursuit of a less advantageous, though a more brilliant fame.

On the 13th of July, 1704, only a single Swedish colonel, at the head of his detachment, obliged the Polish nobility to nominate a new king, on the field of election, called Kolo, near the city of Warsaw. The cardinal-primate of the kingdom, and several bishops, submitted to a Lutheran prince, notwithstanding the menaces and excommunications of the supreme pontiff: in short, every thing gave way to force. All the world knows in what manner Stanislaus Leczinsky was elected king, and how Charles XII. obliged the greatest part of Poland to acknowledge him.

Peter, however, would not abandon the dethroned king, but redoubled his assistance, in proportion to the necessities of his ally; and, while his enemy was making kings, he beat the Swedish generals one after another in Esthonia and Ingria; from thence he passed to the siege of Narva, and gave several vigorous assaults to the town. There were three bastions, famous at least for their names, called Victory, Honour, and Glory. The czar carried them all three sword-in-hand. The besiegers forced their way into the town, where they pillaged and exercised all those cruelties which were but too customary at that time, between the Swedes and Russians.

August 20.] Peter, on this occasion, gave an example that ought to have gained him the affections of all his new subjects: he ran every where in person, to put a stop to the pillage and slaughter, rescues several women out of the clutches of the brutal soldiery, and, after having, with his own hand, killed two of those ruffians who had refused to obey his orders, he enters the town-house, whither the citizens had ran in crowds for shelter, and laying his sword, yet reeking with blood, upon the table—'This sword,' said he, 'is not stained with the blood of your fellow citizens, but with that of my own soldiers, which I have spilt to save your lives'.

CHAP. XIV.

Peter the Great keeps possession of all Ingria, while Charles XII. is triumphant in other places.—Rise of Menzikoff.—Petersburg secured.—The czar executes his designs notwithstanding the victories of the king of Sweden.[69]

1704.

Peter being now master of all Ingria, conferred the government of that province upon Menzikoff; and at the same time gave him the title of prince, and the rank of major-general. Pride and prejudice might, in other countries, find means to gainsay, that a pastry cook's boy should be raised to be a general and governor, and to princely dignity; but Peter had already accustomed his subjects to see, without surprise, every thing given to merit, and nothing to mere nobility. Menzikoff, by a lucky accident, had, while a boy, been taken from his original obscurity, and placed in the czar's family,[70] where he learnt several languages, and acquired a knowledge of public affairs, both in the cabinet and field; and having found means to ingratiate himself with his master, he afterwards knew how to render himself necessary. He greatly forwarded the works at Petersburg, of which he had the direction; several brick and stone houses were already built, with an arsenal and magazines; the fortifications were completed, but the palaces were not built till some time afterwards.

Peter was scarcely settled in Narva, when he offered fresh succours to the dethroned king of Poland; he promised him a body of troops over and above the twelve thousand men he had already sent him, and actually dispatched general Repnin (Aug. 19.) from the frontiers of Lithuania, with six thousand horse, and the same number of foot. All this while he did not lose sight of his colony of Petersburg: the buildings went on very fast; his navy encreased daily; several ships and frigates were on the stocks at Olmutz; these he took care to see finished, and brought them himself into the harbour of Petersburg.

Oct. 11.] Each time he returned to Moscow, was distinguished by triumphal entries. In this manner did he revisit it this year, from whence he made only one excursion, to be present at the launching of his first ship of eighty guns upon the Woronitz, (Dec. 30.) of which ship he himself had drawn the dimensions the preceding year.

May, 1705.] As soon as the campaign could be opened in Poland, he hastened to the army, which he had sent to the assistance of Augustus, on the frontiers of that kingdom; but, while he was thus supporting his ally, a Swedish fleet put to sea, to destroy Petersburg, and the fortress of Cronslot, as yet hardly finished. This fleet consisted of twenty-two ships of war, from fifty-four to sixty-four guns each, besides six frigates, two bomb-ketches, and two fire-ships. The troops that were sent on this expedition, made a descent on the little island of Kotin; but a Russian colonel, named Tolbogwin, who commanded a regiment there, ordered his soldiers to lie down flat on their bellies, while the Swedes were coming on shore, and then suddenly rising up, they threw in so brisk and well directed a fire, that the Swedes were put into confusion, and forced to retreat with the utmost precipitation to their ships, leaving behind them all their dead, and upwards of three hundred prisoners. (June 7.)

However, their fleet still continued hovering about the coast, and threatened Petersburg. They made another descent, and were repulsed as before (June 25.): a body of land-forces were also advancing from Wiburn,[71] under the command of the Swedish general Meidel, and took their route by Shlusselburg: this was the most considerable attempt that Charles had yet made upon those territories, which Peter had either conquered or new formed. The Swedes were every where repulsed, and Petersburg remained in security.

Peter, on the other hand, advanced towards Courland, with a design to penetrate as far as Riga. His plan was to make himself master of Livonia, while Charles XII. was busied in reducing the Poles entirely under the obedience of the new king he had given them. The czar was still at Wilnaw in Lithuania, and his general Sheremeto was approaching towards Mittau, the capital of Courland; but there he was met by general Levenhaupt, already famous by several victories, and a pitched battle was fought between the two armies at a place called Gemavershoff, or Gemavers.

In all those actions where experience and discipline decide the day, the Swedes, though inferior in number, had the advantage. The Russians were totally defeated, (June 28.) and lost their artillery. Peter, notwithstanding the loss of three battles, viz. at Gemavers, at Jacobstadt, and at Narva, always retrieved his losses, and even converted them to his advantage.

After the battle of Gemavers, he marched his army into Courland; came before Mittau, made himself master of the town, and afterwards laid siege to the citadel, which he took by capitulation.

Sept. 14, 1705.] The Russian troops at that time had the character of distinguishing their successes by rapine and pillage; a custom of too great antiquity in all nations. But Peter, at the taking of Narva, had made such alterations in this custom, that the Russian soldiers appointed to guard the vaults where the grand dukes of Courland were buried, in the castle of Mittau, perceiving that the bodies had been taken out of their tombs, and stripped of their ornaments, refused to take possession of their post, till a Swedish colonel had been first sent for to inspect the condition of the place; who gave them a certificate that this outrage had been committed by the Swedes themselves.

A rumour which was spread throughout the whole empire, that the czar had been totally defeated at the battle of Gemavers, proved of greater prejudice to his affairs, than even the loss of that battle. The remainder of the ancient strelitzes in garrison at Astracan, emboldened by this false report, mutinied, and murdered the governor of the town. Peter was obliged to send marshal Sheremeto with a body of forces to quell the insurrection, and punish the mutineers.

Every thing seemed now to conspire against the czar; the success and valour of Charles XII.; the misfortunes of Augustus; the forced neutrality of Denmark; the insurrection of the ancient strelitzes; the murmurs of a people, sensible of the restraint, but not of the utility of the late reform; the discontent of the grandees, who found themselves subjected to military discipline; and, lastly, the exhausted state of the finances, were sufficient to have discouraged any prince except Peter: but he did not despond, even for an instant. He soon quelled the revolt, and having provided for the safety of Ingria, and secured the possession of the citadel of Mittau, in spite of the victorious Levenhaupt, who had not troops enough to oppose him; he found himself at liberty to march an army through Samojitia and Lithuania.

He now shared with Charles XII. the glory of giving laws to Poland. He advanced as far as Tikoczin: where he had an interview for the second time with king Augustus; when he endeavoured to comfort him under his misfortunes, promising to revenge his cause, and, at the same time, made him a present of some colours, which Menzikoff had taken from the troops of his rival. The two monarchs afterwards went together to Grodno, the capital of Lithuania, where they staid till the 15th of December. At their parting, Peter presented him both men and money, and then, according to his usual custom, went to pass some part of the winter at Moscow, (30 Dec.) to encourage the arts and sciences there, and to enforce his new laws there, after having made a very difficult and laborious campaign.

CHAP. XV.

While Peter is strengthening his conquests, and improving the police of his dominion, his enemy Charles XII. gains several battles: gives laws to Poland and Saxony, and to Augustus, notwithstanding a victory gained by the Russians.—Augustus resigns the crown, and delivers up Patkul, the czar's ambassador.—Murder of Patkul, who is sentenced to be broke upon the wheel.

1706.

Peter was hardly returned to Moscow, when he heard that Charles XII. after being every where victorious, was advancing towards Grodno, to attack the Russian troops. King Augustus had been obliged to fly from Grodno, and retire with precipitation towards Saxony, with four regiments of Russian dragoons; a step which both weakened and discouraged the army of his protector. Peter found all the advances to Grodno occupied by the Swedes, and his troops dispersed.

While he was with the greatest difficulty assembling his troops in Lithuania, the famous Schullemburg, who was the last support Augustus had left, and who afterwards gained so much glory by the defence of Corfu against the Turks, was advancing on the side of Great Poland, with about twelve thousand Saxons, and six thousand Russians, taken from the body troops with which the czar had entrusted that unfortunate prince. Schullemburg expected with just reason, that he should be able to prop the sinking fortunes of Augustus; he perceived that Charles XII. was employed in Lithuania, and that there was only a body of ten thousand Swedes under general Renschild to interrupt his march; he therefore advanced with confidence as far as the frontiers of Silesia; which is the passage out of Saxony into Upper Poland. When he came near the village of Fraustadt, on the frontiers of that kingdom, he met marshal Renschild, who was advancing to give him battle.

Whatever care I take to avoid repeating what has been already mentioned in the history of Charles XII., I am obliged in this place to take notice once more, that there was in the Saxon army a French regiment, that had been taken prisoners at the famous battle of Hochsted (or Blenheim) and obliged to serve in the Saxon troops. My memoirs say, that this regiment had the charge of the artillery, and add, that the French, struck with the fame and reputation of Charles XII., and discontented with the Saxon service, laid down their arms as soon as they came in sight of the enemy (Feb.), and desired to be taken into the Swedish army, in which they continued to the end of the war. This defection was as the beginning, or signal of a total overthrow to the Russian army, of which no more than three battalions were saved, and almost every man of these was wounded; and as no quarter was granted, the remainder was cut in pieces.

Norberg, the chaplain, pretends, that the Swedish word at this battle was, 'In the name of God,' and that of the Russians, 'Kill all;' but it was the Swedes who killed all in God's name. The czar himself declares, in one of his manifestoes,[72] that a number of Russians, Cossacks, and Calmucks, that had been made prisoners, were murdered in cool blood three days after that battle. The irregular troops on both sides had accustomed their generals to these cruelties, than which greater were never committed in the most barbarous times. I had the honour to hear king Stanislaus himself say, that in one of those engagements which were so frequent in Poland, a Russian officer who had formerly been one of his friends, came to put himself under his protection, after the defeat of the corps he commanded; and that the Swedish general Steinbock shot him dead with a pistol, while he held him in his arms.

This was the fourth battle the Russians had lost against the Swedes, without reckoning the other victories of Charles XII. in Poland. The czar's troops that were in Grodno, ran the risk of suffering a still greater disgrace, by being surrounded on all sides; but he fortunately found means to get them together, and even to strengthen them with new reinforcements. But necessitated at once to provide for the safety of this army, and the security of his conquests in Ingria, he ordered prince Menzikoff to march with the army under his command eastward, and from thence southward as far as Kiow.

While his men were upon their march, he repairs to Shlusselburg, from thence to Narva, and to his colony of Petersburg (August), and puts those places in a posture of defence. From the Baltic he flies to the banks of the Boristhenes, to enter into Poland by the way of Kiow, making it still his chief care to render those victories of Charles, which he had not been able to prevent, of as little advantage to the victor as possible. At this very time he meditated a new conquest; namely, that of Wibourg, the capital of Carelia, situated on the gulf of Finland. He went in person to lay siege to this place, but for this time it withstood the power of his arms; succours arrived in season, and he was obliged to raise the siege. (Oct.) His rival, Charles XII. did not, in fact, make any conquests, though he gained so many battles: he was at that time in pursuit of king Augustus in Saxony, being always more intent upon humbling that prince, and crushing him beneath the weight of his superior power and reputation, than upon recovering Ingria, that had been wrested from him by a vanquished enemy.

He spread terror through all Upper Poland, Silesia, and Saxony. King

Augustus's whole family, his mother, his wife, his son, and the principal nobility of the country, were retired into the heart of the empire. Augustus now sued for peace, choosing rather to trust himself to the mercy of his conqueror, than in the arms of his protector. He entered into a treaty which deprived him of the crown of Poland, and covered him at the same time with ignominy. This was a private treaty, and was to be concealed from the czar's generals, with whom he had taken refuge in Poland, while Charles XII. was giving laws in Leipsic, and acting as absolute master throughout his electorate.

His plenipotentiaries had already signed the fatal treaty (Sept. 14.), by which he not only divested himself of the crown of Poland, but promised never more to assume the title of king; at the same time he recognized Stanislaus, renounced his alliance with the czar his benefactor; and, to complete his humiliation, engaged to deliver up to Charles XII. John Reinold Patkul, the czar's ambassador and general in the Russian service, who was then actually fighting in his cause. He had some time before ordered Patkul to be arrested upon false suspicions, contrary to the law of nations; and now, in direct violation of these laws, he delivered him up to the enemy. It had been better for him to have died sword-in-hand, than to have concluded such a treaty; a treaty, which not only robbed him of his crown, and of his reputation, but likewise endangered his liberty, because he was at that time in the power of prince Menzikoff in Posnania, and the few Saxons that he had with him, were paid by the Russians.

Prince Menzikoff was opposed in that district by a Swedish army, reinforced with a strong party of Poles, in the interest of the new king Stanislaus, under the command of general Meyerfeld; and not knowing that Augustus had engaged in a treaty with the enemies of Russia, had proposed to attack them, and Augustus did not dare to refuse. The battle was fought near Calish (Oct. 19.), in the palatinate belonging to Stanislaus; this was the first pitched battle the Russians had gained against the Swedes. Prince Menzikoff had all the glory of the action, four thousand of the enemy were left dead on the field, and two thousand five hundred and ninety-eight were made prisoners.

It is difficult to comprehend how Augustus could be prevailed on, after this battle, to ratify a treaty which deprived him of all the fruits of his victory. But Charles was still triumphant in Saxony, where his very name spread terror. The success of the Russians appeared so inconsiderable, and the Polish party against Augustus was so strong, and, in fine, that monarch was so ill-advised, that he signed the fatal convention. Neither did he stop here: he wrote to his envoy Finkstein a letter, that was, if possible, more shameful than the treaty itself; for therein he asked pardon for having obtained a victory, 'protesting, that the battle had been fought against his will; that the Russians and the Poles, his adherents, had obliged him to it; that he had, with a view of preventing it, actually made some movements to abandon Menzikoff; that Meyerfeld might have beaten him, had he made the most of that opportunity; that he was ready to restore all the Swedish prisoners, or to break with the Russians; and that, in fine, he would give the king of Sweden all possible satisfaction,' for having dared to beat his troops.

This whole affair, unparalleled and inconceivable as it is, is, nevertheless, strictly true. When we reflect, that, with all this weakness, Augustus was one of the bravest princes in Europe, we may plainly perceive, that the loss or preservation, the rise or decline of empires, are entirely owing to fortitude of mind.

Two other circumstances concurred to complete the disgrace of the king of Poland elector of Saxony, and heighten the abuse which Charles XII. made of his good fortune; the first was his obliging Augustus to write a letter of congratulation to the new king Stanislaus on his election: the second was terrible, he even compelled Augustus to deliver up Patkul, the czar's ambassador and general.[73] It is sufficiently known to all Europe, that this minister was afterwards broke alive upon the wheel at Casimir, in the month of September, 1707. Norberg, the chaplain, confesses that the orders for his execution were all written in Charles's own hand.

There is not a civilian in all Europe, nay even the vilest slave, but must feel the whole horror of this barbarous injustice. The first crime of this unfortunate man was, the having made an humble representation of the rights and privileges of his country, at the head of six Livonian gentlemen, who were sent as deputies from the whole province: having been condemned to die for fulfilling the first of duties, that of serving his country agreeable to her laws. This iniquitous sentence put him in full possession of a right, which all mankind derive from nature, that of choosing his country. Being afterwards made ambassador to one of the greatest monarchs in the universe, his person thereby became sacred. On this occasion the law of force violated that of nature and nations. In former ages cruelties of this kind were hidden in the blaze of success, but now they sully the glory of a conqueror.

CHAP. XVI.

Attempts made to set up a third king of Poland.—Charles XII. sets out from Saxony with a powerful army, and marches through Poland in a victorious manner.—Cruelties committed.—Conduct of the czar.—Successes of the king of Sweden, who at length advances towards Russia.

1707.

Charles XII. enjoyed the fruits of his good fortune in Altranstadt near Leipsic, whither the Protestant princes of the German empire repaired in droves to pay homage to him, and implore his protection. He received ambassadors from almost all the potentates in Europe. The emperor Joseph implicitly followed his directions. Peter then perceiving that king Augustus had renounced his protection and his own crown, and that a part of the Polish nation had acknowledged Stanislaus, listened to the proposals made him by Yolkova, of choosing a third king.

A diet was held at Lublin, in which several of the palatines were proposed; and among others, Prince Ragotski was put upon the list; that prince, who was so long kept in prison, when young, by the emperor Leopold, and who afterwards when he procured his liberty, was his competitor for the throne of Hungary.

This negotiation was pushed very far, and Poland was on the point of having three kings at one time. Prince Ragotski not succeeding, Peter thought to bestow the crown on Siniauski, grand general of the republic; a person of great power and interest, and head of a third party, that would neither acknowledge the dethroned king, nor the person elected by the opposed party.

In the midst of these troubles, there was a talk of peace, as is customary on the like occasions. Besseval the French envoy in Saxony interposed, in order to bring about a reconciliation between the czar and the king of Sweden. It was thought at that time by the court of France, that Charles, having no longer either the Russians or Poles to fight against, might turn his arms against the emperor Joseph, with whom he was not on very good terms, and on whom he had imposed several laws during his stay in Saxony. But Charles made answer, that he would treat with the czar in Moscow. It was on this occasion that Peter said, 'My brother Charles wants to act the Alexander, but he shall not find a Darius in me.'

The Russians however were still in Poland, and were in the city of Warsaw, while the king whom Charles XII. had set over the Poles was hardly acknowledged by that nation. In the mean time, Charles was enriching his army with the spoils of Saxony.

Aug. 22.] At length he began his march from Altranstadt, at the head of an army of forty-five thousand men; a force which it seemed impossible for the czar to withstand, seeing he had been entirely defeated by eight thousand only at Narva.

Aug. 27.] It was in passing by the walls of Dresden, that Charles made that very extraordinary visit to king Augustus, which, as Norberg says, 'will strike posterity with admiration.' It was running an unaccountable risk, to put himself in the power of a prince whom he had deprived of his kingdom. From thence he continued his march through Silesia, and re-entered Poland.

This country has been entirely ravaged by war, ruined by factions, and was a prey to every kind of calamity. Charles continued advancing with his army through the province of Muscovia, and chose the most difficult ways he could take. The inhabitants, who had taken shelter in the morasses, resolved to make him at least pay for his passage. Six thousand peasants dispatched an old man of their body to speak to him: this man who was of a very extraordinary figure, clad in white, and armed with two carabines, made a speech to Charles; but as the standers by did not well understand what he said, they, without any further ceremony, dispatched him in his harangue, and before their king's face. The peasants, in a rage, immediately withdrew, and took up arms. All who could be found were seized, and obliged to hang one another; the last was compelled to put the rope about his neck himself, and to be his own executioner. All their houses were burnt to the ground. This fact is attested by Norberg, who was an eye-witness, and therefore cannot be contradicted, as it cannot be related without inspiring horror.

1708, Feb. 6.] Charles being arrived within a few leagues of Grodno in Lithuania, is informed of the czar's being there in person with a body of troops; upon which, without staying to deliberate, he takes only eight hundred of his guards, and sets out for Grodno. A German officer, named Mulfels, who commanded a body of troops, posted at one of the gates of the town, making no doubt, when he saw Charles, but that he was followed by his whole army, instead of disputing the passage with him, leaves it open, and takes to flight. The alarm is now spread through the whole town; every one imagines the whole Swedish army already entered; the few Russians who made any resistance, are cut in pieces by the Swedish guards; and all the officers assure the czar, that the victorious army had made itself master of the place. Hereupon Peter retreats behind the ramparts, and Charles plants a guard of thirty men at the very gate through which the czar had just before entered.

In this confusion some of the Jesuits, whose college had been taken to accommodate the king of Sweden, as being the handsomest structure in the place, went by night to the czar, and for this time told the whole truth. Upon this, Peter immediately returns into the town, and forces the Swedish guards. An engagement ensues in the streets and public places; but, at length, the whole Swedish army appearing in sight, the czar is obliged to yield to superior numbers, and leaves the town in the hands of the victor, who made all Poland tremble.

Charles had augmented his forces in Livonia and Finland, and Peter had every thing to fear, not only for his conquests on this side, together with those in Lithuania, but also for his ancient territories, and even for the city of Moscow itself. He was obliged then to provide at once for the safety of all these different places, at such a distance from each other. Charles could not make any rapid conquest to the eastward of Lithuania in the depth of winter, and in a marshy country, subject to epidemical disorders, which had been spread by poverty and famine, from Warsaw, as far as Minski. Peter posted his troops so as to command the passes of the rivers, (April 8.) guarded all the important posts, and did every thing in his power to impede the marches of his enemy, and afterwards hastened to put things in a proper situation at Petersburg.

Though Charles was lording it in Poland, he took nothing from the czar; but Peter, by the use he made of his new fleet, by landing his troops in Finland, by the taking and dismantling the town of Borgau, (May 22.) and by seizing a great booty, was procuring many real and great advantages to himself, and distressing his enemy.

Charles, after being detained a long time in Lithuania, by continual rains, at length reached the little river of Berezine, some few leagues from the Boristhenes. Nothing could withstand his activity: he threw a bridge over the river in sight of the Russians; beat a detachment that guarded the passage, and got to Holozin on the river Bibitsch, where the czar had posted a considerable body of troops to check the impetuous progress of his rival. The little river of Bibitsch is only a small brook in dry weather; but at this time it was swelled by the rains to a deep and rapid stream. On the other side was a morass, behind which the Russians had thrown up an intrenchment for above a quarter of a league, defended by a large and deep ditch, and covered by a parapet, lined with artillery. Nine regiments of horse, and eleven of foot, were advantageously posted in these lines, so that the passage of the river seemed impracticable.

The Swedes, according to the custom of war, got ready their pontoons, and erected batteries to favour their passage; but Charles, whose impatience to engage would not let him brook the least delay, did not wait till the pontoons were ready. Marshal Schwerin, who served a long time under him, has assured me several times, that one day that they were to come to action, observing his generals to be very busy in concerting the necessary dispositions, said tartly to them, 'When will you have done with this trifling?' and immediately advanced in person at the head of his guards, which he did particularly on this memorable day.

He flung himself into the river, followed by his regiment of guards. Their numbers broke the impetuosity of the current, but the water was as high as their shoulders, and they could make no use of their firelocks. Had the artillery of the parapet been but tolerably well served, or had the infantry but levelled their pieces in a proper manner, not a single Swede would have escaped.

July 25.] The king, after wading the river, passed the morass on foot. As soon as the army had surmounted these obstacles within sight of the Russians, they drew up in order of battle, and attacked the enemies intrenchments seven different times, and it was not till the seventh attack that the Russians gave way. By the accounts of their own historians, the Swedes took but twelve field-pieces, and twenty-four mortars.

It was therefore evident, that the czar had at length succeeded in disciplining his troops, and this victory of Holozin, while it covered Charles XII. with glory, might have made him sensible of the many dangers he must have to encounter in adventuring into such distant countries, where his army could march only in small bodies, through woods, morasses, and where he would be obliged to fight out every step of his way; but the Swedes, being accustomed to carry all before them, dreaded neither danger nor fatigue.[74]

CHAP. XVII.

Charles XII. crosses the Boristhenes, penetrates into the Ukraine, but concerts his measures badly.—One of his armies is defeated by Peter the Great: he loses his supply of provisions and ammunition: advances forward through a desert country: his adventures in the Ukraine.

1708.

At last Charles arrives on the borders of the Boristhenes, at a small town called Mohilow. This was the important spot where it was to be determined, whether he should direct his march eastward, towards Moscow; or southwards, towards the Ukraine. His own army, his friends, his enemies, all expected that he would direct his course immediately for the capital of Russia. Which ever way he took, Peter was following him from Smolensko with a strong army; no one expected that he would turn towards the Ukraine. He was induced to take this strange resolution by Mazeppa, hetman of the Cossacks, who, being an old man of seventy and without children, ought to have thought only of ending his days in peace: gratitude should have bound him to the czar, to whom he was indebted for his present dignity; but whether he had any real cause of complaint against that prince, or that he was dazzled with the lustre of Charles's exploits, or whether, in time, he thought to make himself independent, he betrayed his benefactor, and privately espoused the interests of the king of Sweden, flattering himself with the hopes of engaging his whole nation in a rebellion with himself.

Charles made not the least doubt of subduing the Russian empire, as soon as his troops should be joined by so warlike a people as the Cossacks. Mazeppa was to furnish him with what provisions, ammunition, and artillery, he should want; besides these powerful succours, he was to be joined by an army of sixteen or seventeen thousand men, out of Livonia, under the command of general Levenhaupt, who was to bring with him a prodigious quantity of warlike stores and provisions. Charles was not at the trouble of reflecting, whether the czar was within reach of attacking the army, and depriving him of these necessary supplies. He never informed himself whether Mazeppa was in a condition to observe his promises; if that Cossack had credit enough to change the disposition of a whole nation, who are generally guided only by their own opinion; or whether his army was provided with sufficient resources in case of an accident; but imagined, if Mazeppa should prove deficient in abilities or fidelity, he could trust in his own valour and good fortune. The Swedish army then advanced beyond the Boristhenes towards the Desna; it was between these two rivers, that he expected to meet with Mazeppa. His march was attended with many difficulties and dangers, on account of the badness of the road, and the many parties of Russians that were hovering about these regions.

Sept. 11.] Menzikoff, at the head of some horse and foot, attacked the king's advanced guard, threw them into disorder, and killed a number of his men. He lost a great number of his own, indeed, but that did not discourage him. Charles immediately hastened to the field of battle, and with some difficulty repulsed the Russians, at the hazard of his own life, by engaging a party of dragoons, by whom he was surrounded. All this while Mazeppa did not appear, and provisions began to grow scarce. The Swedish soldiers, seeing their king share in all their dangers, fatigues, and wants, were not dispirited; but though they admired his courage, they could not refrain from murmuring at his conduct.

The orders which the king had sent to Levenhaupt to march forward with all haste, to join him with the necessary supplies, were not delivered by twelve days so soon as they should have been. This was a long delay as circumstances then stood. However, Levenhaupt at length began his march; Peter suffered him to pass the Boristhenes, but as soon as his army was got between that river and the lesser ones, which empty themselves into it, he crossed over after him, and attacked him with his united forces, which had followed in different corps at equal distances from one another. This battle was fought between the Boristhenes and the Sossa.[75]

Prince Menzikoff was upon his return with the same body of horse, with which he had lately engaged Charles XII. General Baur followed him, and the czar himself headed the flower of his army. The Swedes imagined they had to deal with an army of forty thousand men, and the same was believed for a long time on the faith of their relation; but my late memoirs inform me, that Peter had only twenty thousand men in this day's engagement, a number not much superior to that of the enemy: but his vigour, his patience, his unwearied perseverance, together with that of his troops, animated by his presence, decided the fate, not of that day only, but of three successive days, during which the fight was renewed at different times.

They made their first attack upon the rear of the Swedish army, near the village of Lesnau, from whence this battle borrows its name. This first shock was bloody, without proving decisive. Levenhaupt retreated into a wood, and thereby saved his baggage. (Oct. 7.) The next morning, when the Swedes were to be driven from this wood, the fight was still more bloody, and more to the advantage of the Russians. Here it was that the czar, seeing his troops in disorder, cried out to fire upon the runaways, and even upon himself, if they saw him turn back. The Swedes were repulsed, but not thrown into confusion.

At length a reinforcement of four thousand dragoons arriving, he fell upon the Swedes a third time; who retreated to a small town called Prospock, where they were again attacked; they then marched towards the Desna, the Russians still pursuing them: yet they were never broken, but lost upwards of eight thousand men, seventeen pieces of cannon, and forty-four colours: the czar took fifty-six officers and near nine hundred private men prisoners; and the great convoy of provisions and ammunition that were going to Charles's army, fell into the hands of the conqueror.

This was the first time that the czar in person gained a pitched battle, against an enemy who had distinguished himself by so many victories over his troops: he was employed in a general thanksgiving for his success, when he received advice that general Apraxin had lately gained an advantage over the enemy in Ingria, (Sept. 17,) some leagues from Narva, an advantage less considerable indeed than that of Lesnau; but this concurrence of fortunate events greatly raised the hopes and courage of his troops.

Charles XII. heard of these unfortunate tidings just as he was ready to pass the Desna, in the Ukraine. Mazeppa at length joined him; but instead of twenty thousand men, and an immense quantity of provisions, which he was to have brought with him, he came with only two regiments, and appeared rather like a fugitive applying for assistance, than a prince, who was bringing powerful succours to his ally. This Cossack had indeed begun his march with near fifteen or sixteen thousand of his people, whom he had told, at their first setting out, that they were going against the king of Sweden; that they would have the glory of stopping that hero on his march, and that he would hold himself eternally obliged to them for so great a service.

But when they came within a few leagues of the Desna, he made them acquainted with his real design. These brave people received his declaration with disdain: they refused to betray a monarch, against whom they had no cause of complaint, for the sake of a Swede, who had invaded their country with an armed force, and who, after leaving it, would be no longer able to defend them, but must abandon them to the mercy of the incensed Russians, and of the Poles, once their masters, and always their enemies: they accordingly returned home, and gave advice to the czar of the defection of their chief: Mazeppa found himself left with only two regiments, the officers of which were in his own pay.

He was still master of some strong posts in the Ukraine, and in particular of Bathurin, the place of his residence, looked upon as the capital of the country of the Cossacks: it is situated near some forests on the Desna, at a great distance from the place where Peter had defeated general Levenhaupt. There were always some Russian regiments quartered in these districts. Prince

Menzikoff was detached from the czar's army, and got thither by round-about marches. Charles could not secure all the passes; he did not even know them all, and had neglected to make himself master of the important post of Starowdoub, which leads directly to the Bathurin, across seven or eight leagues of forest, through which the Desna directs its course. His enemy had always the advantage of him, by being better acquainted with the country.

Menzikoff and prince Galitzin, who had accompanied him, easily made their passage good, and presented themselves before the town of Bathurin, (Nov. 14,) which surrendered almost without resistance, was plundered, and reduced to ashes. The Russians made themselves masters of a large magazine destined for the use of the king of Sweden, and of all Mazeppa's treasures. The Cossacks chose another hetman, named Skoropasky, who was approved by the czar, who being willing to impress a due sense of the enormous crime of treason on the minds of the people, by a striking example of justice, the archbishop of Kiow, and two other prelates, were ordered to excommunicate Mazeppa publicly, (Nov. 22,) after which he was hanged in effigy, and some of his accomplices were broken upon the wheel.

In the meanwhile, Charles XII. still at the head of about twenty-five or twenty-seven thousand Swedes, who were reinforced by the remains of Levenhaupt's army, and the addition of between two or three thousand men, whom Mazeppa had brought with him, and still infatuated with the same notion of making all the Ukraine declare for him, passed the Desna at some distance from Bathurin, and near the Boristhenes, in spite of the czar's troops which surrounded him on all sides; part of whom followed close in the rear, while another part lined the opposite side of the river to oppose his passage.

He continued his march through a desert country, where he met with nothing but burned or ruined villages. The cold began to set in at the beginning of December so extremely sharp, that in one of his marches near two thousand of his men perished before his eyes: the czar's troops did not suffer near so much, being better supplied; whereas the king of Sweden's army, being almost naked, was necessarily more exposed to the inclemency of the weather.

In this deplorable situation, count Piper, chancellor of Sweden, who never gave his master other than good advice, conjured him to halt, and pass at least the severest part of the winter in a small town of the Ukraine, called Romna, where he might intrench himself, and get some provisions by the help of Mazeppa; but Charles replied, that—He was not a person to shut himself up in a town. Piper then intreated him to re-pass the Desna and the Boristhenes, to return back into Poland, to put his troops into winter quarters, of which they stood so much in need, to make use of the Polish cavalry, which was absolutely necessary; to support the king he had nominated, and to keep in awe the partisans of Augustus, who began already to bestir themselves. Charles answered him again—That this would be flying before the czar, that the season would grow milder, and that he must reduce the Ukraine, and march on to Moscow.[76]

January, 1709.] Both armies remained some weeks inactive, on account of the intenseness of the cold, in the month of January, 1709; but as soon as the men were able to make use of their arms, Charles attacked all the small posts that he found in his way; he was obliged to send parties on every side in search of provisions; that is to say, to scour the country twenty leagues round, and rob all the peasants of their necessary subsistence. Peter, without hurrying himself, kept a strict eye upon all his motions, and suffered the Swedish army to dwindle away by degrees.

It is impossible for the reader to follow the Swedes in their march through these countries: several of the rivers which they crossed are not to be found in the maps: we must not suppose, that geographers are as well acquainted with these countries, as we are with Italy, France, and Germany: geography is, of all the arts, that which still stands the most need of improvement, and ambition has hitherto been at more pains to desolate the face of the globe, than to give a description of it.

We must content ourselves then with knowing, that Charles traversed the whole Ukraine in the month of February, burning the villages wherever he came, or meeting with others that had been laid in ashes by the Russians. He advancing south-east, came to those sandy deserts, bordered by mountains that separate the Nogay Tartars from the Don Cossacks. To the eastward of those mountains are the altars of Alexander. Charles was now on the other side of the Ukraine, in the road that the Tartars take to Russia; and when he was got there, he was obliged to return back again to procure subsistence: the inhabitants, having retired with all their cattle into their dens and lurking-places, would sometimes defend their subsistence against the soldiers, who came to deprive them of it. Such of these poor wretches, who could be found, were put to death, agreeably to what are falsely called, the rules of war. I cannot here forbear transcribing a few lines from Norberg.[77] 'As an instance,' says he, 'of the king's regard to justice, I shall insert a note, which he wrote with his own hand to colonel Heilmen.

> 'Colonel,
>
> 'I am very well pleased that you have taken those peasants, who carried off a Swedish soldier; as soon as they are convicted of the crime, let them be punished with death, according to the exigency of the case.

'Charles; and lower down, Budis.'

Such are the sentiments of justice and humanity shewn by a king's confessor; but, had the peasants of the Ukraine had it in their power to hang up some of those regimented peasants of East Gothland, who thought themselves entitled to come so far to plunder them, their wives, and families, of their subsistence, would not the confessors and chaplains of these Ukrainers have had equal reason to applaud their justice?

Mazeppa had for a considerable time, been in treaty with the Zaporavians, who dwell about the two shores of the Boristhenes, and of whom part inhabit the islands on that river. It is this division that forms the nation, of whom mention has already been made in the first chapter of this history, and who have neither wives nor families, and subsist entirely by rapine. During the winter they heap up provisions in their islands, which they afterwards go and sell in the summer, in the little town of Pultowa; the rest dwell in small hamlets, to the right and left of this river. All together choose a particular hetman, and this hetman is subordinate to him of the Ukraine. The person, at that time at the head of the Zaporavians, came to meet Mazeppa; and these two barbarians had an interview, at which each of them had a horse's tail, and a club borne before him, as ensigns of honour.

To shew what this hetman of the Zaporavians and his people were, I think it not unworthy of history, to relate the manner in which this treaty was concluded. Mazeppa gave a great feast to the hetman of the Zaporavians, and his principal officers, who were all served in plate. As soon as these chiefs had made themselves drunk with brandy, they took an oath (without stirring from table) upon the Evangelists, to supply Charles with men and provisions; after which they carried off all the plate and other table-furniture. Mazeppa's steward ran after them, and remonstrated, that such behaviour ill-suited with the doctrine of the Gospels, on which they had so lately sworn. Some of Mazeppa's domestics were for taking the plate away from them by force; but the Zaporavians went in a body to complain to Mazeppa, of the unparalleled affront offered to such brave fellows, and demanded to have the steward delivered up to them, that they might punish him according to law. This was accordingly complied with, and the Zaporavians, according to law, tossed this poor man from one to another like a ball, and afterwards plunged a knife to his heart.

Such were the new allies that Charles XII. was obliged to receive; part of whom he formed into a regiment of two thousand men; the remainder marched in separate bodies against the Cossacks and Calmucks of the czar's party, that were stationed about that district.

The little town of Pultowa, with which those Zaporavians carry on a trade, was filled with provisions, and might have served Charles for a place of arms. It is situated on the river Worsklaw, near a chain of mountains, which command it on the north side. To the eastward is a vast desert. The western part is the most fruitful, and the best peopled. The Worsklaw empties itself into the Boristhenes, about fifteen leagues lower down; from Pultowa, one may go northward, through the defiles, which communicate with the road to Moscow, a passage used by the Tartars. It is very difficult of access, and the precautions taken by the czar had rendered it almost impervious; but nothing appeared impossible to Charles, and he depended upon marching to Moscow, as soon as he had made himself master of Pultowa: with this view he laid siege to that town in the beginning of May.

CHAP. XVIII.

Battle of Pultowa.

Here it was that Peter expected him; he had disposed the several divisions of his army at convenient distances for joining each other, and marching all together against the besiegers: he had visited the countries which surround the Ukraine; namely the duchy of Severia, watered by the Desna, already made famous by his victory: the country of Bolcho, in which the Occa has its source; the deserts and mountains leading to the Palus Mæotis; and lately he had been in the neighbourhood of Azoph, where he caused that harbour to be cleansed, new ships to be built, and the citadel of Taganroc to be repaired. Thus did he employ the time that passed between the battles of Lesnau and Pultowa, in preparing for the defence of his dominions. As soon as he heard the Swedes had laid siege to the town, he mustered all his forces; the horse, dragoons, infantry, Cossacks, and Calmucks, advanced from different quarters. His army was well provided with necessaries of every kind; large cannon, field pieces, ammunition of all sorts, provisions, and even medicines for the sick: this was another degree of superiority which he had acquired over his rival.

On the 15th day of June, 1709, he appeared before Pultowa, with an army of about sixty thousand effective men; the river Worsklaw was between him and Charles. The besiegers were encamped on the north-west side of that river, the Russians on the south-east.

Peter ascends the river above the town, fixes his barges, marches over with his army, and draws a long line of intrenchments, (July 3.) which were begun and completed in one night, in the face of the enemy. Charles might then judge, whether the person, whom he had so much despised, and whom he thought of dethroning at Moscow, understood the art of war. This disposition being made, Peter posted his cavalry between two woods, and covered it with several redoubts, lined with artillery. Having thus taken all the necessary measures, (July 6.) he went to reconnoitre the enemy's camp, in order to form the attack.

This battle was to decide the fate of Russia, Poland, and Sweden, and of two monarchs, on whom the eyes of all Europe were fixed. The greatest part of those nations, who were attentive to these important concerns, were equally ignorant of the place where these two princes were, and of their situation: but knowing that Charles XII. had set out from Saxony, at the head of a victorious army, and that he was driving his enemy every where before him, they no longer doubted that he would at length entirely crush him; and that, as he had already given laws to Denmark, Poland, and Germany, he would now dictate conditions of peace in the Kremlin of Moscow, and make a new czar, after having already made a new king of Poland. I have seen letters from several public ministers to their respective courts, confirming this general opinion.

The risk was far from being equal between these two great rivals. If Charles lost a life, which he had so often and wantonly exposed, there would after all have been but one hero less in the world. The provinces of the Ukraine, the frontiers of Lithuania, and of Russia, would then rest from their calamities, and a stop would be put to the general devastation which had so long been their scourge. Poland would, together with her tranquillity, recover her lawful prince, who had been lately reconciled to the czar, his benefactor; and Sweden, though exhausted of men and money, might find motives of consolation under her heavy losses.

But, if the czar perished, those immense labours, which had been of such utility to mankind, would be buried with him, and the most extensive empire in the world would again relapse into the chaos from whence it had been so lately taken.

There had already been some skirmishes between the detached parties of the Swedes and Russians, under the walls of the town. In one of these rencounters, (June 27.) Charles had been wounded by a musket-ball, which had shattered the bones of his foot: he underwent several painful operations, which he bore with his usual fortitude, and had been confined to his bed for several days. In this condition he was informed, that Peter intended to give him battle; his notions of honour would not suffer him to wait to be attacked in his intrenchments. Accordingly he gave orders for quitting them, and was carried himself in a litter. Peter the Great acknowledges, that the Swedes attacked the redoubts, lined with artillery, that covered his cavalry, with such obstinate valour, that, notwithstanding the strongest resistance, supported by a continual fire, the enemy made themselves masters of two redoubts. Some writers say, that when the Swedish infantry found themselves in possession of the two redoubts, they thought the day their own, and began to cry out— Victory. The chaplain, Norberg, who was at some great distance from the field of battle, amongst the baggage (which was indeed his proper place) pretends, that this was a calumny; but, whether the Swedes cried victory or not, it is certain they were not victorious. The fire from the other redoubts was kept up without ceasing, and the resistance made by the Russians, in every part, was as firm as the attack of their enemies was vigorous. They did not make one irregular movement; the czar drew up his army without the intrenchments in excellent order, and with surprising dispatch.

The battle now became general. Peter acted as major-general; Baur commanded the right wing, Menzikoff the left, and Sheremeto the centre. The action lasted about two hours: Charles, with a pistol in his hand, went from rank to rank, carried in a litter, on the shoulders of his drabans; one of which was killed by a cannon-ball, and at the same time the litter was shattered in pieces. He then ordered his men to carry him upon their pikes; for it would have been difficult, in so smart an action, let Norberg say as he pleases, to find a fresh litter ready made. Peter received several shots through his clothes and his hat; both princes were continually in the midst of the fire, during the whole action. At length, after two hours desperate engagement, the Swedes were taken on all sides, and fell into confusion; so that Charles was obliged to fly before him, whom he had hitherto held in so much contempt. This very hero, who could not mount his saddle during the battle, now fled for his life on horseback; necessity lent him strength in his retreat: he suffered the most excruciating pain, which was increased by the mortifying reflection of being vanquished without resource. The Russians reckoned nine thousand two hundred and twenty-four Swedes left dead on the field of battle, and between two and three thousand made prisoners in the action, the chief of which was cavalry.

Charles XII. fled with the greatest precipitation, attended by the remains of his brave army, a few field-pieces, and a very small quantity of provisions and ammunition. He directed his march southward, towards the Boristhenes, between the two rivers Workslaw and Psol, or Sol, in the country of the Zaporavians. Beyond the Boristhenes, are vast deserts, which lead to the frontiers of Turkey. Norberg affirms, that the victors durst not pursue Charles; and yet he acknowledges, that prince Menzikoff appeared on the neighbouring heights, (July 12.) with ten thousand horse, and a considerable train of artillery, while the king was passing the Boristhenes.

Fourteen thousand Swedes surrendered themselves prisoners of war to these ten thousand Russians; and Levenhaupt, who commanded them, signed the fatal capitulation, by which he gave up those Zaporavians who had engaged in the service of his master, and were then in the fugitive army. The chief persons taken prisoners in the battle, and by the capitulation, were count Piper, the first minister, with two secretaries of state, and two of the cabinet; field-marshal Renschild, the generals Levenhaupt, Slipenbak, Rozen, Stakelber, Creutz, and Hamilton, with three general aides-de-camp, the auditor-general of the army, fifty-nine staff-officers, five colonels, among whom was the prince of Wirtemberg; sixteen thousand nine hundred and forty-two private men and non-commissioned officers: in short, reckoning the king's own domestics, and others, the conqueror had no less than eighteen thousand seven hundred and forty-six prisoners in his power: to whom, if we add nine thousand two hundred and twenty-four slain in battle, and nearly two thousand that passed the Boristhenes with Charles, it appears, plainly, that he had, on that memorable day, no less than twenty-seven thousand effective men under his command.[78]

Charles had begun his march from Saxony with forty-five thousand men, Levenhaupt had brought upwards of sixteen thousand out of Livonia, and yet scarce a handful of men was left of all this powerful army; of a numerous train of artillery, part lost in his marches, and part buried in the morasses; he had now remaining only eighteen brass cannon, two howitzers, and twelve mortars; and, with inconsiderable force, he had undertaken the siege of Pultowa, and had attacked an army provided with a formidable artillery. Therefore he is, with justice, accused of having shewn more courage than prudence, after his leaving Germany. On the side of the Russians, there were no more than fifty-two officers and one thousand two hundred and ninety- three private men killed; an undeniable proof, that the disposition of the Russian troops was better than those of Charles, and that their fire was infinitely superior to that of the Swedes.

We find, in the memoirs of a foreign minister to the court of Russia, that Peter, being informed of Charles's design to take refuge in Turkey, wrote a friendly letter to him, intreating him not to take so desperate a resolution, but rather to trust himself in his hands, than in those of the natural enemy of all Christian princes. He gave him, at the same time, his word of honour, not to detain him prisoner, but to terminate all their differences by a reasonable peace. This letter was sent by an express as far as the river Bug, which separates the deserts of the Ukraine from the grand seignior's dominions. As the messenger did not reach that place till Charles had entered Turkey, he brought back the letter to his master. The same minister adds further, that he had this account from the very person who was charged with the letter.[79] This anecdote is not altogether improbable; but I do not meet with it either in Peter's journals, or in any of the papers entrusted to my care. What is of greater importance, in relation to this battle, was its being the only one, of the many that have stained the earth with blood, that, instead of producing only destruction, has proved beneficial to mankind, by enabling the czar to civilize so considerable a part of the world.

There have been fought more than two hundred pitched battles in Europe, since the commencement of this century to the present year. The most signal, and the most bloody victories, have produced no other consequences than the reduction of a few provinces ceded afterwards by treaties, and retaken again by other battles. Armies of a hundred thousand men have frequently engaged each other in the field; but the greatest efforts have been attended with only slight and momentary successes; the most trivial causes have been productive of the greatest effects. There is no instance, in modern history, of any warthat has compensated, by even a better good, for the many evils it has occasioned: but, from the battle of Pultowa, the greatest empire under the sun has derived its present happiness and prosperity.

CHAP. XIX.

Consequences of the battle of Pultowa.—Charles XII. takes refuge among the Turks.—Augustus, whom he had dethroned, recovers his dominions.—Conquests of Peter the Great.

The chief prisoners of rank were now presented to the conqueror, who ordered their swords to be returned, and invited them to dinner. It is a well known fact, that, on drinking to the officers, he said, 'To the health of my masters in the art of war.' However, most of his masters, particularly the subaltern officers, and all the private men, were soon afterwards sent into Siberia. There was no cartel established here for exchange of prisoners between the Russians and Swedes; the czar, indeed, had proposed one before the siege of Pultowa, but Charles rejected the offer, and his troops were in every thing the victims of his inflexible pride.

It was this unseasonable obstinacy that occasioned all the misfortunes of this prince in Turkey, and a series of adventures, more becoming a hero of romance than a wise or prudent king; for, as soon as he arrived at Bender, he was advised to write to the grand-vizier, as is the custom among the Turks; but this he thought would be demeaning himself too far. The like obstinacy embroiled him with all the ministers of the Porte, one after another, in short, he knew not how to accommodate himself either to times or circumstances.
[80]

The first news of the battle of Pultowa produced a general revolution in minds and affairs in Poland, Saxony, Sweden, and Silesia. Charles, while all powerful in those parts, had obliged the emperor Joseph to take a hundred and five churches from the catholics in favour of the Silesians of the confession of Augsburg. The catholics then no sooner received news of the defeat of Charles, than they repossessed themselves of all the Lutheran temples. The Saxons now thought of nothing but being revenged for the extortions of a conqueror, who had robbed them, according to their own account, of twenty- three millions of crowns.

The king of Poland, their elector, immediately protested against the abdication that had been extorted from him, and being now reconciled to the czar (Aug. 3.), he left no stone unturned to reascend the Polish throne. Sweden, overwhelmed with consternation, thought her king for a long time dead, and in this uncertainty the senate knew not what to resolve.

Peter in the mean time determined to make the best use of his victory, and therefore dispatched marshal Sheremeto with an army into Livonia, on the frontiers of which province that general had so often distinguished himself. Prince Menzikoff was sent in haste with a numerous body of cavalry to second the few troops left in Poland, to encourage the nobles who were in the interest of Augustus to drive out his competitor, who was now considered in no better light than a rebel, and to disperse a body of Swedes and troops that were still left in that kingdom under the command of general Crassau.

The czar soon after sets out in person, marches through the province of Kiow, and the palatinates of Chelm and Upper Volhinia, and at length arrives at Lublin, where he concerts measures with the general of Lithuania. He then reviews the crown troops, who all take the oath of allegiance to king Augustus, from thence he proceeds to Warsaw, and at Thera enjoyed the most glorious of all triumphs (Sept. 18.), that of receiving the thanks of a king, whom he had reinstated in his dominions. There it was that he concluded a treaty against Sweden, with the kings of Denmark, Poland, and Prussia (Oct. 7.): in which he was resolved to recover from Charles all the conquests of Gustavus Adolphus. Peter revived the ancient pretensions of the czars to Livonia, Ingria, Carelia, and part of Finland; Denmark laid claim to Scania, and the king of Prussia to Pomerania.

Thus had Charles XII. by his unsuccessful valour, shook the noble edifice that had been erected by the prosperous bravery of his ancestor Gustavus Adolphus. The Polish nobility came in on all sides to renew their oaths to their king, or to ask pardon for having deserted him; and almost the whole kingdom acknowledged Peter for its protector.

To the victorious arms of the czar, to these new treaties, and to this sudden revolution, Stanislaus had nothing to oppose but a voluntary resignation: he published a writing called Universale, in which he declares himself ready to resign the crown, if the republic required it.

Peter, having concerted all the necessary measures with the king of Poland, and ratified the treaty with Denmark, set out directly to finish his negotiation with the king of Prussia. It was not then usual for sovereign princes to perform the function of their own ambassadors. Peter was the first who introduced this custom, which has been followed by very few. The elector of Brandenburg, the first king of Prussia, had a conference with the czar at Marienverder, a small town situated in the western part of Pomerania, and built by the old Teutonic knights, and included in the limits of Prussia, lately erected into a kingdom. This country indeed was poor, and of a small extent; but its new king, whenever he travelled, displayed the utmost magnificence; with great splendour he had received czar Peter at his first passing through his dominions, when that prince quitted his empire to go in search of instruction among strangers. But he received the conqueror of Charles XII. in a still more pompous manner. (Oct. 20.) Peter for this time concluded only a defensive treaty with him, which afterwards, however, completed the ruin of Sweden.

Not an instant of time was lost. Peter, having proceeded with the greatest dispatch in his negotiations, which elsewhere are wont to take up so much time, goes and joins his army, then before Riga, the capital of Livonia; he began by bombarding the place (Nov. 21.), and fired off the three first bombs himself; then changed the siege into a blockade; and, when well assured that Riga could not escape him, he repaired to his city of Petersburg, to inspect and forward the works carrying on there, the new buildings, and finishing of his fleet; and having laid the keel of a ship of fifty-four guns, (Dec. 3.) with his own hands, he returned to Moscow. Here he amused himself with assisting in the preparations for the triumphal entry, which he exhibited in the capital. He directed every thing relating to that festival, and was himself the principal contriver and architect.

He opened the year 1710 with this solemnity, so necessary to his subjects, whom it inspired with notions of grandeur, and was highly pleasing to every one who had been fearful of seeing those enter their walls as conquerors, over whom they now triumphed. Seven magnificent arches were erected, under which passed in triumph, the artillery, standards, and colours, taken from the enemy, with their officers, generals, and ministers, who had been taken prisoners, all on foot, amidst the ringing of bells, the sound of trumpets, the discharge of a hundred pieces of cannon, and the acclamations of an innumerable concourse of people, whose voices rent the air as soon as the cannon ceased firing. The procession was closed by the victorious army, with the generals at its head; and Peter, who marched in his rank of major-general. At each triumphal arch stood the deputies of the several orders of the state; and at the last was a chosen band of young gentlemen, the sons of boyards, clad in Roman habits, who presented a crown of laurels to their victorious monarch.

This public festival was followed by another ceremony, which proved no less satisfactory than the former. In the year 1708 happened an accident the more disagreeable to Peter, as his arms were at that time unsuccessful. Mattheof, his ambassador to the court of London, having had his audience of leave of queen Anne, was arrested for debt, at the suit of some English merchants, and carried before a justice of peace to give security for the monies he owed there. The merchants insisted that the laws of commerce ought to prevail before the privileges of foreign ministers; the czar's ambassador, and with him all the public ministers, protested against this proceeding, alleging, that their persons ought to be always inviolable. The czar wrote to queen Anne, demanding satisfaction for the insult offered him in the person of his ambassador.

But the queen had it not in her power to gratify him; because, by the laws of England, tradesmen were allowed to prosecute their debtors, and there was no law that excepted public ministers from such prosecution.[81] The murder of Patkul, the czar's ambassador, who had been executed the year before by the order of Charles XII. had encouraged the English to shew so little regard to a character which had been so cruelly profaned. The other public ministers who were then at the court of London, were obliged to be bound for the czar's ambassador; and at length all the queen could do in his favour, was to prevail on her parliament to pass an act, by which no one for the future could arrest an ambassador for debt; but after the battle of Pultowa, the English court thought proper to give satisfaction to the czar.

The queen made by a formal embassy an excuse for what had passed. Mr. Whitworth,[82] the person charged with this commission, began his harangue with the following words.—(Feb. 16.) 'Most high and mighty emperor.' He told the czar that the person who had presumed to arrest his ambassador, had been imprisoned and rendered infamous. There was no truth in all this, but it was sufficient that he said so, and the title of emperor, which the queen had not given Peter before the battle of Pultowa, shewed the consideration he had now acquired in Europe.

This title had been already granted him in Holland, not only by those who had been his fellow-workmen in the dock-yards at Saardam, and seemed to interest themselves most in his glory, but likewise by the principal persons in the state, who unanimously styled him emperor, and made public rejoicings for his victory, even in the presence of the Swedish minister.

The universal reputation which he had acquired by his victory of Pultowa, was still further increased by his not suffering a moment to pass without making some advantages of it. In the first place, he laid siege to Elbing, a Hans town of Regal Prussia in Poland, where the Swedes had still a garrison. The Russians scaled the walls, entered the town, and the garrison surrendered prisoners of war. (Mar. 11.) This was one of the largest magazines belonging to Charles XII. The conquerors found therein one hundred and eighty-three brass cannon, and one hundred and fifty-seven mortars. Immediately after the reduction of Elbing, Peter re-marched from Moscow to Petersburg (April 2.); as soon as he arrived at this latter place, he took shipping under his new fortress of Cronslot, coasted along the shore of Carelia, and notwithstanding a violent storm, brought his fleet safely before Wiburg, the capital of Carelia in Finland; while his land-forces advanced over the frozen morasses, and in a short time the capital of Livonia beheld itself closely blockaded (June 23.): and after a breach was made in the walls, Wiburg surrendered, and the garrison, consisting of four thousand men, capitulated, but did not receive the honours of war, being made prisoners notwithstanding the capitulation. Peter charged the enemy with several infractions of this kind, and promised to set these troops at liberty, as soon as he should receive satisfaction from the Swedes, for his complaints. On this occasion the king of Sweden was to be consulted, who continued as inflexible as ever; and those soldiers, whom, by a little concession, he might have delivered from their confinement, remained in captivity. Thus did king William III. in 1695, arrest marshal Boufflers, notwithstanding the capitulation of Namur. There have been several instances of such violations of treaties, but it is to be wished there never had been any.

After the taking of this capital, the blockade of Riga was soon changed into a regular siege, and pushed with vigour. They were obliged to break the ice on the river Dwina, which waters the walls of the city. An epidemical disorder, which had raged some time in those parts, now got amongst the besiegers, and carried off nine thousand; nevertheless, the siege was not in the least slackened; it lasted a considerable time, but at length the garrison capitulated (July 15.): and were allowed the honours of war; but it was stipulated by the capitulation, that all the Livonian officers and soldiers should enter into the Russian service, as natives of a country that had been dismembered from that empire, and usurped by the ancestors of Charles XII. But the Livonians were restored to the privileges of which his father had stripped them, and all the officers entered into the czar's service: this was the most noble satisfaction that Peter could take for the murder of his ambassador, Patkul, a Livonian, who had been put to death, for defending those privileges. The garrison consisted of near five thousand men. A short time afterwards the citadel of Pennamund was taken, and the besiegers found in the town and fort above eight hundred pieces of artillery of different kinds.

Nothing was now wanting, to make Peter entirely master of the province of Carelia, but the possession of the strong town of Kexholm, built on an island in the lake of Ladoga, and deemed impregnable; it was bombarded soon after, and surrendered in a short time. (Sep. 19.) The island of Oesel in the sea, bordering upon the north of Livonia, was subdued with the same rapidity. (Sep. 23.)

On the side of Esthonia, a province of Livonia, towards the north, and on the gulf of Finland, are the towns of Pernau and Revel: by the reduction of these Peter completed the conquest of all Livonia. Pernau surrendered after a siege of a few days (Aug. 25.), and Revel capitulated (Sep. 10.) without waiting to have a single cannon fired against it; but the besieged found means to escape out of the hands of the conquerors, at the very time that they were surrendering themselves prisoners of war: for some Swedish ships, having anchored in the road, under favour of the night, the garrison and most of the citizens embarked on board, and when the besiegers entered the town, they were surprised to find it deserted. When Charles XII. gained the victory of Narva little did he expect that his troops would one day be driven to use such artifices.

In Poland, Stanislaus finding his party entirely ruined, had taken refuge in Pomerania, which still belonged to Charles XII. Augustus resumed the government, and it was difficult to decide who had acquired most glory, Charles in dethroning him, or Peter in restoring him to his crown.

The subjects of the king of Sweden were still more unfortunate than that monarch himself. The contagious distemper, which had made such havock over Livonia, passed from thence into Sweden, where, in the city of Stockholm, it carried off thirty thousand persons: it likewise desolated the provinces, already thinned of their inhabitants; for during the space of ten years successively, most of the able-bodied men had quitted their country to follow their master, and perished in foreign climes.

Charles's ill fortune pursued him also in Pomerania: his army had retired thither from Poland, to the number of eleven thousand; the czar, the kings of Denmark and Prussia, the elector of Hanover, and the duke of Holstein, joined together to render this army useless, and to compel general Crassau, who commanded it, to submit to neutrality. The regency of Stockholm, hearing no news of their king, and distracted by the mortality that raged in that city, were glad to sign this neutrality, which seemed to deliver one of its provinces at least from the horrors of war. The emperor of Germany favoured this extraordinary convention, by which it was stipulated, that the Swedish army then in Pomerania should not march from thence to assist their monarch in any other part of the world; nay, it was furthermore resolved in the German empire, to raise an army to enforce the execution of this unparalleled convention. The reason of this was, that the emperor of Germany, who was then at war with France, was in hopes to engage the Swedish army to enter into his service. This whole negotiation was carried on while Peter was subduing Livonia, Esthonia, and Carelia.

Charles XII. who was all this time at Bender, putting every spring in motion to engage the divan to declare war against the czar, received this news as one of the severest blows his untoward fortune had dealt him: he could not brook, that his senate at Stockholm should pretend to tie up the hands of his army, and it was on this occasion that he wrote them word, he would send one of his boots to govern them.

The Danes, in the mean time, were making preparations to invade Sweden; so that every nation in Europe was now engaged in war, Spain, Portugal, Italy, France, Germany, Holland, and England, were contending for the dominions left by Charles II. of Spain; and the whole North was up in arms against Charles XII. There wanted only a quarrel with the Ottoman empire, for every village in Europe to be exposed to the ravages of war. This quarrel happened soon afterwards, when Peter had attained to the summit of his glory, and precisely for that reason.

CHAP. XX.

Campaign of Pruth.

Sultan Achmet III. declared war against Peter I. not from any regard to the king of Sweden, but, as may readily be supposed, merely from a view to his own interest. The Khan of the Crim Tartars could not without dread, behold a neighbour so powerful as Peter I. The Porte had, for some time, taken umbrage at the number of ships which this prince had on the Palus Mæotis, and in the Black Sea, at his fortifying the city of Azoph, and at the flourishing state of the harbour of Taganroc, already become famous; and, lastly, at his great series of successes, and at the ambition which success never fails to augment.

It is neither true, nor even probable, that the Porte should have begun the war against the czar, on the Palus Mæotis, for no other reason than because a Swedish ship had taken a bark on the Baltic, on board of which was found a letter from a minister, whose name has never been mentioned. Norberg tells us, that this letter contained a plan for the conquest of the Turkish empire; that it was carried to Charles XII. who was then in Turkey, and was by him sent to the divan; and that immediately after the receipt of this letter, war was declared. But this story carries the mark of fiction with it. It was the remonstrances of the khan of Tartary, who was more uneasy about the neighbourhood of Azoph, than the Turkish divan, that induced this latter to give orders for taking the field.[83]

It was in the month of August, and before the czar had completed the reduction of Livonia, when Achmet III. resolved to declare war against him. The Turks, at that time, could hardly have had the news of the taking of Riga; and, therefore, the proposal of restoring to the king of Sweden the value in money, of the effects he had lost at the battle of Pultowa, would have been the most absurd thing imaginable, if not exceeded by that of demolishing Petersburg. The behaviour of Charles XII. at Bender, was sufficiently romantic; but the conduct of the Turkish divan would have been much more so, if we suppose it to have made any demands of this kind.

Nov. 1710.] The khan of Tartary, who was the principal instigator of this war, paid Charles a visit in his retreat at Bender. They were connected by the same interests, inasmuch as Europe makes part of the frontiers of Little Tartary. Charles and the khan were the two greatest sufferers by the successes of the czar; but the khan did not command the forces of the grand seignior. He was like one of the feudatory princes of Germany, who served in the armies of the empire with their own troops, and were subject to the authority of the emperor's generals for the time being.

Nov. 29, 1710.] The first step taken by the divan, was to arrest Tolstoy, the czar's ambassador at the Porte, in the streets of Constantinople, together with thirty of his domestics, who, with their master, were all confined in the prison of the Seven Towers. This barbarous custom, at which even savages would blush, is owing to the Turks having always a number of foreign ministers residing amongst them from other courts, whereas they never send any in return. They look upon the ambassadors of Christian princes in no other light than as merchants or consuls; and, having naturally as great a contempt for Christians as they have for Jews, they seldom condescend to observe the laws of nations, in respect to them, unless forced to it; at least, they have hitherto persisted in this barbarous pride.

The famous vizier, Achmet Couprougli, the same who took the island of Candia, under Mahomet IV., insulted the son of the French ambassador, and even carried his brutality so far as to strike him, and afterwards to confine him in prison, without Lewis XIV., proud and lofty as he was, daring to resent it, otherwise than by sending another minister to the Porte. The Christian princes, who are so remarkably delicate on the point of honour amongst themselves, and have even made it a part of the law of nations, seem to be utterly insensible on this head in regard to the Turks.

Never did a crowned head suffer greater affronts in the persons of his ministers, than czar Peter. In the space of a few years, his ambassador at the court of London was thrown into jail for debt, his plenipotentiary at the courts of Poland and Saxony was broke upon the wheel, by order of the king of Sweden; and now his minister at the Ottoman Porte was seized and thrown into a dungeon at Constantinople, like a common felon.[84]

We have already observed, in the first part of this history, that he received satisfaction from queen Anne, of England, for the insult offered to his ambassador at London. The horrible affront he suffered, in the person of Patkul, was washed away in the blood of the Swedes slain at the battle of Pultowa; but fortune permitted the violation of the law of nations by the Turks to pass unpunished.

Jan. 1711.] The czar now found himself obliged to quit the theatre of war in the west, and march towards the frontiers of Turkey. He began by causing ten regiments, which he had in Poland, to advance towards Moldavia.[85] He then ordered marshal Sheremeto to set out from Livonia, with his body of forces; and, leaving prince Menzikoff at the head of affairs at Petersburg, he returned to Moscow, to give orders for opening the ensuing campaign.

Jan. 18.] He now establishes a senate of regency: the regiment of guards begin their march, he issues orders for all the young nobility to follow him to the field, to learn the art of war, and places some of them in the station of cadets, and others in that of subaltern officers. Admiral Apraxin goes to Azoph to take the command by sea and land. These several measures being taken, the czar publishes an ordonnance in Moscow for acknowledging a new empress. This was the person who had been taken prisoner in Marienburg, in the year 1702. Peter had, in 1696, repudiated his wife Eudoxia Lopoukin (or Lapouchin) by whom he had two children. The laws of his church allow ofno divorces; but, had they not, Peter would have enacted a new law to permit them.

The fair captive of Marienburg, who had taken the name of Catherine, had a soul superior to her sex and her misfortunes. She rendered herself so agreeable to the czar, that this prince would have her always near his person. She accompanied him in all his excursions, and most fatiguing campaigns: sharing in his toils, and softening his uneasiness by her natural gaiety, and the great attention she shewed to oblige him on all occasions, and the indifference she expressed for the luxury, dress, and other indulgences, of which the generality of her sex are, in other countries, wont to make real necessities. She frequently softened the passionate temper of the czar, and, by making him more clement and merciful, rendered him more truly great. In a word, she became so necessary to him, that he married her privately, in 1707. He had already two daughters by her, and the following year she bore him a third, who was afterwards married to the duke of Holstein.[86]

March 17, 1711.] The czar made this private marriage known the very day he set out with her to try the fortune of his arms against the Turks. The several dispositions he had made seemed to promise a successful issue. The hetman of the Cossacks was to keep the Tartars in awe, who had already began to commit ravages in the Ukraine. The main body of the Russian army was advancing towards Niester, and another body of troops, under prince Galitzin, were in full march through Poland. Every thing went on favourably at the beginning: for Galitzin having met with a numerous body of Tartars near Kiow, who had been joined by some Cossacks and some Poles of king Stanislaus' party, as also a few Swedes, he defeated them entirely, and killed near five thousand men. These Tartars had, in their march through the open country, made about ten thousand prisoners. It has been the custom of the Tartars, time immemorial, to carry with them a much greater number of cords than scimitars, in order to bind the unhappy wretches they surprise. The captives were all set free, and those who had made them prisoners were put to the sword. The whole Russian army, if it had been assembled together, would have amounted to sixty thousand men. It was to have been farther augmented by the troops belonging to the king of Poland. This prince, who owed every thing to the czar, came to pay him a visit at Jaroslaw, on the river Sana, the 3d of June, 1714, and promised him powerful succours. War was now declared against the Turks, in the name of these two monarchs: but the Polish diet, not willing to break with the Ottoman Porte, refused to ratify the engagement their king had entered into. It was the fate of the czar to have, in the king of Poland, an ally who could never be of any service to him. He entertained the same hopes of assistance from the princes of Moldavia and Walachia, and was, in the like manner, disappointed.

These two provinces ought to have taken this opportunity to shake off the Turkish yoke. These countries were those of the ancient Daci, who, together with the Gepidi, with whom they were intermixed, did, for a long time, disturb the Roman empire. They were at length subdued by the emperor Trajan, and Constantine the First made them embrace the Christian religion. Dacia was one of the provinces of the eastern empire; but shortly after these very people contributed to the ruin of that of the west, by serving under the Odoacers and Theodorics.

They afterwards continued to be subject to the Greek empire; and when the Turks made themselves masters of Constantinople, were governed and oppressed by particular princes; at length they were totally subjected by the Padisha, or Turkish emperor, who now granted them an investiture. The Hospodar, or Waiwod, chosen by the Ottoman Porte to govern these provinces, is always a Christian of the Greek church. The Turks, by this choice, give a proof of their toleration, while our ignorant declaimers are accusing them of persecution. The prince, nominated by the Porte, is tributary to, or rather farms these countries of the grand seignior; this dignity being always conferred on the best bidder, or him who makes the greatest presents to the vizier, in like manner as the Greek patriarch, at Constantinople. Sometimes this government is bestowed on a dragoman, that is to say, the interpreter to the divan. These provinces are seldom under the government of the same Waiwod, the Porte choosing to divide them, in order to be more sure of retaining them in subjection. Demetrius Cantemir was at this time Waiwod of Moldavia. This prince was said to be descended from Tamerlane, because Tamerlane's true name was Timur, and Timur was a Tartarian khan; and so, from the name Tamurkan, say they, came the family of Cantemir.

Bassaraba Brancovan had been invested with the principality of Walachia, but had not found any genealogist to deduce his pedigree from the Tartarian conqueror. Cantemir thought the time now come to shake off the Turkish yoke, and render himself independent by means of the czar's protection. In this view he acted in the very same manner with Peter as Mazeppa had done with Charles XII. He even engaged Bassaraba for the present to join him in the conspiracy, of which he hoped to reap all the benefit himself: his plan being to make himself master of both provinces. The bishop of Jerusalem, who was at that time at Walachia, was the soul of this conspiracy. Cantemir promised the czar to furnish him with men and provisions, as Mazeppa did the king of Sweden, and kept his word no better than he had done.

General Sheremeto advanced towards Jassi, the capital of Moldavia, to inspect and occasionally assist the execution of these great projects. Cantemir came thither to meet him, and was received with all the honours due to a prince: but he acted as a prince in no one circumstance, but that of publishing a manifesto against the Turkish empire. The hospodar of Walachia, who soon discovered the ambitious views of his colleague, quitted his party, and returned to his duty. The bishop of Jerusalem dreading, with reason, the punishment due to his perfidy, fled and concealed himself: the people of Walachia and Moldavia continued faithful to the Ottoman Porte, and those, who were to have furnished provisions for the Russian army, carried them to the Turks.

The vizier, Baltagi Mahomet had already crossed the Danube, at the head of one hundred thousand men, and was advancing towards Jassi, along the banks of the river Pruth (formerly the Hierasus), which falls into the Danube, and which is nearly the boundary of Moldavia and Bessarabia. He then dispatched count Poniatowsky,[87] a Polish gentleman, attached to the fortunes of the king of Sweden, to desire that prince to make him a visit, and see his army. Charles, whose pride always got the better of his interest, would not consent to this proposal: he insisted that the grand vizier should make him the first visit, in his asylum near Bender. When Poniatowsky returned to the Ottoman camp, and endeavoured to excuse this refusal of his master, the vizier, turning to the khan of the Tartars, said, 'This is the very behaviour I expected from this proud pagan.' This mutual pride, which never fails of alienating the minds of those in power from each other, did no service to the king of Sweden's affairs; and indeed that prince might have easily perceived, from the beginning, that the Turks were not acting for his interest, but for their own.

While the Turkish army was passing the Danube, the czar advanced by the frontiers of Poland, and passed the Boristhenes, in order to relieve marshal Sheremeto, who was then on the banks of the Pruth, to the southward of Jassi, and in danger of being daily surrounded by an army of ten thousand Turks, and an army of Tartars. Peter, before he passed the Boristhenes, was in doubt whether he should expose his beloved Catherine to these dangers, which seemed to increase every day; but Catherine, on her side, looked upon this solicitude of the czar, for her ease and safety, as an affront offered to her love and courage; and pressed her consort so strongly on this head, that he found himself under a necessity to consent that she should pass the river with him. The army beheld her with eyes of joy and admiration, marching on horseback at the head of the troops, for she rarely made use of a carriage. After passing the Boristhenes, they had a tract of desert country to pass through, and then to cross the Bog, and afterwards the river Tiras, now called the Niester, and then another desert to traverse, before they came to the banks of the Pruth. Catherine, during this fatiguing march, animated the whole army by her cheerfulness and affability. She sent refreshments to such of the officers who were sick, and extended her care even to the meanest soldier.

July 4, 1711.] At length the czar brought his army in sight of Jassi. Here he was to establish his magazine. Bassaraba, the hospodar of Walachia, who had again embraced the interest of the Ottoman Porte, but still, in appearance, continued a friend to the czar, proposed to that prince to make peace with the Turks, although he had received no commission from the grand vizier for that purpose. His deceit, however, was soon discovered; and the czar contented himself with demanding only provisions for his army, which Bassaraba neither could nor would furnish. It was very difficult to procure any supplies from Poland; and these, which prince Cantemir had promised, and which he vainly hoped to procure from Walachia, could not be brought from thence. These disappointments rendered the situation of the Russian army very disagreeable; and, as an addition to their afflictions, they were infested with an immense swarm of grasshoppers, that covered the face of the whole country, and devoured, or spoiled, every thing where they alighted. They were likewise frequently in want of water during their march through sandy deserts, and beneath a scorching sun: what little they could procure, they were obliged to have brought in vessels to the camp, from a considerable distance.

During this dangerous and fatiguing march, the czar, by a singular fatality, found himself in the neighbourhood of his rival and competitor, Charles; Bender not being above twenty-five leagues from the place where the Russian army was encamped, near Jassi. Some parties of Cossacks made excursions even to the place of that unfortunate monarch's retreat; but the Crim Tartars, who hovered round that part of the country, sufficiently secured him from any attempt that might be made to seize his person; and Charles waited in his camp with impatience, and did not fear the issue of the war.

Peter, as soon as he had established some magazines, marched in haste with his army to the right of the river Pruth. His essential object was to prevent the Turks, who were posted to the left, and towards the head of the river, from crossing it, and marching towards him. This effected, he would then be master of Moldavia and Walachia: with this view, he dispatched general Janus, with the vanguard of the army, to oppose the passage of the Turks; but the general did not arrive till they had already began to cross the river upon their bridges; upon which he was obliged to retreat, and his infantry was closely pursued by the Turks, till the czar came up in person to his assistance.

The grand vizier now marched directly along the river towards the czar. The two armies were very unequal in point of numbers: that of the Turks, which had been reinforced by the Tartarian troops, consisted of nearly two hundred and fifty thousand men, while that of the Russians hardly amounted to thirty-five thousand. There was indeed a considerable body of troops, headed by general Renne, on their march from the other side of the Moldavian mountains; but the Turks had cut off all communication with those parts.

The czar's army now began to be in want of provisions, nor could, without the greatest difficulty, procure water, though encamped at a very small distance from the river; being exposed to a furious discharge from the batteries, which the grand vizier had caused to be erected on the left side of the river, under the care of a body of troops, that kept up a constant fire against the Russians. By this relation, which is strictly circumstantial and true, it appears that Baltagi Mahomet, the Turkish vizier, far from being the pusillanimous, or weak commander, which the Swedes have represented him, gave proofs, on this occasion, that he perfectly well understood his business. The passing the Pruth in the sight of the enemy, obliging him to retreat, and harassing him in that retreat; the cutting off all communication between the czar's army, and a body of cavalry that was marching to reinforce it; the hemming in this army, without the least probability of a retreat; and the cutting off all supplies of water and provisions, by keeping it constantly under the check of the batteries on the opposite side of the river, were manœuvres that in no ways bespoke the unexperienced or indolent general.

Peter now saw himself in a situation even worse than that to which he had reduced his rival, Charles XII. at Pultowa; being, like him, surrounded by a superior army, and in greater want of provisions; and, like him, having confided in the promises of a prince, too powerful to be bound by those promises, he resolved upon a retreat; and endeavoured to return towards Jassi, in order to choose a more advantageous situation for his camp.

July 20, 1711.] He accordingly decamped under favour of the night; but his army had scarcely begun its march, when, at break of day, the Turks fell upon his rear: but the Preobrazinski regiment turning about, and standing firm, did, for a considerable time, check the fury of their onset. The Russians then formed themselves, and made a line of intrenchments with their waggons and baggage. The same day (July 21.) the Turks returned again to the attack, with the whole body of their army; and, as a proof that the Russians knew how to defend themselves, let what will be alleged to the contrary, they also made head against this very superior force for a considerable time, killed a great number of their enemies, who in vain endeavoured to break in upon them.

There were in the Ottoman army two officers belonging to the king of Sweden, namely, count Poniatowsky and the count of Sparre, who had the command of a body of Cossacks in that prince's interest. My papers inform me, that these two generals advised the grand vizier to avoid coming to action with the Russians, and content himself with depriving them of supplies of water and provisions, which would oblige them either to surrender prisoners of war, or to perish with famine. Other memoirs pretend, on the contrary, that these officers would have persuaded Mahomet to fall upon this feeble and half-starved army, in a weak and distressed condition, and put all to the sword. The first of these seems to be the most prudent and circumspect; but the second is more agreeable to the character of generals who had been trained up under Charles XII.

The real fact is, that the grand vizier fell upon the rear of the Russian army, at the dawn of day, which was thrown into confusion, and there remained only a line of four hundred men to confront the Turks. This small body formed itself with amazing quickness, under the orders of a German general, named Alard, who, to his immortal honour, made such rapid and excellent dispositions on this occasion, that the Russians withstood, for upwards of three hours, the repeated attack of the whole Ottoman army, without losing a foot of ground.

The czar now found himself amply repaid for the immense pains he had taken to inure his troops to strict discipline. At the battle of Narva, sixty thousand men were defeated by only eight thousand, because the former were undisciplined; and here we behold a rear-guard, consisting of only eight thousand Russians, sustaining the efforts of one hundred and fifty thousand Turks, killing seven thousand of them, and obliging the rest to return back.

After this sharp engagement, both armies intrenched themselves for that night: but the Russians still continued enclosed, and deprived of all provisions, even water; for notwithstanding they were so near the river Pruth, yet they did not dare approach its banks; for as soon as any parties were sent out to find water, a body of Turks, posted on the opposite shore, drove them back by a furious discharge from their cannon, loaded with chain shot: and the body of the Turkish army, which had attacked that of the czar the day before, continued to play upon them from another quarter, with the whole force of their artillery.

The Russian army appeared now to be lost beyond resource, by its position, by the inequality of numbers, and by the want of provisions. The skirmishes on both sides were frequent and bloody: the Russian cavalry being almost all dismounted, could no longer be of any service, unless by fighting on foot: in a word, the situation of affairs was desperate. It was out of their power to retreat, they had nothing left but to gain a complete victory; to perish to the last man, or to be made slaves by the infidels.

All the accounts and memoirs of those times unanimously agree, that the czar, divided within himself, whether or not he should expose his wife, his army, his empire, and the fruits of all his labours, to almost inevitable destruction; retired to his tent, oppressed with grief, and seized with violent convulsions, to which he was naturally subject, and which the present desperate situation of his affairs brought upon him with redoubled violence. In this condition he remained alone in his tent, having given positive orders, that no one should be admitted to be a witness to the distraction of his mind. But Catherine, hearing of his disorders, forced her way in to him; and, on this occasion, Peter found how happy it was for him that he had permitted his wife to accompany him in this expedition.

A wife, who, like her, had faced death in its most horrible shapes, and had exposed her person, like the meanest soldier, to the fire of the Turkish artillery, had an undoubted right to speak to her husband, and to be heard. The czar accordingly listened to what she had to say, and in the end suffered himself to be persuaded to try and send to the vizier with proposals of peace.

It has been a custom, from time immemorial, throughout the East, that when any people apply for an audience of the sovereign, or his representative, they must not presume to approach them without a present. On this occasion, therefore, Catherine mustered the few jewels that she had brought with her, on this military tour, in which no magnificence or luxury were admitted; to these she added two black foxes' skins, and what ready money she could collect; the latter was designed for a present to the kiaia. She made choice herself of an officer, on whose fidelity and understanding she thought she could depend, who, accompanied with two servants, was to carry the presents to the grand vizier, and afterwards to deliver the money intended for the kiaia into his own hand. This officer was likewise charged with a letter from marshal Sheremeto to the grand vizier. The memoirs of czar Peter mentions this letter, but they take no notice of the other particulars of Catherine's conduct in this business; however, they are sufficiently confirmed by the declaration issued by Peter himself, in 1723, when he caused Catherine to be crowned empress, wherein we find these words:—'She has been of the greatest assistance to us in all our dangers, and particularly in the battle of Pruth, when our army was reduced to twenty-two thousand men.' If the czar had then indeed no more men capable of bearing arms, the service which Catherine did him, on that occasion, was fully equivalent to the honours and dignities conferred upon her. The MS.

journal of Peter the Great observes, that on the day of the bloody battle (on the 20th July), he had thirty-one thousand five hundred and fifty-four foot, and six thousand six hundred and ninety-two horse, the latter almost all dismounted; he must then have lost sixteen thousand two hundred and forty- six men in that engagement. The same memoirs affirm, the loss sustained by the Turks greatly exceeded that of the Russians; for as the former rushed upon the czar's troops pell-mell, and without observing any order, hardly a single fire of the latter missed its effect. If this is fact, the affair of the 20th and 21st of July, was one of the most bloody that had been known for many ages.

We must either suspect Peter the Great of having been mistaken, in his declaration at the crowning of the empress, when he acknowledges 'his obligations to her of having saved his army, which was reduced to twenty-two thousand men,' or accuse him of a falsity in his journal, wherein he says, that the day on which the above battle was fought, his army, exclusive of the succours he expected from the other side the Moldavian mountains, amounted to thirty-one thousand five hundred and fifty-four foot, and six thousand six hundred and ninety-two horse. According to this calculation, the battle of Pruth must have been by far more terrible than the historians or memorials have represented on either side. There must certainly be some mistake here, which is no uncommon thing in the relation of campaigns, especially when the writer enters into a minute detail of circumstances. The surest method, therefore, on these occasions, is to confine ourselves to the principal events, the victory and the defeat; as we can very seldom know, with any degree of certainty, the exact loss on either side.

But however here the Russian army might be reduced in point of numbers, there were still hopes that the grand vizier, deceived by their vigorous and obstinate resistance, might be induced to grant them peace, upon such terms as might be honourable to his master's arms, and at the same time not absolutely disgraceful to those of the czar. It was the great merit of Catherine to have perceived this possibility, at a time when her consort and his generals expected nothing less than inevitable destruction.

Norberg, in his History of Charles XII. quotes a letter, sent by the czar to the grand vizier, in which he expresses himself thus:—'If, contrary to my intentions, I have been so unhappy as to incur the displeasure of his highness, I am ready to make reparation for any cause of complaint he may have against me; I conjure you, most noble general, to prevent the further effusion of blood; give orders, I beseech you, to put a stop to the dreadful fire of your artillery, and accept the hostage I herewith send you.'

This letter carries all the marks of falsity with it, as do indeed most of the random pieces of Norberg: it is dated 11th July, N. S. whereas no letter was sent to Baltagi Mahomet till the 21st, N. S. neither was it the czar who wrote to the vizier, but his general Sheremeto: there were no such expressions made use of as—'if the czar has had the misfortune to incur the displeasure of his highness;' such terms being suitable only to a subject, who implores the pardon of his sovereign, whom he has offended. There was no mention made of any hostage, nor was any one sent. The letter was carried by an officer, in the midst of a furious cannonade on both sides. Sheremeto, in his letter, only reminded the vizier of certain overtures of peace that the Porte had made at the beginning of the campaign, through the mediation of the Dutch and English ministers, and by which the divan demanded that the fort and harbour of Taganroc should be given up, which were the real subjects of the war.

21st July, 1711.] Some hours elapsed before the messenger received an answer from the grand vizier, and it was apprehended that he had either been killed by the enemy's cannon, or that they detained him prisoner. A second courier was therefore dispatched, with duplicates of the former letters, and a council of war was immediately held, at which Catherine was present. At this council ten general officers signed the following resolution:—

'Resolved, If the enemy will not accept the conditions proposed, and should insist upon our laying down our arms, and surrendering at discretion, that all the ministers and general officers are unanimously of opinion, to cut their way through the enemy sword in hand.'

In consequence of this resolution, a line of intrenchments was thrown round the baggage, and the Russians marched some few paces out of their camp, towards the enemy, when the grand vizier caused a suspension of arms to be proclaimed between the two armies.

All the writers of the Swedish party have treated the grand vizier as a cowardly and infamous wretch, who had been bribed to sell the honour of his master's arms. In the same manner have several authors accused count Piper of receiving money from the duke of Marlborough, to persuade the king of Sweden to continue the war against the czar; and have laid to the charge of the French minister, that he purchased the peace of Seville for a stipulated sum. Such accusations ought never to be advanced but on very strong proofs. It is very seldom that a minister will stoop to such meannesses, which are always discovered, sooner or later, by those who have been entrusted with the payment of the money, or by the public registers, which never lie. A minister of state stands as a public object to the eyes of all Europe. His credit and influence depend wholly upon his character, and he is always sufficiently rich to be above the temptation of becoming a traitor.

The place of viceroy of the Turkish empire is so illustrious, and the profits annexed to it, in time of war, so immense, there was such a profusion of every thing necessary, and even luxurious, in the camp of Baltagi Mahomet, and, on the other hand, so much poverty and distress in that of the czar, that surely the grand vizier was rather in a condition to give than to receive. The trifling present of a woman, who had nothing to send but a few skins and some jewels, in compliance with the established custom of all courts, or rather those in particular of the East, can never be considered in the light of a bribe. The frank and open conduct of Baltagi Mahomet seems at once to give the lie to the black accusations with which so many writers have stained their relations. Vice chancellor Shaffiroff paid the vizier a public visit in his tent: every thing was transacted in the most open manner, on both sides; and indeed it could not be otherwise. The very first article of the negotiation was entered upon in the presence of a person wholly devoted to the king of Sweden, a domestic of count Poniatowsky, who was himself one of that monarch's generals. This man served as an interpreter, and the several articles were publicly reduced to writing by the vizier's chief secretary, Hummer Effendi. Moreover, count Poniatowsky was there in person. The present sent to the kiaia was offered probably in form, and every thing was transacted agreeable to the oriental customs. Other presents were made by the Turks in return; so that there was not the least appearance of treachery or contrivance. The motives which determined the vizier to consent to the proposals offered him, were, first that the body of troops under the command of general Renne, on the borders of the river Sireth, in Moldavia, had already crossed three rivers, and were actually in the neighbourhood of the Danube, where Renne had already made himself master of the town and castle of Brahila, defended by a numerous garrison, under the command of a basha. Secondly, the czar had likewise another body of troops advancing through the frontiers of Poland; and, lastly, it is more than probable that the vizier was not fully acquainted with the extreme scarcity that was felt in the Russian camp. One enemy seldom furnishes another with an exact account of his provisions and ammunition; on the contrary, either side are accustomed rather to make a parade of plenty, even at a time when they are in the greatest necessity. There can be no artifices practised to gain intelligence of the true state of an adversary's affairs, by means of spies, between the Turks and the Russians. The difference of their dress, of their religion, and of their language, will not permit it. They are, moreover, strangers to that desertion which prevails in most of our armies; and, consequently, the grand vizier could not be supposed to know the desperate condition to which the czar's army was reduced.

Baltagi, who was not fond of war, and who, nevertheless, had conducted this very well, thought that his expedition would be sufficiently successful, if he put his master in possession of the towns and harbours which made the subject of the war, stopt the progress of the victorious army under Renne, and obliged that general to quit the banks of the Danube, and return back into Russia, and for ever shut the entrance of the Palus Mæotis, the Cimmerian Bosphorus, and the Black Sea, against an enterprising prince; and, lastly, if he avoided taking these certain advantages, on the hazard of a new battle (in which, after all, despair might have got the better of superiority of numbers). The preceding day only he had beheld his janissaries repulsed with loss; and there wanted not examples of many victories having been gained by the weaker over the strong. Such then were Mahomet's reasons for accepting the proposals of peace. His conduct, however, did not merit the approbation of Charles's officers, who served in the Turkish army, nor of the khan of Tartary. It was the interest of the latter, and his followers, to reject all terms of accommodation which would deprive them of the opportunity of ravaging the frontiers of Russia and Poland. Charles XII. desired to be revenged on his rival, the czar: but the general, and the first minister of the Ottoman empire, was neither influenced by the private thirst of revenge, which animated the Christian monarch, nor by the desire of booty, which actuated the Tartar chief.

As soon as the suspension of arms was agreed to, and signed, the Russians purchased of the Turks the provisions, of which they stood in need. The articles of the peace were not signed at that time, as is related by La Motraye, and which Norberg has copied from him. The vizier, among other conditions, demanded that the czar should promise not to interfere any more in the Polish affairs. This was a point particularly insisted upon by count Poniatowsky; but it was, in fact, the interest of the Ottoman crown, that the kingdom of Poland should continue in its then defenceless and divided state; accordingly this demand was reduced to that of the Russian troops evacuating the frontiers of Poland. The khan of Tartary, on his side, demanded a tribute of forty thousand sequins. This point, after being long debated, was at length given up.

The grand vizier insisted a long time, that prince Cantemir should be delivered up to him, as Patkul had been to the king of Sweden. Cantemir was exactly in the same situation as Mazeppa had been. The czar caused that hetman to be arraigned and tried for his defection, and afterwards to be executed in effigy. The Turks were not acquainted with the nature of such proceeding; they knew nothing of trials for contumacy, nor of public condemnations. The affixing a sentence on any person, and executing him in effigy, were the more unusual amongst them, as their law forbids the representation of any human likeness whatever. The vizier in vain insisted on Cantemir's being delivered up; Peter peremptorily refused to comply, and wrote the following letter with his own hand, to his vice-chancellor Shaffiroff.

'I can resign to the Turks all the country, as far as Curtzka, because I have hopes of being able to recover it again; but I will, by no means, violate my faith, which, once forfeited, can never be retrieved. I have nothing I can properly call my own, but my honour. If I give up that, I cease to be longer a king.'

At length the treaty was concluded, and signed, at a village called Falksen, on the river Pruth. Among other things, it was stipulated, that Azoph, and the territories belonging thereto, should be restored, together with all the ammunition and artillery that were in the place, before the czar made himself master thereof, in 1696. That the harbour of Taganroc, in the Zabach Sea, should be demolished, as also that of Samara, on the river of the same name; and several other fortresses. There was likewise another article added, respecting the king of Sweden, which article alone, sufficiently shews the little regard the vizier had for that prince; for it was therein stipulated, that the czar should not molest Charles, in his return to his dominions, and that afterwards the czar and he might make peace with the other, if they were so inclined.

It is pretty evident by the wording of this extraordinary article, that Baltagi Mahomet had not forgot the haughty manner in which Charles XII. had behaved to him a short time before, and it is not unlikely that this very behaviour of the king of Sweden might have been one inducement with Mahomet to comply so readily with his rival's proposals for peace. Charles's glory depended wholly on the ruin of the czar: but we are seldom inclinable to exalt those who express a contempt for us: however, this prince, who refused the vizier a visit in his camp, on his invitation, when it was certainly his interest to have been upon good terms with him, now came thither in haste and unasked, when the work which put an end to all his hopes was on the point of being concluded. The vizier did not go to meet him in person, but contented himself with sending two of his bashas, nor would he stir out of his tent, till Charles was within a few paces of him.

This interview passed, as every one knows, in mutual reproaches. Several historians have thought, that the answer which the vizier made to the king of Sweden, when that prince reproached him with not making the czar prisoner, when he might have done it so easily, was the reply of a weak man. 'If I had taken him prisoner,' said Mahomet, 'who would there be to govern his dominions?'

It is very easy, however, to comprehend, that this was the answer of a man who was piqued with resentment, and these words which he added—'For it is not proper that every crowned head should quit his dominions'—sufficiently shewed that he intended to mortify the refugee of Bender.

Charles gained nothing by his journey, but the pleasure of tearing the vizier's robe with his spurs; while that officer, who was in a condition to make him repent this splenetic insult, seemed not to notice it, in which he was certainly greatly superior to Charles. If any thing could have made that monarch sensible, in the midst of his life, how easily fortune can put greatness to the blush, it would have been the reflection, that at the battle of Pultowa, a pastry-cook's boy had obliged his whole army to surrender at discretion; and in this of Pruth a wood-cutter was the arbiter of his fate, and that of his rival the czar: for the vizier, Baltagi Mahomet, had been a cutter of wood in the grand seignior's seraglio, as his name implied; and, far from being ashamed of that title, he gloried in it: so much do the manners of the eastern people differ from ours.

When the news of this treaty reached Constantinople, the grand seignior was so well pleased, that he ordered public rejoicings to be made for a whole week, and Mahomet, the kiaia, or lieutenant-general, who brought the tidings to the divan, was instantly raised to the dignity of boujouk imraour, or master of the horse: a certain proof that the sultan did not think himself ill served by his vizier.

Norberg seems to have known very little of the Turkish government, when he says, that 'the grand seignior was obliged to keep fair with Baltagi Mahomet, that vizier having rendered himself formidable.' The janissaries indeed have often rendered themselves formidable to their sultans; but there is not one example of a vizier, who has not been easily sacrificed to the will or orders of his sovereign, and Mahomet was in no condition to support himself by his own power. Besides, Norberg manifestly contradicts himself, by affirming in the same page, that the janissaries were irritated against Mahomet, and that the sultan stood in dread of his power.

The king of Sweden was now reduced to the necessity of forming cabals in the Ottoman court; and a monarch, who had so lately made kings by his own power, was now seen waiting for audience, and offering memorials and petitions which were refused.

Charles ran through all the ambages of intrigue, like a subject who endeavours to make a minister suspected by his master. In this manner he acted against Mahomet, and against those who succeeded him. At one time he addressed himself to the sultana Valide by means of a Jewess, who had admission into the seraglio; at another, he employed one of the eunuchs for the same purpose. At length he had recourse to a man who was to mingle among the grand seignior's guards, and, by counterfeiting a person out of his senses, to attract the attention of the sultan, and by that means deliver into his own hand a memorial from Charles. From all these various schemes, the king of Sweden drew only the mortification of seeing himself deprived of his thaim; that is to say, of the daily pension which the Porte of its generosity had assigned him for his subsistence, and which amounted to about one thousand five hundred French livres.[88] The grand vizier, instead of remitting this allowance to him as usual, sent him an order, in the form of a friendly advice, to quit the grand seignior's dominions.

Charles, however, was absolutely determined not to depart, still flattering himself with the vain hope, that he should once more re-enter Poland and Russia with a powerful army of Turks. Every one knows what was the issue of his inflexible boldness in the year 1714, and how he engaged an army of janissaries, Spahis, and Tartars, with only himself, his secretaries, his valet de chambre, cook, and stable men; that he was taken prisoner in that country, where he had been treated with the greatest hospitality; and that he at length got back to his own kingdom in the disguise of a courier, after having lived five years in Turkey: from all which it remains to be acknowledged, that if there was reason in the conduct of this extraordinary prince, it was a reason of a very different nature to that of other men.

CHAP. XXI.

Conclusion of the Affairs of Pruth.

It is necessary in this place to repeat an event already related in the History of Charles XII. It happened during the suspension of arms which preceded the treaty of Pruth, that two Tartarian soldiers surprised and took prisoners two Italian officers belonging to the czar's army, and sold them to an officer of the Turkish janissaries. The vizier being informed of this breach of public faith, punished the two Tartars with death. How are we to reconcile this severe delicacy with the violation of the law of nations in the person of Tolstoy, the czar's ambassador, whom this very vizier caused to be arrested in the streets of Constantinople, and afterwards imprisoned in the castle of the Seven Towers? There is always some reason for the contradictions we find in the actions of mankind. Baltagi Mahomet was incensed against the khan of Tartary, for having opposed the peace he had lately made, and was resolved to shew that chieftain that he was his master.

The treaty was no sooner concluded, than the czar quitted the borders of the Pruth, and returned towards his own dominions, followed by a body of eight thousand Turks, whom the vizier had sent as an army of observation to watch the motions of the Russian army during its march, and also to serve as an escort or safeguard to them against the wandering Tartars which infested those parts.

Peter instantly set about accomplishing the treaty, by demolishing the fortresses of Samara and Kamienska; but the restoring of Azoph, and the demolition of the port of Taganroc, met with some difficulties in the execution. According to the terms of the treaty it was necessary to distinguish the artillery and ammunition which belonged to the Turks in Azoph before that place was taken by the czar, from those which had been sent thither after it fell into his hands. The governor of the place spun out this affair to a tedious length, at which the Porte was greatly incensed, and not without reason: the sultan was impatient to receive the keys of Azoph. The vizier promised they should be sent from time to time, but the governor always found means to delay the delivery of them. Baltagi Mahomet lost the good graces of his master, and with them his place. The khan of Tartary and his other enemies made such good use of their interest with the sultan, that the grand vizier was deposed, several bashas were disgraced at the same time; but the grand seignior, well convinced of this minister's fidelity, did not deprive him either of his life or estate, but only sent him to Mytilene to take on him the command of that island. This simple removal from the helm of affairs (Nov. 1711,), and the continuing to him his fortunes, and above all the giving him the command in Mytilene, sufficiently contradicts all that Norberg has advanced, to induce us to believe that this vizier had been corrupted with the czar's money.

Norberg asserts furthermore, that the Bostangi basha, who came to divest him of his office, and to acquaint him of the grand seignior's sentence, declared him at the same time, 'a traitor, one who had disobeyed the orders of his sovereign lord, had sold himself to the enemy for money, and was found guilty of not having taken proper care of the interests of the king of Sweden.' In the first place, this kind of declarations are not at all in use in Turkey: the orders of the grand seignior always being issued privately, and executed with secresy. Secondly, if the vizier had been declared a traitor, a rebel, and a corrupted person, crimes of this nature would have been instantly punished with death in a country where they are never forgiven. Lastly, if he was punishable for not having sufficiently attended to the interests of the king of Sweden, it is evident that this prince must have had such a degree of influence at the Ottoman Porte, as to have made the other ministers to tremble, who would consequently have endeavoured to gain his good graces; whereas, on the contrary, the basha Jussuf, aga of the janissaries, who succeeded Mahomet Baltagi as grand vizier, had the same sentiments as his predecessor, in relation to Charles's conduct, and was so far from doing him any service that he thought of nothing but how to get rid of so dangerous a guest; and when count Poniatowsky, the companion and confidant of that monarch, went to compliment the vizier on his new dignity, the latter spoke to him thus. 'Pagan, I forewarn thee, that if ever I find thee hatching any intrigues, I will, upon the first notice, cause thee to be thrown into the sea with a stone about thy neck.'

This compliment count Poniatowsky himself relates in the memoirs which he drew up at my request, and is a sufficient proof of the little influence his master had in the Turkish court. All that Norberg has related touching the affairs of that empire, appear to come from a prejudiced person, and one who was very ill informed of the circumstances he pretends to write about. And we may count among the errors of a party-spirit and political falsehoods, every thing which this writer advances unsupported by proofs, concerning the pretended corruption of a grand vizier, that is, of a person who had the disposal of upwards of sixty millions per annum, without being subject to the least account.[89] I have now before me the letter which count Poniatowsky wrote to King Stanislaus immediately after the signing the treaty of Pruth, in which he upbraids Baltagi Mahomet with the slight he shewed to the king of Sweden, his dislike to the war, and the unsteadiness of his temper; but never once hints the least charge of corruption: for he knew too well what the place of grand vizier was, to entertain an idea, that the czar was capable of setting a price upon the infidelity of the second person in the Ottoman empire.

Schaffirow and Sheremeto, who remained at Constantinople as hostages on the part of the czar for his performance of the treaty, were not used in the manner they would have been if known to have purchased this peace, and to have joined with the vizier in deceiving his master. They were left to go at liberty about the city, escorted by two companies of janissaries.

The czar's ambassador Tolstoy having been released from his confinement in the Seven Towers, immediately upon the signing of the treaty of Pruth, the Dutch and English ministers interposed with the new vizier to see the several articles of that treaty put into execution.

Azoph was at length restored to the Turks, and the fortresses mentioned in the treaty were demolished according to stipulation. And now the Ottoman Porte, though very little inclinable to interfere in the differences between Christian princes, could not without vanity behold himself made arbitrator between Russia, Poland, and the king of Sweden; and insisted that the czar should withdraw his troops out of Poland, and deliver the Turkish empire from so dangerous a neighbour; and, desirous that the Christian princes might continually be at war with each other, wished for nothing so much as to send Charles home to his own dominions, but all this while had not the least intention of furnishing him with an army. The Tartars were still for war, as an artificer is willing to seize every opportunity to exercise his calling. The janissaries likewise wished to be called into the field, but more out of hatred against the Christians, their naturally restless disposition, and from a fondness for rapine and licentiousness, than from any other motives. Nevertheless, the English and Dutch ministers managed their negotiations so well, that they prevailed over the opposite party: the treaty of Pruth was confirmed, but with the addition of a new article, by which it was stipulated that the czar should withdraw his forces from Poland within three months, and that the sultan should immediately send Charles XII. out of his dominions.

We may judge from this new treaty whether the king of Sweden had that interest at the Porte which some writers would have us to believe. He was evidently sacrificed on this occasion by the new vizier, basha Jussuf, as he had been before by Baltagi Mahomet. The historians of his party could find no other expedient to colour over this fresh affront, but that of accusing Jussuf of having been bribed like his predecessor. Such repeated imputations, unsupported by any proofs, are rather the clamours of an impotent cabal, than the testimonies of history; but faction, when driven to acknowledge facts, will ever be endeavouring to alter circumstances and motives; and, unhappily, it is thus that all the histories of our times will be handed down to posterity so altered, that they will be unable to distinguish truth from falsehoods.

CHAP. XXII.

Marriage of the czarowitz.—The marriage of Peter and Catherine publicly solemnized.—Catherine finds her brother.

This unsuccessful campaign of Pruth proved more hurtful to the czar than ever the battle of Narva was; for after that defeat he had found means not only to retrieve his losses, but also to wrest Ingria out of the hands of Charles XII.; but by the treaty of Falksten, in which he consented to give up to the sultan his forts and harbours on the Palus Mæotis, he for ever lost his projected superiority in the Black Sea. He had besides an infinite deal of work on his hands; his new establishments in Russia were to be perfected, he had to prosecute his victories over the Swedes, to settle king Augustus firmly on the Polish throne, and to manage affairs properly with the several powers with whom he was in alliance; but the fatigues he had undergone having impaired his health, he was obliged to go to Carlsbad[90] to drink the waters of that place. While he was there he gave orders for his troops to enter Pomerania, who blockaded Stralsund, and took five other towns in the neighbourhood.

Pomerania is the most northern province of Germany, bounded on the east by Prussia and Poland, on the west by Brandenburg, on the south by Mecklenburg, and on the north by the Baltic Sea. It has changed masters almost every century: Gustavus Adolphus got possession of it in his famous thirty years war, and it was afterwards solemnly ceded to the crown of Sweden by the treaty of Westphalia: with a reservation of the little bishopric of Camin, and a few other small towns lying in Upper Pomerania. The whole of this province properly belongs to the elector of Brandenburg, in virtue of a family compact made with the dukes of Pomerania, whose family being extinct in 1637, consequently by the laws of the empire the house of Brandenburg had an undoubted right to the succession; but necessity, the first of all laws, occasioned this family compact to be set aside by the treaty of Osnaburg; after which, almost the whole of Pomerania fell to the lot of the victorious Swedes.

The czar's intention was to wrest from Sweden all the provinces that crown was possessed of in Germany; and, in order to accomplish his design, he found it necessary to enter into a confederacy with the electors of Hanover and Brandenburg, and the king of Denmark. Peter drew up the several articles of the treaty he projected with these powers, and also a complete plan of the necessary operations for rendering him master of Pomerania.

In the meanwhile he went to Torgau, to be present at the nuptials of his son the czarowitz Alexis with the princess of Wolfenbuttel (Oct. 23, 1711.), sister to the consort of Charles VI. emperor of Germany; nuptials which, in the end, proved fatal to his own peace of mind, and to the lives of the unfortunate pair.

The czarowitz was born of the first marriage of Peter the Great to Eudocia Lapoukin, to whom he was espoused in 1689: she was at that time shut up in the monastery of Susdal; their son Alexis Petrowitz, who was born the 1st of March, 1690, was now in his twenty-second year: this prince was not then at all known in Europe; a minister, whose memoirs of the court of Russia have been printed, says in a letter he writes to his master, dated August 25, 1711, that 'this prince was tall and well made, resembled his father greatly, was of an excellent disposition, very pious, had read the Bible five times over, took great delight in the ancient Greek historians, appeared to have a very quick apprehension and understanding, was well acquainted with the mathematics, the art of war, navigation, and hydraulics; that he understood the German language, and was then learning the French, but that his father would never suffer him to go through a regular course of study.'

This character is very different from that which the czar himself gives of his son some time afterwards, in which we shall see with how much grief he reproaches him with faults directly opposite to those good qualities, for which this minister seems so much to admire him.

We must leave posterity, therefore, to determine between the testimony of a stranger, who may have formed too slight a judgment, and the declaration of a parent, who thought himself under a necessity of sacrificing the dictates of nature to the good of his people. If the minister was no better acquainted with the disposition of Alexis than he seems to have been with his outward form, his evidence will have but little weight; for he describes this prince as tall and well made, whereas the memoirs sent me from Petersburg say, that he was neither the one nor the other.

His mother-in-law, Catherine, was not present at his nuptials; for though she was already looked upon as czarina, yet she had not been publicly acknowledged as such: and moreover, as she had only the title of highness given her at the czar's court, her rank was not sufficiently settled to admit of her signing the contract, or to appear at the ceremony in a station befitting the consort of Peter the Great. She therefore remained at Thorn in Polish Prussia. Soon after the nuptials were celebrated, the czar sent the new-married couple away to Wolfenbuttel (Jan. 9, 1712), and brought back the czarina to Petersburg with that dispatch and privacy which he observed in all his journies.

Feb. 19, 1712.] Having now disposed of his son, he publicly solemnized his own nuptials with Catherine, which had been declared in private before. This ceremony was performed with as much magnificence as could be expected in a city but yet in its infancy, and from a revenue exhausted by the late destructive war against the Turks, and that which he was still engaged in against the king of Sweden. The czar gave orders for, and assisted himself in, all the preparations for the ceremony, according to the usual custom; and Catherine was now publicly declared czarina, in reward for having saved her husband and his whole army.

The acclamations with which this declaration was received at Petersburg were sincere: the applauses which subjects confer on the actions of a despotic sovereign are generally suspected; but on this occasion they were confirmed by the united voice of all the thinking part of Europe, who beheld with pleasure, on the one hand, the heir of a vast monarchy with no other glory than that of his birth, married to a petty princess; and, on the other hand, a powerful conqueror, and a law-giver, publicly sharing his bed and his throne with a stranger and a captive, who had nothing to recommend her but her merit: and this approbation became more general as the minds of men grew more enlightened by that sound philosophy, which has made so great a progress in our understandings within these last forty years: a philosophy, equally sublime and discerning, which teaches us to pay only the exterior respect to greatness and authority, while we reserve our esteem and veneration for shining talents and meritorious services.

And here I think myself under an obligation to relate what I have met touching this marriage in the dispatches of count Bassewitz, aulic counsellor at Vienna, and long time minister from Holstein at the court of Russia; a person of great merit, and whose memory is still held in the highest esteem in Germany. In some of his letters he speaks thus: 'The czarina had not only been the main instrument of procuring the czar that reputation which he enjoyed, but was likewise essentially necessary in the preservation of his life. This prince was unhappily subject to violent convulsion fits, which were thought to be the effects of poison which had been given him while he was young. Catherine alone had found the secret of alleviating his sufferings by an unwearied assiduity and attention to whatever she thought would please him, and made it the whole study of her life to preserve a health so valuable to the kingdom and to herself, insomuch, that the czar finding he could not live without her, made her the companion of his throne and bed.' I here only repeat the express words of the writer himself.

Fortune, which has furnished us with many extraordinary scenes in this part of the world, and who had raised Catherine from the lowest abyss of misery and distress to the pinnacle of human grandeur, wrought another extraordinary incident in her favour some few years after her marriage with the czar, and which I find thus related in a curious manuscript of a person who was at that time in the czar's service, and who speaks of it as a thing to which he was eye-witness.

An envoy from king Augustus to the court of Peter the Great, being on his return home through Courland, and having put up at an inn by the way, heard the voice of a person who seemed in great distress, and whom the people of the house were treating in that insulting manner which is but too common on such occasions: the stranger, with a tone of resentment, made answer, that they would not dare to use him thus, if he could but once get to the speech of the czar, at whose court he had perhaps more powerful protectors than they imagined.

The envoy, upon hearing this, had a curiosity to ask the man some questions, and, from certain answers he let fall, and a close examination of his face, he thought he found in him some resemblance of the empress Catherine; and, when he came to Dresden, he could not forbear writing to one of his friends at Petersburg concerning it. This letter, by accident, came to the czar's hands, who immediately sent an order to prince Repnin, then governor of Riga, to endeavour to find out the person mentioned in the letter. Prince Repnin immediately dispatched a messenger to Mittau, in Courland, who, on inquiry, found out the man, and learned that his name was Charles Scavronsky; that he was the son of a Lithuanian gentleman, who had been killed in the wars of Poland, and had left two children then in the cradle, a boy and a girl, who had neither of them received any other education than that which simple nature gives to those who are abandoned by the world. Scavronsky, who had been parted from his sister while they were both infants, knew nothing further of her than that she had been taken prisoner in Marienburg, in the year 1704, and supposed her to be still in the household of prince Menzikoff, where he imagined she might have made some little fortune.

Prince Repnin, agreeable to the particular orders he had received from the czar, caused Scavronsky to be seized, and conducted to Riga, under pretence of some crime laid to his charge; and, to give a better colour to the matter, at his arrival there, a sham information was drawn up against him, and he was soon after sent from thence to Petersburg, under a strong guard, with orders to treat him well upon the road.

When he came to that capital, he was carried to the house of an officer of the emperor's palace, named Shepleff, who, having been previously instructed in the part he was to play, drew several circumstances from the young man in relation to his condition; and, after some time, told him, that although the information, which had been sent up from Riga against him, was of a very serious nature, yet he would have justice done him; but that it would be necessary to present a petition to his majesty for that purpose; that one should accordingly be drawn up in his name, and that he (Shepleff) would find means that he should deliver it into the czar's own hands.

The next day the czar came to dine with Shepleff, at his own house, who presented Scavronsky to him; when his majesty, after asking him abundance of questions was convinced, by the natural answers he gave, that he was really the czarina's brother; they had both lived in Livonia, when young, and the czar found every thing that Scavronsky said to him, in relation to his family affairs, tally exactly with what his wife had told him concerning her brother, and the misfortunes which had befallen her and her brother in the earlier part of their lives.

The czar, now satisfied of the truth, proposed the next day to the empress to go and dine with him at Shepleff's; and, when dinner was over, he gave orders that the man, whom he had examined the day before, should be brought in again. Accordingly he was introduced, dressed in the same clothes he had wore while on his journey to Riga; the czar not being willing that he should appear in any other garb than what his unhappy circumstances had accustomed him to.

He interrogated him again, in the presence of his wife; and the MS. adds, that, at the end, he turned about to the empress, and said these very words:—'This man is your brother; come hither, Charles, and kiss the hand of the empress, and embrace your sister.'

The author of this narrative adds further, that the empress fainted away with surprise; and that, when she came to herself again, the czar said, 'There is nothing in this but what is very natural. This gentlemen is my brother in-law; if he has merit, we will make something of him; if he has not, we must leave him as he is.'

I am of opinion, that this speech shews as much greatness as simplicity, and a greatness not very common. My author says, that Scavronsky remained a considerable time at Shepleff's house; that the czar assigned him a handsome pension, but that he led a very retired life. He carries his relation of this adventure no farther, as he made use of it only to disclose the secret of Catherine's brother: but we know, from other authorities, that this gentleman was afterwards created a count; that he married a young lady of quality, by whom he had two daughters, who were married to two of the principal noblemen in Russia. I leave to those, who may be better informed of the particulars, to distinguish what is fact in this relation, from what may have been added; and shall only say, that the author does not seem to have told this story out of a fondness for entertaining his readers with the marvellous, since his papers were not intended to be published. He is writing freely to a friend, about a thing of which he says he was an eye-witness. He may have been mistaken in some circumstances, but the fact itself has all the appearance of truth; for if this gentleman had known that his sister was raised to so great dignity and power, he would not certainly have remained so many years without having made himself known to her. And this discovery, however extraordinary it may seem, is certainly not more so than the exaltation of Catherine herself; and both the one and the other are striking proofs of the force of destiny, and may teach us to be cautious how we treat as fabulous several events of antiquity, which perhaps are less contradictory to the common order of things, than the adventures of this empress.

The rejoicings made by the czar Peter for his own marriage, and that of his son, were not of the nature of those transient amusements which exhaust the public treasure, and are presently lost in oblivion. He completed his grand foundry for cannon, and finished the admiralty buildings. The highways were repaired, several ships built, and others put upon the stocks; new canals were dug, and the finishing hand put to the grand warehouses, and other public buildings, and the trade of Petersburg began to assume a flourishing face. He issued an ordinance for removing the senate from Moscow to Petersburg, which was executed in the month of April, 1712. By this step he made his new city the capital of the empire, and early he employed a number of Swedish prisoners in beautifying this city, whose foundation had been laid upon their defeat.

CHAP. XXIII.

Taking of Stetin.—Descent upon Finland.—Event of the year 1712.

Peter, now seeing himself happy in his own family, and in his state, and successful in his war against Charles XII. and in the several negotiations which he had entered into with other powers, who were resolved to assist him in driving out the Swedes from the continent, and cooping them up for ever within the narrow isthmus of Scandinavia, began to turn his views entirely towards the north-west coasts of Europe, not laying aside all thoughts of the Palus Mæotis, or Black Sea. The keys of Azoph, which had been so long withheld from the basha, who was to have taken possession of that place for the sultan, his master, were now given up; and, notwithstanding all the endeavours of the king of Sweden, the intrigues of his friends at the Ottoman Porte, and even some menaces of a new war on the part of the Turks, both that nation and the Russian empire continued at peace.

Charles XII. still obstinate in his resolution not to depart from Bender, tamely submitted his hopes and fortunes to the caprice of a grand vizier; while the czar was threatening all his provinces, arming against him the king of Denmark, and the elector of Hanover, and had almost persuaded the king of Prussia, and even the Poles and Saxons, to declare openly for him.

Charles, ever of the same inflexible disposition, behaved in the like manner towards his enemies, who now seemed united to overwhelm him, as he had done in all his transactions with the Ottoman Porte; and, from his lurking- place in the deserts of Bessarabia, defied the czar, the kings of Poland, Denmark, and Prussia, the elector of Hanover (soon afterwards king of England), and the emperor of Germany, whom he had so greatly offended, when he was traversing Silesia with his victorious troops, and who now shewed his resentment, by abandoning him to his ill fortune, and refused to take under his protection any of those countries, which as yet belonged to the Swedes in Germany.

1712.] It would have been no difficult matter for him to have broken the league which was forming against him, would he have consented to cede Stetin, in Pomerania, to Frederick (the first) king of Prussia, and elector of Brandenburg, who had a lawful claim thereto; but Charles did not then look upon Prussia as a power of any consequence: and indeed neither he, nor any other person, could at that time foresee, that this petty kingdom, and the electorate of Brandenburg, either of which were little better than deserts, would one day become formidable. Charles therefore would not listen to any proposal of accommodation, but determined rather to stake all than to give up any thing, sent orders to the regency of Stockholm, to make all possible resistance, both by sea and land: and these orders were obeyed, notwithstanding that his dominions were almost exhausted of men and money. The senate of Stockholm fitted out a fleet of thirteen ships of the line, and every person capable of bearing arms came voluntarily to offer their service: in a word, the inflexible courage and pride of Charles seemed to be infused into all his subjects, who were almost as unfortunate as their master.

It can hardly be supposed, that Charles's conduct was formed upon any regular plan. He had still a powerful party in Poland, which assisted by the Crim Tartars, might indeed have desolated that wretched country, but could not have replaced Stanislaus on the throne; and his hope of engaging the Ottoman Porte to espouse his cause, or convincing the divan that it was their interest to send ten or twelve thousand men to the assistance of his friends, under pretence that the czar was supporting his ally, Augustus, in Poland, was vain and chimerical.

Sep. 1712.] Nevertheless, he continued still at Bender, to wait the issue of these vain projects, while the Russians, Danes, and Saxons, were overrunning Pomerania. Peter took his wife with him on this expedition. The king of Denmark had already made himself master of Stade, a sea-port town in the duchy of Bremen, and the united forces of Russia, Saxony, and Denmark, were already before Stralsund.

Oct. 1712.] And now king Stanislaus, seeing the deplorable state of so many provinces, the impossibility of his recovering the crown of Poland, and the universal confusion occasioned by the inflexibility of Charles, called a meeting of the Swedish generals, who were covering Pomerania with an army of eleven thousand men, as the last resource they had left in those provinces.

When they were assembled, he proposed to them to make their terms with king Augustus, offering himself to be the victim of this reconciliation. On this occasion, he made the following speech to them, in the French language, which he afterwards left in writing, and which was signed by nine general officers, amongst whom happened to be one Patkul, cousin-german to the unfortunate Patkul, who lost his life on the wheel, by the order of Charles XII.

'Having been hitherto the instrument of procuring glory to the Swedish arms, I cannot think of proving the cause of their ruin. I therefore declare myself ready to sacrifice the crown, and my personal interests, to the preservation of the sacred person of their king, as I can see no other method of releasing him from the place where he now is.'

Having made this declaration (which is here given in his own words), he prepared to set out for Turkey, in hopes of being able to soften the inflexible temper of his benefactor, by the sacrifice he had made for him. His ill fortune would have it, that he arrived in Bessarabia at the very time that Charles, after having given his word to the sultan, that he would depart from Bender, and having received the necessary remittances for his journey, and an escort for his person, took the mad resolution to continue there, and opposed a whole army of Turks and Tartars, with only his own domestics. The former, though they might easily have killed him, contented themselves with taking him prisoner. At this very juncture, Stanislaus arriving, was seized himself; so that two Christian kings were prisoners at one time in Turkey.

At this time, when all Europe was in commotion, and that France had just terminated a war equally fatal against one part thereof, in order to settle the grandson of Lewis XIV. on the throne of Spain, England gave peace to France, and the victory gained by Marshal Villars at Denain in Flanders, saved that state from its other enemies. France had been, for upwards of a century, the ally of Sweden, and it was the interest of the former, that its ally should not be stript of his possessions in Germany. Charles, unhappily, was at such a distance from his dominions, that he did not even know what was transacting in France.

The regency of Stockholm, by a desperate effort, ventured to demand a sum of money from the French court, at a time when its finances were at so low an ebb, that Lewis XIV. had hardly money enough to pay his household servants. Count Sparre was sent with a commission to negotiate this loan, in which it was not to be supposed he would succeed. However, on his arrival at Versailles, he represented to the marquis de Torci the inability of the regency to pay the little army which Charles had still remaining in Pomerania, and which was ready to break up and dispute of itself on account of the long arrears due to the men; and that France was on the point of beholding the only ally she had left, deprived of those provinces which were so necessary to preserve the balance of power; that indeed his master, Charles, had not been altogether so attentive to the interests of France in the course of his conquests as might have been expected, but that the magnanimity of Lewis XIV. was at least equal to the misfortunes of his royal brother and ally. The French minister, in answer to this speech, so effectually set forth the incapacity of his court to furnish the requested succours, that count Sparre despaired of success.

It so happened, however, that a private individual did that which Sparre had lost all hopes of obtaining. There was at that time in Paris, a banker, named Samuel Bernard, who had accumulated an immense fortune by making remittances for the government to foreign countries, and other private contracts. This man was intoxicated with a species of pride very rarely to be met with from people of his profession. He was immoderately fond of every thing that made an éclat, and knew very well, that one time or another the government would repay with interest those who hazarded their fortune to supply its exigencies. Count Sparre went one day to dine with him, and took care to flatter his foible so well, that before they rose from table the banker put six hundred thousand livres[91] into his hand; and then immediately waiting on the marquis de Torci, he said to him—'I have lent the crown of Sweden six hundred thousand livres in your name, which you must repay me when you are able.'

Count Steinbock, who at that time commanded Charles's army in Pomerania, little expected so seasonable a supply; and seeing his troops ready to mutiny, to whom he had nothing to give but promises, and that the storm was gathering fast upon him, and being, moreover, apprehensive of being surrounded by the three different armies of Russia, Denmark, and Saxony, desired a cessation of arms, on the supposition that Stanislaus' abdication would soften the obstinacy of Charles, and that the only way left him to save the forces under his command, was by spinning out the time in negotiations. He therefore dispatched a courier to Bender, to represent to the king of Sweden the desperate state of his finances and affairs, and the situation of the army, and to acquaint him that he had under these circumstances, found himself necessitated to apply for a cessation of arms, which he should think himself very happy to obtain. The courier had not been dispatched above three days, and Stanislaus was not yet set out on his journey to Bender, when Steinbock received the six hundred thousand livres from the French banker above-mentioned; a sum, which was at that time an immense treasure in a country so desolated. Thus unexpectedly reinforced with money, which is the grand panacea for all disorders of state, Steinbock found means to revive the drooping spirits of his soldiery; he supplied them with all they wanted, raised new recruits, and in a short time saw himself at the head of twelve thousand men, and dropping his former intention of procuring a suspension of arms, he sought only for an opportunity of engaging the enemy.

This was the same Steinbock, who in the year 1710, after the defeat of Pultowa, had revenged the Swedes on the Danes by the eruption he made into Scania, where he marched against and engaged them with only a few militia, whom he had hastily gathered together, with their arms slung round them with ropes, and totally defeated the enemy. He was, like all the other generals of Charles XII. active and enterprising; but his valour was sullied by his brutality: as an instance of which, it will be sufficient to relate, that having, after an engagement with the Russians, given orders to kill all the prisoners, and perceiving a Polish officer in the service of the czar, who had caught hold on king Stanislaus' stirrup, then on horseback, in order to save his life, he, Steinbock, shot him dead with his pistol in that prince's arms, as has been already mentioned in the life of Charles XII. and king Stanislaus has declared to the author of this History, that had he not been withheld by his respect and gratitude to the king of Sweden, he should immediately have shot Steinbock dead upon the spot.

Dec. 9, 1712.] General Steinbock now marched by the way of Wismar to meet the combined forces of the Russians, Danes, and Saxons, and soon found himself near the Danish and Saxon army, which was advanced before that of the Russians about the distance of three leagues. The czar sent three couriers, one after another, to the king of Denmark, beseeching him to wait his coming up, and thereby avoid the danger which threatened him, if he attempted to engage the Swedes with an equality of force; but the Danish monarch, not willing to share with any one the honour of a victory which he thought sure, advanced to meet the Swedish general, whom he attacked near a place called Gadebusch. This day's affair gave a further proof of the natural enmity that subsisted between the Swedes and Danes. The officers of these two nations fought with most unparalleled inveteracy against each other, and neither side would desist till death terminated the dispute.

Steinbock gained a complete victory before the Russian army could come up to the assistance of the Danes, and the next day received an order from his master, Charles, to lay aside all thoughts of a suspension of arms, who, at the same time, upbraided him for having entertained an idea so injurious to his honour, and for which he told him he could make no reparation, but by conquering or perishing. Steinbock had happily obviated the orders and the reproach by the victory he had gained.

But this victory was like that which had formerly brought such a transient consolation to king Augustus, when in the torrent of his misfortunes he gained the battle of Calish against the Swedes, who were conquerors in every other place, and which only served to aggravate his situation, as this of Gadebusch only procrastinated the ruin of Steinbock and his army.

When the king of Sweden received the news of Steinbock's success, he looked upon his affairs as retrieved, and even flattered himself with hopes to engage the Ottoman Porte to declare for him, who at that time seemed disposed to come to a new rupture with the czar: full of these fond imaginations, he sent orders to general Steinbock to fall upon Poland, being still ready to believe, upon the least shadow of success, that the day of Narva, and those in which he gave laws to his enemies, were again returned. But unhappily he too soon found these flattering hopes utterly blasted by the affair of Bender, and his own captivity amongst the Turks.

The whole fruits of the victory at Gadebusch were confined to the surprising in the night-time, and reducing to ashes, the town of Altena, inhabited by traders and manufacturers, a place wholly defenceless, and which, not having been in arms, ought, by all the laws of war and nations, to have been spared; however, it was utterly destroyed, several of the inhabitants perished in the flames, others escaped with their lives, but naked, and a number of old men, women, and children, perished with the cold and fatigue they suffered, at the gates of Hamburg. Such has too often been the fate of several thousands of men for the quarrels of two only; and this cruel advantage was the only one gained by Steinbock; for the Russians, Danes, and Saxons pursued him so closely, that he was obliged to beg for an asylum in Toningen, a fortress in the duchy of Holstein, for himself and army.

This duchy was at that time subjected to the most cruel ravages of any part of the North, and its sovereign was the most miserable of all princes. He was nephew to Charles XII. and it was on his father's account, who had married Charles's sister, that that monarch carried his arms even into the heart of Copenhagen, before the battle of Narva, and for whom he likewise made the treaty of Travendahl, by which the dukes of Holstein were restored to their rights.

This country was in part the cradle of the Cimbri, and of the old Normans, who overrun the province of Neustria, in France, and conquered all England, Naples, and Sicily; and yet, at this present time, no state pretends less to make conquests than this part of the ancient Cimbrica Chersonesus, which consists only of two petty duchies; namely, that of Sleswic, belonging in common to the king of Denmark and the duke of Holstein, and that of Gottorp, appertaining to the duke alone. Sleswic is a sovereign principality; Holstein is a branch of the German empire, called the Roman empire.

The king of Denmark, and the duke of Holstein-Gottorp, were of the same family; but the duke, nephew to Charles XII. and presumptive heir to his crown, was the natural enemy of the king of Denmark, who had endeavoured to crush him in the very cradle. One of his father's brothers, who was bishop of Lubec, and administrator of the dominions of his unfortunate ward, now beheld himself in the midst of the Swedish army, whom he durst not succour, and those of Russia, Denmark, and Saxony, that threatened his country with daily destruction. Nevertheless, he thought himself obliged to try to save Charles's army, if he could do it without irritating the king of Denmark, who had made himself master of his country, which he exhausted, by raising continual contributions.

This bishop and administrator was entirely governed by the famous baron Gortz, the most artful and enterprising man of his age, endowed with a genius amazingly penetrating, and fruitful in every resource: with talents equal to the boldest and most arduous attempts; he was as insinuating in his negotiations as he was hardy in his projects; he had the art of pleasing and persuading in the highest degree, and knew how to captivate all hearts by the vivacity of his genius, after he had won them by the softness of his eloquence. He afterwards gained the same ascendant over Charles XII. which he had then over the bishop; and all the world knows, that he paid with his life the honour he had of governing the most ungovernable and obstinate prince that ever sat upon a throne.

Gortz had a private conference with general Steinbock,[92] at which he promised to deliver him up the fortress of Toningen,[93] without exposing the bishop administrator, his master, to any danger: and, at the same time, gave the strongest assurances to the king of Denmark, that he would defend the place to the uttermost. In this manner are almost all negotiations carried on, affairs of state being of a very different nature from those of private persons; the honour of ministers consisting wholly in success, and those of private persons in the observance of their promises.

General Steinbock presented himself before Toningen: the commandant refused to open the gates to him, and by this means put it out of the king of Denmark's power to allege any cause of complaint against the bishop administrator; but Gortz causes an order to be given in the name of the young duke, a minor, to suffer the Swedish army to enter the town. The secretary of the cabinet, named Stamke, signs this order in the name of the duke of Holstein: by this means Gortz preserves the honour of an infant who had not as yet any power to issue orders; and he at once serves the king of Sweden, to whom he was desirous to make his court, and the bishop administrator his master, who appeared not to have consented to the admission of the Swedish troops. The governor of Toningen, who was easily gained, delivered up the town to the Swedes, and Gortz excused himself as well as he could to the king of Denmark, by protesting that the whole had been transacted without his consent.

The Swedes retired partly within the walls, and partly under the cannon of the town: but this did not save them: for general Steinbock was obliged to surrender himself prisoner of war, together with his whole army, to the number of eleven thousand men, in the same manner as about sixteen thousand of their countrymen had done at the battle of Pultowa.

By this convention it was agreed, that Steinbock with his officers and men might be ransomed or exchanged. The price for the general's ransom was fixed at eight thousand German crowns;[94] a very trifling sum, but which Steinbock however was not able to raise; so that he remained a prisoner in

Copenhagen till the day of his death.

The territories of Holstein now remained at the mercy of the incensed conqueror. The young duke became the object of the king of Denmark's vengeance, and was fated to pay for the abuse which Gortz had made of his name: thus did the ill fortune of Charles XII. fall upon all his family.

Gortz perceiving his projects thus dissipated, and being still resolved to act a distinguished part in the general confusion of affairs, recalled to mind a scheme which he had formed to establish a neutrality in the Swedish territories in Germany.

The king of Denmark was ready to take possession of Toningen; George, elector of Hanover, was about to seize Bremen and Verden, with the city of Stade; the new-made king of Prussia, Frederick William, cast his views upon Stetin, and czar Peter was preparing to make himself master of Finland; and all the territories of Charles XII. those of Sweden excepted, were going to become the spoils of those who wanted to share them. How then could so many different interests be rendered compatible with a neutrality? Gortz entered into negotiation at one and the same time with all the several princes who had any views in this partition; he continued night and day passing from one province to the other; he engaged the governor of Bremen and Verden to put those two duchies into the hands of the elector of Hanover by way of sequestration, so that the Danes should not take possession of them for themselves: he prevailed with the king of Prussia to accept jointly with the duke of Holstein, of the sequestration of Stetin and Wismar, in consideration of which, the king of Denmark was to act nothing against Holstein, and was not to enter Toningen. It was most certainly a strange way of serving Charles XII. to put his towns into the hands of those who might choose if they would ever restore them; but Gortz, by delivering these places to them as pledges, bound them to a neutrality, at least for some time; and he was in hopes to be able afterwards to bring Hanover and Brandenburg to declare for Sweden: he prevailed on the king of Prussia whose ruined dominions stood in need of peace, to enter into his views, and in short he found means to render himself necessary to all these princes, and disposed of the possessions of Charles XII. like a guardian, who gives up one part of his ward's estate to preserve the other, and of a ward incapable of managing his affairs himself; and all this without any regular authority or commission, or other warrant for his conduct, than full powers given him by the bishop of Lubec, who had no authority to grant such powers from Charles himself.

Such was the baron de Gortz, and such his actions, which have not hitherto been sufficiently known. There have been instances of an Oxenstiern, a Richlieu, and an Alberoni, influencing the affairs of all parts of Europe; but that the privy counsellor of a bishop of Lubec should do the same as they, without his conduct being avowed by any one, is a thing hitherto unheard of.

June, 1713.] Nevertheless he succeeded to his wishes in the beginning; for he made a treaty with the king of Prussia, by which that monarch engaged, on condition of keeping Stetin in sequestration, to preserve the rest of Pomerania for Charles XII. In virtue of this treaty, Gortz made a proposal to the governor of Pomerania, Meyerfeld, to give up the fortress of Stetin to the king of Prussia for the sake of peace, thinking that the Swedish governor of Stetin would prove as easy to be persuaded as the Holsteiner who had the command of Toningen; but the officers of Charles XII. were not accustomed to obey such orders. Meyerfeld made answer, that no one should enter Stetin but over his dead body and the ruins of the place, and immediately sent notice to his master of the strange proposal. The messenger at his arrival found Charles prisoner at Demirtash, in consequence of his adventure at Bender, and it was doubtful, at that time, whether he would not remain all his life in confinement in Turkey, or else be banished to some of the islands in the Archipelago, or some part of Asia under the dominion of the Ottoman Porte. However Charles from his prison sent the same orders to Meyerfeld, as he had before done to Steinbock; namely, rather to perish than to submit to his enemies, and even commanded him to take his inflexibility for his example.

Gortz, finding that the governor of Stetin had broke in upon his measures, and would neither hearken to a neutrality nor a sequestration, took it into his head, not only to sequester the town of Stetin of his own authority, but also the city of Stralsund, and found means to make the same kind of treaty (June, 1713,) with the king of Poland, elector of Saxony, for that place, which he had done with the elector of Brandenburg for Stetin. He clearly saw how impossible it would be for the Swedes to keep possession of those places without either men or money, while their king was a captive in Turkey, and he thought himself sure of turning aside the scourge of war from the North by means of these sequestrations. The king of Denmark himself at length gave into the projects of Gortz: the latter had gained an entire ascendant over prince Menzikoff, the czar's general and favourite, whom he had persuaded that the duchy of Holstein must be ceded to his master, and flattered the czar with the prospect of opening a canal from Holstein into the Baltic Sea; an enterprise perfectly conformable to the inclination and views of this royal founder: and, above all, he laboured to insinuate to him, that he might obtain a new increase of power, by condescending to become one of the powers of the empire, which would entitle him to a vote in the diet of Ratisbon, a right that he might afterwards for ever maintain by that of arms.

In a word, no one could put on more different appearances, adapt himself to more opposite interests, or act a more complicated part, than did this skilful negotiator; he even went so far as to engage prince Menzikoff to ruin the very town of Stetin, which he was endeavouring to save; and in which, at length, to his misfortune, he succeeded but too well.

When the king of Prussia saw a Russian army before Stetin, he found that place would be lost to him, and remain in the possession of the czar. This was just what Gortz expected and waited for. Prince Menzikoff was in want of money; Gortz got the king of Prussia to lend him four hundred thousand crowns: he afterwards sent a message to the governor of the place, to know of him—whether he would rather choose to see Stetin in ashes, and under the dominion of Russia, or to trust it in the hands of the king of Prussia, who would engage to restore it to the king, his master?—The commandant at length suffered himself to be persuaded, and gave up the place, which Menzikoff entered; and, in consideration of the four hundred thousand crowns, delivered it afterwards, together with all the territories thereto adjoining, into the hands of the king of Prussia, who, for form's sake, left therein two battalions of the troops of Holstein, and has never since restored that part of Pomerania.

From this period, the second king of Prussia, successor to a weak and prodigal father, laid the foundation of that greatness, to which his state has since arrived by military discipline and economy.

The baron de Gortz, who put so many springs in motion, could not, however, succeed in prevailing on the Danes to spare the duchy of Holstein, or forbear taking possession of Toningen. He failed in what appeared to have been his first object, though he succeeded in all his other views, and particularly in that of making himself the most important personage of the North, which, indeed, was his principal object.

The elector of Hanover then had secured to himself Bremen and Verden, of which Charles XII. was now stripped. The Saxon army was before Wismar (Sept. 1715); Stetin was in the hands of the king of Prussia; the Russians were ready to lay siege to Stralsund, in conjunction with the Saxons; and these latter had already landed in the island of Rugen, and the czar, in the midst of the numberless negotiations on all sides, while others were disputing about neutralities and partitions, makes a descent upon Finland. After having himself pointed the artillery against Stralsund, he left the rest to the care of his allies and prince Menzikoff, and, embarking in the month of May, on the Baltic Sea, on board a ship of fifty guns, which he himself caused to be built at Petersburg, he sailed for the coast of Finland, followed by a fleet of ninety- two whole, and one hundred and ten half-gallies, having on board near sixteen thousand troops. He made his descent at Elsingford, (May 22. N. S. 1713.) the most southern part of that cold and barren country, lying in 61 degrees north latitude; and, notwithstanding the numberless difficulties he had to encounter, succeeded in his design. He caused a feint attack to be made on one side of the harbour, while he landed his troops on the other, and took possession of the town. He then made himself master of Abo, Borgo, and the whole coast. The Swedes now seemed not to have one resource left; for it was at this very time, that their army, under the command of general Steinbock, was obliged to surrender prisoners of war at Toningen.

These repeated disasters which befel Charles, were, as we have already shewn, followed by the loss of Bremen, Verden, Stetin, and a part of Pomerania; and that prince himself, with his ally and friend, Stanislaus, were afterwards both prisoners in Turkey: nevertheless, he was not to be undeceived in the flattering notion he had entertained of returning to Poland, at the head of an Ottoman army, replacing Stanislaus on the throne, and once again making his enemies tremble.

CHAP. XXIV.

Successes of Peter the Great.—Return of Charles XII. into his own dominions.

Peter, while he was following the course of his conquests, completed the establishment of his navy, brought twelve thousand families to settle in Petersburg, kept all his allies firm to his person and fortunes, not withstanding they had all different interests and opposite views; and with his fleet kept in awe all the sea-ports of Sweden, on the gulfs of Finland andBothnia.

Prince Galitzin, one of his land-generals, whom he had formed himself, as he had done all his other officers, advanced from Elsingford, where the czar had made his descent, into the midst of the country, near the village of Tavasthus, which was a post that commanded the gulf of Bothnia, and was defended by a few Swedish regiments, and about eight thousand militia. In this situation, a battle was unavoidable, (Mar. 13, 1714.) the event of which proved favourable to the Russians, who entirely routed the whole Swedish army, and penetrated as far as Vaza, so that they were now masters of about eighty leagues of country.

The Swedes were still in possession of a fleet, with which they kept the sea. Peter had, for a considerable time, waited with impatience for an opportunity of establishing the reputation of his new marine. Accordingly he set out from Petersburg, and having got together a fleet of sixteen ships of the line, and one hundred and eighty galleys, fit for working among the rocks and shoals that surround the island of Aland, and the other islands in the Baltic Sea, bordering upon the Swedish coast, he fell in with the fleet of that nation near their own shores. This armament greatly exceeded his in the largeness of the ships, but was inferior in the number of galleys, and more proper for engaging in the open sea, than among rocks, or near the shore. The advantage the czar had in this respect was entirely owing to himself: he served in the rank of rear-admiral on board his own fleet, and received all the necessary orders from admiral Apraxin. Peter resolved to make himself master of the island of Aland, which lies only twelve leagues off the Swedish coast; and, though obliged to pass full in view of the enemy's fleet, he effected this bold and hazardous enterprise. His galleys forced a passage through the enemy, whose cannon did not fire low enough to hurt them, and entered Aland; but as that coast is almost surrounded with rocks, the czar caused eighty small galleys to be transported by men over a point of land, and launched into the sea, at a place called Hango, where his large ships were at anchor. Erenschild, the Swedish rear-admiral, thinking that he might easily take or sink all these galleys, stood in shore, in order to reconnoitre their situation, but was received with so brisk a fire from the Russian fleet, that most of his men were killed or wounded; and all the galleys and praams he had brought with him were taken, together with his own ship. (Aug. 8.) The admiral himself endeavoured to escape in a boat, but being wounded, was obliged to surrender himself prisoner, and was brought on board the galley where the czar was, navigating it himself. The scattered remains of the Swedish fleet made the best of their way home; and the news of this accident threw all Stockholm into confusion, which now began to tremble for its own safety.

Much about the same time, colonel Scouvalow Neuschlof attacked the only remaining fortress on the western side of Finland, and made himself master of it, after a most obstinate resistance on the part of the besieged.

This affair of Aland was, next to that of Pultowa, the most glorious that had ever befallen the arms of Peter the Great, who now saw himself master of Finland, the government of which he committed to prince Galitzin, and returned to Petersburg (Sept. 15.), victorious over the whole naval force of Sweden, and more than ever respected by his allies; the stormy season now approaching, not permitting him to remain longer with his ships in the Finlandish and Bothnic seas. His good fortune also brought him back to his capital, just as the czarina was brought to bed of a princess, who died, however, about a year afterwards. He then instituted the order of St. Catherine, in honour of his consort,[95] and celebrated the birth of his daughter by a triumphal entry, which was of all the festivals to which he had accustomed his subjects, that which they held in the greatest esteem. This ceremony was ushered in by bringing nine Swedish galleys, and seven praams filled with prisoners, and rear-admiral Erenschild's own ship, into the harbour of Cronstadt.

The cannon, colours, and standards, taken in the expedition to Finland, and which had come home in the Russian admiral's ship, were brought on this occasion to Petersburg, and entered that metropolis in order of battle. A triumphal arch, which the czar had caused to be erected, and which, as usual, was made from a model of his own, was decorated with the insignia of his conquests. Under this arch the victors marched in procession, with admiral Apraxin, at their head; then followed the czar in quality of rear-admiral, and the other officers according to their several ranks. They were all presented one after another to the vice-admiral Rodamonoski, who, at this ceremony represented the sovereign. This temporary vice-emperor distributed gold medals amongst all the officers, and others of silver to the soldiers and sailors. The Swedish prisoners likewise passed under the triumphal arch, and admiral Erenschild followed immediately after the czar, his conqueror. When they came to the place where the vice-czar was seated on his throne, admiral Apraxin presented to him rear-admiral Peter, who demanded to be made vice-admiral, in reward for his services. It was then put to the vote, if his request should be granted; and it may easily be conceived that he had the majority on his side.

After this ceremony was over, which filled every heart with joy, and inspired every mind with emulation, with a love for his country, and a thirst of fame, the czar made the following speech to those present: a speech which deserves to be transmitted to the latest posterity.

'Countrymen and friends! what man is there among you, who could have thought, twenty years ago, that we should one day fight together on the Baltic Sea, in ships built by our own hands; and that we should establish settlements in countries conquered by our own labours and valour?—Greece is said to have been the ancient seat of the arts and sciences: they afterwards took up their abode in Italy, from whence they spread themselves through every part of Europe. It is now our turn to call them ours, if you will second my designs, by joining study to obedience. The arts circulate in this globe, as the blood does in the human body; and perhaps they may establish their empire amongst us, on their return back to Greece, their mother country; and I even venture to hope, that we may one day put the most civilized nations to the blush, by our noble labours and the solid glory resulting therefrom.'

Here is the true substance of this speech, so every way worthy of a great founder, and which has lost its chief beauties in this, and every other translation; but the principal merit of this eloquent harangue is, its having been spoken by a victorious monarch, at once the founder and lawgiver of his empire.

The old boyards listened to this speech with greater regret for the abolition of their ancient customs, than admiration of their master's glory; but the young ones could not hear him without tears of joy.

The splendour of these times were further heightened by the return of the Russian ambassadors from Constantinople, (Sept. 15, 1714.) with a confirmation of the peace with the Turks: an ambassador sent by Sha Hussein from Persia, had arrived some time before with a present to the czar of an elephant and five lions. He received, at the same time, an ambassador from Mahomet Babadir, khan of the Usbeck Tartars, requesting his protection against another tribe of Tartars; so that both extremities of Asia and Europe seemed to join to offer him homage, and add to his glory.

The regency of Stockholm, driven to despair by the desperate situation of their affairs, and the absence of their sovereign, who seemed to have abandoned his dominions, had come to a resolution no more to consult him in relation to their proceedings; and, immediately after the victory the czar gained over their navy, they sent to the conqueror to demand a passport, for an officer charged with proposals of peace. The passport was sent; but, just as the person appointed to carry on the negotiation was on the point of setting out, the princess Ulrica Eleonora, sister to Charles XII. received advice from the king her brother, that he was preparing, at length, to quit Turkey, and return home to fight his own battles. Upon this news the regency did not dare to send the negotiator (whom they had already privately named) to the czar; and, therefore, resolved to support their ill-fortune till the arrival of Charles to retrieve it.

In effect, Charles, after a stay of five years and some months in Turkey, set out from that kingdom in the latter end of October, 1714. Every one knows that he observed the same singularity in his journey, which characterized all the actions of his life. He arrived at Stralsund the 22d of November following. As soon as he got there, baron de Gortz came to pay his court to him; and, though he had been the instrument of one part of his misfortunes, yet he justified his conduct with so much art, and filled the imagination of Charles with such flattering hopes, that he gained his confidence, as he had already done that of every other minister and prince with whom he had entered into any negotiations. In short, he made him believe, that means might be foundto draw off the czar's allies, and thereby procure an honourable peace, or at least to carry on the war upon an equal footing; and from this time Gortz gained a greater ascendancy over the mind of the king of Sweden than ever count Piper had.

The first thing which Charles did after his arrival at Stralsund was to demand a supply of money from the citizens of Stockholm, who readily parted with what little they had left, as not being able to refuse any thing to a king, who asked only to bestow, who lived as hard as the meanest soldier, and exposed his life equally in defence of his country. His misfortunes, his captivity, his return to his dominions, so long deprived of his presence, were arguments which prepossessed alike his own subjects and foreigners in his favour, who could not forbear at once to blame and admire, to compassionate and to assist him. His reputation was of a kind totally differing from that of Peter the Great: it consisted not in cherishing the arts and sciences, in enacting laws, in establishing a form of government, nor in introducing commerce among his subjects; it was confined entirely to his own person. He placed his chief merit in a valour superior to what is commonly called courage. He defended his dominions with a greatness of soul equal to that valour, and aimed only to inspire other nations with awe and respect for him: hence he had more partizans than allies.

CHAP. XXV.

State of Europe at the return of Charles XII. Siege of Stralsund.

When Charles XII. returned to his dominions in the year 1714, he found the state of affairs in Europe very different from that in which he had left them. Queen Anne of England was dead, after having made peace with France. Lewis XIV. had secured the monarchy of Spain for his grandson the duke of Anjou, and had obliged the emperor Charles VI. and the Dutch to agree to a peace, which their situation rendered necessary to them; so that the affairs of Europe had put on altogether a new face.

Those of the north had undergone a still greater change. Peter was become sole arbiter in that part of the world: the elector of Hanover, who had been called to fill the British throne, had views of extending his territories in Germany, at the expense of Sweden, who had never had any possessions in that country, but since the reign of the great Gustavus. The king of Denmark aimed at recovering Scania, the best province of Sweden, which had formerly belonged to the Danes. The king of Prussia, as heir to the dukes of Pomerania, laid claim to a part of that province. On the other hand, the Holstein family, oppressed by the king of Denmark, and the duke of Mecklenburg, almost at open war with his subjects, were suing to Peter the Great to take them under his protection. The king of Poland, elector of Saxony, was desirous to have the duchy of Courland annexed to Poland; so that, from the Elbe to the Baltic Sea, Peter the First was considered as the support of the several crowned heads, as Charles XII. had been their greatest terror.

Many negotiations were set on foot after the return of Charles to his dominions, but nothing had been done. That prince thought he could raise a sufficient number of ships of war and privateers, to put a stop to the rising power of the czar by sea; with respect to the land war, he depended upon his own valour; and Gortz, who was on a sudden become his prime minister, persuaded him, that he might find means to defray the expense, by coining copper money, to be taken at ninety-six times less than its real value, a thing unparalleled in the histories of any state; but in the month of April, 1715, the first Swedish privateers that put to sea were taken by the czar's men of war, and a Russian army marched into the heart of Pomerania.

The Prussians, Danes, and Saxons, now sat down with their united forces before Stralsund, and Charles XII. beheld himself returned from his confinement at Demirtash and Demirtoca on the Black Sea, only to be more closely pent up on the borders of the Baltic.

We have already shewn, in the history of this extraordinary man, with what haughty and unembarrassed resolution he braved the united forces of his enemies in Stralsund; and shall therefore, in this place, only add a single circumstance, which, though trivial, may serve to shew the peculiarity of his character. The greatest part of his officers having been either killed or wounded during the siege, the duty fell hard upon the few who were left. Baron de Reichel, a colonel, having sustained a long engagement upon the ramparts, and being tired out by repeated watchings and fatigues, had thrown himself upon a bench to take a little repose; when he was called up to mount guard again upon the ramparts. As he was dragging himself along, hardly able to stand, and cursing the obstinacy of the king his master, who subjected all those about him to such insufferable and fruitless fatigues, Charles happened to overhear him. Upon which, stripping off his own cloak, he spread it on the ground before him, saying, 'My dear Reichel, you are quite spent; come, I have had an hour's sleep, which has refreshed me, I'll take the guard for you, while you finish your nap, and will wake you when I think it is time;' and so saying, he wrapt the colonel up in his cloak; and, notwithstanding all his resistance, obliged him to lie down to sleep, and mounted the guard himself.

It was during this siege that the elector of Hanover, lately made king of England, purchased of the king of Denmark the province of Bremen and Verden, with the city of Stade, (Oct. 1715.) which the Danes had taken from Charles XII. This purchase cost king George eight hundred thousand German crowns. In this manner were the dominions of Charles bartered away, while he defended the city of Stralsund, inch by inch, till at length nothing was left of it but a heap of ruins, which his officers compelled him to leave; (Dec. 1713.) and, when he was in a place of safety, general Ducker delivered up those ruins to the king of Prussia.

Some time afterwards, Ducker, being presented to Charles, that monarch reproached him with having capitulated with his enemies; when Ducker replied, 'I had too great a regard for your majesty's honour, to continue to defend a place which you was obliged to leave.' However the Prussians continued in possession of it no longer than the year 1721, when they gave it up at the general peace.

During the siege of Stralsund, Charles received another mortification, which would have been still more severe, if his heart had been as sensible to the emotions of friendship, as it was to those of fame and honour. His prime minister, count Piper, a man famous throughout all Europe, and of unshaken fidelity to his prince (notwithstanding the assertions of certain rash persons, or the authority of a mistaken writer): this Piper, I say, had been the victim of his master's ambition ever since the battle of Pultowa. As there was as that time no cartel for the exchange of prisoners subsisting between the Russians and Swedes, he had remained in confinement at Moscow; and though he had not been sent into Siberia, as the other prisoners were, yet his situation was greatly to be pitied. The czar's finances at that time were not managed with so much fidelity as they ought to be, and his many new establishments required an expense which he could with difficulty answer. In particular, he owed a considerable sum of money to the Dutch, on account of two of their merchant-ships which had been burnt on the coast of Finland, in the descent the czar had made on that country. Peter pretended that the Swedes were to make good the damage, and wanted to engage count Piper to charge himself with this debt: accordingly he was sent for from Moscow to Petersburg, and his liberty was offered him, in case he could draw upon Sweden letters of exchange to the amount of sixty thousand crowns. It is said he actually did draw bills for this sum upon his wife at Stockholm, but that she being unable or unwilling to take them up, they were returned, and the king of Sweden never gave himself the least concern about paying the money. Be this as it may, count Piper was closely confined in the castle of Schlusselburg, where he died the year after, at the age of seventy. His remains were sent to the king of Sweden, who gave them a magnificent burial; a vain and melancholy return to an old servant, for a life of suffering, and so deplorable an end!

Peter was satisfied with having got possession of Livonia, Esthonia, Carelia, and Ingria, which he looked upon as his own provinces, and to which he had, moreover, added almost all Finland, which served as a kind of pledge, in case his enemies should conclude a peace. He had married one of his nieces to Charles Leopold, duke of Mecklenburg, in the month of April of the same year, (1715.) so that all the sovereigns of the north were now either his allies or his creatures. In Poland, he kept the enemies of king Augustus in awe; one of his armies, consisting of about eight thousand men, having, without any loss, quelled several of those confederacies, which are so frequent in that country of liberty and anarchy: on the other hand, the Turks, by strictly observing their treaties, left him at full liberty to exert his power, and execute his schemes in their utmost extent.

In this flourishing situation of his affairs, scarcely a day passed without being distinguished by new establishments, either in the navy, the army, or the legislature: he himself composed a military code for the infantry.

Nov. 8.] He likewise founded a naval academy at Petersburg; dispatched Lange to China and Siberia, with a commission of trade; set mathematicians to work, in drawing charts of the whole empire; built a summer's palace at Petershoff; and at the same time built forts on the banks of the Irtish, stopped the incursions and ravages of the Bukari[96] on the one side, and, on the other, suppressed the Tartars of Kouban.

1715.] His prosperity seemed now to be at its zenith, by the empress Catherine's being delivered of a son, and an heir to his dominions being given him, in a prince born to the czarowitz Alexis; but the joy for these happy events, which fell out within a few days of each other, was soon damped by the death of the empress's son; and the sequel of this history will shew us, that the fate of the czarowitz was too unfortunate, for the birth of a son to this prince to be looked upon as a happiness.

The delivery of the czarina put a stop for some time to her accompanying, as usual, her royal consort in all his expeditions by sea and land; but, as soon as she was up again, she followed him to new adventures.

CHAP. XXVI.

New travels of the czar.

Wismar was at this time besieged by the czar's allies. This town, which belonged of right to the duke of Mecklenburg, is situated on the Baltic, about seven leagues distant from Lubec, and might have rivalled that city in its extensive trade, being once one of the most considerable of the Hans Towns, and the duke of Mecklenburg exercised therein a full power of protection, rather than of sovereignty. This was one of the German territories yet remaining to the Swedes, in virtue of the peace of Westphalia: but it was now obliged to share the same fate with Stralsund. The allies of the czar pushed the siege with the greatest vigour, in order to make themselves masters of it before that prince's troops should arrive; but Peter himself coming before the place in person, after the capitulation, (Feb. 1716,) which had been made without his privacy, made the garrison prisoners of war. He was not a little incensed, that his allies should have left the king of Denmark in possession of a town which was the right of a prince, who had married his niece; and his resentment on this occasion (which that artful minister, de Gortz, soon after turned to his own advantage) laid the first foundation of the peace, which he meditated to bring about between the czar and Charles XII.

Gortz took the first opportunity to insinuate to the czar, that Sweden was sufficiently humbled, and that he should be careful not to suffer Denmark and Prussia to become too powerful. The czar joined in opinion with him, and as he had entered into the war, merely from motives of policy, whilst Charles carried it on wholly on the principles of a warrior; he, from that instant, slackened in his operations against the Swedes, and Charles, every where unfortunate in Germany, determined to risk one of those desperate strokes which success only can justify, and carried the war into Norway.

In the meantime, Peter was desirous to make a second tour through Europe. He had undertaken his first, as a person who travelled for instruction in the arts and sciences: but this second he made as a prince, who wanted to dive into the secrets of the several courts. He took the czarina with him to Copenhagen, Lubec, Schwerin, and Nystadt. He had an interview with the king of Prussia at the little town of Aversburg, from thence he and the empress went to Hamburg, and to Altena, which had been burned by the Swedes, and which they caused to be rebuilt. Descending the Elbe as far as Stade, they passed through Bremen, where the magistrates prepared a firework and illuminations for them, which formed, in a hundred different places, these words—'Our deliverer is come amongst us.' At length he arrived once more at Amsterdam, (Dec. 17, 1716,) and visited the little hut at Saardam, where he had first learned the art of ship-building, about eighteen years before, and found his old dwelling converted into a handsome and commodious house, which is still to be seen, and goes by the name of the Prince's House.

It may easily be conceived, with what a kind of idolatry he was received by a trading and seafaring set of people, whose companion he had heretofore been, and who thought they saw in the conqueror of Pultowa, a pupil who had learned from them to gain naval victories; and had, after their example, established trade and navigation in his own dominions. In a word, they looked upon him as a fellow-citizen, who had been raised to the imperial dignity.

The life, the travels, the actions of Peter the Great, as well as of his rival, Charles of Sweden, exhibit a surprising contrast to the manners which prevail amongst us, and which are, perhaps, rather too delicate; and this may be one reason, that the history of these two famous men so much excites our curiosity.

The czarina had been left behind at Schwerin indisposed, being greatly advanced in her pregnancy; nevertheless, as soon as she was able to travel, she set out to join the czar in Holland, but was taken in labour at Wesel, and there delivered of a prince, (Jan. 14, 1717,) who lived but one day. It is not customary with us for a lying-in-woman to stir abroad for some time; but the czarina set out, and arrived at Amsterdam in ten days after her labour. She was very desirous to see the little cabin her husband had lived and worked in. Accordingly, she and the czar went together, without any state or attendance, excepting only two servants, and dined at the house of a rich ship-builder of Saardam, whose name was Kalf, and who was one of the first who had traded to Petersburg. His son had lately arrived from France, whither Peter was going. The czar and czarina took great pleasure in hearing an adventure of this young man, which I should not mention here, only as it may serve to shew the great difference between the manners of that country and ours.

Old Kalf, who had sent this son of his to Paris, to learn the French tongue, was desirous that he should live in a genteel manner during his stay there; and accordingly had ordered him to lay aside the plain garb which the inhabitants of Saardam are in general accustomed to wear, and to provide himself with fashionable clothes at Paris, and to live, in a manner, rather suitable to his fortune than his education; being sufficiently well acquainted with his son's disposition to know, that this indulgence would have no bad effect on his natural frugality and sobriety.

As a calf is in the French language called veau, our young traveller, when he arrived at Paris, took the name of De Veau. He lived in a splendid manner, spent his money freely, and made several genteel connexions. Nothing is more common at Paris, than to bestow, without reserve, the title of count and marquis, whether a person has any claim to it or not, or even if he is barely a gentleman. This absurd practice has been allowed by the government, in order that, by thus confounding all ranks, and consequently humbling the nobility, there might be less danger of civil wars, which, in former times, were so frequent and destructive to the peace of the state. In a word, the title of marquis and count, with possessions equivalent to that dignity, are like those of knight, without being of any order; or abbé, without any church preferment; of no consequence, and not looked upon by the sensible part of the nation.

Young Mr. Kalf was always called the count de Veau by his acquaintance and his own servants: he frequently made one in the parties of the princesses; he played at the duchess of Berri's, and few strangers were treated with greater marks of distinction, or had more general invitations among polite company. A young nobleman, who had been always one of his companions in these parties, promised to pay him a visit at Saardam, and was as good as his word: when he arrived at the village, he inquired for the house of count Kalf; when, being shewn into a carpenter's work-shop, he there saw his former gay companion, the young count, dressed in a jacket and trowsers, after the Dutch fashion, with an axe in his hand, at the head of his father's workmen. Here he was received by his friend, in that plain manner to which he had been accustomed from his birth, and from which he never deviated. The sensible reader will forgive this little digression, as it is a satire on vanity, and a panegyric on true manners.

The czar continued three months in Holland, during which he passed his time in matters of a more serious nature than the adventure just related. Since the treaties of Nimeguen, Ryswic, and Utrecht, the Hague had preserved the reputation of being the centre of negotiations in Europe. This little city, or rather village, the most pleasant of any in the North, is chiefly inhabited by foreign ministers, and by travellers, who come for instruction to this great school. They were, at that time, laying the foundation of a great revolution in Europe. The czar, having gotten intelligence of the approaching storm, prolonged his stay in the Low Countries, that he might be nearer at hand, to observe the machinations going forward, both in the North and South, and prepare himself for the part which it might be necessary for him to act therein.

CHAP. XXVII.

Continuation of the Travels of Peter the Great.—Conspiracy of baron Gortz.—Reception of the czar in France.

He plainly saw that his allies were jealous of his power, and found that there is often more trouble with friends than with enemies.

Mecklenburg was one of the principal subjects of those divisions, which almost always subsist between neighbouring princes, who share in conquests. Peter was not willing that the Danes should take possession of Wismar for themselves, and still less that they should demolish the fortifications, and yet they did both the one and the other.

He openly protected the duke of Mecklenburg, who had married his niece, and whom he regarded like a son-in-law, against the nobility of the country, and the king of England as openly protected these latter. On the other hand, he was greatly discontented with the king of Poland, or rather with his minister, count Flemming, who wanted to throw off that dependance on the czar, which necessity and gratitude had imposed.

The courts of England, Poland, Denmark, Holstein, Mecklenburg, and Brandenburg, were severally agitated with intrigues and cabals.

Towards the end of the year 1716, and beginning of 1717, Gortz, who, as Bassewitz tells us in his Memoirs, was weary of having only the title of counsellor of Holstein, and being only private plenipotentiary to Charles XII. was the chief promoter of these intrigues, with which he intended to disturb the peace of all Europe. His design was to bring Charles XII. and the czar together, not only with a view to finish the war between them, but to unite them in friendship, to replace Stanislaus on the crown of Poland, and to wrest Bremen and Verden out of the hands of George I., king of England, and even to drive that prince from the English throne, in order to put it out of his power to appropriate to himself any part of the spoils of Charles XII.

There was at the same time a minister of his own character, who had formed a design to overturn the two kingdoms of England and France: this was cardinal Alberoni, who had more power at that time in Spain, than Gortz had in Sweden, and was of as bold and enterprising a spirit as himself, but much more powerful, as being at the head of affairs in a kingdom infinitely more rich, and never paid his creatures and dependants in copper money.

Gortz, from the borders of the Baltic Sea, soon formed a connexion with Alberoni in Spain. The cardinal and he both held a correspondence with all the wandering English who were in the interest of the house of Stuart. Gortz made visits to every place where he thought he was likely to find any enemies of king George, and went successively to Germany, Holland, Flanders, and Lorrain, and at length came to Paris, about the end of the year 1716. Cardinal Alberoni began, by remitting to him in Paris a million of French livres, in order (to use the cardinal's expression) to set fire to the train.

Gortz proposed, that Charles XII. should yield up several places to the czar, in order to be in a condition to recover all the others from his enemies, and that he might be at liberty to make a descent in Scotland, while the partisans of the Stuart family should make an effectual rising in England: after their former vain attempts to effect these views, it was necessary to deprive the king of England of his chief support, which at that time was the regent of France. It was certainly very extraordinary, to see France in league with England, against the grandson of Lewis XIV., whom she herself had placed on the throne of Spain, at the expence of her blood and treasure, notwithstanding the strong confederacy formed to oppose him; but it must be considered, that every thing was now out of its natural order, and the interests of the regent not those of the kingdom. Alberoni, at that time, was carrying on a confederacy in France against this very regent.[97] And the foundations of this grand project were laid almost as soon as the plan itself had been formed. Gortz was the first who was let into the secret, and was to have made a journey into Italy in disguise, to hold a conference with the pretender, in the neighbourhood of Rome; from thence he was to have hastened to the Hague, to have an interview with the czar, and then to have settled every thing with the king of Sweden.

The author of this History is particularly well informed of every circumstance here advanced, for baron Gortz proposed to him to accompany him in these journies; and, notwithstanding he was very young at that time, he was one of the first witnesses to a great part of these intrigues.

Gortz returned from Holland in the latter part of 1716, furnished with bills of exchange from cardinal Alberoni, and letters plenipotentiary from Charles XII. It is incontestable that the Jacobite party were to have made a rising in England, while Charles, in his return from Norway, was to make a descent in the north of Scotland. This prince, who had not been able to preserve his own dominions on the continent, was now going to invade and overrun those of his neighbours, and just escaped from his prison in Turkey, and from amidst the ruins of his own city of Stralsund, Europe might have beheld him placing the crown of Great Britain on the head of James III. in London, as he had before done that of Poland on Stanislaus at Warsaw.

The czar, who was acquainted with a part of Gortz's projects, waited for the unfolding of the rest, without entering into any of his plans, or indeed knowing them all. He was as fond of great and extraordinary enterprises as Charles XII., Gortz, or Alberoni; but then it was as the founder of a state, a lawgiver, and a sound politician; and perhaps Alberoni, Gortz, and even Charles himself, were rather men of restless souls, who sought after great adventures, than persons of solid understanding, who took their measures with a just precaution; or perhaps, after all, their ill successes may have subjected them to the charge of rashness and imprudence.

During Gortz's stay at the Hague, the czar did not see him, as it would have given too much umbrage to his friends the states-general, who were in close alliance with, and attached to, the party of the king of England; and even his ministers visited him only in private, and with great precaution, having orders from their master to hear all he had to offer, and to flatter him with hopes, without entering into any engagement, or making use of his (the czar's) name in their conferences. But, notwithstanding all these precautions, those who understood the nature of affairs, plainly saw by his inactivity, when he might have made a descent upon Scania with the joint fleets of Russia and Denmark, by his visible coolness towards his allies, and the little regard he paid to their complaints, and lastly, by this journey of his, that there was a great change in affairs, which would very soon manifest itself.

In the month of January, 1717, a Swedish packet-boat, which was carrying letters over to Holland, being forced by a storm upon the coast of Norway, put into harbour there. The letters were seized, and those of baron de Gortz and some other public ministers being opened, furnished sufficient evidence of the projected revolution. The court of Denmark communicated these letters to the English ministry, who gave orders for arresting the Swedish minister, Gillembourg, then at the court of London, and seizing his papers; upon examining which they discovered part of his correspondence with the Jacobites.

Feb. 1717.] King George immediately wrote to the states-general, requiring them to cause the person of baron Gortz to be arrested, agreeable to the treaty of union subsisting between England and that republic for their mutual security. But this minister, who had his creatures and emissaries in every part, was quickly informed of this order; upon which he instantly quitted the Hague, and was got as far as Arnheim, a town on the frontiers, when the officers and guards, who were in pursuit of him, and who are seldom accustomed to use such diligence in that country, came up with and took him, together with all his papers: he was strictly confined and severely treated; the secretary Stank, the person who had counterfeited the sign manual of the young duke of Holstein, in the affair of Toningen, experienced still harsher usage. In fine, the count of Gillembourg, the Swedish envoy to the court of Great Britain, and the baron de Gortz, minister plenipotentiary from Charles XII. were examined like criminals, the one at London, and the other at Arnheim, while all the foreign ministers exclaimed against this violation of the law of nations.

This privilege, which is much more insisted upon than understood, and whose limits and extent have never yet been fixed, has, in almost every age, received violent attacks. Several ministers have been driven from the courts where they resided in a public character, and even their persons have been more than once seized upon, but this was the first instance of foreign ministers being interrogated at the bar of a court of justice, as if they were natives of the country. The court of London and the states-general laid aside all rules upon seeing the dangers which menaced the house of Hanover; but, in fact, this danger, when once discovered, ceased to be any longer danger, at least at that juncture.

The historian Norberg must have been very ill informed, and have had a very indifferent knowledge of men and things, or at least have been strangely blinded by partiality, or under severe restrictions from his own court, to endeavour to persuade his readers, that the king of Sweden had not a very great share in this plot.

The affront offered to his ministers fixed Charles more than ever in his resolution to try every means to dethrone the king of England. But here he found it necessary, once in his life time, to make use of dissimulation. He disowned his ministers and their proceedings, both to the regent of France and the states-general; from the former of whom he evicted a subsidy, and with the latter it was for his interest to keep fair. He did not, however, give the king of England so much satisfaction, and his ministers, Gortz and Gillembourg, were kept six months in confinement, and this repeated insult animated in him the desire of revenge.

Peter, in the midst of all these alarms and jealousies, kept himself quiet, waiting with patience the event of all from time; and having established such good order throughout his vast dominions, as that he had nothing to fear, either at home or from abroad, he resolved to make a journey to France. Unhappily he did not understand the French language, by which means he was deprived of the greatest advantage he might have reaped from his journey; but he thought there might be something there worthy observation, and he had a mind to be a nearer witness of the terms on which the regent stood with the king of England, and whether that prince was staunch to his alliance.

Peter the Great was received in France as such a monarch ought to be.

Marshal Tessé was sent to meet him, with a number of the principal lords of the court, a company of guards and the king's coaches; but he, according to his usual custom, travelled with such expedition, that he was at Gournay when the equipages arrived at Elbeuf. Entertainments were made for him in every place on the road where he chose to partake of them. On his arrival he was received in the Louvre, where the royal apartments were prepared for him, and others for the princes Kourakin and Dolgorouki, the vice-chancellor Shaffiroff, the ambassador Tolstoy, the same who had suffered in his person that notorious violation of the laws of nations in Turkey, and for the rest of his retinue. Orders were given for lodging and entertaining him in the most splendid and sumptuous manner: but Peter, who was come only to see what might be of use to him, and not to suffer these ceremonious triflings, which were a restraint upon his natural plainness, and consumed a time that was precious to him, went the same night to take up his lodgings at the other end of the city in the hotel of Lesdiguiére, belonging to marshal Villeroi, where he was entertained at the king's expense in the same manner as he would have been at the Louvre. The next day (May 8, 1717.) the regent of France went to make him a visit in the before mentioned hotel, and the day afterwards the young king, then an infant, was sent to him under the care of his governor, the marshal de Villeroi, whose father had been governor to Lewis XIV. On this occasion, they, by a polite artifice, spared the czar the troublesome restraint of returning this visit immediately after receiving it, by allowing an interview of two days for him to receive the respects of the several corporations of the city; the second night he went to visit the king: the household were all under arms, and they brought the young king quite to the door of the czar's coach. Peter, surprised and uneasy at the prodigious concourse of people assembled about the infant monarch, took him in his arms, and carried him in that manner for some time.

Certain ministers, of more cunning than understanding, have pretended in their writings, that marshal de Villeroi wanted to make the young king of France take the upper hand on this occasion, and that the czar made use of this stratagem to overturn the ceremonial under the appearance of good nature and tenderness; but this notion is equally false and absurd. The natural good breeding of the French court, and the respect due to the person of Peter the Great, would not permit a thought of turning the honours intended him into an affront. The ceremonial consisted in doing every thing for a great monarch and a great man, that he himself could have desired, if he had given any attention to matters of this kind. The journeys of the emperor Charles IV. Sigismund, and Charles V. to France, were by no means comparable, in point of splendour, to this of Peter the Great. They visited this kingdom only from motives of political interest, and at a time when the arts and sciences, as yet in their infancy, could not render the era of their journey so memorable: but when Peter the Great, on his going to dine with the duke d'Antin, in the palace of Petitbourg, about three leagues out of Paris, saw his own picture, which had been drawn for the occasion, brought on a sudden, and placed in a room where he was, he then found that no people in the world knew so well how to receive such a guest as the French.

He was still more surprised, when, on going to see them strike the medals in the long gallery of the Louvre, where all the king's artists are so handsomely lodged; a medal, which they were then striking, happening to fall to the ground, the czar stooped hastily down to take it up, when he beheld his own head engraved thereon, and on the reverse a Fame standing with one foot upon a globe, and underneath these words from Virgil—'Vires acquirit eundo;' an allusion equally delicate and noble, and elegantly adapted to his travels and his fame. Several of these medals in gold were presented to him, and to all those who attended him. Wherever he went to view the works of any artists, they laid the master-pieces of their performances at his feet, which they besought him to accept. In a word, when he visited the manufactories of the Gobelins, the workshop of the king's statuaries, painters, goldsmiths, jewellers, or mathematical instrument-makers, whatever seemed to strike his attention at any of those places, were always offered him in the king's name.

Peter, who was a mechanic, an artist, and a geometrician, went to visit the academy of sciences, who received him with an exhibition of every thing they had most valuable and curious; but they had nothing so curious as himself. He corrected, with his own hand, several geographical errors in the charts of his own dominions, and especially in those of the Caspian Sea. Lastly, he condescended to become one of the members of that academy, and afterwards continued a correspondence in experiments and discoveries with those among whom he had enrolled himself as a simple brother. If we would find examples of such travellers as Peter, we must go back to the times of a Pythagoras and an Anacharsis, and even they did not quit the command of a mighty empire, to go in search of instruction.

And here we cannot forbear recalling to the mind of the reader the transport with which Peter the Great was seized on viewing the monument of cardinal Richelieu. Regardless of the beauties of the sculpture, which is a master-piece of its kind, he only admired the image of a minister who had rendered himself so famous throughout Europe by disturbing its peace, and restored to France that glory which she had lost after the death of Henry IV. It is well known, that, embracing the statue with rapture, he burst forth into this exclamation —'Great man! I would have bestowed one half of my empire on thee, to have taught me to govern the other.' And now, before he quitted France, he was desirous to see the famous madame de Maintenon, whom he knew to be, in fact, the widow of Lewis XIV. and who was now drawing very near her end; and his curiosity was the more excited by the kind of conformity he found between his own marriage and that of Lewis; though with this difference between the king of France and him, that he had publickly married an heroine, whereas Lewis XIV. had only privately enjoyed an amiable wife.

The czarina did not accompany her husband in this journey: he was apprehensive that the excess of ceremony would be troublesome to her, as well as the curiosity of a court little capable of distinguishing the true merit of a woman, who had braved death by the side of her husband both by sea and land, from the banks of the Pruth to the coast of Finland.

CHAP. XXVIII.

Of the return of the czar to his dominions.—Of his politics and occupations.

The behaviour of the Sorbonne to Peter, when he went to visit the mausoleum of cardinal Richelieu, deserves to be treated of by itself.

Some doctors of this university were desirous to have the honour of bringing about a union between the Greek and Latin churches. Those who are acquainted with antiquity need not be told, that the Christian religion was first introduced into the west by the Asiatic Greeks: that it was born in the east, and that the first fathers, the first councils, the first liturgies, and the first rites, were all from the east; that there is not a single title or office in the hierarchy, but was in Greek, and thereby plainly shews the same from whence they are all derived to us. Upon the division of the Roman empire, it was next to impossible, but that sooner or later there must be two religions as well as two empires, and that the same schism should arise between the eastern and western Christians, as between the followers of Osman and the Persians.

It is this schism which certain doctors of the Sorbonne thought to crush all at once by means of a memorial which they presented to Peter the Great, and effect what Pope Leo XI. and his successors had in vain laboured for many ages to bring about, by legates, councils, and even money. These doctors should have known, that Peter the Great, who was the head of the Russian church, was not likely to acknowledge the pope's authority. They expatiated in their memorial on the liberties of the Gallican church, which the czar gave himself no concern about. They asserted that the popes ought to be subject to the councils, and that a papal decree is not an article of faith: but their representations were in vain; all they got by their pains, was to make the pope their enemy by such free declarations, at the same time that they pleased neither the czar nor the Russian church.

There were, in this plan of union, certain political views, which the good fathers did not understand, and some points of controversy which they pretended to understand, and which each party explained as they thought proper. It was concerning the Holy Ghost, which, according to the Latin church, proceeds from the Father and Son, and which, at present, according to the Greeks, proceeds from the Father through the Son, after having, for a considerable time, proceeded from the Father only: on this occasion they quoted a passage in St. Epiphanius, where it is said, 'That the Holy Ghost is neither brother to the Son, nor grandson to the Father.'

But Peter, when he left Paris, had other business to mind, than that of clearing up passages in St. Epiphanius. Nevertheless, he received the memorial of the Sorbonne with his accustomed affability. That learned body wrote to some of the Russian bishops, who returned a polite answer, though the major part of them were offended at the proposed union. It was in order to remove any apprehensions of such a union, that Peter, some time afterwards, namely, in 1718, when he had driven the jesuits out of his dominions, instituted the ceremony of a burlesque conclave.

He had at his court an old fool, named Jotof, who had learned him to write, and who thought he had, by that trivial service, merited the highest honours and most important posts: Peter, who sometimes softened the toils of government, by indulging his people in amusements, which befitted a nation as yet not entirely reformed by his labours, promised his writing-master, to bestow on him one of the highest dignities in the world; accordingly, he appointed him knéz papa, or supreme pontiff, with an appointment of two thousand crowns, and assigned him a house to live in, in the Tartarian quarter at Petersburg. He was installed by a number of buffoons, with great ceremony, and four fellows who stammered were appointed to harangue him on the accession. He created a number of cardinals, and marched in procession at their head, and the whole sacred college was made drunk with brandy. After the death of this Jotof, an officer, named Buturlin, was made Pope: this ceremony has been thrice renewed at Moscow and Petersburg, the ridiculousness of which, though it appeared of no moment, yet has by its ridiculousness confirmed the people in their aversion to a church, which pretended to the supreme power, and whose church had anathematized so many crowned heads. In this manner did the czar revenge the cause of twenty emperors of Germany, ten kings of France, and a number of other sovereigns; and this was all the advantage the Sorbonne gained from its impolitic attempt to unite the Latin and Greek churches.

The czar's journey to France proved of more utility to his kingdom, by bringing about a connexion with a trading and industrious people, than could have arisen from the projected union between two rival churches; one of which will always maintain its ancient independence, and the other its new superiority.

Peter carried several artificers with him out of France, in the same manner as he had done out of England; for every nation, which he visited, thought it an honour to assist him in his design of introducing the arts and sciences into his new-formed state, and to be instrumental in this species of new creation.

In this expedition, he drew up a sketch of a treaty of commerce with France, and which he put into the hands of his ministers at Holland, as soon as he returned thither, but it was not signed by the French ambassador, Chateauneuf, till the 15th August, 1717, at the Hague. This treaty not only related to trade, but likewise to bringing about peace in the North. The king of France and the elector of Brandenburg accepted of the office of mediators, which Peter offered them. This was sufficient to give the king of England to understand, that the czar was not well pleased with him, and crowned the hopes of baron Gortz, who from that time, left nothing undone to bring about a union between Charles and Peter, to stir up new enemies against George I. and to assist cardinal Alberoni in his schemes in every part of Europe. Gortz now paid and received visits publicly from the czar's ministers at the Hague, to whom he declared, that he was invested with full power from the court of Sweden to conclude a peace.

The czar suffered Gortz to dispose all his batteries, without assisting therein himself, and was prepared either to make peace with the king of Sweden, or to carry on the war, and continued still in alliance with the kings of Denmark, Poland, and Russia, and in appearance with the elector of Hanover.

It was evident, that he had no fixed design, but that of profiting of conjunctures and circumstances, and that his main object was to complete the general establishments he had set on foot. He well knew, that the negotiations and interests of princes, their leagues, their friendships, their jealousies, and their enmities, were subject to change with each revolving year, and that frequently not the smallest traces remain of the greatest efforts in politics. A simple manufactory, well established, is often of more real advantage to a state than twenty treaties.

Peter having joined the czarina, who was waiting for him in Holland, continued his travels with her. They crossed Westphalia, and arrived at Berlin in a private manner. The new king of Prussia was as much an enemy to ceremonious vanities, and the pomp of a court, as Peter himself; and it was an instructive lesson to the etiquette of Vienna and Spain, the punctilio of Italy, and the politesse of the French court, to see a king, who only made use of a wooden elbow-chair, who went always in the dress of a common soldier, and who had banished from his table, not only all the luxuries, but even the more moderate indulgences of life.

The czar and czarina observed the same plain manner of living; and had Charles been with them, the world might have beheld four crowned heads, with less pomp and state about them than a German bishop, or a cardinal of Rome. Never were luxury and effeminacy opposed by such noble examples.

It cannot be denied, that if one of our fellow-subjects had, from mere curiosity, made the fifth part of the journeys that Peter I. did for the good of his kingdom, he would have been considered as an extraordinary person, and one who challenged our consideration. From Berlin he went to Dantzic, still accompanied by his wife, and from thence to Mittau, where he protected his niece, the duchess of Courland, lately become a widow. He visited all the places he had conquered, made several new and useful regulations in Petersburg; he then goes to Moscow, where he rebuilds the houses of several persons that had fallen to ruin; from thence he transports himself to Czaritsin, on the river Wolga, to stop the incursions of the Cuban Tartars, constructs lines of communication from the Wolga to the Don, and erects forts at certain distances, between the two rivers. At the same time he caused the military code, which he had lately composed, to be printed, and erected a court of justice, to examine into the conduct of his ministers, and to retrieve the disorders in his finances; he pardons several who were found guilty, and punishes others. Among the latter was the great prince Menzikoff himself, who stood in need of the royal clemency. But a sentence more severe, which he thought himself obliged to utter against his own son, filled with bitterness those days, which were, in other respects, covered with so much glory.

CHAP. XXIX.

Proceedings against prince Alexis Petrowitz.

Peter the Great, at the age of seventeen, had married, in the year 1689, Eudocia Theodora, or Theodorouna Lapoukin. Bred up in the prejudices of her country, and incapable of surmounting them like her husband, the greatest opposition he met with in erecting his empire, and forming his people, came from her: she was, as is too common to her sex, a slave to superstition; every new and useful alteration she looked upon as a species of sacrilege; and every foreigner, whom the czar employed to execute his great designs, appeared to her no better than as corruptors and innovators.

Her open and public complaints gave encouragement to the factious, and those who were the advocates for ancient customs and manners. Her conduct, in other respects, by no means made amends for such heavy imperfections. The czar was at length obliged to repudiate her in 1696, and shut her up in a convent at Susdal, where they obliged her to take the veil under the name of Helena.

The son, whom he had by her in 1690, was born unhappily with the disposition of his mother, and that disposition received additional strength from his very first education. My memoirs say, that he was entrusted to the care of superstitious men, who ruined his understanding for ever. 'Twas in vain that they hoped to correct these first impressions, by giving him foreign preceptors; their very quality of being foreigners disgusted him. He was not born destitute of genius; he spoke and wrote German well; he had a tolerable notion of designing, and understood something of mathematics: but these very memoirs affirm, that the reading of ecclesiastical books was the ruin of him. The young Alexis imagined he saw in these books a condemnation of every thing which his father had done. There were some priests at the head of the malçontents, and by the priests he suffered himself to be governed.

They persuaded him that the whole nation looked with horror upon the enterprises of Peter; that the frequent illnesses of the czar promised but a short life; and that his son could not hope to please the nation, but by testifying his aversion for all changes of custom. These murmurs, and these counsels, did not break out into an open faction or conspiracy, but every thing seemed to tend that way, and the tempers of the people were inflamed.

Peter's marriage with Catherine in 1707, and the children which he had by her, began to sour the disposition of the young prince. Peter tried every method to reclaim him: he even placed him at the head of the regency for a year; he sent him to travel; he married him in 1711, at the end of the campaign of Pruth, to the princess of Brunswick. This marriage was attended with great misfortunes. Alexis, now twenty years old, gave himself up to the debauchery of youth, and that boorishness of ancient manners he so much delighted in. These irregularities almost brutalized him. His wife, despised, ill-treated, wanting even necessaries, and deprived of all comforts, languished away in disappointment, and died at last of grief, the first of November, 1715.

She left the prince Alexis one son; and according to the natural order, this son was one day to become heir to the empire. Peter perceived with sorrow, that when he should be no more, all his labours were likely to be destroyed by those of his own blood. After the death of the princess, he wrote a letter to his son, equally tender and resolute: it finished with these words: ‘I will still wait a little time, to see if you will correct yourself; if not, know that I will cut you off from the succession, as we lop off a useless member. Don’t imagine, that I mean only to intimidate you; don’t rely upon the title of being my only son; for if I spare not my own life for my country, and the good of my people, how shall I spare you? I will rather choose to leave my kingdom to a foreigner who deserves it, than to my own son, who makes himself unworthy of it.’

This is the letter of a father, but it is still more the letter of a legislator; it shews us, besides, that the order of succession was not invariably established in Russia, as in other kingdoms, by those fundamental laws which take away from fathers the right of disinheriting their children; and the czar believed he had an undoubted prerogative to dispose of an empire which he had founded.

At this very time the empress Catherine was brought to bed of a prince, who died afterwards in 1719. Whether this news sunk the courage of Alexis, or whether it was imprudence or bad counsel, he wrote to his father, that he renounced the crown, and all hopes of reigning. ‘I take God to witness,’ says he, ‘and I swear by my soul that I will never pretend to the succession. I put my children into your hands, and I desire only a provision for life.’

The czar wrote him a second letter, as follows:[98]—‘You speak of the succession, as if I stood in need of your consent in the disposal thereof. I reproached you with the aversion you have shewn to all kind of business, and signified to you, that I was highly dissatisfied with your conduct in general; but to these particulars you have given me no answer. Paternal exhortations make no impression on you, wherefore I resolved to write you this once for the last time. If you despise the advice I give you while I am alive, what regard will you pay to them after my death? But though you had the inclination at present to be true to your promises, yet a corrupt priesthood will be able to turn you at pleasure, and force you to falsify them. They have no dependance but upon you. You have no sense of gratitude towards him who gave you your being. Have you ever assisted him in toils and labours since you arrived at the age of maturity? Do you not censure and condemn, nay, even affect to hold in detestation, whatever I do for the good of my people? In a word, I have reason to conclude, that if you survive me, you will overturn every thing that I have done. Take your choice, either endeavour to make yourself worthy of the throne, or embrace a monastic state. I expect your answer, either in writing, or by word of mouth, otherwise I shall treat you as a common malefactor.'

This letter was very severe, and it was easy for the prince to have replied, that he would alter his conduct; instead of which, he only returned a short answer to his father, desiring permission to turn monk.[100]

This resolution appeared altogether unnatural; and it may furnish matter of surprise, that the czar should think of travelling, and leaving a son at home so obstinate and ill-affected; but, at the same time, his doing so, is next to a proof, that he thought he had no reason to apprehend a conspiracy from that son.

The czar, before he set out for Germany and France, went to pay his son a visit. The prince, who was at that time ill, or at least feigned himself so, received his father in his bed, where he protested, with the most solemn oaths, that he was ready to retire into a cloister. The czar gave him six months to consider of it, and then set out on his travels with the czarina.

No sooner was he arrived at Copenhagen, than he heard (what he might reasonably expect) that the czarowitz conversed only with factions and evil-minded persons, who strove to feed his discontent. Upon this the czar wrote to him, that he had to choose between a throne and a convent; and that, if he had any thoughts of succeeding him, he must immediately set out and join him at Copenhagen.

But the confidants of the prince remonstrating to him how dangerous it would be to trust himself in a place where he could have no friends to advise him, and where he would be exposed to the anger of an incensed father, and the machinations of a revengeful step-mother; he, under pretence of going to join his father at Copenhagen, took the road to Vienna, and threw himself under the protection of the emperor Charles VI. his brother-in-law, intending to remain at his court till the death of the czar.

This adventure of the czarowitz was nearly the same as that of Lewis XI. of France, who, when he was dauphin, quitted the court of his father Charles VII. and took refuge with the duke of Burgundy; but the dauphin was much more culpable than Alexis, inasmuch as he married in direct opposition to his father's will, raised an army against him, and threw himself into the arms of a prince, who was Charles's declared enemy, and refused to hearken to the repeated remonstances of his father, to return back to his court.

The czarowitz, on the contrary, had married only in compliance with his father's orders, had never rebelled against him, nor raised an army, nor taken refuge in the dominions of an enemy, and returned to throw himself at his feet, upon the very first letter he received from him; for, as soon as Peter knew that his son had been at Vienna, and had afterwards retired to Tyrol,and from thence to Naples, which, at that time, belonged to the emperor, he dispatched Romanzoff, a captain of his guards, and the privy-counsellor Tolstoy, with a letter written with his own hand, and dated at Spa, the 21st of July, N. S. 1717. They found the prince at Naples, in the castle of St. Elme, and delivered to him his father's letter, which was as follows:—

'I now write to you for the last time, to acquaint you, that you must instantly comply with my orders, which will be communicated to you by Tolstoy and Romanzoff. If you obey, I give you my sacred word and promise, that I will not punish you; and that, if you will return home, I will love you more than ever; but, if you do not, I, as your father, and in virtue of the authority which God has given me over you, denounce against you my eternal curse; and, as your sovereign, declare to you, that I will find means to punish your disobedience, in which I trust God himself will assist me, and espouse the just cause of an injured parent and king.

'For the rest, remember that I have never laid any restraint upon you. Was I obliged to leave you at liberty to choose your way of life? Had I not the power in my own hands to oblige you to conform to my will? I had only to command, and make myself obeyed.'

The viceroy of Naples found it no difficult matter to persuade the czarowitz to return to his father. This is an incontestable proof that the emperor had no intention to enter into any engagements with the prince, that might give umbrage to his father. Alexis therefore returned with the envoys, bringing with him his mistress, Aphrosyne, who had been the companion of his elopement.

We may consider the czarowitz as an ill-advised young man, who had gone to Vienna and to Naples, instead of going to Copenhagen, agreeable to the orders of his father and sovereign. Had he been guilty of no other crime than this, which is common enough with young and giddy persons, it wascertainly very excusable. The prince determined to return to his father, on the faith of his having taken God to witness, that he not only would pardon him, but that he would love him better than ever. But it appears by the instructions given to the two envoys who went to fetch him, and even by the czar's own letter, that his father required him to declare the persons who had been his counsellors, and also to fulfil the oath he had made of renouncing the succession.

It seemed difficult to reconcile this exclusion of the czarowitz from the succession, with the other part of the oath, by which the czar had bound himself in his letter, namely that of loving his son better than ever. Perhaps divided between paternal love, and the justice he owed to himself and people, as a sovereign, he might limit the renewal of his affection to his son in a convent, instead of to that son on a throne: perhaps, likewise, he was in hopes to reduce him to reason, and to render him worthy of the succession at last, by making him sensible of the loss of a crown which he had forfeited by his own indiscretion. In a circumstance so uncommon, so intricate, and so afflicting, it may be easily supposed that the minds of both father and son were under equal perturbation, and hardly consistent with themselves.

The prince arrived at Moscow on the 13th of February, N. S. 1717; and the same day went to throw himself at his father's feet, who was returned to the city from his travels. They had a long conference together, and a report was immediately spread through the city, that the prince and his father were reconciled, and that all past transactions were buried in oblivion. But the next day, orders were issued for the regiments of guards to be under arms at break of day, and for all the czar's ministers, boyards, and counsellors, to repair to the great hall of the castle; as also for the prelates, together with two monks of St. Basile, professors of divinity, to assemble in the cathedral, at the tolling of the great bell. The unhappy prince was then conducted to the great castle like a prisoner, and being come in his father's presence, threw himself in tears at his feet, and presented a writing, containing a confession of his faults, declaring himself unworthy of the succession, and imploring only that his life might be spared.[101]

The czar, raising up his son, withdrew with him into a private room, where he put many questions to him, declaring to him at the same time, that if he concealed any one circumstance relating to his elopement, his life should answer for it. The prince was then brought back to the great hall, where the council was assembled, and the czar's declaration, which had been previously prepared, was there publicly read in his presence.[102]

In this piece the czar reproaches his son with all those faults we have before related, namely, his little application to study, his connexions with the favourers of the ancient customs and manners of the country, and his ill-behaviour to his wife.—'He has even violated the conjugal faith,' saith the czar in his manifesto, 'by giving his affection to a prostitute of the most servile and low condition, during the life-time of his lawful spouse.' It is certain that Peter himself had repudiated his own wife in favour of a captive, but that captive was a person of exemplary merit, and the czar had just cause for discontent against his wife, who was at the same time his subject. The czarowitz, on the contrary, had abandoned his princess for a young woman, hardly known to any one, and who had no other merit but that of personal charms. So far there appears some errors of a young man, which a parent ought to reprimand in secret, and which he might have pardoned.

The czar, in his manifesto, next reproaches his son with his flight to Vienna, and his having put himself under the emperor's protection; and adds, that he had calumniated his father, by telling the emperor that he was persecuted by him; and that he had compelled him to renounce the succession; and, lastly, that he had made intercession with the emperor to assist him with an armed force.

Here it immediately occurs, that the emperor could not, with any propriety, have entered into a war with the czar on such an occasion; nor could he have interposed otherwise between an incensed father and a disobedient son, than by his good offices to promote a reconciliation. Accordingly we find, that Charles VI. contented himself with giving a temporary asylum to the fugitive prince, and readily sent him back on the first requisition of the czar, in consequence of being informed of the place his son had chosen for his retreat.

Peter adds, in this terrible piece, that Alexis had persuaded the emperor, that he went in danger of his life, if he returned back to Russia. Surely it was in some measure justifying these complaints of the prince, to condemn him to death at his return, and especially after so solemn a promise to pardon him; but we shall see, in the course of this history, the cause which afterwards moved the czar to denounce this ever-memorable sentence. For the presentlet us turn our eyes upon an absolute prince, pleading against his son before an august assembly.—

'In this manner,' says he, 'has our son returned; and although, by his withdrawing himself and raising calumnies against us, he has deserved to be punished with death, yet, out of our paternal affection, we pardon his crimes; but, considering his unworthiness, and the series of his irregular conduct, we cannot in conscience leave him the succession to the throne of Russia; foreseeing that, by his vicious courses, he would, after our decease, entirely destroy the glory of our nation, and the safety of our dominions, which we have recovered from the enemy.

'Now, as we should pity our states and our faithful subjects, if, by such a successor, we should throw them back into a much worse condition than ever they were yet; so, by the paternal authority, and, in quality of sovereign prince, in consideration of the safety of our dominions, we do deprive our said son Alexis, for his crimes and unworthiness, of the succession after us to our throne of Russia, even though there should not remain one single person of our family after us.

'And we do constitute and declare successor to the said throne after us, our second son, Peter,[103] though yet very young, having no successor that is older.

‘We lay upon our said son Alexis our paternal curse, if ever at any time he pretends to, or reclaims, the said succession.

‘And we desire our faithful subjects, whether ecclesiastics or seculars, of all ranks and conditions, and the whole Russian nation, in conformity to this constitution and our will, to acknowledge and consider our son Peter, appointed by us to succeed, as lawful successor, and agreeably to this our constitution, to confirm the whole by oath before the holy altar, upon the holy gospel, kissing the cross.

‘And all those who shall ever at any time oppose this our will, and who, from this day forward, shall dare to consider our son Alexis as successor, or assist him for that purpose, declare them traitors to us and our country. And we have ordered that these presents shall be every where published and promulgated, to the end that no person may pretend ignorance.’

It would seem that this declaration had been prepared beforehand for the occasion, or that it had been drawn up with astonishing dispatch: for the czarowitz did not return to Moscow till the 13th of February, and his renunciation in favour of the empress Catherine’s son is dated the 14th.

The prince on his part signed his renunciation, whereby he acknowledges his exclusion to be just, as having merited it by his own fault and unworthiness; ‘And I do hereby swear,’ adds he, ‘in presence of God Almighty in the Holy Trinity, to submit in all things to my father’s will,’ &c.

These instruments being signed, the czar went in procession to the cathedral, where they were read a second time, when the whole body of clergy signed their approbation with their seals at the bottom, to a copy prepared for that purpose.[104] No prince was ever disinherited in so authentic a manner. There are many states in which an act of this kind would be of no validity; but in Russia, as in ancient Rome, every father has a power of depriving his son of his succession, and this power was still stronger in a sovereign than in a private subject, and especially in such a sovereign as Peter.

But, nevertheless, it was to be apprehended, that those who had encouraged the prince in his opposition to his father’s will, and had advised him to withdraw himself from his court, might one day endeavour to set aside a renunciation which had been procured by force, and restore to the eldest son that crown which had been violently snatched from him to place on the head of a younger brother by a second marriage. In this case it was easy to foresee a civil war, and a total subversion of all the great and useful projects which Peter had so much laboured to establish; and therefore the present matter in question was to determine between the welfare of near eighteen millions of souls (which was nearly the number which the empire of Russia contained at that time), and the interest of a single person incapable of governing. Hence it became necessary to find out those who were disaffected, and accordingly the czar a second time threatened his son with the most fatal consequences if he concealed any thing: and the prince was obliged to undergo a judicial examination by his father, and afterwards by the commissioners appointed for that purpose.

One principal article of the charge brought against him, and that which served chiefly to his condemnation, was, a letter from one Beyer, the emperor's resident at the court of Russia, dated at Petersburg, after the flight of the prince. This letter makes mention of a mutiny in the Russian army then assembled at Mecklenburg, and that several officers talked of clapping up Catherine and her son in the prison where the late empress, whom Peter had repudiated, was then confined, and of placing the czarowitz on the throne, as soon as he could be found out and brought back. These idle projects fell to the ground of themselves, and there was not the least appearance that Alexis had ever countenanced them. The whole was only a piece of news related by a foreigner; the letter itself was not directed to the prince, and he had only a copy thereof transmitted him while at Vienna.

But a charge of a more grievous nature appeared against him, namely, the heads of a letter written with his own hand, and which he had sent, while at the court of Vienna, to the senators and prelates of Russia, in which were the following very strong assertions:—'The continual ill-treatment which I have suffered without having deserved it, have at length obliged me to consult my peace and safety by flight. I have narrowly escaped being confined in a convent, by those who have already served my mother in the same manner. I am now under the protection of a great prince, and I beseech you not to abandon me in this conjuncture.'

The expression, *in this conjuncture*, which might be construed into a seditious meaning, appeared to have been blotted out, and then inserted again by his own hand, and afterwards blotted out a second time; which shewed it to be the action of a young man disturbed in his mind, following the dictates of his resentment, and repenting of it at the very instant. There were only the copies of these letters found: they were never sent to the persons they were designed for, the court of Vienna having taken care to stop them; a convincing proof that the emperor never intended to break with the czar, or to assist the son to take up arms against his father.

Several witnesses were brought to confront the prince, and one of them, named Afanassief, deposed, that he had formerly heard him speak these words,—'I shall mention something to the bishops, who will mention it again to the lower clergy, and they to the parish priests, and the crown will be placed on my head whether I will or not.'

His own mistress, Aphrosyne, was likewise brought to give evidence against him. The charge, however, was not well supported in all its parts; there did not appear to have been any regular plan formed, any chain of intrigues, or any thing like a conspiration or combination, nor the least shadow of preparation for a change in the government. The whole affair was that of a son, of a depraved and factious disposition, who thought himself injured by his father, who fled from him, and who wished for his death; but this son was heir to the greatest monarchy in our hemisphere, and in his situation and place he could not be guilty of trivial faults.

After the accusations of his mistress, another witness was brought against him, in relation to the former czarina his mother, and the princess Mary his sister. He was charged with having consulted the former in regard to his flight, and of having mentioned it to the princess Mary. The bishop of Rostow, who was the confidant of all three, having been seized, deposed, that the two princesses, who were then shut up in a convent, had expressed their wishes for a revolution in affairs that might restore them their liberty, and had even encouraged the prince, by their advice, to withdraw himself out of the kingdom. The more natural their resentment was, the more it was to be apprehended. We shall see, at the end of this chapter, what kind of a person the bishop of Rostow was, and what had been his conduct.

The czarowitz at first denied several facts of this nature which were alleged against him, and by this very behaviour subjected himself to the punishment of death, with which his father had threatened him in case he did not make an open and sincere confession.

At last, however, he acknowledged several disrespectful expressions against his father, which were laid to his charge, but excused himself by saying, he had been hurried away by passion and drink.

The czar himself drew up several new interrogations. The fourth ran as follows:—

'When you found by Beyer's letter that there was a mutiny among the troops in Mecklenburg, you seemed pleased with it; you must certainly have had some reason for it; and I imagine you would have joined the rebels even during my life-time?'

This was interrogating the prince on the subject of his private thoughts, which, though they might be revealed to a father, who may, by his advice, correct them, yet might they also with justice be concealed from a judge, who decides only upon acknowledged facts. The private sentiments of a man's heart have nothing to do in a criminal process, and the prince was at liberty either to deny them or disguise them, in such manner as he should think best for his own safety, as being under no obligation to lay open his heart, and yet we find him returning the following answer: 'If the rebels had called upon me during your life-time, I do verily believe I should have joined them, supposing I had found them sufficiently strong.'

It is hardly conceivable that he could have made this reply of himself, and it would be full as extraordinary, at least according to the custom in our part of the world, to condemn a person for confessing that he might have thought in a certain manner in a conjuncture that never happened.

To this strange confession of his private thoughts, which had till then been concealed in the bottom of his heart, they added proofs that could hardly be admitted as such in a court of justice in any other country.

The prince, sinking under his misfortunes, and almost deprived of his senses, studied within himself, with all the ingenuity of fear, for whatever could most effectually serve for his destruction; and at length acknowledged, that in private confession to the archpriest James, he had wished his father dead; and that his confessor made answer, 'God will pardon you this wish: we all wish the same.'

The canons of our church do not admit of proofs resulting from private confession, inasmuch as they are held inviolable secrets between God and the penitent: and both the Greek and Latin churches are agreed, that this intimate and secret correspondence between a sinner and the Deity are beyond the cognizance of a temporal court of justice. But here the welfare of a kingdom and a king were concerned. The archpriest, being put to the torture, confirmed all that the prince had revealed; and this trial furnished the unprecedented instance of a confessor accused by his penitent, and that penitent by his own mistress. To this may be added another singular circumstance, namely, the archbishop of Rezan having been involved in several accusations on account of having spoken too favourably of the young czarowitz in one of his sermons, at the time that his father's resentment first broke out against him; that weak prince declared, in his answer to one of the interrogations, that he had depended on the assistance of that prelate, at the same time that he was at the head of the ecclesiastical court, which the czar had consulted in relation to this criminal process against his son, as we shall see in the course of this chapter.

There is another remark to be made in this extraordinary trial, which we find so very lamely related in the absurd History of Peter the Great, by the pretended bojar Nestersuranoy, and that is the following:

Among other answers which the czarowitz Alexis made to the first question put to him by his father, he acknowledges, that while he was at Vienna, finding that he could not be admitted to see the emperor, he applied himself to count Schonborn, the high chamberlain, who told him, the emperor would not abandon him, and that as soon as occasion should offer, by the death of his father, that he would assist him to recover the throne by force of arms. 'Upon which,' adds the prince, 'I made him the following answer: "This is what I by no means desire: if the emperor will only grant me his protection for the present, I ask no more."' This deposition is plain, natural, and carries with it strong marks of the truth; for it would have been the height of madness to have asked the emperor for an armed force to dethrone his father, and no one would have ventured to have made such an absurd proposal, either to the emperor, prince Eugene, or to the council. This deposition bears date in the month of February, and four months afterwards, namely, after the 1st of July, and towards the latter end of the proceedings against the czarowitz, that prince is made to say, in the last answers he delivered in writing:—

'Being unwilling to imitate my father in any thing, I endeavoured to secure myself the succession by any means whatever, *excepting such as were just.* I attempted to get it by a foreign assistance; and, had I succeeded, and that the emperor had fulfilled *what he had promised me*, to replace me on the throne of Russia even by force of arms, I would have left nothing undone to have got possession of it. For instance, if the emperor had demanded of me, in return for his services, a body of my own troops to fight for him against any power whatever, that might be in arms against him, or a large sum of money to defray the charges of a war, I should have readily granted every thing he asked, and should have gratified his ministers and generals with magnificent presents. I would at my own expense have maintained the auxiliary troops he might have furnished to put me in possession of the crown; and, in a word, I should have thought nothing too much to have accomplished my ends.'

This answer seems greatly strained, and appears as if the unhappy deponent was exerting his utmost efforts to appear more culpable than he really was; nay, he seems to have spoken absolutely contrary to truth in a capital point. He says the emperor had promised to procure him the crown by force of arms. This is absolutely false: Schonborn had given him hopes that, after the death of his father, the emperor might assist him to recover his birth-right; but the emperor himself never made him any promise. And lastly, the matter in question was not if he should take arms against his father, but if he should succeed him after his death?

By this last deposition he declares what he believes he should have done, had he been obliged to dispute his birth-right, which he had not formally renounced till after his journey to Vienna and Naples. Here then we have a second deposition, not of any thing he had already done, and the actual commission of which, would have subjected him to the rigorous inquiry of the law, but of what he imagines he should have done had occasion offered, and which consequently is no subject of a juridical inquiry. Thus does he twice together accuse himself of private thoughts that he might have entertained in a future time. The known world does not produce an instance of a man tried and condemned for vague and inconsequential notions that came into his head, and which he never communicated to any one; nor is there a court of justice in Europe that will hear a man accuse himself of criminal thoughts; nay, we believe that they are not punished by God himself, unless accompanied by a fixed resolution to put them in practice.

To these natural reflections it may be answered, that the czarowitz had given his father a just right to punish him, by having withheld the names of several of the accomplices of his flight. His pardon was promised him only on condition of making a full and open confession, which he did not till it was too late. Lastly, after so public an affair, it was not in human nature that Alexis should ever forgive a brother in favour of whom he had been disinherited; therefore, it was thought better to punish one guilty person, than to expose a whole nation to danger, and herein the rigour of justice and reasons of state acted in concert.

We must not judge of the manners and laws of one nation by those of others. The czar was possessed of the fatal, but incontestable right of punishing his son with death, for the single crime of having withdrawn himself out of the kingdom against his consent; and he thus explains himself in his declaration addressed to the prelates and others, who composed the high courts of justice. 'Though, according to all laws, civil and divine, and especially those of this empire, which grant an absolute jurisdiction to fathers over their children (even fathers in private life) we have a full and unlimited power to judge our son for his crimes according to our pleasure, without asking the advice of any person whatsoever: yet, as men are more liable to prejudice and partiality in their own affairs, than in those of others, and as the most eminent and expert physicians rely not on their judgment concerning themselves, but call in the advice and assistance of others; so we, under the fear of God, and an awful dread of offending him, in like manner make known our disease, and apply to you for a cure; being apprehensive of eternal death, if ignorant perhaps of the nature of our distemper, we should attempt to cure ourselves; and the rather as in a solemn appeal to Almighty God, I have signed, sworn, and confirmed a promise of pardon to my son, in case he should declare to me the truth.

'And though he has violated this promise, by concealing the most important circumstances of his rebellious design against us; yet that we may not in any thing swerve from our obligations, we pray you to consider this affair with seriousness and attention, and report what punishment he deserves without favour or partiality either to him or me; for should you apprehend that he deserves but a slight punishment, it will be disagreeable to me. I swear to you by the great God and his judgments, that you have nothing to fear on this head.

'Neither let the reflection of your being to pass sentence on the son of your prince have any influence on you, but administer justice without respect of persons, and destroy not your own souls and mine also, by doing any thing to injure our country, or upbraid our consciences in the great and terrible day of judgment.'

The czar afterwards addressed himself to the clergy,[105] by another declaration to the same purpose; so that every thing was transacted in the most authentic manner, and Peter's behaviour through the whole of this affair was so open and undisguised, as shewed him to be fully satisfied of the justice of his cause.

On the first of July the clergy delivered their opinion in writing. In fact, it was their opinion only, and not a judgment, which the czar required of them. The beginning is deserving the attention of all Europe.

'This affair (say the prelates and the rest of the clergy) does in no wise fall within the verge of the ecclesiastical court, nor is the absolute power invested in the sovereign of the Russian empire subject to the cognizance of his people; but he has an unlimited power of acting herein as to him shall seem best, without any inferior having a right to intermeddle therein.'

After their preamble they proceed to cite several texts of scripture, particularly Leviticus, wherein it is said, 'Cursed be he that curseth his father or mother;' and the gospel of St. Matthew, which repeats this severe denunciation. And they concluded, after several other quotations,[106] with these remarkable words:

'If his majesty is inclinable to punish the offender according to his deeds and the measure of his crimes, he has before him the examples in the Old Testament, if on the other hand, he is inclined to shew mercy, he has a pattern in our Lord Jesus Christ, who receives the prodigal son, when returning with a contrite heart, who set free the woman taken in adultery, whom the law sentenced to be stoned to death, and who prefers mercy to burnt-offerings. He has likewise the example of David, who spared his son Absalom, who had rebelled against and persecuted him, saying to his captains, when going forth to the fight, "Spare my son Absalom." The father was here inclinable to mercy, but divine Justice suffered not the offender to go unpunished.

'The heart of the czar is in the hands of God; let him take that side to which it shall please the Almighty to direct him.'

This opinion was signed by eight archbishops and bishops, four archpriests, and two professors of divinity; and, as we have already observed, the metropolitan archbishop of Rezan, the same with whom the prince had held a correspondence, was the first who signed.

As soon as the clergy had signed this opinion, they presented it to the czar. It is easy to perceive that this body was desirous of inclining his mind to clemency; and nothing can be more beautiful than the contrast between the mercy of Jesus Christ, and the rigour of the Jewish law, placed before the eyes of a father, who was the prosecutor of his own son.

The same day the czarowitz was again examined for the last time, and signed his final confession in writing, wherein he acknowledges himself 'to have been a bigot in his youthful days, to have frequented the company of priests and monks, to have drank with them, and to have imbibed from their conversations the first impressions of dislike to the duties of his station, and even to the person of his father.'

If he made this confession of his own accord, it shews that he must have been ignorant of the mild advice the body of clergy, whom he thus accuses, had lately given his father; and it is a still stronger proof, how great a change the czar had wrought in the manners of the clergy of his time, who, from a state of the most deplorable ignorance, were in so short a time become capable of drawing up a writing, which for its wisdom and eloquence might have been owned, without a blush, by the most illustrious fathers of the church.

It is in this last confession that the czarowitz made that declaration on which we have already commented, viz. that he endeavoured to secure to himself the succession by any means whatever, except such as were just.

One would imagine, by this last confession, that the prince was apprehensive he had not rendered himself sufficiently criminal in the eyes of his judges, by his former self-accusations, and that, by giving himself the character of a dissembler and a bad man, and supposing how he might have acted had he been the master, he was carefully studying how to justify the fatal sentence which was about to be pronounced against him, and which was done on the 5th of July. This sentence will be found, at length, at the end of this volume; therefore, we shall only observe in this place that it begins, like the opinion of the clergy, by declaring, that 'it belongs not to subjects to take cognizance of such an affair, which depends solely on the absolute will of the sovereign, whose authority is derived from God alone;' and then, after having set forth the several articles of the charge brought against the prince, the judges express themselves thus: 'What shall we think of a rebellious design, almost unparalleled in history, joined to that of a horrid parricide against him, who was his father in a double capacity?'

Probably these words have been wrong translated from the trial printed by order of the czar; for certainly there have been instances in history of much greater rebellions; and no part of the proceedings against the czarowitz discover any design in him of killing his father. Perhaps, by the word parricide, is understood the deposition made by the prince, that one day he declared at confession, that he had wished for the death of his father. But, how can a private declaration of a secret thought, under the seal of confession, be a double parricide?

Be this as it may, the czarowitz was unanimously condemned to die, but no mention was made in the sentence of the manner in which he was to suffer. Of one hundred and forty-four judges, there was not one who thought of a lesser punishment than death. Whereas, an English tract, which made a great noise at that time, observes, that if such a cause had been brought before an English parliament, there would not have been one judge out of one hundred and forty-four, that would have inflicted even a penalty.

There cannot be a stronger proof of the difference of times and places. The consul Manlius would have been condemned by the laws of England to lose his own life, for having put his son to death; whereas he was admired and extolled for that action by the rigid Romans: but the same laws would not punish a prince of Wales for leaving the kingdom, who, as a peer of the realm, has a right to go and come when he pleases.[107] A criminal design, not perpetrated, is not punishable by the laws in England[108] or France, but it is in Russia. A continued formal and repeated disobedience of commands would, amongst us, be considered only an error in conduct, which ought to be suppressed; but, in Russia, it was judged a capital crime in the heir of a great empire, whose ruin might have been the consequence of that disobedience. Lastly, the czarowitz was culpable towards the whole nation, by his design of throwing it back into that state of darkness and ignorance, from which his father had so lately delivered it.

Such was the acknowledged power of the czar, that he might put his son to death for disobedience to him, without consulting any one; nevertheless, he submitted the affair to the judgment of the representatives of the nation, so that it was in fact the nation itself who passed sentence on the prince; and Peter was so well satisfied with the equity of his own conduct, that he voluntarily submitted it to the judgment of every other nation, by causing the whole proceedings to be printed and translated into several languages.

The law of history would not permit us to disguise or palliate aught in the relation of this tragic event. All Europe was divided in its sentiments, whether most to pity a young prince, prosecuted by his own father, and condemned to lose his life, by those who were one day to have been his subjects; or the father, who thought himself under a necessity to sacrifice his own son to the welfare of his nation.

It was asserted in several books, published on this subject, that the czar sent to Spain for a copy of the proceedings against Don Carlos, who had been condemned to death by his father, king Philip II. But this is false, inasmuchas Don Carlos was never brought to his trial: the conduct of Peter I. was totally different from that of Philip. The Spanish monarch never made known to the world the reasons for which he had confined his son, nor in what manner that prince died. He wrote letters on this occasion to the pope and the empress, which were absolutely contradictory to each other. William prince of Orange accused Philip publicly of having sacrificed his son and his wife to his jealousy, and to have behaved rather like a jealous and cruel husband, and an unnatural and murderous father, than a severe and upright judge. Philip suffered this accusation against him to pass unanswered: Peter, on the contrary, did nothing but in the eye of the world; he openly declared, that he preferred his people to his own son, submitted his cause to the judgment of the principal persons of his kingdom, and made the whole world the judge of their proceedings and his own.

There was another extraordinary circumstance attending this unhappy affair, which was, that the empress Catherine, who was hated by the czarowitz, and whom he had publicly threatened with the worst of treatment, whenever he should mount the throne, was not in any way accessary to his misfortunes; and was neither accused, nor even suspected by any foreign minister residing at the court of Russia, of having taken the least step against a son-in-law, from whom she had so much to fear. It is true, indeed, that no one pretends to say she interceded with the czar for his pardon: but all the accounts of these times, and especially those of the count de Bassewitz, agree, that she was greatly affected with his misfortunes.

I have now before me the memoirs of a public minister, in which I find the following words: 'I was present when the czar told the duke of Holstein, that the czarina Catherine, had begged of him to prevent the sentence passed upon the czarowitz, being publicly read to that prince. 'Content yourself,' said she, 'with obliging him to turn monk; for this public and formal condemnation of your son will reflect an odium on your grandson.'

The czar, however, would not hearken to the intercession of his spouse; he thought there was a necessity to have the sentence publicly read to the prince himself, in order that he might have no pretence left to dispute this solemn act, in which he himself acquiesced, and that being dead in law, he could never after claim a right to the crown.

Nevertheless, if, after the death of Peter, a formidable party had arose in favour of Alexis, would his being dead in law have prevented him from ascending the throne?

The prince then had his sentence read to him: and the memoirs I have just mentioned observe, that he fell into a fit on hearing these words: 'The laws divine and ecclesiastical, civil and military, condemn to death, without mercy, those whose attempts against their father and their sovereign have been fully proved.' These fits it is said, turned to an apoplexy, and it was with great difficulty he was recovered at that time. Afterwards, when he came a little to himself, and in the dreadful interval, between life and death, he sent for his father to come to him: the czar accordingly went, and both father and son burst into a flood of tears. The unhappy culprit asked his offended parent's forgiveness, which he gave him publicly: then, being in the agonies of death, extreme unction was administered to him in the most solemn manner, and soon after he expired in the presence of the whole court, the day after the fatal sentence had been pronounced upon him. His body was immediately carried to the cathedral, where it lay in state, exposed to public view for four days, after which it was interred in the church of the citadel, by the side of his late princess; the czar and czarina assisting at the funeral.

And here I think myself indispensably obliged to imitate, in some measure, the conduct of the czar; that is to say, to submit to the judgment of the public, the several facts which I have related with the most scrupulous exactness, and not only the facts themselves, but likewise the various reports which were propagated in relation to them, by authors of the first credit. Lamberti, the most impartial of any writer on this subject and at the same time the most exact, and who has confined himself to the simple narrative of the original and authentic pieces, relating to the affairs of Europe, seems in this matter to have departed from that impartiality and discernment for which he is so remarkable; for he thus expresses himself.

'The czarina, ever anxious for the fortune of her own son, did not suffer the czar to rest till she had obliged him to commence the proceedings against the czarowitz, and to prosecute that unhappy prince to death: and, what is still more extraordinary, the czar, after having given him the knout (which is a kind of torture) with his own hand, was himself his executioner, by cutting off his head, which was afterwards so artfully joined to the body, that the separation could not be perceived, when it was exposed to public view. Some little time afterwards, the czarina's son died, to the inexpressible regret of her and the czar. This latter, who had beheaded his own son, coming now to reflect, that he had no successor, grew exceedingly ill-tempered. Much about that time also, he was informed, that his spouse, the czarina, was engaged in a secret and criminal correspondence with prince Menzikoff. This, joined to the reflection, that she had been the cause of his putting to death with his own hand his eldest son, made him conceive a design to strip her of the imperial honours, and shut her up in a convent, in the same manner as he had done his first wife, who is still living there. It was a custom with the czar to keep a kind of diary of his private thoughts in his pocket book, and he had accordingly entered therein a memorandum of this his intention. The czarina having found means to gain over to her interest all the pages of the czar's bed- chamber, one of them finding his pocket-book, which he had carelessly left on the table, brought it to Catherine, who upon reading this memorandum, immediately sent for prince Menzikoff, and communicated it to him, and, in a day or two afterwards, the czar was seized with a violent distemper, of which he died. This distemper was attributed to poison, on account of its being so sudden and violent, that it could not be supposed to proceed from a natural cause, and that the horrible act of poisoning was but too frequently used in Russia.'

These accusations, thus handed down by Lamberti, were soon spread throughout Europe; and, as there still exist a great number of pieces, both in print and manuscript, which may give a sanction to the belief of this fact to the latest posterity, I think it is my duty to mention, in this place, what is come to my knowledge from unexceptionable authority.

In the first place, then, I take it upon me to declare, that the person who furnished Lamberti with this strange anecdote, was in fact a native of Russia, but of a foreign extraction, and who himself did not reside in that country, at the time this event happened, having left it several years before. I was formerly acquainted with him; he had been in company with Lamberti, at the little town of Nyon,[109] whither that writer had retired, and where I myself have often been. This very man declared to me, that he had never told this story to Lamberti, but in the light of a report, which had been handed about at that time.

This example may suffice to shew, how easy it was in former times, before the art of printing was found out, for one man to destroy the reputation of another, in the minds of whole nations, by reason that manuscript histories were in a few hands only, and not exposed to general examination and censure, or of the observations of contemporaries, as they now are. A single line in Tacitus or Sallust, nay, even in the authors of the most fabulous legends was enough to render a great prince odious to the half of mankind, and to perpetuate his name with infamy to successive generations.

How was it possible that the czar could have beheaded his son with his own hand, when extreme unction was administered to the latter in the presence of the whole court? Was he dead when the sacred oil was poured upon his head? When or how could this dissevered head have been rejoined to its trunk? It is notorious, that the prince was not left alone a single moment, from the first reading of his sentence to him to the instant of his death.

Besides, this story of the czar's having had recourse to the sword, acquits him at least of having made use of poison. I will allow, that it is somewhat uncommon, that a young man in the vigour of his days should die of a sudden fright, occasioned by hearing the sentence of his own death read to him, and especially when it was a sentence that he expected; but, after all, physicians will tell us that this is not a thing impossible.

If the czar dispatched his son by poison, as so many authors would persuade us, he by that means deprived himself of every advantage he might expect from this fatal process, in convincing all Europe that he had a right to punish every delinquent. He rendered all the reasons for pronouncing the condemnation of the czarowitz suspected; and, in fact, accused himself. If he was desirous of the death of his son, he was in possession of full power to have caused the sentence to be put in execution: would a man of any prudence then, would a sovereign, on whom the eyes of all his neighbours were fixed, have taken the base and dastardly method of poisoning the person, over whose devoted head he himself already held the sword of justice? Lastly, would he have suffered his memory to have been transmitted to posterity as an assassin and a poisoner, when he could so easily have assumed the character of an upright though severe judge?

It appears then, from all that has been delivered on this subject in the preceding pages, that Peter was more the king than the parent; and that he sacrificed his own son to the sentiments of the father and lawgiver of his country, and to the interest of his people, who, without this wholesome severity, were on the verge of relapsing again into that state from which he had taken them. It is evident that he did not sacrifice this son to the ambition of a step-mother, or to the son he had by her, since he had often threatened the czarowitz to disinherit him, before Catherine brought him that other son, whose infirm infancy gave signs of a speedy death, which actually happened in a very short time afterwards. Had Peter taken this important step merely to please his wife, he must have been a fool, a madman, or a coward; neither of which, most certainly, could be laid to his charge. But he foresaw what would be the fate of his establishments, and of his new-born nation, if he had such a successor as would not adopt his views. The event has verified this foresight:

the Russian empire is become famous and respectable throughout Europe, from which it was before entirely separated; whereas, had the czarowitz succeeded to the throne, every thing would have been destroyed. In fine, when this catastrophe comes to be seriously considered, the compassionate heart shudders, and the rigid applauds.

This great and terrible event is still fresh in the memories of mankind; and it is frequently spoken of as a matter of so much surprise, that it is absolutely necessary to examine what contemporary writers have said of it. One of these hireling scribblers, who has taken on him the title of historian, speaks thus of it in a work which he has dedicated to count Bruhl, prime minister to his Polish majesty, whose name indeed may seem to give some weight to what he advances. 'Russia was convinced that the czarowitz owed his death to poison, which had been given him by his mother-in-law.' But this accusation is overturned by the declaration which the czar made to the duke of Holstein, that the empress Catherine had advised him to confine his son in a monastery.

With regard to the poison which the empress is said to have given afterwards to her husband, that story is sufficiently destroyed by the simple relation of the affair of the page and pocket-book. What man would think of making such a memorandum as this, 'I must remember to confine my wife in a convent?' Is this a circumstance of so trivial a nature, that it must be setdown lest it should be forgotten? If Catherine had poisoned her son-in-law and her husband she would have committed crimes; whereas, so far from being suspected of cruelty, she had a remarkable character for lenity and sweetness of temper.

It may now be proper to shew what was the first cause of the behaviour of the czarowitz, of his flight, and of his death, and that of his accomplices, who fell by the hands of the executioner. It was owing then to mistaken notions in religion, and to a superstitious fondness for priests and monks. That this was the real source from whence all his misfortunes were derived, is sufficiently apparent from his own confession, which we have already set before the reader, and in particular, by that expression of the czar in his letter to his unhappy son, 'A corrupt priesthood will be able to turn you at pleasure.'

The following is, almost word for word, the manner in which a certain ambassador to the court of Russia explains these words.—Several ecclesiastics, says he, fond of the ancient barbarous customs, and regretting the authority they had lost by the nation having become more civilized, wished earnestly to see prince Alexis on the throne, from whose known disposition they expected a return of those days of ignorance and superstition which were so dear to them. In the number of these was Dozitheus, bishop of Rostow. This prelate feigned a revelation from St. Demetrius, and that the saint had appeared to him, and had assured him as from God himself, that the czar would not live above three months; that the empress Eudocia, who was then confined in the convent of Susdal (and had taken the veil under the name of sister Helena), and the princess Mary the czar's sister, should ascend the throne and reign jointly with prince Alexis. Eudocia and the princess Mary were weak enough to credit this imposture, and were even so persuaded of the truth of this prediction, that the former quitted her habit and the convent, and throwing aside the name of sister Helena, reassumed the imperial title and the ancient dress of the czarina's, and caused the name of her rival Catherine to be struck out of the form of prayer. And when the lady abbess of the convent opposed these proceedings, Eudocia answered her haughtily—That as Peter had punished the strelitzes who had insulted his mother, in like manner would prince Alexis punish those who had offered an indignity to his. She caused the abbess to be confined to her apartment. An officer named Stephen Glebo was introduced into the convent; this man Eudocia made use of as the instrument of her designs, having previously won him over to her interest by heaping favours on him. Glebo caused Dozitheus's prediction to be spread over the little town of Susdal, and the neighbourhood thereof. But the three months being nearly expired, Eudocia reproached the bishop with the czar's being still alive, 'My father's sins,' answered Dozitheus, 'have been the cause of this; he is still in purgatory, and has acquainted me therewith.' Upon this Eudocia caused a thousand masses for the dead to be said, Dozitheus assuring her that this would not fail of having the desired effect: but in about a month afterwards, he came to her and told, that his father's head was already out of purgatory; in a month afterwards he was freed as far as his waist, so that then he only stuck in purgatory by his feet; but as soon as they should be set free, which was the most difficult part of the business, the czar would infallibly die.

The princess Mary, persuaded by Dozitheus, gave herself up to him, on condition that his father should be immediately released from purgatory, and the prediction accomplished, and Glebo continued his usual correspondence with the old czarina.

It was chiefly on the faith of these predictions that the czarowitz quitted the kingdom, and retired into a foreign country, to wait for the death of his father. However the whole scheme was soon discovered; Dozitheus and Glebo were seized; the letters of the princess Mary to Dozitheus, and those of sister Helena to Glebo, were read in the open senate. In consequence of which, the princess Mary was shut up in the fortress of Schusselbourg, and the old czarina removed to another convent, where she was kept a close prisoner. Dozitheus and Glebo, together with the other accomplices of these idle and superstitious intrigues, were put to the torture, as were likewise the confidants of the czarowitz's flight. His confessor, his preceptor, and the steward of his household, all died by the hands of the executioner.

Such then was the dear and fatal price at which Peter the Great purchased the happiness of his people, and such were the numberless obstacles he had to surmount in the midst of a long and dangerous war without doors, and an unnatural rebellion at home. He saw one half of his family plotting against him, the majority of the priesthood obstinately bent to frustrate his designs, and almost the whole nation for a long time opposing its own felicity, of which as yet it was not become sensible. He had prejudices to overcome, and discontents to sooth. In a word, there wanted a new generation formed by his care, who would at length entertain the proper ideas of happiness and glory, which their fathers were not able to comprehend or support.

CHAP. XXX.

Works and establishments in 1718, and the following years.

Throughout the whole of the foregoing dreadful catastrophe, it appeared clearly, that Peter had acted only as the father of his country, and that he considered his people as his family. The punishments he had been obliged to inflict on such of them, who had endeavoured to obstruct or impede the happiness of the rest, were necessary, though melancholy sacrifices, made to the general good.

1718.] This year, which was the epoch of the disinheriting and death of his eldest son, was also that of the greatest advantage he procured to his subjects, by establishing a general police hitherto unknown; by the introduction or improvement of manufactures and works of every kind, by opening new branches of trade, which now began to flourish, and by the construction of canals, which joined rivers, seas, and people, that nature had separated from each other. We have here none of those striking events which charm common readers; none of those court-intrigues which are the food of scandal and malice, nor of those great revolutions which amaze the generality of mankind; but we behold the real springs of public happiness, which the philosophic eye delights to contemplate.

He now appointed a lieutenant-general of police over the whole empire, who was to hold his court at Petersburg, and from thence preserve order from one end of the kingdom to the other. Extravagance in dress, and the still more dangerous extravagance of gaming, were prohibited under severe penalties; schools for teaching arithmetic, which had been first set on foot in 1716, were now established in many towns in Russia. The hospitals, which had been began, were now finished, endowed, and filled with proper objects.

To these we may add the several useful establishments which had been projected some time before, and which were completed a few years afterwards. The great towns were now cleared of those innumerable swarms of beggars, who will not follow any other occupation but that of importuning those who are more industrious than themselves, and who lead a wretched and shameful life at the expense of others: an abuse too much overlooked in other nations.

The rich were obliged to build regular and handsome houses in Petersburg, agreeable to their circumstances, and, by a master-stroke of police, the several materials were brought carriage free to the city, by the barks and waggons which returned empty from the neighbouring provinces.

Weights and measures were likewise fixed upon an uniform plan, in the same manner as the laws. This uniformity, so much, but in vain desired, in states that have for many ages been civilized, was established in Russia without the least difficulty or murmuring; and yet we fancy that this salutary regulation is impracticable amongst us.

The prices of the necessaries of life were also fixed. The city of Petersburg was well lighted with lamps during the night; a convenience which was first introduced in Paris by Louis XIV., and to which Rome is still a stranger. Pumps were erected for supplying water in cases of fire; the streets were well paved, and rails put up for the security of foot passengers: in a word, every thing was provided that could minister to safety, decency, and good order, and to the quicker dispatch and convenience of the inland trade of the country. Several privileges were granted to foreigners, and proper laws enacted to prevent the abuse of those privileges. In consequence of these useful and salutary regulations, Petersburg and Moscow put on a new face.

The iron and steel manufactories received additional improvements, especially those which the czar had founded at about ten miles distance from Petersburg, of which he himself was the first superintendant, and wherein no less than a thousand workmen were employed immediately under his eye. He went in person to give directions to those who farmed the corn-mills, powder- mills, and mills for sawing timber, and to the managers of the manufactories for cordage and sail-cloth, to the brick-makers, slaters, and the cloth-weavers. Numbers of workmen in every branch came from France to settle under him; these were the fruits he reaped from his travels.

He established a board of trade, which was composed of one half natives, and the other half foreigners, in order that justice might be equally distributed to all artists and workmen. A Frenchman settled a manufactory for making fine looking-glass at Petersburg, with the assistance of prince Menzikoff. Another set up a loom for working curious tapestry, after the manner of the Gobelins; and this manufactory still meets with great encouragement. A third succeeded in making of gold and silver thread, and the czar ordered that no more than four thousand marks of gold or silver should be expended in these works in the space of a year; by this means to prevent the too great consumption of bullion in the kingdom.

He gave thirty thousand rubles, that is, about one hundred and fifty thousand French livres,[110] together with all the materials and instruments necessary for making the several kinds of woollen stuffs. By this useful bounty he was enabled to clothe all his troops with the cloth made in his own country;

whereas, before that time, it was purchased from Berlin and other foreign kingdoms.

They made as fine linen cloth in Moscow as in Holland; and at his death there were in that capital and at Jaroslaw, no less than fourteen linen and hempen manufactories.

It could certainly never be imagined, at the time that silk sold in Europe for its weight in gold, that one day there would arise on the banks of the lake Ladoga, in the midst of a frozen region, and among unfrequented marshes, a magnificent and opulent city, where the silks of Persia should be manufactured in as great perfection as at Ispahan. Peter, however, undertook this great phenomenon in commerce, and succeeded in the attempt. The working of iron mines was carried to their highest degree of perfection; several other mines of gold and silver were discovered, and the council of mines was appointed to examine and determine, whether the working ofthese would bring in a profit adequate to the expense.

But, to make so many different arts and manufactures flourish, and to establish so many various undertakings, it was not alone sufficient to grant patents, or to appoint inspectors: it was necessary that our great founder should behold all these pass under his own eye in their beginnings, and work at them with his own hands, in the same manner as we have already seen him working at the construction, the rigging, and the sailing of a ship. When canals were to be dug in marshy and almost impassable grounds, he was frequently seen at the head of the workmen digging the earth, and carrying it away himself.

In this same year (1718) he formed the plan of the canal and sluices of Ladoga: this was intended to make a communication between the Neva and another navigable river, in order for the more easy conveyance of merchandize to Petersburg, without taking the great circuit of the lake Ladoga, which, on account of the storms that prevailed on the coast, was frequently impassable for barks or small vessels. Peter levelled the ground himself, and they still preserve the tools which he used in digging up and carrying off the earth. The whole court followed the example of their sovereign, and persisted in a work, which, at the same time, they looked upon as impracticable; and it was finished after his death: for not one of his projects, which had been found possible to be effected, wasabandoned.

The great canal of Cronstadt, which is easily drained of its waters, and wherein they careen and clean the men of war, was also began at the same time that he was engaged in the proceedings against his son.

In this year also he built the new city of Ladoga. A short time afterwards, he made the canal which joins the Caspian Sea to the gulf of Finland and to the ocean. The boats, after sailing up the Wolga, came first to the communication of two rivers, which he joined for that purpose; from thence, by another canal, they enter into the lake of Ilmen, and then fall into the canal of Ladoga, from whence goods and merchandizes may be conveyed by sea to all parts of the world.

In the midst of these labours, which all passed under his inspection, he carried his views from Kamschatka to the most eastern limits of his empire, and caused two forts to be built in these regions, which were so long unknown to the rest of the world. In the meantime, a body of engineers, who were draughted from the marine academy established in 1715, were sent to make the tour of the empire, in order to form exact charts thereof, and lay before mankind the immense extent of country which he had civilized and enriched.

CHAP. XXXI.

Of the trade of Russia.

The Russian trade without doors was in a manner annihilated before the reign of Peter. He restored it anew, after his accession to the throne. It is notorious, that the current of trade has undergone several changes in the world. The south part of Russia was before the time of Tamerlane, the staple of Greece, and even of the Indies; and the Genoese were the principal factors. The Tanais and the Boristhenes were loaded with the productions of Asia: but when Tamerlane, towards the end of the fourteenth century, had conquered the Taurican Chersonesus, afterwards called Crimea or Crim Tartary, and when the Turks became masters of Azoph, this great branch of trade was totally destroyed. Peter formed the design of reviving it, by getting possession of Azoph; but the unfortunate campaign of Pruth wrested this city out of his hands, and with it all his views on the Black Sea: nevertheless he had it still in his power to open as extensive a road to commerce through the Caspian Sea. The English who, in the end of the fifteenth, and beginning of the sixteenth century, had opened a trade to Archangel, had endeavoured to do the same likewise by the Caspian Sea, but failed in all their attempts for this purpose.

It has been already observed, that the father of Peter the Great caused a ship to be built in Holland, to trade from Astracan to the coast of Persia. This vessel was burnt by the rebel Stenkorazin, which put an immediate stop to any views of trading on a fair footing with the Persians. The Armenians, who are the factors of that part of Asia, were received by Peter the Great into Astracan; every thing was obliged to pass through their hands, and they reaped all the advantage of that trade; as is the case with the Indian traders, and the Banians, and with the Turks, as well as several nations in Christendom, and the Jews: for those who have only one way of living, are generally very expert in that art on which they depend for a support; and others pay a voluntary tribute to that knowledge in which they know themselves deficient.

Peter had already found a remedy for this inconvenience, in the treaty which he made with the sophi of Persia, by which all the silk, which was not used for the manufactories in that kingdom, was to be delivered to the Armenians of Astracan, and by them to be transported into Russia.

The troubles which arose in Persia soon overturned this arrangement; and in the course of this history, we shall see how the sha, or emperor of Persia, Hussein, when persecuted by the rebels, implored the assistance of Peter; and how that monarch, after having supported a difficult war against the Turks and the Swedes, entered Persia, and subjected three of its provinces. But to return to the article of trade.

Of the Trade with China.

The undertaking of establishing a trade with China seemed to promise the greatest advantages. Two vast empires, bordering on each other, and each reciprocally possessing what the other stood in need of, seemed to be both under the happy necessity of opening a useful correspondence, especially after the treaty of peace, so solemnly ratified between these two empires in the year 1689, according to our way of reckoning.

The first foundation of this trade had been laid in the year 1653. There was at that time two companies of Siberian and Bukarian families settled in Siberia. Their caravans travelled through the Calmuck plains; after they had crossed the deserts of Chinese Tartary, and made a considerable profit by their trade; but the troubles which happened in the country of thc Calmucks, and the disputes between the Russians and the Chinese, in regard to the frontiers, put a stop to this commerce.

After the peace of 1689, it was natural for the two great nations to fix on some neutral place, whither all the goods should be carried. The Siberians, like all other nations, stood more in need of the Chinese, than these latter did of them; accordingly permission was asked of the emperor of China, to send caravans to Pekin, which was readily granted. This happened in the beginning of the present century.

It is worthy of observation, that the emperor Camhi had granted permission for a Russian church in the suburbs of Pekin; which church was to be served by Siberian priests, the whole at the emperor's own expense, who was so indulgent to cause this church to be built for the accommodation of several families of eastern Siberia; some of whom had been prisoners before the peace of 1680, and the others were adventurers from their own country, who would not return back again after the peace of Niptchou. The agreeable climate of Pekin, the obliging manners of the Chinese, and the ease with which they found a handsome living, determined them to spend the rest of their days in China. The small Greek church could not become dangerous to the peace of the empire, as those of the Jesuits have been to that of other nations; and moreover, the emperor Camhi was a favourer of liberty of conscience. Toleration has, in all times, been the established custom in Asia, as it was in former times all over the world, till the reign of the Roman emperor Theodosius I. The Russian families, thus established in China, having intermarried with the natives, have since quitted the Christian religion, but their church still subsists.

It was stipulated, that this church should be for the use of those who come with the Siberian caravans, to bring furs and other commodities wanted at Pekin. The voyage out and home, and the stay in the country, generally took up three years. Prince Gagarin, governor of Siberia, was twenty years at the head of this trade. The caravans were sometimes very numerous; and it was difficult to keep the common people, who made the greatest number, within proper bounds.

They passed through the territories of a Laman priest, who is a kind of Tartarian sovereign, resides on the sea-coast of Orkon, and has the title of Koutoukas: he is the vicar of the grand Lama, but has rendered himself independent, by making some change in the religion of the country, where the Indian tenet of metempsychosis is the prevailing opinion. We cannot find a more apt comparison for this priest than in the bishops of Lubeck and Osnaburg, who have shaken off the dominion of the church of Rome. The caravans, in their march, sometimes committed depredations on the territories of this Tartarian prelate, as they did also on those of the Chinese. This irregular conduct proved an impediment to the trade of those parts; for the Chinese threatened to shut the entrance into their empire against the Russians, unless a stop was put to these disorders. The trade with China was at that time very advantageous to the Russians, who brought from thence gold, silver, and precious stones, in return for their merchandize. The largest ruby in the world was brought out of China to prince Gagarin, who sent it to prince Menzikoff; and it is now one of the ornaments of the imperial crown.

The exactions put in practice by prince Gagarin were of great prejudice to that trade, which had brought him so much riches; and, at length, they ended in his own destruction; for he was accused before the court of justice, established by the czar, and sentenced to lose his head, a year after the condemnation of the czarowitz, and the execution of all those who had been his accomplices.

About the same time, the emperor Camhi, perceiving his health to decay, and knowing, by experience, that the European mathematicians were much more learned in their art than those of his own nation, thought that the European physicians must also have more knowledge than those of Pekin, and therefore sent a message to the czar, by some ambassadors who were returning from China to Petersburg, requesting him to send him one of his physicians. There happened at that time to be an English surgeon at Petersburg, who offered to undertake the journey in that character; and accordingly set out in company with a new ambassador, and one Laurence Lange, who has left a description of that journey. This embassy was received, and all the expense of it defrayed with great pomp, by Camhi. The surgeon, at his arrival, found the emperor in perfect health, and gained the reputation of a most skilful physician. The caravans who followed this embassy made prodigious profits; but fresh excesses having been committed by this very caravan, the Chinese were so offended thereat, that they sent back Lange, who was at that time resident from the czar at the Chinese court, and with him all the Russian merchants established there.

The emperor Camhi dying, his son Yontchin, who had as great a share of wisdom, and more firmness than his father, and who drove the Jesuits out of his empire, as the czar had done from Russia in 1718, concluded a treaty with Peter, by which the Russian caravans were no more to trade on the frontiers of the two empires. There are only certain factors, dispatched in the name of the emperor or empress of Russia, and these have liberty to enter Pekin, where they are lodged in a vast house, which the emperor of China formerly assigned for the reception of the envoys from Corea: but it is a considerable time since either caravans or factors have been sent from Russia thither so that the trade is now in a declining way, but may possibly soon be revived.

Of the Trade of **PETERSBURG,** *and the other ports of the* **RUSSIAN EMPIRE.**

There were at this time above two hundred foreign vessels traded to the new capital, in the space of a year. This trade has continued increasing, and has frequently brought in five millions (French money) to the crown. This was greatly more than the interest of the money which this establishment had cost. This trade, however, greatly diminished that of Archangel, and was precisely what the founder desired; for the port of Archangel is too dangerous, and at too great distance from other ports: besides that, a trade which is carried on immediately under the eye of an assiduous sovereign, is always the most advantageous. That of Livonia continued still on the same footing. The trade of Russia in general has proved very successful; its ports have received from one thousand to twelve hundred vessels in a year, and Peter discovered the happy expedient of joining utility to glory.

CHAP. XXXII.

Of the laws.

It is well known, that good laws are scarce, and that the due execution of them is still more so. The greater the extent of any state, and the variety of people of which it is composed, the more difficult it is to unite them by the same body of laws. The father of czar Peter formed a digest or code under the title of *Oulogenia*, which was actually printed, but it by no means answered the end intended.

Peter, in the course of his travels, had collected materials for repairing this great structure, which was falling to decay in many of its parts. He gathered many useful hints from the governments of Denmark, Sweden, England, Germany, and France, selecting from each of these different nations what he thought most suitable to his own.

There was a court of boyards or great men, who determined all matters *en dernier ressort*. Rank and birth alone gave a seat in this assembly; but the czar thought that knowledge was likewise requisite, and therefore this court was dissolved.

He then instituted a procurator-general, assisted by four assistors, in each of the governments of the empire. These were to overlook the conduct of the judges, whose decrees were subject to an appeal to the senate which he established. Each of those judges was furnished with a copy of the *Oulogenia*, with additions and necessary alterations, until a complete body of laws could be formed.

It was forbid to these judges to receive any fees, which, however moderate, are always an abusive tax on the fortunes and properties of those concerned in suits of law. The czar also took care that the expenses of the court were moderate, and the decisions speedy. The judges and their clerks had salaries appointed them out of the public treasury, and were not suffered to purchase their offices.

It was in the year 1718, at the very time that he was engaged in the process against his son, that he made the chief part of these regulations. The greatest part of the laws he enacted were borrowed from those of the Swedes, and he made no difficulty to admit to places in his courts of judicature such Swedish prisoners who were well versed in the laws of their own country, and who, having learnt the Russian language, were willing to continue in that kingdom.

The governor of each province and his assistors had the cognizance of private causes within such government; from them there was an appeal to the senate; and if any one, after having been condemned by the senate, appealed to the czar himself, and such appeal was found unjust, he was punished with death: but to mitigate the rigour of this law, the czar created a master of the requests, who received the petitions of those who had affairs depending in the senate, or in the inferior courts, concerning which the laws then in force were not sufficiently explanatory.

At length, in 1722, he completed his new code, prohibiting all the judges, under pain of death, to depart therefrom in their decrees, or to set up their own private opinions in place of the general statutes. This dreadful ordonnance was publicly fixed up, and still remains in all the courts of judicature of the empire.

He erected every thing anew; there was not, even to the common affairs of society, aught but what was his work. He regulated the degrees between man and man, according to their posts and employments, from the admiral and the field-marshal to the ensign, without any regard to birth.

Having always in his own mind, and willing to imprint it on those of his subjects, that services are preferable to pedigree, a certain rank was likewise fixed for the women; and she who took a seat in a public assembly, that did not properly belong to her, was obliged to pay a fine.

By a still more useful regulation, every private soldier, on being made an officer, instantly became a gentleman; and a nobleman, if his character had been impeached in a court of justice, was degraded to a plebeian.

After the settling of these several laws and regulations, it happened that the increase of towns, wealth, and population in the empire, new undertakings, and the creation of new employs, necessarily introduced a multitude of new affairs and unforeseen cases, which were all consequences of that success which attended the czar in the general reformation of his dominions.

The empress Elizabeth completed the body of laws which her father had begun, in which she gave the most lively proofs of that mildness and clemency for which she was so justly famed.

CHAP. XXXIII.

Of Religion.

At this time Peter laboured more than ever to reform the clergy. He had abolished the patriarchal office, and by this act of authority had alienated the minds of the ecclesiastics. He was determined that the imperial power should be free and absolute, and that of the church respected, but submissive. His design was, to establish a council of religion, which should always subsist, but dependent on the sovereign, and that it should give no laws to the church, but such as should be approved of by the head of the state, of which the church was a part. He was assisted in this undertaking by the archbishop of Novogorod, named Theophanes Procop, or Procopowitz, i.e. son of Procop.

This prelate was a person of great learning and sagacity: his travels through the different parts of Europe had afforded him opportunities of remarks on the several abuses which reign amongst them. The czar, who had himself been a witness of the same, had this great advantage in forming all his regulations, that he was possessed of an unlimited power to choose what was useful, and reject what was dangerous. He laboured, in concert with the archbishop, in the years 1718 and 1719, to effect his design. He established a perpetual synod, to be composed of twelve members, partly bishops, and partly archpriests, all to be chosen by the sovereign. This college was afterwards augmented to fourteen.

The motives of this establishment were explained by the czar in a preliminary discourse. The chief and most remarkable of these was, 'That under the administration of a college of priests, there was less danger of troubles and insurrections, than under the government of a single head of the church; because the common people, who are always prone to superstition, might, by seeing one head of the church, and another of the state, be led to believe that they were in fact two different powers.' And hereupon he cites as an example, the divisions which so long subsisted between the empire and the papal see, and which stained so many kingdoms with blood.

Peter thought, and openly declared, that the notion of two powers in a state, founded on the allegory of the two swords, mentioned in the apostles, was absurd and erroneous.

This court was invested with the ecclesiastical power of regulating all penances, and examining into the morals and capacity of those nominated by the court to bishoprics, to pass judgment *en dernier ressort* in all causes relating to religion, in which it was the custom formerly to appeal to the patriarch, and also to take cognizance of the revenues of monasteries, and the distribution of alms.

This synod had the title of *most holy*, the same which the patriarchs were wont to assume, and in fact the czar seemed to have preserved the patriarchal dignity, but divided among fourteen members, who were all dependant on the crown, and were to take an oath of obedience, which the patriarchs never did. The members of this holy synod, when met in assembly, had the same rank as the senators; but they were like the senate, all dependant on the prince. But neither this new form of church administration, nor the ecclesiastical code, were in full vigour till four years after its institution, namely in 1722. Peter at first intended, that the synod should have the presentation of those whom they thought most worthy to fill the vacant bishoprics. These were to be nominated by the emperor, and consecrated by the synod, Peter frequently presided in person at the assembly. One day that a vacant see was to be filled, the synod observed to the emperor, that they had none but ignorant persons to present to his majesty: 'Well, then,' replied the czar, 'you have only to pitch upon the most honest man, he will be worth two learned ones.'

It is to be observed, that the Greek church has none of that motley order called secular abbots. The *petit collet* is unknown there, otherwise than by the ridiculousness of its character, but by another abuse (as every thing in this world must be subject to abuse) the bishops and prelates are all chosen from the monastic orders. The first monks were only laymen, partly devotees, and partly fanatics, who retired into the deserts, where they were at length gathered together by St. Basil, who gave them a body of rules, and then they took vows, and were reckoned as the lower order of the church, which is the first step to be taken to arise at higher dignities. It was this that filled all Greece and Asia with monks. Russia was overrun with them. They became rich, powerful, and though excessively ignorant, they were, at the accession of Peter to the throne, almost the only persons who knew how to write. Of this knowledge they made such an abuse, when struck and confounded with the new regulations which Peter introduced in all the departments of government, that he was obliged in 1703 to issue an edict, forbidding the use of pen and ink to the monks, without an express order from the archimandrite, or prior of the convent, who in that case was responsible for the behaviour of those to whom he granted this indulgence.

Peter designed to make this a standing law, and at first he intended, that no one should be admitted into any order under fifty years of age; but that appeared too late an age, as the life of man being in general so limited, there was not time sufficient for such persons to acquire the necessary qualifications for being made bishops; and therefore, with the advice of his synod, he placed it at thirty years complete, but never under; at the same time expressly prohibiting any person exercising the profession of a soldier, or an husbandman, to enter into a convent, without an immediate order from the emperor, or the synod, and to admit no married man upon any account, even though divorced from his wife; unless that wife should at the same time embrace a religious life of her own pure will, and that neither of them had any children. No person in actual employ under government can take the habit, without an express order of the state for that purpose. Every monk is obliged to work with his own hands at some trade. The nuns are never to go without the walls of their convent, and at the age of fifty are to receive the tonsure, as did the deaconesses of the primitive church; but if, before undergoing that ceremony, they have an inclination to marry, they are not only allowed, but even exhorted so to do. An admirable regulation in a country where population is of infinitely greater use than a monastic life.

Peter was desirous that those unhappy females, whom God has destined to people a kingdom, and who, by a mistaken devotion, annihilated in cloisters that race of which they would otherwise become mothers, should at least be of some service to society, which they thus injure; and therefore ordered, that they should all be employed in some handy works, suitable to their sex. The empress Catherine took upon herself the care of sending for several handicrafts over from Brabant and Holland, whom she distributed among these convents, and, in a short time, they produced several kinds of work, which the empress and her ladies always wore as a part of their dress.

There cannot perhaps be any thing conceived more prudent than these institutions; but what merits the attention of all ages, is the regulation which Peter made himself, and which he addressed to the synod in 1724. The ancient ecclesiastical institution is there very learnedly explained, and the indolence of the monkish life admirably well exposed; and he not only recommends an application to labour and industry, but even commands it; and that the principal occupation of those people should be, to assist and relieve the poor. He likewise orders, that sick and infirm soldiers shall be quartered in the convents, and that a certain number of monks shall be set apart to take care of them, and that the most strong and healthy of these shall cultivate the lands belonging to those convents. He orders the same regulations to be observed in the monasteries for women, and that the strongest of these shall take care of the gardens, and the rest to wait on sick or infirm women, who shall be brought from the neighbouring country into the convents for that purpose. He also enters into the minutest details relating to these services; and lastly, he appoints certain monasteries of both sexes for the reception and education of orphans.

In reading this ordinance of Peter the Great, which was published the 31st January, 1724, one would imagine it to have been framed by a minister of state and a father of the church.

Almost all the customs in the Russian church are different from those of ours. As soon as a man is made a sub-deacon, we prohibit him from marrying, and he is accounted guilty of sacrilege if he proves instrumental to the population of his country. On the contrary, when any one has taken a sub-deacon's order in Russia, he is obliged likewise to take a wife, and then may rise to the rank of priest, and arch-priest, but he cannot be made a bishop, unless he is a widower and a monk.

Peter forbid all parish-priests from bringing up more than one son to the service of the church, unless it was particularly desired by the parishioners; and this he did, lest a numerous family might in time come to tyrannize over the parish. We may perceive in these little circumstances relating to church- government, that the legislator had always the good of the state in view, and that he took every precaution to make the clergy properly respected, without being dangerous, and that they should be neither contemptible nor powerful.

In those curious memoirs, composed by an officer who was a particular favourite of Peter the Great, I find the following anecdote:—One day a person reading to the czar that number of the English Spectator, in which a parallel is drawn between him and Lewis XIV. 'I do not think,' said Peter, 'that I deserve the preference that is here given me over that monarch; but I have been fortunate enough to have the superiority over him in one essential point, namely, that of having obliged my clergy to live in peace and submission; whereas my brother Lewis has suffered himself to be ruled by his.'

A prince, whose days were almost wholly spent in the fatigues of war, and his nights in the compiling laws for the better government of so large an empire, and in directing so many great labours, through a space of two thousand leagues, must stand in need of some hours of amusement. Diversions at that time were neither so noble or elegant as they now are, and therefore we must not wonder if Peter amused himself with the entertainment of the sham conclave, of which mention has been already made, and other diversions of the same stamp, which were frequently at the expense of the Romish church, to which he had a great dislike, and which was very pardonable in a prince of the Greek communion, who was determined to be master in his own dominions. He likewise gave several entertainments of the same kind at the expense of the monks of his own country; but of the ancient monks, whose follies and bigotry he wished to ridicule, while he strove to reform the new.

We have already seen that previous to his publishing his church-laws, he created one of his fools pope, and celebrated the feast of the sham conclave.

This fool, whose name was Jotof, was between eighty and ninety. The czar took it into his head to make him marry an old widow of his own age, and to have their nuptials publicly solemnized; he caused the invitation to the marriage guests to be made by four persons who were remarkable for stammering. The bride was conducted to church by decrepit old men, four of the most bulky men that could be found in Russia acted as running footmen. The music were seated in a waggon drawn by bears, whom they every now and then pricked with goads of iron, and who, by their roaring, formed a full base, perfectly agreeable to the concert in the cart. The married couple received the benediction in the cathedral from the hands of a deaf and blind priest, who, to appear more ridiculous, wore a large pair of spectacles on his nose. The procession, the wedding, the marriage-feast, the undressing and putting to bed of the bride and bridegroom, were all of a piece with the rest of this burlesque ceremony.

We may perhaps be apt to look upon this as a trivial and ridiculous entertainment for a great prince; but is it more so than our carnival? or to see five or six hundred persons with masks on their faces, and dressed in the most ridiculous manner, skipping and jumping about together, for a whole night in a large room, without speaking a word to each other?

In fine, were the ancient feasts of the fools and the ass, and the abbot of the cuckolds, which were formerly celebrated in our churches, much superior, or did our comedies of the foolish mother exhibit marks of a greater genius?

CHAP. XXXIV.

The congress of Aland or Oeland. Death of Charles XII., &c. The treaty of Nystadt.

These immense labours, this minute review of the whole Russian empire, and the melancholy proceedings against his unhappy son, were not the only objects which demanded the attention of the czar; it was necessary to secure himself without doors, at the same time that he was settling order and tranquillity within. The war with Sweden was still carried on, though faintly, in hopes of approaching peace.

It is a known fact, that in the year 1717, cardinal Alberoni, prime minister to Philip V. of Spain, and baron Gortz, who had gained an entire ascendant over the mind of Charles XII. had concerted a project to change the face of affairs in Europe, by effecting a reconciliation between this last prince and the czar, driving George I. from the English throne, and replacing Stanislaus on that of Poland, while cardinal Alberoni was to procure the regency of France for his master Philip. Gortz, as has been already observed, had opened his mind on this head to the czar himself. Alberoni had begun a negotiation with prince Kourakin, the czar's ambassador at the Hague, by means of the Spanish ambassador, Baretti Landi, a native of Mantua, who had, like the cardinal, quitted his own country to live in Spain.

Thus a set of foreigners were about to overturn the general system, for masters under whose dominion they were not born, or rather for themselves. Charles XII. gave into all these projects, and the czar contented himself with examining them in private. Since the year 1716 he had made only feeble efforts against Sweden, and those rather with a view to oblige that kingdom to purchase peace by restoring those places it had taken in the course of the war, than with an intent to crush it altogether.

The baron Gortz, ever active and indefatigable in his projects, had prevailed on the czar to send plenipotentiaries to the island of Oeland to set on foot a treaty of peace. Bruce, a Scotchman, and grand master of the ordnance in Russia, and the famous Osterman, who was afterwards at the head of affairs, arrived at the place appointed for the congress exactly at the time that the czarowitz was put under arrest at Moscow. Gortz and Gillembourg were already there on the part of Charles XII. both impatient to bring about a reconciliation between that prince and Peter, and to revenge themselves on the king of England. It was an extraordinary circumstance that there should be a congress, and no cessation of arms. The czar's fleet still continued cruising on the coasts of Sweden, and taking the ships of that nation. Peter thought by keeping up hostilities to hasten the conclusion of a peace, of which he knew the Swedes stood greatly in need, and which must prove highly glorious to the conqueror.

Notwithstanding the little hostilities which still continued, every thing bespoke the speedy approach of peace. The preliminaries began by mutual acts of generosity, which produce stronger effects than many hand-writings. The czar sent back without ransom marshal Erenschild, whom he had taken prisoner with his own hands, and Charles in return did the same by Trubetskoy and Gallowin, who had continued prisoners in Sweden ever since the battle of Narva.

The negotiations now advanced apace, and a total change was going to be made in the affairs of the North. Gortz proposed to the czar to put the duchy of Mecklenburg into his hands. Duke Charles, its sovereign, who had married a daughter of czar John, Peter's elder brother, was at variance with the nobility of the country, who had taken arms against him. And Peter, who looked upon that prince as his brother-in-law, had an army in Mecklenburg ready to espouse his cause. The king of England, elector of Hanover,declared on the side of the nobles. Here was another opportunity of mortifying the king of England, by putting Peter in possession of Mecklenburg, who, being already master of Livonia, would by this means, in a short time, become more powerful in Germany than any of its electors. The duchy of Courland was to be given to the duke of Mecklenburg, as an equivalent for his own, together with a part of Prussia at the expense of Poland, who was to have Stanislaus again for her king. Bremen and Verden were to revert to Sweden; but these provinces could not be wrested out of the hands of the king of England but by force of arms; accordingly Gortz's project was (as we have already said) to effect a firm union between Peter and Charles XII., and that not only by the bands of peace, but by an offensive alliance, in which case they were jointly to send an army into Scotland. Charles XII. after having made himself master of Norway, was to make a descent on Great Britain, and he fondly imagined he should be able to set a new sovereign on the throne of those kingdoms, after having replaced one of his own choosing on that of Poland. Cardinal Alberoni promised both Peter and Charles to furnish them with subsidies. The fall of the king of England would, it was supposed, draw with it that of his ally, the regent of France, who being thus deprived of all support, was to fall a victim to the victorious arms of Spain, and the discontent of the French nation.

Alberoni and Gortz now thought themselves secure of totally overturning the system of Europe, when a cannon ball from the bastions of Frederickshal in

Norway confounded all their mighty projects. Charles XII. was killed, the Spanish fleet was beaten by that of England, the conspiracy which had been formed in France was discovered and quelled, Alberoni was driven out of Spain, and Gortz was beheaded at Stockholm; and of all this formidable league, so lately made, the czar alone retained his credit, who by not having put himself in the power of any one, gave law to all his neighbours.

At the death of Charles XII. there was a total change of measures in Sweden. Charles had governed with a despotic power, and his sister Ulrica was elected Queen on express condition of renouncing arbitrary government. Charles intended to form an alliance with the czar against England and its allies, and the new government of Sweden now joined those allies against theczar.

The congress at Oeland, however, was not broken up; but the Swedes, now in league with the English, flattered themselves that the fleets of that nation sent into the Baltic would procure them a more advantageous peace. A body of Hanoverian troops entered the dominions of the duke of Mecklenburg (Feb. 1716.), but were soon driven from thence by the czar's forces.

Peter likewise had a body of troops in Poland, which kept in awe both the party of Augustus, and that of Stanislaus; and as to Sweden, he had a fleet always ready, either to make a descent on their coasts, or to oblige the Swedish government to hasten matters in the congress. This fleet consisted of twelve large ships of the line, and several lesser ones, besides frigates and galleys. The czar served on board this fleet as vice-admiral, under the command of admiral Apraxin.

A part of this fleet signalized itself in the beginning against a Swedish squadron, and, after an obstinate engagement, took one ship of the line, and two frigates. Peter, who constantly endeavoured, by every possible means, to encourage and improve the navy he had been at so much pains to establish, gave, on this occasion, sixty thousand French livres[111] in money among the officers of this squadron, with several gold medals, besides conferring marks of honour on those who principally distinguished themselves.

About this time also the English fleet under admiral Norris came up the Baltic, in order to favour the Swedes. Peter, who well knew how far he could depend on his new navy, was not to be frightened by the English, but boldly kept the sea, and sent to know of the English admiral if he was come only as a friend to the Swedes, or as an enemy to Russia? The admiral returned for answer, that he had not as yet any positive orders from his court on that head: however Peter, notwithstanding this equivocal reply, continued to keep the sea with his fleet.

The English fleet, which in fact was come thither only to shew itself, and thereby induce the czar to grant more favourable conditions of peace to the Swedes, went to Copenhagen, and the Russians made some descents on the Swedish coast, and even in the neighbourhood of Copenhagen, (July 1719.) where they destroyed some copper mines, burnt about fifteen thousand houses, and did mischief enough to make the Swedes heartily wish for a speedy conclusion of the peace.

Accordingly the new queen of Sweden pressed a renewal of the negotiations; Osterman himself was sent to Stockholm, and matters continued in this situation during the whole of the year 1719.

The following year the prince of Hesse, husband to the queen of Sweden, and now become king, in virtue of her having yielded up the sovereign power in his favour, began his reign by sending a minister to the court of Petersburg, in order to hasten the so much desired peace; but the war was still carried on in the midst of these negotiations.

The English fleet joined that of the Swedes, but did not yet commit any hostilities, as there was no open rupture between the courts of Russia and England, and admiral Norris even offered his master's mediation towards bringing about a peace; but as this offer was made with arms in hand, it rather retarded than facilitated the negotiations. The coasts of Sweden, and those of the new Russian provinces in the Baltic, are so situated, that the former lay open to every insult, while the latter are secured by their difficult access. This was clearly seen when admiral Norris, after having thrown off the mask, (June 1720.) made a descent in conjunction with the Swedish fleet on a little island in the province of Esthonia, called Narguen, which belonged to the czar, where they only burnt a peasant's house; but the Russians at the same time made a descent near Wasa, and burnt forty-one villages, and upwards of one thousand houses, and did an infinite deal of damage to the country round about. Prince Galitzin boarded and took four Swedish frigates, and the English admiral seemed to have come only to be spectator of that pitch of glory to which the czar had raised his infant navy; for he had but just shewn himself in those seas, when the Swedish frigates were carried in triumph into the harbour of Cronslot before Petersburg.[112] On this occasions methinks the English did too much if they came only as mediators, and too little if as enemies.

Nov. 1720.] At length, the new king of Sweden demanded a cessation of arms; and as he found the menaces of the English had stood him in no stead, he had recourse to the duke of Orleans, the French regent; and this prince, at once an ally of Russia and Sweden, had the honour of effecting a reconciliation between them. (Feb. 1721.) He sent Campredon, his plenipotentiary, to the court of Petersburg, and from thence to that of

Stockholm. A congress was opened at Nystadt,[113] but the czar would not agree to a cessation of arms till matters were on the point of being concluded and the plenipotentiaries ready to sign. He had an army in Finland ready to subdue the rest of that province, and his fleets were continually threatening the Swedish coasts, so that he seemed absolute master of dictating the terms of peace; accordingly they subscribed to whatever he thought fit to demand. By this treaty he was to remain in perpetual possession of all that his arms had conquered, from the borders of Courland to the extremity of the gulf of Finland, and from thence again of the whole extent of the country of Kexholm, and that narrow slip of Finland which stretches out to the northward of the neighbourhood of Kexholm; so that he remained master of all Livonia, Esthonia, Ingria, Carelia, with the country of Wybourg, and the neighbouring isles, which secured to him the sovereignty of the sea, as likewise of the isles of Oessel, Dago, Mona, and several others: the whole forming an extent of three thousand leagues of country, of unequal breadth, and which altogether made a large kingdom, that proved the reward of twenty years' immense pains and labour.

The peace was signed at Nystadt the 10th September, 1721, N. S. by the Russian minister Osterman, and general Bruce.

Peter was the more rejoiced at that event, as it freed him from the necessity of keeping such large armies on the frontiers of Sweden, as also from any apprehensions on the part of England, or of the neighbouring states, and left him at full liberty to exert his whole attention to the modelling of his empire, in which he had already made so successful a beginning, and to cherish arts and commerce, which he had introduced among his subjects, at the expense of infinite labour and industry.

In the first transports of his satisfaction, we find him writing in these terms to his plenipotentiaries; 'You have drawn up the treaty as if we ourself had dictated and sent it to you to offer the Swedes to sign. This glorious event shall be ever present to our remembrance.'

All degrees of people, throughout the Russian empire, gave proofs of their satisfaction, by the most extraordinary rejoicings of all kinds, and particularly at Petersburg. The triumphal festivals, with which the czar had entertained his people during the course of the war, were nothing to compare to these rejoicings for the peace, which every one hailed with unutterable satisfaction. The peace itself was the most glorious of all his triumphs; and what pleased more than all the pompous shows on the occasion, was a free pardon and general release granted to all prisoners, and a general remission of all sums due to the royal treasury for taxes throughout the whole empire, to the day of the publication of the peace. In consequence of which a multitude of unhappy wretches, who had been confined in prison, were set at liberty, excepting only those guilty of highway-robbery, murder, or treason.[114]

It was at this time that the senate decreed Peter the titles of *Great*, *Emperor*, and *Father of his Country*. Count Golofkin, the high chancellor, made a speech to the czar in the great cathedral, in the name of all the orders of the state, the senators crying aloud, *Long live our emperor and father!* in which acclamations they were joined by the united voice of all the people present. The ministers of France, Germany, Poland, Denmark, and the states-general, waited on him, with their congratulations, on the titles lately bestowed on him, and formally acknowledged for emperor him who had been always publicly known in Holland by that title, ever since the battle of Pultowa. The names of *Father*, and of *Great*, were glorious epithets, which no one in Europe could dispute him; that of *Emperor* was only a honorary title, given by custom to the sovereigns of Germany, as titular kings of the Romans; and it requires time before such appellations come to be formally adopted by those courts where forms of state and real glory are different things. But Peter was in a short time after acknowledged emperor by all the states of Europe, excepting only that of Poland, which was still divided by factions, and the pope, whose suffrage was become of very little significance, since the court of Rome had lost its credit in proportion as other nations became more enlightened.

CHAP. XXXV.

Conquests in Persia.

The situation of Russia is such, as necessarily obliges her to keep up certain connexions with all the nations that lie in the fifth degree of north latitude. When under a bad administration, she was a prey by turns to the Tartars, the Swedes, and the Poles; but when governed by a resolute and vigorous prince, she became formidable to all her neighbours. Peter began his reign by an advantageous treaty with the Chinese. He had waged war at one and the same time against the Swedes and the Turks, and now prepared to lead his victorious armies into Persia.

At this time Persia began to fall into that deplorable state, in which we now behold her. Let us figure to ourselves the thirty years' war in Germany, the times of the league, those of the massacre of St. Bartholomew, and the reigns of Charles VI. and of king John in France, the civil wars in England, the long and horrible ravages of the whole Russian empire by the Tartars, or their invasion of China; and then we shall have some slight conception of the miseries under which the Persian empire has so long groaned.

A weak and indolent prince, and a powerful and enterprising subject, are sufficient to plunge a whole nation into such an abyss of disasters. Hussein, sha, shaic, or sophi of Persia, a descendant of the great sha Abbas, who sat at this time on the throne of Persia, had given himself wholly up to luxury and effeminacy: his prime minister committed acts of the greatest violence and injustice, which this great prince winked at, and this gave rise to forty years' desolation and bloodshed.

Persia, like Turkey, has several provinces, all governed in a different manner; she has subjects immediately under her dominion, vassals, tributary princes, and even nations, to whom the court was wont to pay a tribute, under the name of subsidies; for instance, the people of Daghestan, who inhabit the branches of mount Caucasus, to the westward of the Caspian Sea, which was formerly a part of the ancient Albania; for all nations have changed their appellation and their limits. These are now called Lesgians, and are mountaineers, who are rather under the protection, than the dominion, of Persia; to these the government paid subsidies for defending the frontiers.

At the other extremity of the empire, towards the Indies, was the prince of Candahar, who commanded a kind of martial militia, called Aghwans. This prince of Candahar was a vassal of the Persian, as the hospodars of Walachia and Moldavia are of the Turkish empire: this vassalage was not hereditary, but exactly the same with the ancient feudal tenures established throughout Europe, by that race of Tartars who overthrew the Roman empire. The Aghwan militia, of which the prince of Candahar was the head, was the same with the Albanians on the coasts of the Caspian Sea, in the neighbourhood of Daghestan, and a mixture of Circassians and Georgians, like the ancient Mamelucks who enslaved Egypt. The name of Aghwans is a corruption; Timur, whom we call Tamerlane, had led these people into India, and they remained settled in the province of Candahar, which sometimes belonged to the Mogul empire, and sometimes to that of Persia. It was these Aghwans and Lesgians who began the revolution.

Mir-Weis, or Meriwitz, intendant of the province, whose office was only to collect the tributes, assassinated the prince of Candahar, armed the militia, and continued master of the province till his death, which happened in 1717. His brother came quietly to the succession, by paying a slight tribute to the Persian court. But the son of Mir-Weis, who inherited the ambition of his father, assassinated his uncle, and began to erect himself into a conqueror. This young man was called Mir-Mahmoud, but he was known in Europe only by the name of his father, who had begun the rebellion. Mahmoud reinforced his Aghwans, by adding to them all the Guebres he could get together. These Guebres were an ancient race of Persians, who had been dispersed by the caliph Omar, and who still continued attached to the religion of the Magi (formerly flourished in the reign of Cyrus), and were always secret enemies to the new Persians. Having assembled his forces, Mahmoud marched into the heart of Persia, at the head of a hundred thousand men.

At the same time the Lesgians or Albanians, who, on account of the troublesome times, had not received their subsidies from the court of Persia, came down from their mountains with an armed force, so that the flames of civil war were lighted up at both ends of the empire, and extended themselves even to the capital.

These Lesgians ravaged all that country which stretches along the western borders of the Caspian Sea, as far as Derbent, or the Iron Gate. In this country is situated the city of Shamache, about fifteen leagues distant from the sea, and is said to have been the ancient residence of Cyrus, and by the Greeks called Cyropolis, for we know nothing of the situation or names of these countries, but what we have from the Greeks; but as the Persians never had a prince called Cyrus, much less had they any city called Cyropolis. It is much in the same manner that the Jews, who commenced authors when they were settled in Alexandria, framed a notion of a city called Scythopolis, which, said they, was built by the Scythians in the neighbourhood of Judea, as if either

Scythians or ancient Jews could have given Greek names to their towns.

The city of Shamache was very rich. The Armenians, who inhabit in the neighbourhood of this part of the Persian empire, carried on an immense traffic there, and Peter had lately established a company of Russian merchants at his own expense, which company became very flourishing. The Lesgians made themselves masters of this city by surprise, plundered it, and put to death all the Russians who traded there under the protection of shah Hussein, after having stripped all their warehouses. The loss on this occasion was said to amount to four millions of rubles.

Peter upon this sent to demand satisfaction of the emperor Hussein, who was then disputing the throne with the rebel Mahmoud, who had usurped it, and likewise of Mahmoud himself. The former of these was willing to do the czar justice, the other refused it; Peter therefore resolved to right himself, and take advantage of the distractions in the Persian empire.

Mir-Mahmoud still pushed his conquests in Persia. The sophi hearing that the emperor of Russia was preparing to enter the Caspian Sea, in order to revenge the murder of his subjects at Shamache, made private application to him, by means of an Armenian, to take upon him at the same time the defence of Persia.

Peter had for a considerable time formed a project to make himself master of the Caspian Sea, by means of a powerful naval force, and to turn the tide of commerce from Persia and a part of India through his own dominions. He had caused several parts of this sea to be sounded, the coasts to be surveyed, and exact charts made of the whole. He then set sail for the coast of Persia the 15th day of May, 1722. Catherine accompanied him in this voyage, as she had done in the former. They sailed down the Wolga as far as the city of Astracan. From thence he hastened to forward the canals which were to join the Caspian, the Baltic, and the Euxine seas, a work which has been since executed in part under the reign of his grandson.

While he was directing these works, the necessary provisions for his expedition were arrived in the Caspian Sea. He was to take with him twenty- two thousand foot, nine thousand dragoons, fifteen thousand Cossacks, and three thousand seamen, who were to work the ships, and occasionally assist the soldiery in making descents on the coast. The horse were to march over land through deserts where there was frequently no water to be had, and afterwards to pass over the mountains of Caucasus, where three hundred men are sufficient to stop the progress of a whole army; but the distracted condition in which Persia then was, warranted the most hazardous enterprises.

The czar sailed about a hundred leagues to the southward of Astracan, till he came to the little town of Andrewhoff. It may appear extraordinary to hear of the name of Andrew on the coasts of the Hyrcanian Sea; but some Georgians, who were formerly a sect of Christians, had built this town, which the Persians afterwards fortified; but it fell an easy prey to the czar's arms. From thence he continued advancing by land into the province of Daghestan, and caused manifestoes to be circulated in the Turkish and Persian languages.[115] It was necessary to keep fair with the Ottoman Porte, who reckoned among its subjects, not only the Circassians and Georgians, who border upon this country, but also several powerful vassals, who had of late put themselves under the protection of the grand seignior.

Among others there was one very powerful, named Mahmoud d'Utmich, who took the title of sultan, and had the courage to attack the czar's troops, by which he was totally defeated, and the story says, that his whole country was made a bonfire on the occasion.

Sept. 14, 1722.] In a short time afterwards Peter arrived at the city of Derbent, by the Persians and Turks called Demir Capi, that is, the Iron Gate, and so named from having formerly had an iron gate at the south entrance. The city is long and narrow, its upper part joins to a rocky branch of Mount Caucasus, and the walls of the lower part are washed by the sea, which in violent storms make a breach over them. These walls might pass for one of the wonders of antiquity, being forty feet in height, and six in breadth, defended with square towers at the distance of every fifty feet. The whole work seems one uniform piece, and is built of a sort of brown free-stone mixed with pounded shells, which served as mortar, so that the whole forms a mass harder than marble. The city lies open from the sea, but part of it next the land appears impregnable. There are still some ruins of an old wall like that of China, which must have been built in the earliest times of antiquity, and stretched from the borders of the Caspian Sea to the Pontus Euxinus; and this was probably a rampart raised by the ancient kings of Persia against those swarms of barbarians which dwelt between those two seas.

According to the Persian tradition, the city of Derbent was partly repaired and fortified by Alexander the Great. Arrian and Quintus Curtius tell us, that Alexander absolutely rebuilt this city. They say indeed that it was on the banks of the Tanais or Don, but then in their time the Greeks gave the name of Tanais to the river Cyrus, which runs by the city. It would be a contradiction to suppose that Alexander should build a harbour in the Caspian Sea, on a river that opens into the Black Sea.

There were formerly three or four other ports in different parts of the Caspian Sea, all which were probably built with the same view; for the several nations inhabiting to the west, east, and north of that sea, have in all times been barbarians, who had rendered themselves formidable to the rest of the world, and from hence principally issued those swarms of conquerors who subjugated Asia and Europe.

And here I must beg leave to remark, how much pleasure authors in all ages have taken to impose upon mankind, and how much they have preferred a vain show of eloquence to matter of fact. Quintus Curtius puts into the mouths of Scythians an admirable speech full of moderation and philosophy, as if the Tartars of those regions had been all so many sages, and that Alexander had not been the general nominated by the Greeks against the king of Persia, sovereign of the greatest part of southern Scythia and the Indies. Other rhetoricians, thinking to imitate Quintus Curtius, have studied to make us look upon those savages of Caucacus and its dreary deserts, who lived wholly upon rapine and bloodshed, as the people in the world most remarkable for austere virtue and justice, and have painted Alexander, the avenger of Greece, and the conqueror of those who would have enslaved him and his country, as a public robber, who had ravaged the world without justice or reason.

Such writers do not consider, that these Tartars were never other than destroyers, and that Alexander built towns in the very country which they inhabited; and in this respect I may venture to compare Peter the Great to Alexander; like him he was assiduous and indefatigable in his pursuits, a lover and friend of the useful arts; he surpassed him as a lawgiver, and like him endeavoured to change the tide of commerce in the world, and built and repaired at least as many towns as that celebrated hero of antiquity.

On the approach of the Russian army, the governor of Derbent resolved not to sustain a siege, whether he thought he was not able to defend the place, or that he preferred the czar's protection to that of the tyrant Mahmoud; brought the keys of the town and citadel (which were silver) and presented them to Peter, whose army peaceably entered the city, and then encamped on the sea-shore.

The usurper, Mahmoud, already master of great part of Persia, in vain endeavoured to prevent the czar from taking possession of Derbent: he stirred up the neighbouring Tartars, and marched into Persia to the relief of the place; but, too late, for Derbent was already in the hands of theconqueror.

Peter however was not in a condition to push his successes any further at this time. The vessels which were bringing him a fresh supply of provisions, horses, and recruits, had been cast away near Astracan, and the season was far spent. He therefore returned to Moscow, Jan. 5. which he entered in triumph; and after his arrival (according to custom) gave a strict account of his expedition to the vice-czar Romadanowski, thus keeping up this extraordinary farce, which, says his eulogium, pronounced in the academy of sciences at

Paris, ought to have been performed before all the monarchs of the earth.

The empire of Persia continued to be divided between Hussein and the usurper Mahmoud. The first of these thought to find a protector in the czar, and the other dreaded him as an avenger, who was come to snatch the fruits of his rebellion out of his hands. Mahmoud exerted all his endeavours to stir up the Ottoman Porte against Peter, and for this purpose sent an embassy to Constantinople, while the princes of Daghestan, who were under the protection of the grand seignior, and had been stript of their territories by the victorious army of Peter, cried aloud for vengeance. The divan was now alarmed for the safety of Georgia, which the Turks reckon in the number of their dominions.

The grand seignior was on the point of declaring war against the czar, butwas prevented by the courts of Vienna and Paris. The emperor of Germany at the same time declared, that if Russia should be attacked by the Turks, he must be obliged to defend it. The marquis de Bonac, the French ambassador at Constantinople, made a dextrous use of the menaces of the imperial court, and at the same time insinuated, that it was contrary to the true interest of the Turkish empire, to suffer a rebel and an usurper to set the example of dethroning sovereigns, and that the czar had done no more than what the grand seignior himself ought to have done.

During these delicate negotiations, Mir Mahmoud was advanced to the gates of Derbent, and had laid waste all the neighbouring country in order to cutoff all means of subsistence from the Russian army. That part of ancient Hyrcania, now called Ghilan, was reduced to a desert, and the inhabitants threw themselves under the protection of the Russians, whom they looked upon as their deliverers.

In this they followed the example of the sophi himself. That unfortunate prince sent a formal embassy to Peter the Great, to request his assistance; but the ambassador was hardly departed, when the rebel, Mir Mahmoud, seized on Ispahan and the person of his master.

Thamaseb, the son of the dethroned sophi, who was taken prisoner, found means to escape out of the tyrant's hands, and got together a body of troops, with which he gave the usurper battle. He seconded his father's entreaties to Peter the Great for his protection, and sent to the ambassador the same instructions which Shah Hussein had given him.

This ambassador, whose name was Ishmael Beg, found that his negotiations had proved successful, even before he arrived in person; for, on landing at Astracan, he learnt that general Matufkin was going to set out with fresh recruits to reinforce the army in Daghestan. The dey of Baku or Bachu, which with the Persians gives to the Caspian Sea the name of the Sea of Bacou, was not yet taken. The ambassador therefore gave the Russian general a letter for the inhabitants, in which he exhorted them in his master's name to submit to the emperor of Russia. The ambassador then proceeded to Petersburg, and general Matufkin departed to lay siege to the city of Bachu. (Aug. 1723.) The Persian ambassador arrived at the czar's court the very day that tidings were brought of the reduction of that city.

Baku is situate near Shamache, but is neither so well peopled, nor so rich as the latter. It is chiefly remarkable for the naptha, with which it furnishes all Persia. Never was treaty so speedily concluded as that of Ishmael Beg. (Sept. 1723.) Czar Peter promised to march with his forces into Persia, in order to revenge the death of his subjects, and to succour Thamaseb against the usurper of his crown, and the new sophi in return was to cede to him, not only the towns of Bachu and Derbent, but likewise the provinces of Ghilan, Mazanderan, and Asterabath.

Ghilan is, as we have already observed, the ancient South Hyrcania; Mazanderan, which joins to it, is the country of the Mardi, or Mardians; and Asterabath borders upon Mazanderan. These were the three principal provinces of the ancient Median kings; so that Peter beheld himself, by the means of arms and treaties, in possession of the original kingdom of Cyrus.

It may not be foreign to our subject to observe, that by the articles of this convention, the prices of necessaries to be furnished to the army were settled. A camel was to cost only sixty franks (about twelve rubles) a pound of bread no more than five farthings, the same weight of beef about six. These prices furnish a convincing proof of the plenty he found in these countries, that possessions in land are of the most intrinsic value, and that money, which is only of nominal worth, was at that time very scarce.

Such was the deplorable state to which Persia was then reduced, that the unfortunate sophi Thamaseb, a wanderer in his own kingdom, and flying before the face of the rebel, Mahmoud, who had dipt his hands in the bloodof his father and his brothers, was necessitated to entreat the court of Russia and the Turkish divan to accept of one part of his dominions to preserve for him the rest.

It was agreed then, between czar Peter, sultan Achmet III. and the sophi Thamaseb, that the first of these should keep the three provinces above- named, and that the Porte should have Casbin, Tauris, and Erivan, besides what she had already taken from the usurper. Thus was this noble kingdom dismembered at once by the Russians, the Turks, and the Persians themselves.

And now the emperor Peter might be said to extend his dominions from the furthest part of the Baltic Sea, beyond the southern limits of the Caspian. Persia still continued a prey to violations and devastations, and its natives, till then opulent and polite, were now sunk in poverty and barbarism, while the Russian people had arisen from indigence and ignorance to a state of riches and learning. One single man, by a resolute and enterprising genius, had brought his country out of obscurity; and another, by his weakness and indolence, had brought destruction upon his.

Hitherto we know very little of the private calamities which for so long a time spread desolation over the face of the Persian empire. It is said, that shah Hussein was so pusillanimous as to place with his own hands the tiara or crown of Persia on the head of the usurper Mahmoud, and also that this Mahmoud afterwards went mad. Thus the lives of so many thousands of men depend on the caprice of a madman or a fool. They add furthermore, that Mahmoud, in one of his fits of frenzy, put to death with his own hand all the sons and nephews of the shah Hussein to the number of a hundred; and that he caused the gospel of St. John to be read upon his head, in order to purify himself, and to receive a cure for his disorder. These and such like Persian fables have been circulated by our monks, and afterwards printed in Paris.

The tyrant, after having murdered his uncle, was in his turn put to death by his nephew Eshreff, who was as cruel and bloody a tyrant as Mahmoud himself.

Shah Thamaseb still continued imploring the assistance of Russia. This Thamaseb or shah Thomas, was assisted and afterwards replaced on the throne by the famous Kouli Khan, and was again dethroned by the same Kouli Khan.

The revolutions and wars which Russia had afterwards to encounter against the Turks, and in which she proved victorious, the evacuating the three provinces in Persia, which cost Russia more to keep than they were worth, are events which do not concern Peter the Great, as they did not happen till several years after his death; it may suffice to observe, that he finished his military career by adding three provinces to his empire on the part next to Persia, after having just before added the same number on that side next to Sweden.

CHAP. XXXVI.

Of the Coronation of the Empress Catherine I. and the Death of Peter the Great.

Peter, at his return from his Persian expedition, found himself in a better condition than ever to be the arbiter of the North. He now openly declared himself the protector of Charles XII. whose professed enemy he had been for eighteen years. He sent for the duke of Holstein, nephew to that monarch, to his court, promised him his eldest daughter in marriage, and began to make preparations for supporting him in his claims on the duchy of Holstein Sleswick, and even engaged himself so to do by a treaty of alliance, (Feb. 1724.) which he concluded with the crown of Sweden.

He continued the works he had begun all over his empire, to the further extremity of Kamtshatka, and for the better direction of them, established an academy of sciences at Petersburg. The arts began now to flourish on every side: manufactures were encouraged, the navy was augmented, the army well provided, and the laws properly enforced. He now enjoyed his glory in full repose; but was desirous of sharing it in a new manner with her who, according to his own declaration, by remedying the disaster of the campaign of Pruth, had been in some measure the instrument of his acquiring that glory.

Accordingly, the coronation of his consort Catherine was performed at Moscow, in presence of the duchess of Courland, his eldest brother's daughter, and the duke of Holstein, his intended son-in-law. (May 28, 1724.) The declaration which he published on this occasion merits attention: he therein cites the examples of several Christian princes who had placed the crown on the heads of their consorts, as likewise those of the heathen emperors, Basilides, Justinian, Heraclius, and Leo, the philosopher. He enumerates the services Catherine had done to the state, and in particular in the war against the Turks,—'Where my army,' says he, 'which had been reduced to 22,000 men, had to encounter an army above 200,000 strong.' He does not say, in this declaration, that the empress was to succeed to the crown after his death; but this ceremony, which was altogether new and unusual in the Russian empire, was one of those means by which he prepared the minds of his subjects for such an event. Another circumstance that might perhaps furnish a stronger reason to believe that he destined Catherine to succeed him on the throne, was, that he himself marched on foot before her the day of her coronation, as captain of a new company, which he had created under the name of the *knights of the empress*.

When they arrived at the cathedral, Peter himself placed the crown on her head; and when she would have fallen down and embraced his knees, he prevented her; and, at their return from the church, caused the sceptre and globe to be carried before her. The ceremony was altogether worthy an emperor; for on every public occasion Peter shewed as much pomp and magnificence as he did plainness and simplicity in his private manner of living.

Having thus crowned his spouse, he at length determined to give his eldest daughter, Anna Petrowna, in marriage to the duke of Holstein. This princess greatly resembled her father in the face, was very majestic, and of a singular beauty. She was betrothed to the duke of Holstein on the 24th of November, 1724, but with very little ceremony. Peter having for some time past found his health greatly impaired, and this, together with some family uneasiness, that perhaps rather increased his disorder, which in a short time proved fatal, permitted him to have but very little relish for feasts or public diversions in this latter part of his life. [116] The empress Catherine had at that time a young man for the chamberlain of her household, whose name was Moens de la Croix, a native of Russia, but of Flemish parents, remarkably handsome and genteel. His sister, madame de Balc, was bed-chamber-woman to the empress, and these two had entirely the management of her household. Being both accused of having taken presents, they were sent to prison, and afterwards brought to their trial by express order of the czar; who, by an edict in the year 1714, had forbidden any one holding a place about court to receive any present or other gratuity, on pain of being declared infamous, and suffering death; and this prohibition had been several times renewed.

The brother and sister were found guilty, and received sentence, and all those who had either purchased their services or given them any gratuity in return for the same, were included therein, except the duke of Holstein and his minister count Bassewitz: as it is probable that the presents made by that prince, to those who had a share in bringing about his marriage with the czar's daughter, were not looked upon in a criminal light.

Moens was condemned to be beheaded, and his sister (who was the empress's favourite) to receive eleven strokes of the knout. The two sons of this lady, one of whom was an officer in the household, and the other a page, were degraded, and sent to serve as private soldiers in the army in Persia.

These severities, though they shock our manners, were perhaps necessary in a country where the observance of the laws is to be enforced only by the most terrifying rigour. The empress solicited her favourite's pardon; but the czar, offended at her application, peremptorily refused her, and, in the heat of his passion, seeing a fine looking-glass in the apartment, he, with one blow of his fist, broke it into a thousand pieces; and, turning to the empress, 'Thus,' said he, 'thou seest I can, with one stroke of my hand, reduce this glass to its original dust.' Catherine, in a melting accent, replied, 'It is true, you have destroyed one of the greatest ornaments of your palace, but do you think that palace is the more charming for its loss?' This answer appeased the emperor's wrath; but all the favour that Catherine could obtain for her bed-chamber- woman was, that she should receive only five strokes of the knout instead of eleven.

I should not have related this anecdote, had it not been attested by a public minister, who was eye-witness of the whole transaction, and who, by having made presents to the unfortunate brother and sister, was perhaps himself one of the principal causes of their disgrace and sufferings. It was this affair that emboldened those who judge of every thing in the worst light, to spread the report that Catherine hastened the death of her husband, whose choleric disposition filled her with apprehensions that overweighed the gratitude she owed him for the many favours he had heaped upon her.

These cruel suspicions were confirmed by Catherine's recalling to court her woman of the bed-chamber immediately upon the death of the czar, and reinstating her in her former influence. It is the duty of an historian to relate the public reports which have been circulated in all times in states, on the decease of princes who have been snatched away by a premature death, as if nature was not alone sufficient to put a period to the existence of a crowned head as well as that of a beggar; but it is likewise the duty of an historian to shew how far such reports were rashly or unjustly formed.

There is an immense distance between the momentary discontent which may arise from the morose or harsh behaviour of a husband, and the desperate resolution of poisoning that husband, who is at the same time our sovereign and benefactor in the highest degree. The danger attending such a design would have been as great as it was criminal. Catherine had at that time a powerful party against her, who epoused the cause of the son of the deceased czarowitz. Nevertheless, neither that faction, nor any one person about the court, once suspected the czarina; and the vague rumours which were spread on this head were founded only on the mistaken notions of foreigners, who were very imperfectly acquainted with the affair, and who chose to indulge the wretched pleasure of accusing of heinous crimes those whom they thought interested to commit them. But it was even very doubtful whether this was at all the case with Catherine. It was far from being certain that she was to succeed her husband. She had been crowned indeed, but only in the character of wife to the reigning sovereign, and not as one who was to enjoy the sovereign authority after his death.

Peter, in his declaration, had only ordered this coronation as a matter of ceremony, and not as conferring a right of governing. He therein only cited the examples of emperors, who had caused their consorts to be crowned, but not of those who had conferred on them the royal authority. In fine, at the very time of Peter's illness, several persons believed that the princess Anna Petrowna would succeed him jointly with her husband the duke of Holstein, or that the czar would nominate his grandson for his successor; therefore, so far from Catherine's being interested in the death of the emperor, she rather seemed concerned in the preservation of his life.

It is undeniable, that Peter had, for a considerable time, been troubled with an abscess in the bladder, and a stoppage of urine. The mineral waters of Olnitz, and some others, which he had been advised to use, had proved of very little service to him, and he had found himself growing sensibly weaker, ever since the beginning of the year 1724. His labours, from which he would not allow himself any respite, increased his disorder, and hastened his end: (Jan. 1723.) his malady became now more and more desperate, he felt burning pains, which threw him into an almost constant delirium,[117] whenever he had a moment's interval, he endeavoured to write, but he could only scrawl a few lines that were wholly unintelligible; and it was with the greatest difficulty that the following words, in the Russian language, could be distinguished:
—'*Let every thing be given to* ——'

He then called for the princess Anna Petrowna, in order to dictate to her, but by that time she could come to his bed-side, he had lost his speech, and fell into a fit, which lasted sixteen hours. The empress Catherine did not quit his bed-side for three nights together. At length, he breathed his last in her arms, on the 28th of Jan. 1725. about four o'clock in the morning.

His body was conveyed into the great hall of the palace, accompanied by all the imperial family, the senate, all the principal personages of state, and an innumerable concourse of people. It was there exposed on a bed of state, and every one was permitted to approach and kiss his hand, till the day of his interment, which was on the 10-21st of March, 1725.[118]

It has been thought, and it has been asserted in print, that he had appointed his wife Catherine to succeed him in the empire, by his last will, but the truth is, that he never made any will, or at least none that ever appeared; a most astonishing negligence in so great a legislator, and a proof that he did not think his disorder mortal.

No one knew, at the time of his death, who was to succeed him: he left behind him his grandson Peter, son of the unfortunate Alexis, and his eldest daughter Anna, married to the duke of Holstein. There was a considerable faction in favour of young Peter; but prince Menzikoff, who had never had any other interests than those of the empress Catherine, took care to be beforehand with all parties, and their designs; and accordingly, when the czar was upon the point of giving up the ghost, he caused the empress to remove into another apartment of the palace, where all their friends were assembled ready: he had the royal treasures conveyed into the citadel, and secured the guards in his interest, as likewise the archbishop of Novogorod; and then they held a private council, in presence of the empress Catherine, and one Macarof, a secretary, in whom they could confide, at which the duke of Holstein's minister assisted.

At the breaking up of this council, the empress returned to the czar's bed-side, who soon after yielded up the ghost in her arms. As soon as his death was made known, the principal senators and general officers repaired to the palace, where the empress made a speech to them, which prince Menzikoff answered in the name of all present. The empress being withdrawn, they proceeded to consider the proper forms to be observed on the occasion, when Theophanes, archbishop of Pleskow, told the assembly, that, on the eve of the coronation of the empress Catherine, the deceased czar had declared to him, that his sole reason for placing the crown on her head, was, that she might wear it after his death; upon which the assembly unanimously signed the proclamation, and Catherine succeeded her husband on the throne the very day of his death.

Peter the Great was regretted by all those whom he had formed, and the descendants of those who had been sticklers for the ancient customs soon began to look on him as their father: foreign nations, who have beheld the duration of his establishments, have always expressed the highest admiration for his memory, acknowledging that he was actuated by a more than common prudence and wisdom, and not by a vain desire of doing extraordinary things. All Europe knows that though he was fond of fame, he coveted it only for noble principles; that though he had faults, they never obscured his noble qualities, and that, though, as a man, he was liable to errors, as a monarch he was always great: he every way forced nature, in his subjects, in himself, by sea and land: but he forced her only to render her more pleasing and noble. The arts, which he transplanted with his own hands, into countries, till then in a manner savage, have flourished, and produced fruits which are lasting testimonies of his genius, and will render his memory immortal, since they now appear as natives of those places to which he introduced them. The civil, political, and military government, trade, manufactures, the arts and the sciences, have all been carried on, according to his plan, and by an event not to be paralleled in history: we have seen four women successively ascend the throne after him, who have maintained, in full vigour, all the great designs he accomplished, and have completed those which he had begun.

The court has undergone some revolutions since his death, but the empire has not suffered one. Its splendour was increased by Catherine I. It triumphed over the Turks and the Swedes under Anna Petrowna; and under Elizabeth it conquered Prussia, and a part of Pomerania; and lastly, it has tasted the sweets of peace, and has seen the arts flourish in fulness and security in the reign of Catherine the Second.[119]

Let the historians of that nation enter into the minutest circumstances of the new creation, the wars and undertakings of Peter the Great: let them rouse the emulation of their countrymen, by celebrating those heroes who assisted this monarch in his labours, in the field, and in the cabinet. It is sufficient for a stranger, a disinterested admirer of merit, to have endeavoured to set to view that great man, who learned of Charles XII. to conquer him, who twice quitted his dominions, in order to govern them the better, who worked with his own hands, in almost all the useful and necessary arts, to set an example of instruction to his people, and who was the founder and the father of his empire.[120]

Princes, who reign over states long since civilized, may say to themselves, 'If a man, assisted only by his own genius, has been capable of doing such great things in the frozen climes of ancient Scythia, what may not be expected from us, in kingdoms where the accumulated labours of many ages have rendered the way so easy?'

ORIGINAL PIECES

RELATIVE TO THIS HISTORY, AGREEABLE TO THE TRANSLATIONS MADE AT THEIR FIRST PUBLICATION, BY ORDER OF CZAR PETER I.

SENTENCE

Pronounced against the CZAROWITZ ALEXIS, *June 24th, 1718.*

By virtue of an express ordinance issued by his czarish majesty, and signed by his own hand, on the 13th of June, for the judgment of the czarowitz Alexis Petrowitz, in relation to his crimes and transgressions against his father and sovereign; the undernamed ministers and senators, estates military and civil, after having assembled several times in the regency chamber of the senate of Petersburg, and having heard read the original writings and testimonies given against the czarowitz, as also his majesty's admonitory letters to that prince, and his answers to them in his own writing, and other acts relating to the process, and likewise the criminal informations, declarations and confessions of the czarowitz, partly written with his own hand, and partly delivered by word of mouth to his father and sovereign, before the several persons undernamed, constituted by his czarish majesty's authority to the effect of the present judgment, do acknowledge and declare, that though according to the laws of the Russian empire, it belongs not to them, the natural subjects of his czarish majesty's sovereign dominions, to take cognizance of an affair of this nature, which for its importance depends solely on the absolute will of the sovereign, whose power, unlimited by any law, is derived from God alone; yet, in submission to his ordinance who hath given them this liberty, and after mature reflection, observing the dictates of their consciences without fear, flattery, or respect of persons, having nothing before their eyes but the divine laws applicable to the present case, the canons and rules of councils, the authority of the holy fathers and doctors of the church, and taking also for their rule the instruction of the archbishops and clergy assembled at Petersburg on this occasion, and conforming themselves to the laws and constitutions of this empire, which are agreeable to those of other nations, especially the Greeks and the Romans, and other Christian princes; they unanimously agreed and pronounced the czarowitz Alexis Petrowitz *to be worthy of death*, for the aforesaid crimes and capital transgressions against his sovereign and father, he being his czarish majesty's son and subject; and that, notwithstanding the promise given by his czarish majesty to the czarowitz, in a letter sent by M. Tolstoy and captain Romanzoff, dated from Spaw, the 10th of July, 1717, to pardon his elopement if he voluntarily returned, as the czarowitz himself acknowledges with gratitude, in his answer to that letter, dated from Naples, the 4th of October, 1717, wherein he returns thanks to his majesty for the pardon he had promised him solely on condition of his speedy and voluntary return; yet he hath forfeited and rendered himself unworthy of that pardon, by renewing and continuing his former transgressions, as is fully set forth in his majesty's manifesto of the 3d of February, in this present year, and for not returning voluntarily and of his own accord.

And although his majesty did, upon the arrival of the czarowitz at Moscow, and his humbly confessing in writing his crimes, and asking pardon for them, take pity on him, as is natural for every father to act towards a son, and at the audience, held in the great hall of the castle, dated the said 3d day of February, did promise him full pardon for all his crimes and transgressions, it was only on condition that he would declare, without reserve or restriction, all his designs, and who were his counsellors and abettors therein, but that if he concealed any one person or thing, that in such case the promised pardon should be null and void, which conditions the czarowitz did at that time accept and receive, with all outward tokens of gratitude and obedience, solemnly swearing on the holy cross and the blessed evangelists, and in the presence of all those assembled at that time and for that purpose in the cathedral church, that he would faithfully, and without reserve, declare the whole truth.

His majesty did also the next day confirm to the czarowitz in writing the said promise, in the interrogatories which hereafter follow, and which his majesty caused to be delivered to him, having first written at the begining what follows:

'As you did yesterday receive your pardon, on condition that you would confess all the circumstances of your flight, and whatever relates thereto; but if you concealed any part thereof, you should answer for it with your life; and, as you have already made some confessions, it is expected of you, for our more full satisfaction, and your own safety, to commit the same to writing, in such order as shall in the course of your examination be pointed out to you.'

And at the end, under the seventh question, there was again written, with his czarish majesty's own hand:

'Declare to us, and discover whatever hath any relation to this affair, though it be not here expressed, and clear yourself as if it were at confession; for if you conceal any thing that shall by any other means be afterwards discovered, do not impute the consequence to us, since you have been already told, that in such case the pardon granted you should be null and void.'

Notwithstanding all which, the answers and confessions of the czarowitz were delivered without any sincerity; he not only concealing many of his accomplices, but also the capital circumstances relating to his own transgressions, particularly his rebellious design in usurping the throne even in the life-time of his father, flattering himself that the populace would declare in his favour; all which hath since been fully discovered in the criminal process, after he had refused to make a discovery himself, as hath appeared by the above presents.

Thus it hath appeared by the whole conduct of the czarowitz, as well as by the confessions which he both delivered in writing, and by word of mouth, particularly, that he was not disposed to wait for the succession in the manner in which his father had left it to him after his death, according to equity, and the order of nature which God has established; but intended to take the crown off the head of his father, while living, and set it upon his own, not only by a civil insurrection, but by the assistance of a foreign force, which he had actually requested.

The czarowitz has hereby rendered himself unworthy of the clemency and pardon, promised him by the emperor his father; and since the laws divine and ecclesiastical, civil and military, condemn to death, without mercy, not only those whose attempts against their father and sovereign have been proved by testimonies and writings; but even such as have been convicted of an intention to rebel, and of having formed a base design to kill their sovereign, and usurp the throne; what shall we think of a rebellious design, almost unparalleled in history, joined to that of a horrid parricide, against him who was his father in a double capacity; a father of great lenity and indulgence, who brought up the czarowitz from the cradle with more than paternal care and tenderness; who earnestly endeavoured to form him for government, and with incredible pains, and indefatigable application, to instruct him in the military art, and qualify him to succeed to so great an empire? with how much stronger reason does such a design deserve to be punished with death?

It is therefore with hearts full of affliction, and eyes streaming with tears, that we, as subjects and servants, pronounce this sentence; considering that it belongs not to us to give judgment in a case of so great importance, and especially to pronounce against the son of our most precious sovereign lord the czar. Nevertheless, it being his pleasure that we should act in this capacity, we, by these presents, declare our real opinion, and pronounce this sentence of condemnation with a pure and Christian conscience, as we hope to be able to answer for it at the just, awful, and impartial tribunal of Almighty God.

We submit, however, this sentence, which we now pass, to the sovereign power, the will, and merciful revisal of his czarish majesty, our most gracious sovereign.

THE PEACE OF NYSTADT.

In the name of the Most Holy and undivided Trinity.

Be it known by these presents, that whereas a bloody, long, and expensive war has arisen and subsisted for several years past, between his late majesty king Charles XII. of glorious memory, king of Sweden, of the Goths, and Vandals, &c. &c. his successors to the throne of Sweden, the lady Ulrica queen of Sweden, of the Goths and Vandals, &c. and the kingdom of Sweden, on the one part; and between his czarish majesty Peter the First, emperor of all the Russias, &c. and the empire of Russia, on the other part; the two powers have thought proper to exert their endeavours to find out means to put a period to those troubles, and prevent the further effusion of so much innocent blood; and it has pleased the Almighty to dispose the hearts of both powers, to appoint a meeting of their ministers plenipotentiary, to treat of, and conclude a firm, sincere and lasting peace, and perpetual friendship between the two powers, their dominions, provinces, countries, vassals, subjects, and inhabitants; namely, Mr. John Lilienstedt, one of the most honourable privy- council to his majesty the king of Sweden, his kingdom and chancery, and baron Otto Reinhold Stroemfeld, intendant of the copper mines and fiefs of Dalders, on the part of his said majesty; and on the part of his czarish majesty, count Jacob Daniel Bruce, his general adjutant, president of the colleges of mines and manufactories, and knight of the order of St. Andrew and the White Eagle, and Mr. Henry John Frederic Osterman, one of his said majesty's privy-counsellors in his chancery: which plenipotentiary ministers, being assembled at Nystadt, and having communicated to each other their respective commissions, and imploring the divine assistance, did enter upon this important and salutary enterprise, and have, by the grace and blessing of God, concluded the following peace between the crown of Sweden and his czarish majesty.

Art. 1. There shall be now and henceforward a perpetual and inviolable peace, sincere union, and indissoluble friendship, between his majesty Frederic the First, king of Sweden, of the Goths and Vandals, his successors to the crown and kingdom of Sweden, his dominions, provinces, countries, villages, vassals, subjects, and inhabitants, as well within the Roman empire as out of said empire, on the one side; and his czarish majesty Peter the First, emperor of all the Russias, &c. his successors to the throne of Russia, and all his countries, villages, vassals, subjects, and inhabitants, on the other side; in such wise, that for the future, neither of the two reconciled powers shall commit, or suffer to be committed, any hostility, either privately or publicly, directly or indirectly, nor shall in any wise assist the enemies of each other, on any pretext whatever, not contract any alliance with them, that may be contrary to this peace, but shall always maintain and preserve a sincere friendship towards each other, and as much as in them lies, support their mutual honour, advantage and safety; as likewise prevent, to the utmost of their power, any injury or vexation with which either of the reconciled parties may be threatened by any other power.

Art. 2. It is further mutually agreed upon betwixt the two parties, that a general pardon and act of oblivion for all hostilities committed during the war, either by arms or otherwise, shall be strictly observed, so far as that neither party shall ever henceforth either call to mind, or take vengeance for the same, particularly in regard to persons of state, and subjects who have entered into the service of either of the two parties during the war, and have thereby become enemies to the other, except only the Russian Cossacks, who enlisted in the service of the king of Sweden, and whom his czarish majesty will not consent to have included in the said general pardon, notwithstanding the intercession made for them by the king of Sweden.

Art. 3. All hostilities, both by sea and land, shall cease both here and in the grand duchy of Finland in fifteen days, or sooner, if possible, after the regular exchange of the ratifications; and to this intent the conclusion of the peace shall be published without delay. And in case that, after the expiration of the said term, any hostilities should be committed by either party, either by sea or land, in any manner whatsoever, through ignorance of the conclusion of the peace, such offence shall by no means prejudice the conclusion of said peace; on the contrary, each shall make a reciprocal exchange of both men and effects that may be taken after the said term.

Art. 4. His majesty the king of Sweden does, by the present treaty, as well for himself as for his successors to the throne and kingdom of Sweden, cede to his czarish majesty, and his successors to the Russian empire, in full, irrevocable and everlasting possession, the provinces which have been taken by his czarish majesty's arms from the crown of Sweden during this war, viz. Livonia, Esthonia, Ingria, and a part of Carelia, as likewise the district of the fiefs of Wybourg specified hereafter in the article for regulating the limits;the towns and fortresses of Riga, Dunamund, Pernau, Revel, Dorpt, Nerva, Wybourg, Kexholm, and the other towns, fortresses, harbours, countries, districts, rivers, and coasts, belonging to the provinces: as likewise theislands of Oesel, Dagoe, Moen, and all the other islands from the frontiers of Courland, towards the coasts of Livonia, Esthonia, and Ingria, and on the east side of Revel, and in the road of Wybourg, towards the south-east, with all the present inhabitants of those islands, and of the aforesaid provinces, towns, and countries; and in general, all their appurtenances, dependencies, prerogatives, rights, and advantages, without exception, in like manner as the crown of Sweden possessed them.

To which purpose, his majesty the king of Sweden renounces for ever, in the most solemn manner, as well for his own part, as for his successors, and for the whole kingdom of Sweden, all pretensions which they have hitherto had, or could have, to the said provinces, islands, countries, and towns; and all the inhabitants thereof shall, by virtue of these presents, be discharged from the oath of allegiance, which they have taken to the crown of Sweden, in such wise as that his Swedish majesty, and the kingdom of Sweden, shall never hereafter either claim or demand the same, on any pretence whatsoever; but, on the contrary, they shall be and remain incorporated for ever into the empire of Russia. Moreover, his Swedish majesty, and the kingdom of Sweden, promise by these presents to assist and support from henceforth his czarish majesty, and his successors to the empire of Russia, in the peaceable possession of the said provinces, islands, countries, and towns; and that they will find out and deliver up to the persons authorized by his czarish majesty for that purpose, all the records and papers principally belonging to those places which have been taken away and carried into Sweden during the war.

Art 5. His czarish majesty, in return, promises to evacuate and restore to his Swedish majesty, and the kingdom of Sweden, within the space of four weeks after the exchange of the ratifications of this treaty, or sooner if possible, the grand duchy of Finland, except only that part thereof which has been reserved by the following regulation of the limits which shall belong to his czarish majesty, so that his said czarish majesty, and his successors, never shall have or bring the least claim or demand on the said duchy, on any pretence whatever. His czarish majesty further declares and promises, that certain and prompt payment of two millions of crowns shall be made without any discount to the deputies of the king of Sweden, on condition that they produce and give sufficient receipts, as agreed upon; and the said payment shall be made in such coin as shall be agreed upon by a separate article, which shall be of equal force as if inserted in the body of this treaty.

Art. 6. His majesty the king of Sweden does further reserve to himself, in regard to trade, the liberty of buying corn yearly at Riga, Revel, and Arensbourg, to the amount of fifty thousand rubles, which corn shall be transported from thence into Sweden, without paying duty or any other taxes, on producing a certificate, shewing that such corn has been purchased for the use of his Swedish majesty, or by his subjects, charged with the care of making this purchase by his said majesty; and such right shall not be subject to, or depend on any exigency, wherein his czarish majesty may find it necessary, either on account of a bad harvest, or some other important reasons, to prohibit in general the exportation of corn to any other nation.

Art. 7. His czarish majesty does also promise, in the most solemn manner, that he will in no wise interfere with the private affairs of the kingdom of Sweden, nor with the form of government, which has been regulated and established by the oath of allegiance, and unanimous consent of the states of said kingdom; neither will he assist therein any person whatever, in any manner, directly or indirectly; but, on the contrary, will endeavour to hinder and prevent any disturbance happening, provided his czarish majesty has timely notice of the same, who will on all such occasions act as a sincere friend and good neighbour to the crown of Sweden.

Art. 8. And as they mutually intend to establish a firm sincere and lasting peace, to which purpose it is very necessary to regulate the limits so, that neither of the parties can harbour any jealousy, but that each shall peaceably possess whatever has been surrendered to him by this treaty of peace, they have thought proper to declare, that the two empires shall from henceforth and for ever have the following limits, beginning on the northern coast of the Bothnic gulf, near Wickolax, from whence they shall extend to within half a league of the sea-coast inland, and from the distance of half a league from the sea as far as opposite to Willayoki, and from thence further inland; so that from the sea-side, and opposite to Rohel, there shall be a distance of about three-quarters of a league, in a direct line, to the road which leads from Wibourg to Lapstrand, at three leagues distance from Wibourg, and which proceeds the same distance of three leagues towards the north by Wibourg, in a direct line to the former limits between Russia and Sweden, even before the reduction of the district of Kexholm under the government of the king of Sweden. Those ancient limits extend eight leagues towards the north, from thence they run in a direct line through the district of Kexholm, to the place where the harbour of Porogerai, which begins near the town of Kudumagube, joins to the ancient limits, between Russia and Sweden, so that his majesty the king and kingdom of Sweden, shall henceforth possess all that part lying west and north beyond the above specified limits, and his czarish majesty and the empire of Russia all that part which is situated east and south of the said limits. And as his czarish majesty surrenders from henceforth to his Swedish majesty and the kingdom of Sweden, a part of the district of Kexholm, which belonged heretofore to the empire of Russia, he promises, in the most solemn manner, in regard to himself and successors to the throne of Russia, that he never will make any future claim to this said district of Kexholm, on any account whatever; but the said district shall hereafter be and remain incorporated into the kingdom of Sweden. As to the limits in the country of Lamparque, they shall remain on the same footing as they were before the beginning of this war between the two empires. It is further agreed upon, that commissaries shall be appointed by each party, immediately after the ratification of this treaty to regulate the limits as aforesaid.

Art. 9. His czarish majesty further promises to maintain all the inhabitants of the provinces of Livonia, Esthonia, and Oesel, as well nobles as plebeians, and the towns, magistrates, companies, and trades, in the full enjoyment of the said privileges, customs and prerogatives, which they have enjoyed under the dominion of his Swedish majesty.

Art. 10. There shall not hereafter be any violence offered to the consciences of the inhabitants of the ceded countries; on the contrary, his czarish majesty engages on his side to preserve and maintain the evangelical (Lutheran) religion on the same footing as under the Swedish government, provided there is likewise a free liberty of conscience allowed to those of the Greek religion.

Art. 11. In regard to the reductions and liquidations made in the reign of the late king of Sweden in Livonia, Esthonia, and Oesel, to the great injury of the subjects and inhabitants of those countries, which, conformable to the justice of the affair in question, obliged his late majesty the king of Sweden, of glorious memory, to promise, by an ordinance (which was published the 13th day of April, 1700, that if any one of his subjects could fairly prove, that the goods which had been confiscated were their property justice should be done them, whereby several subjects of the said countries have had such their confiscated effects restored to them) his czarish majesty engages and promises, that justice shall be done to every person, whether residing or not, who has a just claim or pretension to any lands in Livonia, Esthonia, or the province of Oesel, and can make full proof thereof, and that such person shall be reinstated in the possession of his lands and effects.

Art. 12. There shall likewise be immediate restitution made, conformable to the general amnesty regulated and agreed by the second article, to such of the inhabitants of Livonia, Esthonia, and the island of Oesel, who may during this war have joined the king of Sweden, together with all their effects, lands, and houses, which have been confiscated and given to others, as well in the towns of these provinces, as in those of Narva and Wibourg, notwithstanding they may have passed during the said war by inheritance or otherwise into other hands, with any exception or restraint, even though the proprietors should be actually in Sweden, either as prisoners or otherwise; and such restitution shall take place so soon as each person is re-naturalized by his respective government, and produces his documents relating to his right; on the other hand, these proprietors shall by no means lay claim to, or pretend to any part of, the revenues, which may have been received by those who were in possession in consequence of the confiscation, nor to any other compensation for their losses in the war or otherwise. And all persons, who are thus put in re-possession of their effects and lands, shall be obliged to do homage to his czarish majesty, their present sovereign, and further to behave themselves as faithful vassals and subjects; and when they have taken the usual oath of allegiance, they shall be at liberty to leave their own country to go and live in any other, which is in alliance and friendship with the Russian empire, as also to enter into the service of neutral powers, or to continue therein, if already engaged, as they shall think proper. On the other hand, in regard to those, who do not choose to do homage to his czarish majesty, they shall be allowed the space of three years from the publication of the peace, to sell or dispose of their effects, lands, and all belonging to them, to the best advantage, without paying any more than is paid by every other person, agreeably to the laws and statutes of the country. And if hereafter, it should happen that an inheritance should devolve to any person according to the laws of the country, and that such person shall not as yet have taken the oath of allegiance to his czarish majesty, he shall in such case be obliged to take the same at the time of entering on the possession of his inheritance, otherwise to sell off all his effects in the space of one year.

Also those who have advanced money on lands in Livonia, Esthonia, and the island of Oesel, and have lawful security for the same, shall enjoy their mortgages peaceably, until both capital and interest are discharged; on the other hand, the mortgages shall not claim any interest, which expired during the war, and which have not been demanded or paid; but those who in either of these cases have the administration of the said effects, shall be obliged to do homage to his czarish majesty. This likewise extends to all those who remain in his czarish majesty's dominions, and who shall have the same liberty to dispose of their effects in Sweden, and in those countries which have been surrendered to that crown by this peace. Moreover, the subjects of each of the reconciled powers shall be mutually supported in all their lawful claims and demands, whether on the public, or on individuals within the dominions of the two powers, and immediate justice shall be done them, so that every person may be reinstated in the possession of what justly belongs to him.

Art. 13. All contributions in money shall from the signing of this treaty cease in the grand duchy of Finland, which his czarish majesty by the fifth article of this treaty cedes to his Swedish majesty and the kingdom of Sweden; on the other hand the duchy of Finland shall furnish his czarish majesty's troops with the necessary provisions and forage gratis, until they shall have entirely evacuated the said duchy, on the said footing as has been practised heretofore; and his czarish majesty shall prohibit and forbid, under the severest penalties, the dislodging any ministers or peasants of the Finnish nation, contrary to their inclinations, or that the least injury be done to them. In consideration of which, and as it will be permitted his czarish majesty, upon evacuating the said countries and towns, to take with him his great and small cannon, with their carriages and other appurtenances, and the magazines and other warlike stores which he shall think fit. The inhabitants shall furnish a sufficient number of horse and waggons as far as the frontiers; and also, if the whole of this cannot be executed according to the stipulated terms, and that any part of such artillery, &c. is necessitated to be left behind, then, and in such cases, that which is so left shall be properly taken care of, and afterwards delivered to his czarish majesty's deputies, whenever it shall be agreeable to them, and likewise be transported to the frontiers in manner as above. If his czarish majesty's troops shall have found and sent out of the country any deeds or papers belonging to the grand duchy of Finland, strict search shall be made for the same, and all of them that can be found shall be faithfully restored to deputies of his Swedish majesty.

Art. 14. All the prisoners on each side, of whatsoever nation, rank, and condition, shall be set at liberty immediately after the ratification of this treaty, without any ransom, at the same time every prisoner shall either pay or give sufficient security for the payment of all debts by them contracted. The prisoners on each side shall be furnished with the necessary horses and waggons gratis during the time allotted for their return home, in proportion to the distance from the frontiers. In regard to such prisoners, who shall have sided with one or the other party, or who shall choose to settle in the dominions of either of the two powers, they shall have full liberty so to do without restriction: and this liberty shall likewise extend to all those who have been compelled to serve either party during the war, who may in like manner remain where they are, or return home; except such who have voluntarily embraced the Greek religion, in compliance to his czarish majesty; for which purpose each party shall order that the edicts be published and made known in their respective dominions.

Art. 15. His majesty the king, and the republic of Poland, as allies to his czarish majesty, are expressly comprehended in this treaty of peace, and have equal right thereto, as if the treaty of peace between them and the crown of Sweden had been inserted here at full length: to which purpose all hostilities whatsoever shall cease in general throughout all the kingdoms, countries, and patrimonies belonging to the two reconciled parties, whether situated within or out of the Roman empire, and there shall be a solid and lasting peace established between the two aforesaid powers. And as no plenipotentiary on the part of his Polish majesty and the republic of Poland has assisted at this treaty of peace, held at Nystadt, and that consequently they could not at one and the same time renew the peace by a solemn treaty between his majesty the king of Poland and the crown of Sweden, his majesty the king of Sweden does therefore engage and promise, that he will send plenipotentiaries to open the conferences, so soon as a place shall be appointed for the said meeting, in order to conclude, through the mediation of his czarish majesty, a lasting peace between the two crowns, provided nothing is therein contained which may be prejudicial to the treaty of perpetual peace made with his czarish majesty.

Art. 16. A free trade shall be regulated and established as soon as possible, which shall subsist both by sea and land between the two powers, their dominions, subjects, and inhabitants, by means of a separate treaty on this head, to the good and advantage of their respective dominions; and in the mean time the subjects of Russia and Sweden shall have leave to trade freely in the empire of Russia and kingdom of Sweden, so soon as the treaty of peace is ratified, after paying the usual duties on the several kinds of merchandise; so that, the subjects of Russia and Sweden shall reciprocally enjoy the same privileges and prerogatives as are enjoyed by the closest friends of either of the said states.

Art. 17. Restitution shall be made on both sides, after the ratification of the peace, not only of the magazines which were before the commencement of the war established in certain trading towns belonging to the two powers, but also liberty shall be reciprocally granted to the subjects of his czarish majesty and the king of Sweden to establish magazines in the towns, harbours, and other places subject to both or either of the said powers.

Art. 18. If any Swedish ships of war or merchant vessels shall have the misfortune to be wrecked, or cast away by stress of weather, or any other accident, on the coasts and harbours of Russia, his czarish majesty's subjects shall be obliged to give them all aid and assistance in their power to save their rigging and effects, and faithfully to restore whatever may be drove on shore, if demanded, provided they are properly rewarded. And the subjects of his majesty the king of Sweden shall do the same in regard to such Russian ships and effects as may have the misfortune to be wrecked or otherwise lost on the coasts of Sweden; for which purpose, and to prevent all ill treatment, robbing, and plundering, which commonly happens on such melancholy occasions, his czarish majesty and the king of Sweden will cause a most rigorous prohibition to be issued, and all who shall be found transgressing in this point shall be punished on the spot.

Art. 19. And to prevent all possible cause or occasion of misunderstanding between the two parties, in relation to sea affairs, they have concluded and determined, that any Swedish ships of war, of whatever number or size, that shall hereafter pass by any of his czarish majesty's forts or castles, shall salute the same with their cannon, which compliment shall be directly returned in the same manner by the Russian fort or castle; and, *vice versa*, any Russian ships of war, of whatever number or size, that shall hereafter pass by any fort or castle belonging to his Swedish majesty, shall salute the same with a discharge of their cannon, which compliment shall be instantly returned in the same manner by the Swedish fort; and in case any one or more Swedish and Russian ships shall meet at sea, or in any harbour or elsewhere, they shall salute each other with a common discharge, as is usually practised on such occasions between the ships of Sweden and Denmark.

Art. 20. It is mutually agreed between the two powers, no longer to defray the expenses of the ministers of the two powers, as have been done hitherto; but their representative ministers, plenipotentiaries, and envoys, shall hereafter defray their own expenses and those of their own attendants, as well on their journey as during their stay, and back to their respective place of residence. On the other hand, either of the two parties, on receiving timely notice of the arrival of an envoy, shall order that their subjects give them all the assistance that may be necessary to escort them safe on their journey.

Art. 21. His majesty the king of Sweden does on his part comprehend his majesty the king of Great Britain in this treaty of peace, reserving only the differences subsisting between their czarish and his Britannic majesties, which they shall immediately endeavour to terminate in a friendly manner; and such other powers, who shall be named by the two reconciled parties within the space of three months, shall likewise be included in this treaty of peace.

Art. 22. In case any misunderstanding shall hereafter arise between the states and subjects of Sweden and Russia, it shall by no means prejudice this treaty of perpetual peace; which shall nevertheless always be and remain in full force agreeable to its intent, and commissaries shall without delay be appointed on each side to inquire into and adjust all disputes.

Art. 23. All those who have been guilty of high treason, murder, theft, and other crimes, and those who deserted from Sweden to Russia, and from Russia to Sweden, either singly or with their wives and children, shall be immediately sent back, provided the complaining party of the country from whence they made their escape, shall think fit to recal them, let them be of what nation soever, and in the same condition as they were at their arrival, together with their wives and children, as likewise with all they had stolen, plundered, or taken away with them in their flight.

Art. 24. The exchange of the ratification of this treaty of peace, shall be reciprocally made at Nystadt within the space of three weeks, after the day of signing the same, or sooner, if possible. In witness whereof, two copies of this treaty, exactly corresponding with each other, have been drawn up, and confirmed by the plenipotentiary ministers on each side, in virtue of the authority they have received from their respective sovereigns; which copies they have signed with their own hands, and sealed with their own seals. Done at Nystadt, this 30th day of August, in the year of our Lord 1721. O. S.

Jean Liliensted.
Otto Reinhold Stroemfeld.
Jacob Daniel Bruce.
Henry-John-Frederic Osterman.

Ordinance of the Emperor Peter I. for the crowning of the Empress Catherine.

We, Peter the First, emperor and autocrator of all the Russias, &c. to all our officers ecclesiastical, civil, and military, and all others of the Russian nation, our faithful subjects.

No one can be ignorant that it has been a constant and invariable custom among the monarchs of all Christian states, to cause their consorts to be crowned, and that the same is at present practised, and hath frequently been in former times by those emperors who professed the holy faith of the Greek church; to wit, by the emperor Basilides, who caused his wife Zenobia to be crowned; the emperor Justinian, his wife Lucipina; the emperor Heraclius, his wife Martina: the emperor Leo, the philosopher, his wife Mary; and many others, who have in like manner placed the imperial crown on the head of their consorts, and whom it would be too tedious here to enumerate.

It is also well known to every one how much we have exposed our person, and faced the greatest dangers, for the good of our country during the one and twenty years' course of the late war, which we have by the assistance of God terminated in so honourable and advantageous a manner, that Russia hath never beheld such a peace, nor ever acquired so great glory as in the late war. Now the empress Catherine, our dearly beloved wife, having greatly comforted and assisted us during the said war, and also in several other our expeditions, wherein she voluntarily and cheerfully accompanied us, assisting us with her counsel and advice in every exigence, notwithstanding the weakness of her sex, particularly in the battle against the Turks, on the banks of the river Pruth, wherein our army was reduced to twenty thousand men, while that of the Turks amounted to two hundred and seventy thousand, and on which desperate occasion she signalized herself in a particular manner, by a courage and presence of mind superior to her sex, which is well known to all our army, and to the whole Russian empire: therefore, for these reasons, and in virtue of the power which God has given us, we have resolved to honour our said consort Catherine with the imperial crown, as a reward for her painful services; and we propose, God willing, that this ceremony shall be performed the ensuing winter at Moscow. And we do hereby give notice of this our resolution to all who are faithful subjects, in favour of whom our imperial affection is unalterable.

THE END.

S. Johnson & Son, Printers, Livesey St., Manchester.

FOOTNOTES:

[1] A French league contains three English miles.

[2] The Boristhenes, or Dnieper, is one of the largest rivers in Europe; it rises in the Walchonske Forest, runs through Lithuania, the country of the Zoporag Cossacks, and that of the Nagisch Tartars, and falls into the Black Sea near Oczakow. It has thirteen cataracts within a small distance.

[3] The reader will easily perceive, that the whole of this paragraph relates only to the French language, for in English we make no such distinctions in the name of these people, but always call them Russians.

[4] A collection of water lying between the gulf of Finland and lake Onega; it is the largest, and said to contain a greater number of fish than any other in Europe.

[5] We must not confound this river with another of the same name that runs through Lithuania in Poland, and dividing Livonia and Courland, falls into the Baltic at Dunamunder fort, below Riga.

[6] This was by the ancients reckoned among the most famous rivers in the world, and the boundary between Asia and Europe. It issues from St. John's Lake, not far from Tula, and after a long course, divides itself into three arms, and falls into the sea below Azoph.

[7] A promontory of the island of Maggero in the north of Norway, and is the most northern point in Europe.

[8] Grod, or gorod, signifies city in the Russian language.

[9] Memoirs of Strahlemberg, confirmed by those sent me from Russia.

[10] Memoirs sent from Petersburg.

[11] Memoirs sent from Petersburg.

[12] Called also the Ob. This large river issues from the lake Altin in Calmuck Tartary, in Asia, from whence running north it forms the boundary between Europe and Asia, and after traversing a vast tract of above two thousand miles, it falls into a bay of the Frozen Sea.

[13] In the Russian language Irtish. This river runs from N. to S. through all Russia, and falling into the former river, forms part of the boundary between Asia and Europe.

[14] In the Russian language Tobolsky.

[15] His name was Sowastowslaw.

[16] This anecdote is taken from a private MS. entitled 'The Ecclesiastical Government of Russia,' which is like wise deposited in the public library.

[17] See page 35.

[18] Thus the Russians call this young man; but in all French authors we find Romano, that language having no such letter as the W; others again call him Romanoff.

[19] Or Chotsin, a town of Upper Moldavia in European Turkey, well fortified both by nature and art, situated on the Dniester, and subject to the Turks, from whom it was taken by the Russians in 1739.

[20] This must certainly be a mistake of M. de Voltaire, or an error in the press; for the lady here spoken of was the daughter of Matthias Apraxim, a person on whom Theodore had lately conferred nobility.

[21] Extracted wholly from the memoirs sent from Moscow and Petersburg.

[22] Here M. de Voltaire seems to have greatly mistaken the sense of this word. Raspop not being a proper name, in which sense he takes it, but signifies a degraded priest.

[23] We suppose the author means Moscow.

[24] Or Cossano, a small town and abbey in the Milanese. On the Adda, near this place, an obstinate

battle was fought between the Germans and French, in 1705, when prince Eugene defeated the duke of Vendome.

[25] A town and abbey on the borders of Westphalia, in Germany; the abbot of which is a sovereign prince, and has a seat in the imperial diet.

[26] Or Fuld, a town and abbey of Hesse, in Germany; situate on a river of the same name. It is governed by an abbot, who is a prince of the empire.

[27] An imperial city of Suabia, in Germany, situate on the Ifar.

[28] How are we to reconcile this with what the author tells us in the latter part of the third chapter, where he says, that this princess, perceiving that her brother Theodore was near his end, declined retiring to a convent, as was the usual custom of the princesses of the imperial family.

[29] We find, in the memoirs of count Strahlemberg, a Swedish officer, who was taken prisoner at the battle of Pultowa, and continued many years at the court of czar Peter, the following account of the true cause of this extraordinary kind of hydrophobia. When Peter was about five years of age, his mother took him with her in a coach for an airing, and having to pass a dam, where there was a great fall of water the child, who was then sleeping in his nurse's lap, was so terrified by the rushing of the water (the noise of which waked him suddenly out of his sleep), that he was seized with a violent fever, and, after his recovery, he retained such a dread of that element, that he could not bear the sight even of any standing water, much less to hear a running stream.

[30] Memoirs of Petersburg and Moscow.

[31] This should certainly be four years; as we can hardly suppose a boy of fourteen years and a half, would be received into the military service of any country, and much less by the Dutch at that period of time, when they stood in need of able and experienced soldiers, to withstand the attacks of the French, who breathed nothing less than the utter subversion of their state.

[32] General Le Fort's MSS.

[33] General Le Fort's MSS.

[34] Extracted from memoirs sent from China; also from Petersburg, and from letters published in Du Halde's History of China.

[35] A famous and considerable river of the Asiatic part of the empire of Russia, which falls into the eastern ocean. It was formerly called Charan Muran, but at present the Chinese and Mauschurs give it the name of Sagalin Ula. It also bears the several appellations of Jamur, Onon, Helong, Kiang, and Skilka. It is formed by the junction of the rivers Sckilk and Argun, and is navigable to the sea.

[36] Busching, the famous geographer, says, that its whole length is no more than four hundred miles, so that there must be a very great error in one or other of these authors.

[37] Memoirs of the jesuits Pereira and Gerbillon.

[38] 1689, Sept. 8, new style. Memoirs of China.

[39] The present reigning empress Catharine seems even to exceed her aunt in lenity, which together with the superior qualifications of this princess, affords her people the most happy presage of a glorious reign; and it is not without reason, that the most sensible amongst them flatter themselves with the hope, that under this august princess, the Russian empire will arrive at its highest pinnacle of glory.

[40] Le Fort's Memoirs.

[41] It is in consequence of this glorious and equitable distinction, that at this day we find nobility gives no precedence in the court of Russia; nor can the son of a prince appear there in any other rank, than that which his situation in the army gives him; while a private citizen, who by his merit has raised himself above his condition, receives all the honours due to his post; or more properly speaking, to the merit which obtained him that post. A reputation of this kind would, methinks, be attended with great advantages, both in England and France, as it would be a means to raise in the youth of all ranks, a virtuous and noble emulation.

[42] General Le Fort's MSS.

[43] The Petersburg Memoirs, and Memoirs of Le Fort.

[44] Le Fort's MS. memoirs.

[45] Precop, or Perekop, once a fortress on the Isthmus, which joins the peninsula of Crim Tartary to the main land of little Tartary, in European Turkey, and thence considered as the key to that country. It has its name from the ditches cut across for the defence of the peninsula.

[46] These were two scholars from Christ Church Hospital, commonly called blue coat boys.

[47] The czar was particularly fond of this nobleman, because he was a great lover of maritime affairs, frequently rowed and sailed with him upon the water, and gave him what information he could concerning shipping.

[48] Le Fort's MSS. and those of Petersburg.

[49] Le Fort's MSS.

[50] A most extraordinary instance of the obstinate attachment of the Russians to their old customs, happened in the time of the czar Bassilowitz, and undoubtedly influenced him not a little in the severity with which he treated his people. The king of Poland, Stephen Battori, having recovered Livonia, went himself into that province to establish a new form of government. According to the constant custom there, when any peasant, all of whom were treated as slaves, had committed a fault, he was whipped with a rod till the blood came. The king was willing to commute this barbarous punishment for one that was more moderate; but the peasants, insensible of the favour designed them, threw themselves at his feet, and intreated him not to make any alterations in their ancient customs, because they had experienced, that all innovations, far from procuring them the least redress, had always made their burthens sit the heavier on them.

[51] Memoirs of captain Perry, the engineer, employed by Peter the Great, in Russia, and MSS. of Le Fort.

[52] Captain Perry, in p. 184 of his memoirs, says, that these executions being performed in the depth of winter, their bodies were immediately frozen; those who were beheaded, were ordered to be left in the same posture as when executed, in ranks upon the ground, with their heads lying by them: and those who were hanged round the three walls of the city, were left hanging the whole winter, to the view of the people, till the warm weather began to come on in the spring, when they were taken down and buried together in a pit, to prevent infection. This author adds, that there were other gibbets placed on all the public roads leading to Moscow, where others of these rebels were hanged.

[53] MSS. of Le Fort.

[54] Somewhat like those of our blue coat boys in England.

[55] 20th Sept. 1698. It is to be observed, that I always follow the new style in my dates.

[56] Norberg, chaplain and confessor to Charles XII. says, in his history, 'That he had the insolence to complain of oppressions, and that he was condemned to lose his honour and life.' This is speaking like the high-priest of despotism. He should have observed, that no one can deprive a citizen of his honour for doing his duty.

[57] See the History of Charles XII.

[58] A town on the river Lycus, in the province of Assyria, now called Curdestan, where Alexander the Great fought his third and decisive battle, with Darius, king of Persia.

[59] Vol. I. p. 439, of the 4to. edition, printed at the Hague.

[60] The chaplain Norberg, pretends, that, immediately after the battle of Narva, the Grand Seignior wrote a letter of congratulation to the king of Sweden, in these terms. 'The sultan Basha, by the grace of God, to Charles XII. &c.' The letter was dated from the æra of the creation of the world.

[61] See History of Charles XII.

[62] This chapter and the following, are taken entirely from the journal of Peter the Great, sent me from Petersburg.

[63] We must beg leave to remark in this place, that a king of England has the power of doing good in

virtue of his own authority, and may do evil if so disposed, by having a majority in a corrupt parliament; whereas, a king of Poland can neither do good nor evil, not having it in his power to dispose even of a pair of colours.

[64] This seems a mistake; our author probably meant to say Kercholme, because Wibourg is not on the lake Ladoga, but on the gulf of Finland.

[65] Taken from the journal of Peter the Great.

[66] Some writers call it Nyenschantz.

[67] Petersburg was founded on Whitsunday, the 27th May, 1703.

[68] About sixty thousand pounds sterling.

[69] All the foregoing chapters, and likewise those which follow, are taken from the journals of Peter the Great, and the papers sent me from Petersburg, carefully compared with other memoirs.

[70] Menzikoff's parents were vassals of the monastery of Cosmopoly: at the age of thirteen, he went to Moscow, and was taken into the service of a pastry-cook. His employment was singing ballads, and crying puffs and cakes about the streets. One day, as he was following this occupation, the czar happening to hear him, and to be diverted with one of his songs, sent for him, and asked him if he would sell his pies and his basket? The boy answered, that his business was to sell his pies, but he must ask his master's leave to sell his basket; yet as every thing belonged to his prince, his majesty had only to lay his commands upon him. The czar was so pleased with this answer, that he immediately ordered him to court, where he gave him at first a mean employment; but being every day more pleased with his wit, he thought fit to place him about his person, and to make him groom of his bed-chamber, from whence he gradually raised him to the highest preferments. He was tall and well shaped. At his first coming into the czar's service, he inlisted in Le Fort's company, and acquired, under that general's instruction, such a degree of knowledge and skill, as enabled him to command armies, and to become one of the bravest and most successful generals in Russia.

[71] M. de Voltaire calls this city Wibourg, in this and some other places of his history. The French are not always very attentive to the right names of places, but here it is of some consequence. Wibourg is the capital of Jutland in Denmark. Wiburn, the city here meant, is the capital of Carelia in Russian Finland.

[72] The czar's manifesto in the Ukraine, 1709.

[73] The impartiality of an historian obliges us in this place to advertise our readers, that it was not the fault of Augustus, that Patkul was delivered up to the king of Sweden; Augustus having privately sent orders to the commandant of the fort of Konigstein, where Patkul was then confined, to suffer his prisoner to make his escape in time. But the avarice of this officer proved fatal to the life of the unhappy captive, and to the character of his own prince; for while he was endeavouring to make the best bargain he could for himself, the time slipped inconceivably away; and while they were yet debating upon the price of the proposed releasement, the guards sent by Charles came and demanded Patkul in the name of their sovereign. The commandant was forced to obey, and the unhappy victim was delivered up, contrary to the intentions of Augustus.

[74] What would those Swedes say, were they living, to see the pitiful figure their descendants have made in this war.

[75] In the Russian language, Soeza.

[76] This is acknowledged by Norberg himself, vol. ii. p. 263.

[77] Vol. II. page 279.

[78] The Memoirs of Peter the Great, by the pretended boyard Iwan Nestesuranoy, printed at Amsterdam, in 1730, say, that the king of Sweden, before he passed the Boristhenes, sent a general officer with proposals of peace to the czar. The four volumes of these Memoirs are either a collection of untruths and absurdities, or compilations from common newspapers.

[79] This fact is likewise found in a letter, printed before the Anecdotes of Russia, p. 23.

[80] La Motraye, in the relation of his travels, quotes a letter from Charles XII. to the grand vizier; but

this letter is false, as are most of the relations of that mercenary writer; and Norberg himself acknowledges that the king of Sweden never could be prevailed on to write to the grand vizier.

[81] The czar, says the preface to lord Whitworth's account of Russia, who had been absolute enough to civilize savages, had no idea, could conceive none, of the privileges of a nation civilized in the only rational manner by laws and liberties. He demanded immediate and severe punishment of the offenders: he demanded it of a princess, whom he thought interested, to assert the sacredness of the persons of monarchs, even in their representatives; and he demanded it with threats of wreaking his vengeance on all English merchants and subjects established in his dominions. In this light the menaces were formidable; otherwise, happily, the rights of the whole people were more sacred here than the persons of foreign ministers. The czar's memorials urged the queen with the satisfaction which she herself had extorted, when only the boat and servants of the earl of Manchester had been insulted at Venice. That state had broken through the fundamental laws, to content the queen of Great Britain. How noble a picture of government, when a monarch, that can force another nation to infringe its constitution, dare not violate his own? One may imagine with what difficulty our secretaries of state must have laboured through all the ambages of phrase in English, French, German, and Russ, to explain to Muscovite ears and Muscovite understandings, the meaning of indictments, pleadings, precedents, juries, and verdicts; and how impatiently Peter must have listened to promises of a hearing next term? With what astonishment must he have beheld a great queen, engaging to endeavour to prevail on her parliament to pass an act to prevent any such outrage for the future? What honour does it not reflect on the memory of that princess to own to an arbitrary emperor, that even to appease him she dare not put the meanest of her subjects to death uncondemned by law!—There are, says she, in one of her dispatches to him, insuperable difficulties, with respect to the ancient and fundamental laws of the government of our people; which we fear do not permit so severe and rigorous a sentence to be given, as your imperial majesty at first seemed to expect in this case; and we persuade ourself, that your imperial majesty, who are a prince famous for clemency and exact justice, will not require us, who are the guardian and protectress of the laws, to inflict a punishment upon our subjects, which the law does not impower us to do. Words so venerable and heroic, that this broil ought to become history, and be exempted from the oblivion due to the silly squabbles of ambassadors and their privileges. If Anne deserved praise for her conduct on this occasion, it reflects still greater glory on Peter, that this ferocious man should listen to these details, and had moderation and justice enough to be persuaded by the reason of them.

[82] Afterwards created lord Whitworth, by king George I.

[83] The account this chaplain gives of the demands of the grand seignior is equally false and puerile. He says, that sultan Achmet, previous to his declaring war against the czar, sent to that prince a paper, containing the conditions on which he was willing to grant him peace. These conditions, Norberg tells us, were as follows: 'That Peter should renounce his alliance with Augustus, reinstate Stanislaus in the possession of the crown of Poland, restore all Livonia to Charles XII., and pay that prince the value in ready money of what he had taken from him at the battle of Pultowa; and, lastly, that the czar should demolish his newly-built city of Petersburg.' This piece was forged by one Brazey, a half-starved pamphleteer, and author of a work entitled, Memoirs, Satirical, Historical, and Entertaining. It was from this fountain Norberg drew his intelligence; and however he may have been the confessor of Charles XII. he certainly does not appear to have been his confidant.

[84] The new vizier embraced every opportunity of affronting the czar, in the person of his envoy, and particularly in giving the French ambassador the preference. It was customary, on the promotion of the grand vizier, for all the foreign ministers to request an audience of congratulation. Count Tolstoy was the first who demanded that audience; but was answered—That the precedence had always been given to the ambassador of France: whereupon Tolstoy informed the vizier—That he must be deprived of the pleasure of waiting on him at all: which, being maliciously represented, as expressing the utmost contempt of his person, and the khan of Tartary being at the same time instigated to make several heavy complaints against the conduct of the Russians on the frontiers, count Tolstoy was immediately committed to the castle of the Seven Towers.

[85] It is very strange that so many writers always confound Walachia and Moldavia together.

[86] This duke of Holstein, at the time he married the daughter of Peter I. was a prince of very inconsiderable power, though of one of the most ancient houses in Germany. His ancestors had been stripped of great part of their dominions by the kings of Denmark; so that, at the time of this marriage,

he found himself greatly circumscribed in point of possessions; but, from this epoch of his alliance with the czar of Muscovy, we may date the rise of the ducal branch of Holstein, which now fills the thrones of Russia and Sweden, and is likewise in possession of the bishopric of Lubec, which, in all probability, will fall to this house, notwithstanding the late election, which at present is the subject of litigation, the issue of which will, to all appearance, terminate in favour of the prince, son to the present bishop, through the protection of the courts of Vienna and Petersburg. The empress Catherine, who now sits on the throne of Russia is herself descended from this august house, by the side of her mother, who was sister to the king of Sweden, to the prince-bishop of Lubec, and to the famous prince George of Holstein, whose achievements made so much noise during the war. This princess, whose name was Elizabeth, married the reigning prince of Anbak Zerbst, whose house was indisputably the most ancient; and, in former times, the most powerful in all Germany, since they can trace their pedigree from the dukes of Ascania, who were formerly masters of the two electorates of Saxony and Brandenburg, as appears by their armorial bearings, which are, quarterly, the arms of Saxony and Brandenburg. Of this branch of Zerbst there is remaining only the present reigning prince, brother to the empress Catherine, who, in case he should die without issue, will succeed to the principality of Yevern, in East Friesland; from all which it appears already, that the family of Holstein is at present the most powerful in Europe, as being in possession of three crowns in the North.—[Since the above was written important changes have taken place.]

[87] This same count Poniatowsky, who was at that time in the service of Charles XII., died afterwards castellan of Cracovia, and first senator of the republic of Poland, after having enjoyed all the dignities to which a nobleman of that country can attain. His connexions with Charles XII. during that prince's retirement at Bender, first made him taken notice of; and, it is to be wished, for the honour of his memory, that he had waited till the conclusion of a peace between Sweden and Poland, to be reconciled to king Augustus; but following the dictates of ambition, rather than those of strict honour, he sacrificed the interests of both Charles and Stanislaus, to the care of his own fortune; and, while he appeared the most zealous in their cause, he secretly did them all the ill services he could at the Ottoman Porte: to this double dealing he owed the immense fortune of which he was afterwards possessed. He married the princess Czartoriski, daughter of the castellan of Vilna, a lady, for her heroic spirit, worthy to have been born in the times of ancient Rome: when her eldest son, the present grand chamberlain of the crown, had that famous dispute with Count Tarlo, palatine of Lublin; a dispute which made so much noise in all the public papers in the year 1742, this lady, after having made him shoot at a mark every day, for three weeks, in order to be expert at firing, said to him, as he was mounting his horse, to go to meet his adversary—'Go, my son; but, if you do not acquit yourself with honour in this affair, never appear before me again.' This anecdote may serve as a specimen of the character of our heroine. The family of Czartoriski is descended from the ancient Jagellins, who were, for several ages, in lineal possession of the crown of Poland; and is, at this day, extremely rich and powerful, by the alliances it has contracted, but they have never been able to acquire popularity; and so long as count Tarlo (who was killed in a duel with the young count Poniatowsky) lived, had no influence in the dictines, or lesser assembly of the states, because Tarlo, who was the idol of the nobles, and a sworn enemy to the Czartoriski family, carried every thing before him, and nothing was done but according to his pleasure.

[88] About seventy pounds sterling.

[89] French money, which is always counted by livres and makes about three millions sterling.

[90] A town in Bohemia famous for its mineral springs.

[91] About fifty thousand pounds sterling.

[92] Private memoirs of Bassowitz, Jan. 21, 1712.

[93] A town of Sleswic, in Denmark, situated on the river Eyder, fourteen miles from the German Ocean, having a very commodious harbour.

[94] About twelve hundred pounds sterling.

[95] In the preamble to this institution, the czar declared, that it was to perpetuate the memory of her love in his distressed condition on the banks of the river Pruth. He invested her with full power to bestow it on such of her own sex as she should think proper. The ensigns of this order are, a broad white riband, and wore over the right shoulder, with a medal of St. Catherine, adorned with precious stones, and the motto, 'Out of love and fidelity.'

[96] Inhabitants of a small town of Hungarian Dalmatia, with a harbour, from whence the neighbouring sea takes the name of Golfo di Bickariga.

[97] The conspiracy carried on in France by cardinal Alberoni, was discovered in a very singular manner. The Spanish ambassador's secretary, who used frequently to go to the house of one La Follon, a famous procuress of Paris, to amuse himself for an hour or two after the fatigues of business, had appointed a young nymph, whom he was fond of, to meet him there at nine o'clock in the evening, but did not come to her till near two o'clock in the morning. The lady, as may be supposed, reproached him with the little regard he paid to her charms, or his own promise; but he excused himself, by saying, that he had been obliged to stay to finish a long dispatch in ciphers, which was to be sent away that very night by a courier to Spain: so saying, he undressed and threw himself into bed, where he quietly fell asleep. In pulling off his clothes, he had, by accident, dropped a paper out of his pocket, which, by its bulk, raised in the nymph that curiosity so natural to her sex. She picked it up, and read it partly over, when the nature of its contents made her resolve to communicate them to La Follon: accordingly, she framed some excuse for leaving the room, and immediately went to the apartment of the old lady, and opened her budget. La Follon, who was a woman of superior understanding to most in her sphere, immediately saw the whole consequence of the affair; and, after having recommended to the girl, to amuse her gallant as long as possible, she immediately went to waken the regent, to whom she had access at all hours, for matters of a very different nature to the present. This prince, whose presence of mind was equal to every exigency, immediately dispatched different couriers to the frontiers; in consequence of which, the Spanish ambassador's messenger was stopped at Bayonne, and his dispatches taken from him; upon deciphering of which, they were found exactly to agree with the original delivered to the regent by La Follon: upon this the prince of Cellamar, the Spanish ambassador was put under an arrest, and all his papers seized; after which he was sent under a strong guard to the frontiers, where they left him to make the best of his way to his own country. Thus an event, which would have brought the kingdom of France to the verge of destruction, was frustrated by a votary of Venus, and a priestess of the temple of pleasure.

[98] As these letters and answers afford the most striking evidence of the czar's prudence, and the prince's insincerity, and will convey to the reader a clear idea of the grounds and motives of this extraordinary transaction, we have inserted the following translation of them. The first letter from the czar to his son, is dated the 27th of October, 1715, and displays a noble spirit of religion, with the most ardent desire of leaving a successor who should perpetuate his name and glory to future ages.

'Son,' says the czar to him, 'you cannot be ignorant of what is known to all the world, that our people groaned under the oppression of the Swedes, before the beginning of this present war. By the usurped possession of many of our maritime ports, so necessary to our state, they cut us off from all commerce with the rest of mankind; and we saw, with deep regret, that they had even cast a mist over the eyes of persons of the greatest discernment, who tamely brooked their slavery, and made no complaints to us. You know how much it cost us at the beginning of this war, to make ourselves thoroughly experienced, and to stand our ground in spite of all the advantages which our irreconcileable enemies gained over us. The Almighty alone has conducted us by his hand, and conducts us still. We submitted to that probationary state with resignation to the will of God, not doubting but it was he who made us pass through it: he has accepted our submission; and the same enemy, before whom we were wont to tremble, now trembles before us. These are effects, which, under God's assistance, we owe to our labour, and those of our faithful and affectionate sons, and Russian subjects. But while I survey the successes with which God has blessed our arms, if I turn my eyes on the posterity that is to succeed me, my soul is pierced with anguish; and I have no enjoyment of my present happiness, when I carry my views into futurity. All my felicity vanishes away like a dream, since you, my son, reject all means of rendering yourself capable of governing well after me. Your incapacity is voluntary; for you cannot excuse yourself from want of genius: it is inclination alone you want. Far less can you plead the want of bodily strength, as if God had not furnished you sufficiently in that respect: for though your constitution be none the strongest, it cannot be reckoned weak. Yet you will not so much as hear of warlike exercises; though it is by those means we are risen from that obscurity in which we were buried, and have made ourselves known to the nations about us, whose esteem we now enjoy. I am far from desiring you to cherish in yourself a disposition to make war for its own sake, and without just reasons: all I demand of you is, that you would apply yourself to learn the military art; because, without understanding the rules of war, it is impossible to be qualified for government. I might set before your eyes many examples of what I propose to you; but shall only mention the Greeks, with whom we are united by the same profession of faith. Whence came the declension of their empire, but from the neglect of arms? Sloth and inaction have subjected them to tyrants, and that slavery under which they have groaned. You are much mistaken if you imagine it is enough for a prince that he have good generals to act under his orders: no, my son, it is upon the chief himself that the eyes of the world are fixed; they study his inclinations, and easily slide into the imitation of his manners. My brother, during his reign, loved magnificence in dress, and splendid equipages, and horses richly caparisoned; the taste of this country was not much formed that way; but the pleasures of the prince soon became those of the subjects, who are readily led to imitate him both in the objects of his love and disgust. If people are so easily disengaged from things that are only for pleasure, will they not be still more prone to forget, and in process of time wholly to lay aside the use of arms, the exercise of which grows the more irksome the less they are habituated to them? You have no inclination to learn the profession of war; you do not apply yourself to it; and consequently will never know it. How then will you be able to command others, and to judge of the rewards which those subjects deserve who do their duty, or of the punishment due to such as fall short of obedience? You must judge only by other people's eyes; and will be considered as a young bird, which reaching out its beak, is as ready to receive poison as proper nourishment. You say, the infirm state of your health makes you unfit to bear the fatigues of war; but that is a frivolous excuse. I desire you not to undergo the fatigues of that profession, though it is there that all great captains are begun; but I wish you had an inclination to the military art; and reason may give it you, if you have it not from nature. Had you once this inclination, it would occupy your thoughts at all times, even in your hours of sickness. Ask those who remember my brother's reign: his state of health was much more infirm than your's; he could not manage a horse of never so little mettle, nor hardly mount him: yet he loved horses, and perhaps there never will be in the country finer stables than his. Hence you see, that success does not always depend upon personal labour, but upon the inclination. If you think that there are princes, whose affairs fail not to succeed, though they go not to war in person, you are in the right; but if they go not to the field of battle, they have, however, an inclination to go, and are acquainted with the military art. For instance, the late king of France did not always take the field himself; but we know to what a degree he was a lover of war, and how many glorious exploits he performed therein; which made his campaigns be called the theatre and school of the world. The bent of that prince's mind was not turned to military affairs only, he had also a taste for the polite arts, for manufactures, and other institutions, which have made his kingdom more flourishing than any other. After all these remonstrances which I have laid before you, I return to my first subject, which immediately concerns yourself. I am a man, and consequently must die: to whom shall I leave the care of finishing what, by God's grace, I have begun, and of preserving what I have in part recovered? To a son who, like that slothful servant in the gospel, buries his talent in the earth, and neglects to improve what God has committed to his trust? How often have I reproached you for your sullenness and indocility? I have been obliged to chastise you on that account. For these several years past I have hardly spoke to you, because I almost despair of bringing you back to the right way; discouraged and disheartened by the fruitlessness of all my endeavours. You loiter on in supine indolence; abandoning yourself to shameful pleasures, without extending your foresight to the dangerous consequences which such a conduct must produce both to yourself and the whole state: you confine yourself to the government of your own house, and in that station you acquit yourself very ill; St. Paul has told us, 'he that knows not how to govern his own house, how shall he be able to rule the church of God?' In like manner I say to you, since you know not how to manage your domestic affairs, how can you be able to govern a kingdom? I am determined, at last, to signify to you my final purpose; being willing, however, to defer the execution of it for a short time, to see if you will reform: if not, know that I am resolved to deprive you of the succession, as I would lop off a useless branch. Do not imagine, that because I have no other child but you,[99] I mean by this only to intimidate you: I will most certainly execute my resolution; and God requires it of me: for, since I spare not my own life for the sake of my country, and the welfare of my people, why should I allow an effeminate prince to ascend the throne after me, who would sacrifice the interest of the subject to his pleasures? and should he be obliged to expose his life in their behalf, would leave them to perish, rather than redress their grievances. I will call in a mere stranger to the crown, if he be but worthy of that honour, sooner than my own son, if he is unworthy.

'PETER.'

To this letter the czarowitz replied: 'Most gracious sovereign and father, I have read the letter which your majesty sent me of the 27th of October, 1715, after the interment of my wife; and all the answer I can make to it is, that if your majesty is determined to deprive me of the succession to the crown of Russia, on account of my inability, your will be done. I even request it of you very earnestly; because I judge not myself fit for government. My memory is greatly impaired; and without memory there is no managing affairs. The powers both of my body and mind are much weakened by the diseases to which I have been incident, and I am thereby incapacitated for the rule of so great a people. Such a charge requires a man far more vigorous than I am. For these reasons I am not ambitious to succeed you (whom God preserve through a length of years) in the crown of Russia, even though I had no brother, as I have one at present, whom God long preserve. As little will I for the future set up any claim to the succession: to the truth of which I solemnly swear, taking God to be my witness; and in testimony thereof I write and sign these presents. I put my children into your hands: and for myself I ask no more of you than a bare maintenance during my life, leaving the whole to your pleasure.

'Your humble servant and son,

'ALEXIS.'

Peter soon penetrated through the disguise his son had assumed, and therefore wrote him the above letter, dated January 19, 1716, and which he called his 'Last Admonition.'

[99] This letter was written about eight days before the birth of Peter Patrowitz, the czar's second son.

[100] This letter was couched in the following terms:—'Most gracious sovereign and father, yesterday morning I received your letter, of the 19th of this month: my indisposition hinders me from writing to you at large, but I am willing to embrace the monastic state, and I beg your gracious consent thereto.

'Your servant, and unworthy son,

'ALEXIS.'

[101] The prince's renunciation was couched in the following terms:—'I, the undernamed, declare upon the holy gospel, that on account of the crimes I have committed against his czarish majesty, my father and sovereign, as set forth in his manifesto, I am, through my own fault, excluded from the throne of Russia. Therefore I confess and acknowledge that exclusion to be just, as having merited it by my own fault and unworthiness; and I hereby oblige myself, and swear in the presence of Almighty God, in unity of nature, and trinity of persons, as my supreme Judge, to submit in all things to my father's will, never to set up a claim or pretension to the succession, or accept of it under any pretext whatever, acknowledging my brother Peter Petrowitz as lawful successor to the crown. In testimony whereof, I kiss the holy cross, and sign these presents with my own hand.

'ALEXIS.'

[102] As this extraordinary piece cannot fail of being interesting to most part of our readers, we have ventured to subjoin the whole of it in a note, our author having only given some few extracts.

The Czar's Declaration.

Peter I. by the grace of God, czar, emperor of Russia, &c. to all our faithful subjects, ecclesiastical, military, and civil, of all the states of the Russian nation. It is notorious, and well known to the greatest part of our faithful subjects, and chiefly to those who live in the places of our residence, or who are in our service, with how much care and application we have caused our eldest son Alexis to be brought up and educated; having given him for that purpose, from his infancy, tutors to teach him the Russian tongue, and foreign languages, and to instruct him in all arts and sciences, in order not only to bring him up in our Christian orthodox faith of the Greek profession, but also in the knowledge of political and military affairs, and likewise in the constitution of foreign countries, their customs and languages; through the reading of history, and other books, in all manner of sciences, becoming a prince of his high rank, he might acquire the qualifications worthy of a successor to our throne of Great Russia. Nevertheless, we have seen with grief, that all attention and care, for the education and instruction of our son, proved ineffectual and useless, seeing he always swerved from his filial obedience, shewing no application for what was becoming a worthy successor, and slighting the precepts of the masters we had appointed for him; but, on the contrary, frequenting disorderly persons, from whom he could learn nothing good, or that would be advantageous and useful to him. We have not neglected often to endeavour to reclaim, and bring him back to his duty, sometimes by caresses and gentle means, sometimes by reprimands, sometimes by paternal corrections. We have more than once taken him with us into our army and the field, that he might be instructed in the art of war, as one of the chief sciences for the defence of his country; guarding him, at the same time, from all hazard of the succession, though we exposed ourself to manifest perils and dangers. We have at other times left him at Moscow, putting into his hands a sort of regency in the empire, in order to form him in the art of government, and that he might learn how to reign after us. We have likewise sent him into foreign countries, in hopes and expectation, that seeing, in his travels, governments so well regulated, this would excite in him some emulation and an inclination to apply himself to do well. But all our care has been fruitless, and like the seed of the doctrine fallen upon a rock; for he has not only refused to follow that which is good, but even is come to hate it, without shewing any inclination, or disposition, either for military or political affairs; hourly and continually conversing with base and disorderly persons, whose morals are rude and abominable. As we were resolved to endeavour, by all imaginable means, to reclaim him from that disorderly course, and to inspire him with an inclination to converse with persons of virtue and honour; we exhorted him to choose a consort among the chief foreign houses, as is usual in other countries, and hath been practised by our ancestors, the czars of Russia, who have contracted alliances by marriages with other sovereign houses, and we have left him at liberty to make a choice. He declared his inclination for the princess, grand-daughter of the duke of Wolfenbuttle, then reigning, sister-in-law to his imperial majesty the emperor of the Romans, now reigning, and cousin to the king of Great Britain; and having desired us to procure him that alliance, and permit him to marry that princess, we readily consented thereunto, without any regard to the great expense which was necessarily occasioned by that marriage: but, after its consummation, we found ourselves disappointed of the hopes we had, that the change in the condition of our son would produce good fruits, and change his bad inclinations; for, notwithstanding his spouse was, as far as we have been able to observe, a wise, sprightly princess, and of a virtuous conduct, and that he himself had chosen her, he nevertheless lived with her in the greatest disunion, while he redoubled his affection for lewd people, bringing thereby a disgrace upon our house in the eyes of foreign powers to whom that princess was related, which drew upon us many complaints and reproaches. Our frequent advices and exhortations to him, to reform his conduct, proved ineffectual, and he at last violated the conjugal faith, and gave his affection to a prostitute of the most servile and low condition, living publicly in that crime with her, to the great contempt of his lawful spouse, who soon after died; and it was believed that her grief, occasioned by the disorderly life of her husband, hastened the end of her days. When we saw his resolution to persevere in his vicious courses, we declared to him, at the funeral of his consort, that if he did not for the future conform to our will, and apply himself to things becoming a prince, presumptive heir to so great an empire, we would deprive him of the succession, without any regard to his being our only son (our second son was not then born) and that he ought not to rely upon his being such, because we would rather choose for our successor a stranger worthy thereof, than an unworthy son; that we would not leave our empire to such a successor, who would ruin and destroy what we have, by God's assistance, established, and tarnish the glory and honour of the Russian nation, for the acquiring of which we had sacrificed our ease and our health, and willingly exposed our life on several occasions; besides, that the fear of God's judgment would not permit us to leave the government of such vast territories in the hands of one whose insufficiency and unworthiness we were not ignorant of. In short, we exhorted him in the most pressing terms we could make use of, to behave himself with discretion, and gave him time to repent and return to his duty. His answer to these remonstrances was, that he acknowledged himself guilty in all these points; but alleged the weakness of his parts and genius, which did not permit him to apply himself to the sciences, and other functions recommended to him: he owned himself incapable of our succession, and desired us to discharge him from the same. Nevertheless, we continued to exhort him with a paternal affection, and joining menaces to our exhortations; we forgot nothing to bring him back to the right way. The operations of the war having obliged us to repair to Denmark, we left him at Petersburg, to give him time to return to his duty, and amend his ways; and, afterwards, upon the repeated advices we received of the continuance of his disorderly life, we sent him orders to come to us at Copenhagen, to make the campaign, that he might thereby the better form himself. But, forgetting the fear and commandments of God, who enjoins obedience even to private parents, and much more to those who are at the same time sovereigns, our paternal cares had no other return than unheard-of ingratitude; for, instead of coming to us as we ordered, he withdrew, with large sums of money, and his infamous concubine, with whom he continued to live in a criminal course, and put himself under the protection of the emperor, raising against us, his father and his lord, numberless calumnies and false reports, as if we did persecute him, and intended, without cause, to deprive him of the succession; alleging, moreover, that even his life was not safe if he continued with us, and desired the emperor not only to give him refuge in his dominions, but also to protect him against us by force of arms. Every one may judge, what shame and dishonour this conduct of our son hath drawn upon us and our empire, in the face of the whole world; the like instance is hardly to be found in history. The emperor, though informed of his excesses, and how he had lived with his consort, sister-in-law to his imperial majesty, thought fit, however, upon these pressing instances, to appoint him a place where he might reside; and he desired farther, that he might be so private there, that we might not come to the knowledge of it. Meanwhile his long stay having made us fear, out of a tender and fatherly affection for him, that some misfortune had befallen him, we sent persons several ways to get intelligence of him, and, after a great deal of trouble, we were at last informed by the captain of our guard, Alexander Romanzoff, that he was privately kept in an imperial fortress at Tyrol; whereupon we wrote a letter, with our own hand, to the emperor, to desire that he might be sent back to us: but, notwithstanding the emperor acquainted him with our demands, and exhorted him to return to us, and submit to our will, as being his father and lord; yet he alleged, with a great many calumnies against us, that he ought not to be delivered into our hands, as if we had been his enemy, and a tyrant, from whom he had nothing to expect but death. In short, he persuaded his imperial majesty, instead of sending him back at that time to us, to remove him to some remote place in his dominions, namely, Naples in Italy, and keep him there secretly in the castle, under a borrowed name. Nevertheless, we having notice of the place where he was, did thereupon dispatch to the emperor our privy-counsellor, Peter Tolstoy, and the captain of our guard, aforesaid, with a most pressing letter, representing how unjust it would be to detain our son, contrary to all laws, divine and human, according to which private parents, and with much more reason those who are besides invested with a sovereign authority as we are, have an unlimited power over their children, independently of any other judge; and we set forth on one side, the just and affectionate manner with which we had always used our son, and, on the other, his disobedience; representing, in the conclusion, the ill consequences and animosities which the refusal of delivering up our son to us might occasion, because we would not leave this affair in that condition. We, at the same time, ordered those we sent with that letter, to make verbal remonstrances even in more pressing terms, and to declare that we should be obliged to revenge, by all possible methods, such detaining our son. We wrote likewise a letter to him with our own hand, to represent to him the horror and impiety of his conduct, and the enormity of the crime he had committed against us his father, and how God threatened in his laws to punish disobedient children with eternal death: we threatened him, as a father, with our curses, and, as his lord, to declare him a traitor to his country, unless he returned, and obeyed our commands; and gave him assurance, that if he did as we desired, and returned, we would pardon his crime. Our envoys, after many solicitations, and the above representation, made by us in writing, at last obtained leave of the emperor to go and speak to our son, in order to dispose him to return home. The imperial minister gave them at the same time to understand, that our son had informed the emperor that we persecuted him, and that his life was not safe with us, whereby he moved the emperor's compassion, and induced him to take him into his protection; but that the emperor, taking now into his consideration our true and solid representations, promised to use his utmost endeavour to dispose him to return to us; and would, moreover, declare to him, that he could not in justice and equity refuse to deliver him to his father, or have any difference with us on that account. Our envoys, upon their arrival at Naples, having desired to deliver to him our letter, written with our hand, sent us word, that he did refuse to admit them; but that the emperor's viceroy had found means, by inviting him to his house, to present them to him afterwards, much against his will. He did then, indeed, receive our letter, containing our paternal exhortation, and threatening our curse, but without shewing the least inclination to return; alleging still a great many falsities and calumnies against us, as if, by reason of several dangers he had to apprehend from us, he could not, nor would not return; and boasting, that the emperor had not only promised to defend and protect him against us, but even to set him upon the throne of Russia against our will, by force of arms. Our envoys perceiving this evil disposition, tried all imaginable ways to prevail with him to return, they intreated him, they expatiated by turns upon the graciousness of our assurances towards him, and upon our threats in case of disobedience, and that we would even bring him away by force of arms; they declared to him that the emperor would not enter into a war with us on his account, and many other such-like representations did they make to him. But he paid no regard to all this, nor shewed any inclination to return to us, until the imperial viceroy, convinced at last of his obstinacy, told him in the emperor's name, that he ought to return; for that his imperial majesty could not by any law keep him from us, nor, during the present war with Turkey, and also in Italy with Spain, embroil himself with us upon his account. When he saw how the case stood, fearing he should be delivered up to us, whether he would or not, he at length resolved to return home; and declared his mind to our envoys, and to the imperial viceroy: he likewise wrote the same thing to us, acknowledging himself to be a criminal, and blameworthy. Now although our son, by so long a course of criminal disobedience against us, his father and lord, for many years, and particularly for the dishonour he hath cast upon us in the face of the world, by withdrawing himself, and raising calumnies against us, as if we were an unnatural father, and for opposing his sovereign, hath deserved to be punished with death; yet our paternal affection inclines us to have mercy upon him, and we therefore pardon his crimes, and exempt him from all punishment for the same. But considering his unworthiness, we cannot in conscience, leave him after us the succession to the throne of Russia; foreseeing that, by his vicious courses, he would entirely destroy the glory of our nation and the safety of our dominions, which, through God's assistance, we have acquired and established by incessant application; for it is notorious and known to every one, how much it hath cost us, and with what efforts we have not only recovered the provinces which the enemy had usurped from our empire, but also conquered several considerable towns and countries, and with what care we have caused our people to be instructed in all sorts of civil and military sciences, to the glory and advantage of the nation and empire. Now, as we should pity our states and faithful subjects, if, by such a successor, we should throw them back into a much worse condition than ever they were yet; so, by the paternal authority, in virtue of which, by the laws of our empire, any of our subjects may disinherit a son, and give his succession to such other of his sons, as he pleases; and, in quality of sovereign prince, in consideration of the safety of our dominions, we do deprive our said son Alexis, for his crimes and unworthiness, of the succession after us to the throne of Russia, even though there should not remain one single person of our family after us. And we do constitute and declare successor to the said throne after us, our second son Peter, though yet very young, having no successor that is older. We lay upon our said son Alexis our paternal curse, if ever at any time he pretends to, or reclaims, the said succession; and we desire our faithful subjects, whether ecclesiastics or seculars, of all ranks and conditions, and the whole Russian nation, in conformity to this constitution and our will, to acknowledge and consider our said son Peter, appointed by our constitution, to confirm the whole by oath, before the holy altar, upon the holy gospel, kissing the cross; and all those who shall ever, at any time, oppose this our will, and who, from this day forward, shall dare to consider our son Alexis, as successor, or to assist him for that purpose, declare them traitors to us and their country. And we have ordered that these presents shall be every where published and promulgated, to the end that no person may pretend ignorance.—Given at Moscow, the third of February, 1718. Signed with our hand, and sealed with our seal.

'PETER.'

[103] This was the son of the empress Catherine, who died April 15, 1719.

[104] At the same time confirming it by an oath, the form of which was as follows: 'I swear before Almighty God, and upon his holy gospel, that whereas our most gracious sovereign, the czar Peter Alexiowitz, has caused circular letters to be published through his empire, to notify that he has thought fit to exclude his son, prince Alexis Petrowitz, from the throne of Russia, and to appoint for his successor to the crown his second son, the prince royal Peter Petrowitz; I do acknowledge this order and regulation made by his majesty in favour of the said prince Peter Petrowitz, to be just and lawful, and entirely conform and submit myself to the same; promising always to acknowledge the said prince royal Peter Petrowitz for his lawful successor, and to stand by him on all occasions, even to the loss of my life, against all such as shall presume to oppose the said succession; and that I never will, on any pretence whatsoever assist the prince Alexis Petrowitz, nor in any manner whatsoever contribute to procure him the succession. And this I solemnly promise by my oath on the holy gospel, kissing the holy cross thereupon.'

[105] His declaration to the clergy concluded in this manner:—'Though this affair does not fall within the verge of the spiritual, but of the civil jurisdiction, and we have this day referred it to the imperial decision of the secular court, but remembering that passage in the word of God, which requires us on such occasions to consult the priests and elders of the church, in order to know the will of Heaven, and being desirous of receiving all possible instructions in a matter of such importance, we desire of you, the archbishops, and the whole ecclesiastical state, as teachers of the word of God, not to pronounce judgment in this case, but to examine and give us your opinion concerning it, according to the sacred oracles, from whom we may be best informed what punishment my son deserves, and that you will give it us in writing under your hands, that being properly instructed herein, we may lay no burthen on our

conscience. We therefore repose our confidence in you, that, as guardians of the divine laws, as faithful pastors of the Christian flock, and as well affected towards your country, you will act suitable to your dignity, conjuring you by that dignity, and the holiness of your function, to proceed without fear or dissimulation.

[106] Besides the particular passages in holy writ cited on this occasion, which were, Levit. xx. 1, 9. Deut. xxxi. Matt. xx. 1. Mark vii. 9. Rom. i. 28. Ephes vi. 1. those from the constitutions of the empire were as follows: 'If any person, by any ill design, forms any attempt against the health of the czar, or does any thing to his prejudice, and is found inclined to execute his pernicious designs, let him be put to death, after he is convicted thereof.' Stat. 1. 'In like manner, if any one, during the reign of his czarian majesty, through a desire to reign in the empire of Russia, and put the czar to death, shall begin to raise troops with this pernicious view; or if any one shall form an alliance with the enemies of his czarian majesty, or hold a correspondence with them, or assist them to arrive at the government, or raise any other disorder; if any one declare it, and the truth be found out upon such declaration, let the traitor suffer death upon conviction of the treason.' Stat. 2. From the military laws the following citations were made; chap. 3. art. 19. 'If any subject raises men, and takes up arms against the czarian majesty; or if any person forms a design of taking his majesty prisoner, or killing him; or if he offers any violence to him; he and all his abettors and adherents shall be quartered, as guilty of treason, and their goods confiscated.' To which article the following explanation was added: 'They also shall suffer the same punishment, who, though they have not been able to execute their crime, shall be convicted of inclination and desire to commit it; and likewise, those who shall not have discovered it when it came to their knowledge,' chap. 26. art. 37. 'He who forms a design of committing any treason, or any other matter of the like nature, shall be punished with the same capital punishments as if he had actually executed his design.'

[107] M. de Voltaire is mistaken in this point; for, by our laws, no peer of the realm can absent himself from the service of the parliament during its session, without the liberty of the king or the house.

[108] This is another mistake; for it is death by our law to compass or imagine the death of the sovereign.

[109] Or Nions, the capital of Montauban, in Dauphine, in France, situate on the river Aigues, over which is a bridge, said to be a Roman work.

[110] At twenty-four to the pound sterling.

[111] About three thousand pounds sterling.

[112] The czar celebrated this victory by a naval triumph at Petersburg, caused a gold medal to be struck to perpetuate the glory of the action, presented prince Galitzin with a sword set with diamonds, and distributed a large sum of money among the officers and sailors who had given such signal proofs of their valour.

[113] A little town of the Bothnick gulf in North Finland.

[114] Notwithstanding the great rejoicings made on this occasion, Peter was noways inattentive to the affairs of state; but held frequent councils thereon: and being desirous, as his son Peter Petrowitz was dead, to settle the succession on a prince who would follow his maxims, and prosecute the great designs which he had begun for civilizing his people, he ordered public notice to be given, on the 23d of February, to all his subjects inhabiting the city of Moscow, to repair the next day to Castle-church; which they having done, printed papers were delivered to them all, signifying, 'That it was his imperial majesty's pleasure, that every man should swear, and give under his hand, that he would not only approve the choice his majesty would make of a successor, but acknowledge the person he should appoint as emperor and sovereign.' An order was likewise published a few days after at Petersburg, requiring the magistrates and all persons to subscribe the same declaration; and all the grandees of the empire were commanded, on pain of death and confiscation, to repair to Moscow by the latter end of March for that purpose, except those inhabiting Astracan and Siberia, who, living at too great a distance, were excused from giving their personal attendance, and permitted to subscribe before their respective governors. This oath was readily taken by all ranks and degrees of the people, who were well assured that their emperor would make choice of one who was every way worthy of the succession, and capable of supporting the dignity intended for him: but they were still in the dark as to the identical person, though it was generally believed to be prince Nariskin, who was nearly related to the emperor, and

allowed to have all the qualities requisite for his successor: but a little time shewed them, that this conjecture was groundless.

[115] These he published and distributed along the borders of the Caspian Sea, therein declaring—That he came not upon the frontiers of Persia, with an intention of reducing any of the provinces of that kingdom to his obedience, but only to maintain the lawful possessor of them on his throne, and to defend him powerfully, together with his faithful subjects, against the tyranny of Mir Mahmoud, and to obtain satisfaction from him and his Tartars, for the robberies and mischiefs which they had committed in the Russian empire.

[116] Memoirs of Bassewitz.

[117] MS. memoirs of count de Bassewitz.

[118] Catherine paid the last duties to her husband's ashes, with a pomp becoming the greatest monarch that Russia, or perhaps any other country, had ever known; and though there is no court of Europe where splendour and magnificence is carried to a greater height on these occasions than in that of Russia, yet it may with great truth be said, that she even surpassed herself in the funeral honours paid to her great Peter. She purchased the most precious kinds of marble, and employed some of the ablest sculptors of Italy to erect a mausoleum to this hero, which might, if possible, transmit the remembrance of his great actions to the most distant ages. Not satisfied with this, she caused a medal to be struck, worthy of the ancients. On one side was represented the bust of the late emperor, with these words —'*Peter the Great, Emperor and Sovereign of all Russia, born May 30, 1672.* On the reverse was the empress sitting, with the crown on her head, the globe and sceptre by her side on a table, and before her were a sphere, sea charts, plans, mathematical instruments, arms, and a caduceus. At distances, in three different places, were represented an edifice on the sea coast, with a platform before it, a ship and galley at sea, and the late emperor in the clouds, supported by eternity, looking on the empress, and shewing her with his right hand all the treasures he had left her, with these words, 'Behold what I have left you.' In the exergue, 'Deceased 28 January, 1725.' Several of these medals she ordered to be struck in gold, to the weight of fifty ducats and distributed among the foreign ministers, and all the grandees of the empire, as a testimony of her respect and gratitude to the memory of her late husband, to whose generosity she took a pleasure in owning herself indebted for her present elevated station.

Mottley gives us the following, as the czar's epitaph:

Here lieth,
All that could die of a man immortal,
PETER ALEXIOWITZ:
It is almost superfluous to add,
Great Emperor of Russia!
A title,
Which, instead of adding to his glory,
Became glorious by his wearing it.
Let antiquity be dumb,
Nor boast her Alexander, or her Cæsar.
How easy was victory
To leaders who were followed by heroes!
And whose soldiers felt a noble disdain
At being thought less vigilant than their generals!
But he,
Who in this place first knew rest,
Found subjects base and inactive,
Unwarlike, unlearned, untractable;
Neither covetous of fame, nor fearless of danger;
Creatures with the names of men,
But with qualities rather brutal than rational!
Yet, even these
He polished from their native ruggedness;
And, breaking out like a new sun,
To illuminate the minds of a people,

Dispelled their night of hereditary darkness;
And, by force of his invincible influence,
Taught them to conquer
Even the conquerors of Germany.
Other princes have commanded victorious armies;
This commander created them.
Blush, O Art! at a hero who owed thee nothing
Exult, O Nature! for thine was this prodigy.

[119] The distinguished regard which this princess shews for the arts and sciences, and her endeavours to attract the great geniuses of all nations to reside in her dominions, by every possible encouragement, affords the strongest presumptions, that in her reign we shall see a second age of Louis XIV. and of this we have had a recent proof, in the obliging letter which this august princess wrote with her own hand to M. d'Alembert, and the choice she has since made of M. Duplex, a member of the royal academy of sciences at Paris, when the beforementioned gentleman thought fit to decline the gracious offers she made him. In which choice she has shewn that it is not birth nor rank, but true merit and virtue, which she considers as the essential qualifications in a person to whom she would confide the most sacred of all trusts, that of the education of the grand duke, her son. What then may not be expected from the administration of a sovereign so superior to vulgar prejudice? And especially when assisted by a Woronzoff and a Galitzin, both the professed friends and patrons of literature and the fine arts, which they themselves have not disdained to cultivate, when business and the weighty affairs of state have allowed them a few moments leisure.

[120] The following anecdote, communicated by a nobleman of the strictest probity, who was himself an eye-witness of the fact, will give us a clear insight into the character and disposition of Peter I. In one of the many plots which was formed against the life and government of this monarch, there was among the number of those seized a soldier, belonging to his own regiment of guards. Peter being told by his officers that this man had always behaved extremely well, had a curiosity to see him, and learn from his own mouth what might have been his inducement to be concerned in a plot against him; and to this purpose he dressed himself in a plain garb, and so as not to be known by the man again, and went to the prison where he was confined, when, after some conversation, 'I should be glad to know, friend,' said Peter, 'what were your reasons for being concerned in an attempt against the emperor your master, as I am certain that he never did you any injury, but on the contrary, has a regard for you, as being a brave soldier, and one who have always done your duty in the field; and therefore, if you were to shew the least remorse for what you have done, I am persuaded that the emperor would forgive you: but before I interest myself in your behalf, you must tell me what motives you had to join the mutineers; and repeat to you again, that the emperor is naturally so good and compassionate, that I am certain he will give you your pardon.'

'I know little or nothing of the emperor,' replied the soldier, 'for I never saw him but at a distance; but he caused my father's head to be cut off some time ago, for being concerned in a former rebellion, and it is the duty of a son to revenge the death of his father, by that of the person who took away his life. If then the emperor is really so good and merciful as you have represented him, counsel him, for his own safety not to pardon me; for were he to restore me my liberty, the first use I should make of it would be, to engage in some new attempt against his life, nor should I ever rest till I had accomplished my design; therefore the securest method he can take, will be to order my head to be struck off immediately, without which his own life is not in safety.' The czar in vain used all the arguments he could think of, to set before this desperado the folly and injustice of such sentiments; he still persisted in what he had declared, and Peter departed, greatly chagrined at the bad success of his visit, and gave orders for the execution of this man and the rest of his accomplices.

www.ingramcontent.com/pod-product-compliance
Lightning Source LLC
Chambersburg PA
CBHW060807310726
48980CB00002B/265

* 9 7 8 3 7 3 2 6 2 4 8 2 9 *